Be well,
Good Wishes,

TOO LATE TO KILL ME SO:
A Recounting

TOO LATE TO KILL ME SO:
A Recounting

JOE BERRY

Negative Capability Press
Mobile, Alabama

A Negative Capability Press Book

Published in the United States of America by
Negative Capability Press
Mobile, Alabama

Text Copyright © 2015 by Joe Berry
ISBN: 9780942544992
LCCN: 2014956512

Design & Production by HTDesignS
Illustrations by Susan Berry Clanton

Printed in the United States of America

Visit Negative Capability Press
at
negativecapabilitypress.org
facebook.com/negativecapabilitypress

ACKNOWLEDGMENTS

For more than forty years, I have wanted to tell this story. Others have said to write Ann's story while it was fresh in my memory. They do not understand that Ann's life made an indelible impression on me and cannot be forgotten.

My special thanks to Linda Berry, my wife, for her patience, to Susan Berry Clanton, my daughter, for the sketches she contributed to this book, to Linda Hill and Jon Conover for reading my manuscripts, correcting my errors, and urging me on, and last, a lady who told me her name "need not be mentioned." Though contrary to my wish, I follow her suggestion and identify her only as a "Lady." In an act of boldness, I sent her my story of Ann, asking, "Should I pursue this?" She responded, "You are going to write this book, and I am going to help you." She took me by the hand and for two years led me, but in such a wonderful manner, she almost seemed to follow.

Dedicated to the "real" Ann and any of the living consigned to "The City of The Living Dead."

PREFACE

The real "Ann Albert Tatum" was born, lived, and died in a state other than Georgia. To the author's knowledge, her daughters, "Dana" and "Jane" never lived there. Any resemblance of persons, living or dead, in the places depicted is purely coincidental.

To conceal identities, assumed names, places, and dates are used. Some, but not all events, characters, and conversations are creations of the author. In these, the author has created scenes and events that have molded Ann into the novel's fictive character, but her life, marriages, the manner of her husband's death, and her trial for murder are fairly presented.

Ann's life gives witness to the truth found in the words of John Donne that "No man is an island" and she, like so many others of her time, struggled for survival during the Great Depression years and wore its scars. Her life departs from the typical when the scars of later years made the scars of childhood miniscule. Indeed, one man's death diminishes all.

This is a story not only of a violent death, but also of great love and courage. It is a story of life's uncertainties garnished with the hope of a better tomorrow in the light of shattered dreams. This is a story the author has long sought to tell. For those who are certain they could never cause the violent death of another, this narrative may be disturbing, but it is important to understand that we all have a breaking point.

DEATH'S KNELL

On February 18, 1972, the Atlanta police found Ann Tatum sitting on her kitchen floor cradling her dead husband in her arms. A partially eaten sandwich, a half-glass of milk, and a copy of a poem about a butterfly lay on the kitchen table.

Rumor quickly spread that Ann had killed Edward "Ed" Tatum, but those who knew her best responded to this alleged violent act in complete disbelief.

On the same day, Pete Atkinson, Ann's son-in-law, requested the assistance of Job Lee, a small-town lawyer who had never represented a client charged with murder.

CHILD AND BUTTERFLY

"Mama, tell me about the butterfly."

"In a few minutes Ann. Let me get my hands out of this biscuit dough. You go be warming-up the porch swing."

Ann never tired of hearing her mother, Martha Hicks Albert, recite the poem about the lifecycle of a butterfly.

> *Brown and furry*
> *Little caterpillar in a hurry.*
> *Take your walk*
> *To a shady leaf or stalk.*
> *Spin and die*
> *And live again a butterfly.*

Listening to her recite this simple poem was Ann's earliest memory.

Ann's mother and father were born within five miles of each other on small farms outside Summerville, Georgia. They were classmates at Elmore County Consolidated School through the tenth grade when Ellis "Ell" Albert, Jr., dropped out of school to take a job at Pate's Lumber Company a few miles south of Summerville. Martha remained in the same school and graduated in 1926.

Two weeks after graduation, Martha and Ell eloped to Trenton, Georgia, and were married by a probate judge. The newlyweds made their home in a small tenant house on the farm of Ellis Albert, Sr. There, in 1929, Dr. Wimberley delivered a baby girl who was named after her maternal grandmother, Ann Elizabeth Albert.

GREAT DEPRESSION & BY-GONE YEARS

The Great Depression years of the 1930's came early to Ann's family. Considered hard by many, these were the years of Ann's childhood, and she remembered them as a mixture of bitter and sweet. Ann and the Depression were childhood mates.

Having no other point of reference, Ann did not think of these years as difficult ones, for the span of her reach in the first 10-12 years of her life was determined by the distance two mules could pull a wagon in a day's time and return home by night. It would be later in life before she experienced a different lifestyle. Regrettably, at age ten, when a baby sister and a seriously ill mother became a large part of her life, she gained a reference point for comparison. It would be much later in life before she would be able to see the negative footprints of the Great Depression years and the harsh demands of fate that shaped her life. Even in later years, her vision would be obscured by the ominous tolling of death's knell as she tried to hold on to happy memories of her childhood. Her fondest memory was of her mother reciting the butterfly poem. She had learned the poem at her mother's knee but never knew who had written it.

When Martha finished making the pan of biscuits, placed them in the oven, and added wood to the stove's firebox, she called: "Okay, little girl, the biscuits are cooking. I'll wash my hands and meet you at the swing." By the time she reached the front porch, Ann, age four, had the swing in motion.

"Do you ever tire of hearing this same poem? I sometimes tire of telling it. Maybe I could learn a new poem or story to tell you."

"No, Mama. Please tell me about the butterfly."

"How about you tell the poem to me?"

"Please Mama. I can't tell it like you."

"Well, tell me how it begins."

"Brown and furry," Ann began as Martha recited the poem once more.

Ann was not yet twelve years old when her mother died, yet she always recalled her mother going to the barn with bucket in hand to milk the cow. She would hear the stream of milk collide with the bottom of the metal bucket and watch the foam on top of the milk rise and fall as her mother's sure hands pulled the warm milk from the willing cow.

Ann would also picture her mother with hoe in hand, her eyes and face concealed under the shadow of the wide brim hat she wore when attacking the garden weeds. She would recall, too, the anxiety she felt if she couldn't see her mother's face and then the relief when her mother would turn, lift her big hat, and say, "I'm right here little girl."

Ann's single abiding wish in life was having her family safe, under the same roof, and by her side.

Before Ann's baby sister, Betsy, was born, she remembered going with her mother to pick wild blackberries and plums.

"Little girl," Martha would say, "I'm going to mix a tad of this turpentine with some water and wash your feet and legs with it. Otherwise, the chiggers will cover you up. I'll warm some water in the washtub for your bath when we get back."

Ann remembered that once, near a clump of blackberry bushes, she had seen an injured quail on the ground and tried to catch it. The bird had a crippled wing and couldn't fly, but when Ann got close, it would flutter a few feet away.

"Honey, the mother quail is trying to protect her babies," Martha said. "Good mothers always protect their family."

In the last years of her life, Ann would relive moments of her childhood and imagine her parents, her little sister, and the small, frame house in which they lived. She could see the outdoor toilet, the well in the backyard, and the long, slender bucket filled with water as the chain pulled it up and out of the darkness of the earth. She could see the chickens in the yard and hear the crow of the rooster as he fluffed his feathers and pranced around as if he were king. Ann envisioned the mules, harnessed and hitched to the wagon, and could see her daddy in the seat, holding the reins. The mules, Maude and Lucy, would once more stamp their feet and shoo the flies away. She would hear the trace chains rattle as she and her daddy waited for Mama to climb into the wagon and take her seat next to Daddy. At times, Ann could hear her daddy chuckle and say, "Ann, I seem to spend half my life waiting on Mama after she says she's ready to go." And she would hear her mother tell about the October day in 1929 when Dr. Wimberley came to their house to help with Ann's arrival in the world.

In her waning years, Ann's memories returned with absolute fidelity. She tried to shun the bad and hold on to the pleasant ones but she never had complete success except for thoughts of the butterfly. She recalled the songs her mother used to sing, "The Old Spinning Wheel in the Parlor," "Amazing Grace," and "The Sweet By and By." Her mother's voice rang clear and strong and told again of faith and of a land fairer than day where the Father waits to prepare a dwelling place.

Yet, ever in the recesses of Ann's memory was the death of her baby sister, Betsy, who was one and the same as the butterfly. Sometimes Martha referred to Betsy as "Our new little butterfly." On wash days, she would say, "Now Ann, you watch the little butterfly, and be sure she doesn't get too close to the fire under the wash pot." Memories of Betsy, while her mother lived, were pleasant ones, but Ann could not forget her mother's increasing illness and subsequent death as the bell tolled broken dreams always within the mind's hearing.

SURVIVING: TRYING TO GET ON WITH LIFE

In 1939, when Dr. Wimberley made a second trip to the Albert home, economic conditions had improved. Ten years earlier when he had called at the same four-room house for Ann's birth, he'd arrived in a horse-drawn buggy. Now, the fat little doctor drove a 1937 Ford with a V-8 engine for the delivery of Betsy, Ann's new baby sister.

The same improvement could not be said for the Albert family. Ell had lost his job at Pate's Lumber Company. He borrowed his uncle's mules and wagon for Thursday drives to Summerville and frequently stood in line for beans, cheese, and flour, the weekly commodities distributed to the poor by the national government. He worked for the Works Project Administration but barely brought home enough money to provide for his family.

Ann watched from the porch as Dr. Wimberley parked his Ford beneath the large oak tree towering in front of the property. Her daddy walked out to meet the doctor and then escorted him to the bedroom where Martha lay in labor. She was having a difficult time. No prenatal care had been provided, and the doctor was, at first, doubtful that either the mother or the newborn child would survive.

Ann sat on the front porch swing with her daddy while Dr. Wimberley delivered her baby sister. She remembered the serious expression on his face when he walked out and spoke to her daddy.

"Ell, how long has Martha had that cough?"

"About a year, I guess. It seems to be getting worse. Is there a problem?"

"The new baby is weak and will require close attention. Your wife is even weaker. I am concerned about her cough. Her lungs are congested. I don't know what the problem is. It could be one of several things, but a doctor with better skills than I should take a look. There's a new doctor down in Rome. As soon as you can, get Martha down there to see him. His name is Dr. Tom Anderson."

"Dr. Wimberley, I don't have the money. I don't even have the money to pay you. We never even paid you for delivering Ann and that was ten years ago."

"I understand, Ell. Don't worry about paying me. Just see

if you can get Martha down to Rome as soon as you can. I'm concerned about her lungs."

The family was never made aware of the exact nature of Martha's illness when Betsy was born, but based on Dr. Wimberley's words of concern over her cough and lungs, it was assumed she had "consumption," a word often used interchangeably with "tuberculosis." But this was an assumption. The brutal truth was that only people with money could afford to be sick. Martha and her family did not fit that description.

Whatever the cause, Betsy's birth was followed by a steady decline of Martha's health. Ell was never able to take her to Dr. Anderson in Rome. Nor, as far as Ann knew, was Dr. Wimberley ever paid for his visits to the Albert home. Medical care for the Albert Family was essentially nonexistent.

Martha died in 1941. She was buried within a mile of where she was born, at Bethel Baptist Church, alongside her mother and father. Ell was unable to buy a marker for her grave. Her father's gross pay for forty hours of work was $12.00. Their home had neither electricity nor running water. Their toilet sat in back of the house, thirty yards from the back door. No newspaper or magazine ever reached their house, and the nearest radio was at a neighbor's house a half-mile away. In a word, the family was destitute.

To say the two years following Martha's death were trying, demanding, and difficult for Ann is a gross understatement. She became, for all practical purposes, Betsy's "mother." All who witnessed this surrogate role would describe it as a dedicated and determined effort. Ann did her best for her baby sister, but "best" is a relative term, one influenced by many factors beyond Ann's control, and in the end, this best did not prove good enough, for Betsy was never a healthy child. No one will ever know the cause of her poor health and early death, but, as with Martha, the family was too poor to obtain medical care for the child that Ann came to look on as her own. Nothing is gained by speculation, but she looked on Betsy's death as some "fault" of her own and could never shed the feeling that she had been deficient in caring for her baby sister.

William Lones, pastor of the Bethel Church, known tenderly as "Brother Lones" to the family, came to the Albert residence the night of Betsy's death. Not being able to afford the services of a funeral home, relatives bathed and dressed the child's body for burial. They then laid her in a wooden coffin in a bedroom of the Albert home. Family and friends gathered at the Albert home for the sitting. While aunts, uncles, cousins, and neighbors all sat and said goodbye to Betsy, Ann could not bring herself to look at her dead sister.

The ancient practice of "sitting-up with the dead" still prevailed in the South. It had originated several hundred years earlier, arising from death being sometimes obscured by uncertainty and the fear of being buried alive. George Washington had this fear and directed a three-day wait for his burial beyond the date he was said to be dead. Some cultures mandated a three day wait for burial after one was believed to be dead. A bell was attached to the toes of the corpse to signal life with any movement of the foot.

While Brother Lones was at the Albert's, he became concerned that Ann did not express her sorrow and grief for Betsy's death. He invited her to sit on the front porch swing with him. Two kerosene lanterns provided light for the porch and front steps.

"Ann," Brother Lones said, "your father wants me to conduct the service for Betsy's funeral. Is there anything special you'd like me to say?"

Ann's pause was so great that the minister wasn't sure any answer would come. She sat stiff in the swing, staring at a moth fluttering against one of the kerosene lanterns. Finally, she spoke.

"Mama used to tell me a poem about a butterfly. Do you know it?"

"No, Ann. I don't believe I know a poem about a butterfly. Can you tell it to me? I'll try to use it in the service."

Again, Ann took a long time to answer. "Yes, I know it. But it isn't as pretty when I say it."

"I would really like to hear it. Is it a long poem?"

"No sir. It's real short, but it's real pretty the way Mama used to tell it."

"I know that's true. Let me see if I can make myself a note of how it goes."

Taking a notepad from his pocket, Brother Lones coaxed the little girl into sharing the poem. Three times she tried—and failed to complete the poem, always stumbling on the last line. On the fourth try, she said with difficulty "*And live again a butterfly.*" She sat silent for a few moments, and then looked up at the pastor.

"Mr. Lones, do you think it's possible Mama will live again a butterfly?"

The question was both simple and profound. Now, it was Brother Lones' turn to take a long time before answering, "Ann, with God, I think all things are possible. Tell me about the things you and Betsy did together."

"If I had known more," she said, "Betsy would have lived."

The minister was distressed by Ann's answer. "What do you mean?"

"If I had been bigger and smarter, I could have taken care of her."

"Ann, you did a wonderful job of caring for Betsy. You did all that anyone could have done."

A few days later at the funeral service, Brother Lones recited the butterfly poem, and then added, for the benefit of the small congregation: "Ann shared this poem with me, explaining that her mother had taught the poem to her. In sharing the poem, Ann asked a simple question. She asked if it were possible that her mother might live again as a butterfly. Many times before Ann asked me that question, I had spoken of all things being possible with God. But, before Ann asked me, I had never understood. Sometimes it takes the voice of a child to make us fully understand things. In answer to Ann's question, I said to her, and I say to you now, if it is the will of God, we can live again an angel or a butterfly."

THE WORLD THAT AWAITS IS NOT THE WORLD EXPECTED: ANN'S ARREST, 1972

In February, 1972, Ann Elizabeth Albert Tatum was arrested for causing the death of her husband.

The next month, the grand jury of Fulton County, Georgia, indicted her for murder. After her arrest, but before her trial, Ann's family doctor had referred her to Dr. Carl Battle, an Atlanta psychiatrist. Dr. Battle, in seeking to understand his patient, sought and obtained information from various people who knew Ann. This search for information by the doctor brought William Lones to Dr. Battle's office. A marked contrast between these two men would play a role in the preparation for the judicial proceeding to decide Ann Tatum's fate. Dr. Battle, a man of science, would view this encounter of different lives as a matter of chance. Mr. Lones would see this intermingling of lives as a part of God's overarching scheme of things.

William Lones was seven years younger than Dr. Battle and nineteen years older than Ann. He was the ninth of twelve children in his family, all of whom were born in the Waxhaw Community of South Carolina, within a mile of the place where Andrew Jackson was born. In 1918, when William was eight, the Lones family, excluding the three oldest children, moved to Birmingham, Alabama, to live in one of the steel mill villages of that city.

In 1928, William graduated from Ensley High School in Birmingham after managing to avoid trouble during his teenage years living in a tough neighborhood. In 1929, the year Ann was born, he took a job as a heavy equipment operator in Macon, Georgia. While residing in Macon, he married and came under the influence of a Baptist minister who was a graduate of Howard College, a Baptist school in Birmingham. At the urging of this minister, William earned college credits through correspondence classes with Howard College. During the same time, he enrolled as a night student at Macon Junior College, earning one year's credit. He did not earn a college degree.

William Lones was ordained as a Baptist minister in 1933 and employed as the fulltime minister of a small church in Phoenix City, Alabama. At the time, Phoenix City was one of the most corrupt and violent small cities in the United States, a place where most personal disputes were settled with fists, guns, or knives, rather than through prayer. It was a dangerous learning experience for William. In 1935, he welcomed the opportunity to become the pastor of Bethel Baptist Church in northwest Georgia. At that church, he came to know Ann and her family.

Both Carl Battle, a highly educated doctor, and William Lones, a sparsely educated country preacher, viewed Ann's tragedy as a series of events involving conflicting forces. Dr. Battle would be a trial witness. A disabling illness suffered shortly after his meeting with Dr. Battle removed Mr. Lones from the stage on which this drama was reenacted. The information he provided, however, was helpful in the doctor's understanding of his new patient.

DR. BATTLE'S INTERVIEW WITH MR. LONES

BATTLE: Mr. Lones, you state that you were concerned that Ann did not display any signs of grief. Explain what you mean.
LONES: Her little sister had just died. For all practical purposes she had been her sister's mama for about two years. Maybe more, maybe less than that. I do not recall exactly how long. She was devoted to her baby sister. Yet, she didn't cry. She just sat very still and said nothing. It was not a healthy situation; I had never seen anyone who was so close to the deceased act that way.

BATTLE: What did you do?
LONES: I tried to draw her out. I tried to get her to grieve, to talk about Betsy.

BATTLE: What was Ann's reaction?
LONES: Essentially there was none. She indicated she was responsible for Betsy's death.

BATTLE: Do you recall what her words were?
LONES: I can't be exact. That was a long time ago. As best I recall, she said if she had been older, wiser, and stronger, her sister would have lived. She was blaming herself for the child's death. That was clear. That was the scary thing.

BATTLE: Do you recall any of the things that you said to her?
LONES: What could I say? I tried to reassure her, to let her know that she was not at fault, not to blame. But she was just a child herself. She was no more than thirteen or fourteen years old. I tried to reason with her, but reason was out-of-

27

place. The child needed grief, not reason. Grief, I could not give. Grief, she could not find.

BATTLE: How frequently did you see and talk to Ann during this time?
LONES: I saw her for several days. Each day before the funeral and several times over the following two or three weeks.

BATTLE: Did she ever verbalize or show any signs of grief?
LONES: Not that I could see. I could tell the child was tormented by the look on her face. But that lost look was all I ever saw. I guess that's the best way I can express what I saw. She seemed lost. Just a child who was lost in some wilderness, not knowing which way to go. Not knowing which way to run, really. I know it is not good to compare the situation to that of a lost dog, but that is what it reminded me of. I have seen lost dogs looking for a way back home. They will run in one direction looking for home, then they will run the opposite way. They will stop, look, and listen. You can just see the lost look on their face. That's the way Ann looked, That is the best way to describe what I saw.

BATTLE: Did she say anything about running away?
LONES: Oh, no, but I could tell that Ann was lost and needed to run away but did not know where to run.

BATTLE: How frequently did you see Ann the next few years after Betsy died?
LONES: I was the pastor of Bethel Baptist Church at the time, and I continued to be for the next several years. Ell, that's what Ellis, Jr., Ann's father, was called, and Ann were

regular in attendance at Sunday school and the morning service at my church. So I saw Ann each week until she married and went away. That was two or three years, maybe four, after the baby died. I also saw Ann on other occasions; I cannot recall the details. Nevertheless, we had regular contact.

BATTLE: Did she ever say anything else about Betsy's death?
LONES: The talk we had on the porch swing the day before the funeral is the only talk of death that I recall. The only other thing I remember her saying that night was something about a poem. I had asked her if she had any request about what I should say at the funeral. She asked me to recite a poem that she gave me. That is all I recall Ann saying about the death of her sister. There may have been much more said that I do not recall. This happened many years ago.

BATTLE: Did you know Ann's first husband? I understand his name was Lloyd Caine.
LONES: Just slightly. It was during the war, close to the end of the war, maybe early 1945, when I first met the young man. He was from a northern state; I don't know which one. At the time, he was stationed at Fort Benning and came to our community for a few visits with a local boy who was also stationed at Fort Benning. I only saw him a few times and only a few minutes at each time.

BATTLE: Were you aware of Ann's plan to marry Lloyd Caine?
LONES: Yes. Ann talked to me about her plans. She wanted me to conduct the marriage ceremony, but I told her that she needed to know Lloyd better. I said they should give their marriage plans more time. I told her that I could not, in

good faith, marry them.

BATTLE: Was Ann upset or offended that you would not perform the ceremony?

LONES: Oh, no. She was never the type to get offended. She was what I call a "giver" and not a "taker." Being a giver, she didn't let things like my not marrying them upset her.

BATTLE: Tell me more about Ann being a giver.

LONES: Dr. Battle, that's not easy to describe. I will use examples. Some people love to give, some love to take. The givers, like Ann, are the peacemakers in this life. Ann was very much a peacemaker. That is what I mean when I say she was a giver, not a taker.

BATTLE: You are aware that she is charged with the murder of her second husband. There seems to be no dispute that she shot and killed Edward Tatum. How do you reconcile that with her being a peacemaker?

LONES: Doctor, that is a question for which I have no answer. I have been an ordained minister for close to forty years. During that time, I've met and counseled with many people. If I had to choose five people of those I've known who would be the most unlikely to kill someone, Ann would surely be in the five I selected. Any act of violence simply did not seem a part of her nature. There are many things in this life that I do not understand, and this is one of them.

BATTLE: What contacts did you have with Ann after she married Lloyd Caine?

LONES: None while she lived in the northern state. I want

to say Michigan, but I'm not sure about that. I remember she married after the war ended in Europe, but before Japan was bombed and surrendered. She was not yet old enough to marry without her father's consent and Ell had to sign for her. So she was only sixteen, maybe seventeen. After they married, I don't recall seeing her again until she came back home.

BATTLE: Mr. Lones, Ann has told me some things about her first marriage and the reason she left her husband and came back home. I would like for you to tell me the things that she related to you as to why that marriage ended. What is your recollection of her explanation for returning to her father's home?

LONES: As best I recall, she had been married about two years. I had heard that she had a baby girl, but I hadn't seen Ann since she married. About this same time, Ell moved down to Rome, Georgia, maybe before this time, I don't remember the date. But anyway, Ell came by one day and said that Ann was back home with her baby girl, Jane. Ell said that he and Ann needed to talk to me and, in a few days, they came by the church. Ann had little Jane with her; the baby was only a few months old, maybe a year, I'm not sure. It turned out that Ell seemed the one who needed to talk.

BATTLE: About what?

LONES: He said Lloyd Caine had been abusing Ann, was drinking a lot, and involved with another woman. Ann had come back home and was seeking a divorce. She just sat there and let her father do all the talking.

BATTLE: Was that all there was to the conversation?

LONES: No. Ell was upset with Ann because she was not seeking child support and something for herself. Ann didn't have a job, she had no money, and she had a little baby to care for. Ell didn't see how they could make ends meet financially. He seemed a little angry with Ann. I understood his concern.

BATTLE: What did Ann say?

LONES: Not much of anything. She just kept repeating that all she wanted was her baby, that she wanted nothing else from Lloyd Caine. Not too long after that, she got a divorce and all she sought was the custody of little Jane. I guess that illustrates my point that she is a giver, not a taker. All that she wanted was what she carried in her arms.

BATTLE: What were your contacts with Ann after her divorce?

LONES: Hardly any. Shortly after her divorce, I took a church at Waycross, two hundred miles away. This was in late 1947, and I've seen Ann only two or three times since that date. Ann and her child were living with Ell in Rome by then and the only contacts with her that I recall were maybe two times back at Bethel Church for the annual homecoming and cemetery decoration day.

BATTLE: Did you ever know Edward Tatum, her second husband, the man she shot and killed?

LONES: Not that I remember. If we met at all, it would have been just in passing. I do not remember ever meeting him.

AS IF BUTTERFLIES HAD FLOWN AWAY

The things that William Lones related to Dr. Battle were essentially correct. Even before Martha died, a large part of Ann's childhood years were taken from her. All butterflies, it seemed, had flown out of her life.

The bond that had formed between Ann and baby Betsy was both pitiful and beautiful. It was a closeness from which Ann never fully escaped, the unbreakable link in a chain called love. After Betsy's death and for the remainder of her life, Ann was unable to speak more than a few words about her deceased sister.

Ann's attorney interviewed several of her teachers, including Ralph Gibson who had moved to Menlo, Georgia, from Cherokee, North Carolina, when he was fifteen. His mother, a full-blood Cherokee, had instilled a love of classical music in her son; his father, a former professor at Duke University, had implanted a love of history. Gibson's high school grades earned him a full academic scholarship at Vanderbilt University. Following graduation from college, he returned to the hills of northwest Georgia to be a high school teacher. Finding no venue for his piano and classical music skills, he learned to play both a banjo and a fiddle, and, when interviewed by Ann's lawyer, was an active member of a local bluegrass band.

RALPH GIBSON

Almost thirty years after last seeing her, Ann's eighth-grade history teacher, Ralph Gibson, shared his memories of Ann.

Yes, I well remember Ann Albert. I went to high school with both of her parents. Ann was in my history class for eighth and ninth grades. That would have been about 1944 or '45; it was before the war was over.

Ann was always a good girl, one who had been dealt a bad hand to play. Martha, her mother, had died before she came into my class, and then her baby sister died. I do not recall her sister's name. Frankly, Ann had not been given much opportunity to achieve in life. She was never a strong student, this I largely attribute to the difficult hand that life had dealt her. She was shy, dropped out of school a year or so later, and got married. Sometime after that Ell told me that Ann had a baby and had come back home to live. About this time, they moved to Rome and I lost track of Ann and was not aware that she had a second marriage until I heard about her being charged with murdering her husband. If you want to talk to another high school teacher about Ann, I suggest you contact Thrath Curry at Cloudland, Alabama. Curry was her maiden name; I don't recall her married name. You will not have any trouble finding her; there won't be many ladies in Cloudland named "Thrath." She taught home economics at our school and was probably closer to Ann than any other teacher.

PULLING WEEDS & HEARTSTRINGS

Job Lee's inquiry at the Pure Oil Service Station in Cloud-land brought directions from the man who pumped the gas.

"Thrath Curry? You must mean Thrath Appleby. She's the only Thrath we got. The only one I've ever heard of."

"A retired school teacher. I meant to say Thrath Apple-by. I talked to her over the phone and she expects me, but I didn't understand the directions to her house."

The attendant finished pumping the gas, replaced the nozzle in the pump, and wiped his hands on the legs of his pants.

"Buddy, you got a winner. Go to the next crossroads and turn south—that would be to the left. Miss Thrath's house will be about a mile down that road. Look for the house with a porch swing and all the flowers in the yard. She's a tiny little woman and will likely be working around her flowers. Speak up when you talk to her; her hearing's not too good. Eleven and a half gallons. That will be $4.37 for your gas."

The retired teacher was resting in the porch swing rath-er than weeding her flowers when the attorney pulled to a stop. Had Norman Rockwell been looking for the image of a retired teacher, Thrath Appleby would have been a likely choice. She might have been small in height, but her back was ramrod straight and her serious demeanor was accentu-ated by a tight knot of silver hair. Her steel rimmed glasses rested midway down her nose. Her stern "school teacher" ap-pearance belied her compassionate nature.

"You've got to be Job Lee, the lawyer. No one else would

be calling on such a hot day. Join me on the porch while I catch my breath. Keeping control of these weeds is just about beyond my reach."

"You're doing a good job. I don't see a weed in sight."

"Mr. Lee, you remind me of our preacher. Just last week he stopped by and said, 'Thrath, you and the Lord are doing a good job keeping the weeds out of your flowerbeds.' I told him he should see it if the Lord had it by himself. He laughed, but I'm not sure he found my sarcasm funny. That's what happens to old teachers; we retire to pull weeds and upset preachers with irreverent remarks. You've driven all the way from Carrollton to talk about one of my long-ago students. What may I help you with?"

THRATH CURRY APPLEBY

Job Lee, Ann's lawyer interviewed Thrath Curry Appleby:

LEE: Thank you, Mrs. Appleby, for talking to me about Ann Tatum. You knew her as Ann Albert. Please tell me about yourself and the things you recall about Ann.

APPLEBY: Mr. Lee, the first part of your question is easy to answer. I am one of what seems to be ten million retired schoolteachers. After forty years in the classroom, I retired three years ago, and my husband and I sought peace and quiet in the hills of northeast Alabama. I was shocked to receive your call advising that dear little Ann was charged with murder. I still find this almost impossible to believe and

I keep hoping this is a case of mistaken identity.

LEE: No, there is no mistake. Ann Albert Tatum is charged with killing her husband and, regrettably, there is every reason to believe she did. It is my job to try to understand why, in the hope that I can get a jury to understand why. Tell me about your contacts with and observations of Ann. It is my understanding that you taught her in high school.

APPLEBY: Mr. Lee, it's been many years since I last saw little Ann. I still see her as "little," as a child in my classroom. I do not know Ann, the adult. Please do not ask me the dates of my knowing and seeing her. I was teaching what was then called "home economics." This was a required subject for ninth-grade girls. Ann was in the eighth grade and she came to me asking permission to enroll in my class early. She made it known to me that her mother was dead and that she was trying to take care of her baby sister. It simply broke my heart when she asked, "May I get into your class and learn how to be a Mother?" Mr. Lee, those words came from a child. I shall never forget those haunting words. Little Ann wanted to be a mother and she was only a child. I remember asking myself, "What chance in life does this child have?" It was a question for which I had no answer. I loved teaching, but I had no love of questions like that.

LEE: Did she enroll in your eighth-grade class?
APPLEBY: Yes, with the permission of Mr. Burroughs, our principal. Ann's entry into my class became a heart-breaking experience. Her responsibilities at home greatly interfered with her attendance for the first few months of the eighth grade. But the child tried to learn how to be a mother, and I

did my best to teach her. The year was not too far advanced when the baby sister died. I am sorry, but I don't recall the baby's name.

LEE: It was "Betsy."

APPLEBY: Yes, how could I forget? It was little Ann trying to be a mother to Betsy. What a sad, sad arrangement, a child trying to care for a child. She was devastated when Betsy died. It seemed as if her world had come to an end. Even now, these many years later, I am overwhelmed with grief for the little girl.

LEE: Did Ann continue in your class?

APPLEBY: Yes, both the eighth and ninth grades. After Betsy died, she seemed more determined than ever to learn how to be a good mother and homemaker. Mr. Lee, this little girl greatly suffered when her sister died. She would never talk about this death, but I could tell that she needed to. She kept a tight lid on her emotions with her resolve to learn how to be a mother. Little Ann and I became very close, and it hurts me so to know that she is now charged with a crime, a crime against a family member.

LEE: Why do you emphasize "family member?"

APPLEBY: Oh, can't you see? This child loved family; she wanted family. She was breaking her back and mind trying to have a family. She had a deep need for family.

LEE: Did you know Lloyd Caine, Ann's first husband?

APPLEBY: No. As I recall, she had known this boy she planned to marry only a short time. He was from some other state and had not attended our school. I remember that Ann was very excited about the boy when she told me she was getting married. I tried to persuade her to give that more time, but, I am sure, she was compelled to marry.

Lee: Why do you say "compelled?"
Appleby: Mr. Lee, the child wanted a family, one that she could call her own. I have never seen anyone with a stronger desire for family-life, a good family-life. She was a child who was attempting to put a broken egg back together. Not having seen her at that age, it is impossible for you to fully understand her compelling need for a wholesome family.

Lee: Mrs. Appleby, why do you frequently refer to Ann as "Little Ann?"
Appleby: Because I knew her that way. She was just a little child looking for a home. I knew her only as a child. Please tell her that I still love her.

LLOYD CAINE: A WAY OUT

Lloyd Caine was nineteen when he first met Ann Albert. She and her family knew nothing of Caine's past. Had it been known, there was much that might have been helpful. Ann was sixteen and in the tenth grade.

Lloyd Caine, born at Springfield, Ohio, in 1925, was the oldest of seven children. His father was alcoholic and an abusive husband. When Lloyd was thirteen, his unemployed father abandoned his family and moved to Columbus, Ohio. Lloyd went to live with his father and shortly after moving to Columbus, became a problem for both the public school and the local police. He dropped out of school after completing the ninth grade. He was picked up and questioned by the local police on several occasions for suspected burglary but they were unable to establish enough evidence to support an arrest. At seventeen, Lloyd was arrested and convicted of receiving stolen property, a misdemeanor offense. The trial judge deferred sentencing to allow him to join the army. Caine was then assigned to Fort Jackson, South Carolina for his army basic training. He was next assigned to Fort Benning, near Macon, Georgia, where he became friends with another soldier whose family lived within a few miles of Ann's family.

Beginning in early 1945, Caine made several visits to the Summerville area, and met Ann at this time. He was the first young man to ever pay close attention to her. At the time of their first meeting, her previous "dates" had consisted of occasional meetings with boys at church social functions, school events, and a few times when she held hands during a Saturday afternoon visit to the Summerville movie theatre. On Caine's fourth visit, he asked Ann to marry him. The young couple knew very little about each other; Ann knew even less about herself. As one of her teachers said, life had dealt her a difficult hand to play. Almost to a person, those who knew Ann believed she saw marriage as a means of escape, but having no idea where she would be escaping to, nor any good understanding of what she was escaping from.

Ann's father strongly opposed her plan to marry, at first refusing to even discuss the subject with his daughter. Still Ann, in the excited manner of a child, talked to several adults about marriage plans, including Mrs. Hattie Glover ("Miss Hattie to Ann).

Mrs. Glover was living a half-mile from Ann's home when Ann's mother died. During Martha's last illness Miss Hattie, the mother of eleven children, volunteered to come to the Albert home once a week to help Ann with the weekly washing and ironing of clothes.

CHANGES: LAW & LIFE

On July 3, 1972, Job Lee talked to Ann about the recent decision of the United States Supreme Court, under the 8th and 14th Amendments of the United States Constitution, which declared the death penalty an unconstitutional punishment for murder. To Job, this seemed good news for his client. He was somewhat amazed, however, when Ann showed no reaction to this court decision that could possibly save her life. She acted as if the decision had no meaning to her. However, Lee's meeting with Ann brought the name of Hattie Glover to his attention, and he arranged to meet her.

As Job drove from his hometown to meet Mrs. Glover, he recalled that his meeting with Ann ten days earlier had been interrupted by the radio announcement that the

National Convention of the Democratic Party had just nominated South Dakota Senator George McGovern as its standard bearer for the President's seat in Washington. Job agreed with McGovern's opinion that it was time to withdraw the American troops from Indochina, and he wondered about  how national politics might affect Ann's case.

Job Lee was seated in front of another lawyer's office in Calhoun, Georgia waiting for Mrs. Glover's arrival, when a 1963 Ford pulled to a stop in front of the office. The mid-July Georgia weather had stirred new life in buildings with air conditioning units and awakened the stir of handheld funeral parlor fans in the homes with none.

A little, old lady with a badly bowed back got out of the passenger seat of the Ford, and with the aid of a heavy walking stick, made her way toward where Job sat.

"Are you Mrs. Hattie Glover"? he asked.

"What's left of me."

"I am Job Lee, the lawyer who spoke with you by telephone. Thank you for coming today. Let's go inside where it's cool to talk."

HATTIE GLOVER TESTIFIES

LEE: Mrs. Glover, do I have your permission to record our conversation?

GLOVER: Yes, you do. I have never had my talk recorded before.

LEE: Please tell me about your life and family. I will not ask your age.

GLOVER: Mr. Lee, it would do no good to ask, because I really don't know. I can remember my daddy talking about Mr. William Jennings Bryan coming to Huntsville, Alabama when he was running for President. It was about 1900, so I'm old enough to remember that. I have always felt like I was born about 1890, or before. So, I am at least eighty, likely more.

LEE: Where were you born?

GLOVER: In Valley Head, Alabama. That's across the mountain from Summerville.

LEE: Tell me about your life and family.

GLOVER: I was one of ten children. I have done better than Big Mama, that's what we called my mother. She only had ten children. I had eleven. When I was about ten, Big Mama and Daddy moved to Mentone, Alabama. From there, they next moved to Trion, Georgia. I was twenty years old when they made that last move. I met and married Cecil Glover. He grew up in the Trion community.

LEE: Where have you and Mr. Glover lived?

GLOVER: We were married at Calhoun. Not long after we

married, Cecil became a sharecropper on the farm owned by Mr. Ellis Albert, Sr.; he was Ann's granddaddy. We moved to the Albert place and have lived there ever since. My husband died in 1960. The land we live on passed hands after Mr. Ellis died, but we managed to stay on. It's my hope to be living there when I die.

LEE: Mrs. Glover, what formal education do you have?
GLOVER: I have never had the opportunity to darken the door of a schoolhouse. A kind lady, Mrs. Alice Thomas—she was a retired school teacher—taught me to read and write. As my children went to school, I studied their books. I have learned that children are some of the best teachers in the world, at least in my world. Mr. Lee, I have little book learning, but I think I know some things about life.

LEE: Mrs. Glover, I am sure you do. I take it that you came to know Ann Albert Tatum by living on her grandfather's land. Is that the way it happened?
GLOVER: Yes, I was living there when Mr. Ell and Miss Martha married. Miss Martha is long dead now and Mr. Ell is, too. But that is how I came to know both Ann and her baby sister, Betsy. Betsy is long dead, as well.

LEE: Please tell me what you recall about Ann, her mother, and baby sister.
GLOVER: Mr. Lee, when you called me, wanting to talk to me, did I understand you to say that Ann is going to trial for killing her husband?

LEE: Yes, sadly, that is the situation.

GLOVER: My, oh my; I have no reason to doubt your word, but I almost can't believe what you're telling me. I just can't believe it. What does Ann say happened?

LEE: Mrs. Glover, the problem I have is that Ann finds it almost impossible to talk to anyone about what happened. Sometimes she tries, but just can't seem to get the words out. I really wish I could give you a better answer, but I can't. So, I talk to people who know Ann and try to understand. Any help you can give will be greatly appreciated. Please share your recollections with me. I need your help.

GLOVER: My, oh my! Where do I begin talking about Miss Martha and her two girls? Two of them now dead and the other in bad trouble. I knew Miss Martha even before she married Mr. Ell. She was a gentle soul. A gentle soul; I was at her house when old Dr. Wimberley came out to help deliver Ann. I was back at her house when the same doctor came to deliver little Betsy. Ann was about ten years old by then. Maybe older than that. Miss Martha had a bad time birthing Betsy. She was already sick when Betsy came along. She never complained, but I could tell she had been going down-hill for a long time. Nobody ever knew what kind of sickness she had. Dr. Wimberley talked like it might be TB. He wanted Miss Martha to see a doctor in Rome, but they couldn't afford to. That baby girl was only two or three months old when Miss Martha died and Ann was still a child herself. I had started my help with the clothes washing before Miss Martha died. The last year or two of Miss Martha's life was difficult. It was difficult on all the family. The country was still underneath the Depression; I mean it had all of us covered up. Mr. Ell could sometimes find work and other times could not. Cotton sold for a nickel a pound. You could buy a bushel of shelled corn for fifteen cents. We all suffered. Miss Martha and her family, me and my family; we all suffered. But through it all, Miss Martha kept on singing her church songs. Sometimes, I would sing with her. Sometimes little Ann would try to sing with us. She was such a sweet little girl and dearly loved her mama and baby sister. I never did know why, but sometimes Ann would call her little sister a butterfly. My, oh my, Ann did love that sister.

LEE: Mrs. Glover, how did Ann handle her mother's death?
GLOVER: Mr. Lee, that's when Ann's world started falling apart. That's when little Ann got what some folks call the misery of the soul. You have to be a poor person who has lived the life of a sharecropper to understand what misery of the soul is. You have to have worked in the cotton field, hoed the garden, slopped the hogs, cut and hauled the wood, mended the clothes, heard the baby cry from pain, heard the growling of your hungry guts, and feel the sting-of-death to know what misery of the soul is. Ann got it when her mama and Betsy died and I doubt it's ever turned her loose. I hope it has, but now she's accused of killing her husband. My, oh my. That child is still under the misery. Oh, how I wish I could see Ann and hold her close again. It has been so long since I saw her.

LEE: How did Ann handle Betsy's death?
GLOVER: She died again.

LEE: I don't understand what you mean.
GLOVER: When her mama died, Ann died, too. Not on the outside, but a large part of her inside died. That's a big part

46

of the misery. It's a dying of the inside. Most times, it is a slow dying. Ann was hurt when her mama died, even more so when Betsy died. Ann worked so hard trying to be a good mama for Betsy. That child worked her fingers to the bone and bled her heart to death for that baby sister. Mr. Lee, the misery is when you want real bad to do the right thing and can't do it. I have raised eleven children of my own, and now helping raise a yard-full of grandchildren, even great-grand-children. Where you know about law, I know about children and misery. I have never seen any child who tried any harder than Ann did. She was a shy little girl, but, my-oh-my, she was determined. She was determined to keep that family together. Determined to make her mother well, but she died. Determined to make a good home for Betsy, and then she died. Not all folks know what misery of the soul is, but Ann knows.

LEE: Mrs. Glover, from the time Betsy was born until Ann married the soldier from Ohio, how often were you with her?
GLOVER: At least once each week when I went to help with the washing and ironing. Often times, more than that. I could not help her as much as I wanted to. I had a house full of my own family.

LEE: How did she react to Betsy's death?
GLOVER: She dug a hole, crawled in, and pulled the top of the hole in behind her.

LEE: Please explain.
GLOVER: Mr. Lee, for me to even try to explain will make me

cry. Even after all these years, it will make me cry. There are special angels in heaven that need to know when someone you love has died. Ann never let those angels know Betsy had died and that it was time for the angels to give a helping hand.

Lee: I'm sorry, but I don't understand what you're telling me.

Glover: Mr. Lee, special angels watch over us. They look for tears in our eyes that tell them a loved one has died. Ann never called on them for help. She never cried. There were no tears on that child's face. There was no way for the death angels to know it was time to come, hold close, and dry the tears. When I learned Betsy had died, right away I went to Ann's house to hold her in my arms. I went to cry with her, to mourn with her, to send tear signs to the special angels. I held Ann in my arms and cried and cried. But the angels weren't looking for my tears, they were looking for hers. Her tears never came. That little girl never cried for Betsy. I knew it was not a good thing, but there was nothing I could do.

Lee: Did Ann ever talk to you about her sister's death?

Glover: The only thing she would ever say to me were things like, "I should have known better. I should have done better." Mr. Lee, she tried to carry all the load on her two shoulders and she wouldn't ever turn it loose.

Lee: What was her life like after Betsy died?

Glover: She was able to go to school on a regular schedule. She seemed eager to learn things, but she remained an unhappy little girl. She didn't complain, but I know an unhappy child when I see one; I have seen more than a few.

LEE: Did you continue to work in the home each week?
GLOVER: Most of the time. On occasion I would not be able to make it, but most of the time I did.

LEE: With the passage of time, did Ann seem to adjust to Betsy's death?
GLOVER: She tried to cover Betsy up.

LEE: What do you mean?
GLOVER: Mr. Lee, have you ever lost a child?

LEE: No, fortunately, I never have.
GLOVER: Well, I have walked that road and it isn't easy. You have to turn loose the body, but you want to hold on to the spirit. Ann tried to cover up both the body and the spirit of Betsy. She tried to close that door so tight no light could creep through.

LEE: How did she demonstrate this?
GLOVER: By never crying. Never talking. Never showing any tears on her little face. By covering up the baby bed.

LEE: Explain about the baby bed.
GLOVER: Betsy was only about two when she died. I don't remember the exact age, but she was very young. So young she was still sleeping in her baby bed. It was one of those metal baby beds made with the iron rods and knobs. It was painted white, but it was old and some of the paint had been worn or chipped off. The first time I was in the house after the funeral, I saw that someone had put all of Betsy's clothes and playthings in that bed and covered everything with a

sheet. Everything was completely covered so nothing about Betsy could be seen anymore. I asked Ann why everything was covered like that. She said that she wanted it that way, and until she got married, she kept the memory of Betsy covered. Mr. Lee, when we lose a child, we need to walk with the spirit of that child for as long as we live. We need to hold on to pleasant memories of people so everyone knows we remember. Ann did not do it that way. She tried to cover both the body and the spirit. Trying to do it that way got the best of her.

LEE: What do you mean when you say "it got the best of her"?

GLOVER: I mean her marrying that soldier from Ohio when she hardly knew him. Do you know about that marriage?

LEE: Yes, I know part of that history, but I would greatly appreciate your recollections of those events. I know the soldier was named Caine and that Jane was born of that marriage. Tell me what you remember.

GLOVER: It happened about two or three years after Betsy died. Ann was still in school. The soldier came home with another boy from this community, Mr. Wilkins' son, who was in the army. The Caine boy, the one Ann married, came to visit just a few days and only a few times. I do not know how many, but I do know it was not enough for them to get to know each other. Mr. Lee, Ann felt like she was in jail and she wanted to escape. That's the way she felt. About the time Ann started seeing stars in her eyes from the Caine boy. Mr. Ell started calling on Mrs. Rosalie Scott and that did not help Ann's feelings.

LEE: Tell me about Mrs. Scott.

GLOVER: There's not much to tell, but Ann did not see it that way. Mrs. Scott lived about a mile down the road. She had been a widow for years and had lost a son when the war started at Pearl Harbor. Mrs. Scott was a very nice lady, older than Mr. Ell, and they went to the same church. Miss Martha had been dead close to two years before Mr. Ell started sometimes stopping at the Scott place just to talk. That's all there was to it, just talk. They would sit on Mrs. Scott's front porch and talk for a while. Ann did not understand her daddy needed some life of his own. She never said anything, but I could tell it was not to her liking.

LEE: Where was Ell working at this time?

GLOVER: Let me think for a minute. He worked for the WPA for about two years. I bet you don't know it, but folks called the WPA the "We Piddle Around." After the WPA, he did some concrete work for Clarke Construction and after the war started, he went to work for the Summerville Machine Shop. He would have been working at the Machine Shop when he started to visit with Mrs. Scott. There was nothing to it, more than sometimes stopping to talk, but I am sure Ann was uneasy. She had lost her mama, her sister, and now, to her, it looked like she might lose her daddy.

LEE: Did Ell ever remarry?

GLOVER: No, not that I know of. As far as I know, he never married again. Mrs. Scott was older and probably looked on Ell more as a son than anything else. The Bible teaches that we are never given a load too heavy for us to carry, but Ann did not see things that way. That child felt trapped by life and she was looking for a way out. She thought she saw some daylight and she went for it. Mr. Ell was opposed, but he finally gave his consent.

Lee: Did she talk to you about her plan to marry?

Glover: In a roundabout way. She was a shy girl. When Mr. Ell told me that she wanted to marry, I tried to talk to her. I begged her to go slow, to wait awhile and get to know Caine better. She listened, but she did not hear. I could tell that she was looking for a pot-of-gold at the end of a rainbow. She was so young and knew so little about life. I tried to get her to wait, but she thought she saw that pot-of-gold. Ann and that soldier went someplace, and, as I understand, they got married. Mr. Ell told me they had moved to Ohio. The next thing I knew about Ann was a year or two later when she came back home with her baby daughter, Jane. Mr. Ell had moved to Rome by this time. After Ann came back, I saw her little girl for the first time when they came to visit some of their family at the old home place.

Lee: How often did you see Ann after she returned from Ohio?

Glover: Not more than a half dozen times. This would be when she came back for homecoming and Cemetery Decoration Day at her old church. I don't remember the dates. She lived in Rome with her daddy and her aunt for several years, got married again, had another little girl and then moved to Atlanta. The last time I saw Ann, she had a second child with her. I'm sorry, but I do not recall that child's name. What was the name of her second husband?

LEE: Edward Tatum. Ann called him Ed.

GLOVER: Is that the man that she is charged with killing?

LEE: Yes. Did you ever meet him?

GLOVER: Mr. Lee, my old memory is not what it once was. The last time I saw Ann, she had the new baby girl and it seems like I met her new husband. I am not sure. My old mind sometimes plays tricks on me.

LEE: I understand. My mind, though not as old as yours, does the same thing. Mrs. Glover, allow me to ask you some questions of a different nature. Ann is accused of killing her husband in a very violent way. Did Ann ever show signs of being a violent person, of having a violent temper, things like that?

GLOVER: Oh, no Mr. Lee! She was just the opposite. She was as gentle as a kitten. How is she accused of killing her husband?

LEE: Mrs. Glover, she is charged with shooting him several times and, to be honest with you, it appears that is exactly what she did.

GLOVER: Oh, my God have mercy! Mr. Lee that cannot be true! Ann could never intentionally shoot anyone. She is not that kind of person. There is some terrible mistake. I know Ann. I have known her since she was a baby. Mr. Lee, there is something wrong here, very wrong. Ann could not do that.

LEE: I am sorry to tell you, but there appears to be no mistake.

GLOVER: Is Ann in jail?

LEE: No, she has been released on bail. She is at her home, awaiting trial.

GLOVER: Mr. Lee, what is her state of mind? How is her health? How is she holding up?

LEE: Mrs. Glover, she isn't doing well. She is in the first level of Parkinson's disease. She's lost a lot of weight and is very withdrawn. Like when Betsy died, she covered things up. She is not able to share many things with me. That's one of the reasons why I'm talking to people like you. I am having a difficult time understanding what happened in Ann's life that caused her to do the very thing that others, like you, say she is incapable of doing.

GLOVER: If I can get to Atlanta, would I be able to visit with Ann?

LEE: Yes, I am sure that could be arranged. My phone number is on the card I gave you. If you are coming, let me know and I'll be sure that you can see Ann.

GLOVER: Mr. Lee, I am an old woman. Please tell Ann that I would love to see her and give her another good hug. Tell her that, if I can, I will give her another hug.

PIECES OF THE PUZZLE

Slowly and with considerable difficulty, Job started putting together the puzzle pieces of Ann's early life. With the consent of her father, she married Lloyd Caine in 1945. After he was discharged from the army, the couple made their home in Dayton, Ohio. For the first several months in their rented Ohio apartment, all went well. Lloyd worked at his uncle's auto repair shop on Chestnut Street. Ann found work as a sales clerk in a nearby department store, but soon the honeymoon ended.

In their fourth month of marriage, Ann learned that she was pregnant. Five months later, she lost her job and the young couple, with less income and no insurance, began having financial problems. Soon thereafter, Lloyd's alcoholic consumption became a problem, and before the baby was born, he started to physically abuse Ann. In August of 1946, their baby, Jane Marie Caine, was born. The police records of Dayton show seven responses to domestic abuse calls made by Ann during the last two months of her pregnancy and the first four months of the baby's life. The police records show that she declined to sign an affidavit for the arrest of her husband. She didn't want to cause trouble for her family.

In April 1947, Ann and her baby spent the afternoon at the home of Helen Ferguson, an older woman who had taken an interest in Ann and made her welcome in her home. When this lady drove Ann and the baby back to Ann's apartment, Lloyd and a young woman were found inside. Both were nude and highly intoxicated.

Without attempting to gather anything from the apartment, not even a change of clothes, Ann and the baby went home with Mrs. Ferguson. There, she telephoned her father and he wired money to the Dayton Western Union Office for Ann to buy a bus ticket back to Georgia.

STARTING OVER

In her divorce action, Ann only sought the custody of her child. William Lones, in talking to Dr. Battle years later, was correct. Ann was a giver, not a taker.

In preparation for the murder trial, Job Lee interviewed more than thirty people who had known Ann throughout her life. This history revealed that Ann was, and always had been, a passive, non-assertive person. She avoided confrontations and consistently yielded to a stronger personality. Yet, her attorney was confronted with hard evidence that his client had shot her husband once in his chest and seven times in his back as he attempted to run away. On the face of it, the twelve people in the jury box would think Ann was anything but non-aggressive.

SEARCHING AND MATURING

The intervening years between the time Ann returned to Georgia with her baby and the time she shot and killed her second husband were a blend of the difficult, the happy, and the tragic.

Ell Albert and Aunt Bee were waiting at the Rome bus station when Ann and her new baby arrived from Ohio. She and her baby were pitiful to behold. The bus trip, scheduled for two days, had taken four. The bus from Dayton was late in arrival at Lexington, and this caused Ann to miss her connecting bus and created a twelve hour delay. Her second

bus had mechanical problems at Norris, Tennessee, which caused a ten hour roadside delay before a replacement bus arrived. None of the buses had toilet faculties. Missed connections in both Knoxville and Chattanooga created more confusion and added to the delay. Ann, having left all her clothing in her apartment at Dayton, wore, for the fourth day, an ill-fitting dress that Mrs. Ferguson had given her. The dozen diapers Mrs. Ferguson had purchased for the trip had all been used and the last diaper was past due for a change. The weather had turned unexpectedly cold and the weary travelers stepped shivering from the bus. Aunt Bee took them to her house, got them bathed and fed, and then privately went to her bedroom and cried.

Ann was starting over, trying to build on the fragmented pieces of a life that experienced many difficulties, but her father and her aunt provided much support. With their help, Ann was able to attend a secretarial school in Rome. After completing this course of study and training, she found employment in the office of a supervisor who worked at the large paper mill on the west side of Rome.

The six years between Ann's return to Georgia and her

second marriage in 1953 were busy ones—secretarial school followed by employment, caring for little Jane, and helping Aunt Bee with housekeeping and cooking. This left little time for social activity, but when time permitted, involvement in a few activities at the Jackson Street Baptist Church of Rome was Ann's only diversion.

It was at this church that Ann made the acquaintance of a retired high school history teacher, Wallace Henry. He had earned his bachelor's degree in history at Clemson University and his master's degree, also in history, at the University of Georgia. He had taught in various public schools in Georgia for forty years. Now retired, he worked as a volunteer counselor with the division of the local courts that handled juvenile cases. Ann was drawn to this man for two reasons; he was kind and considerate, and he reminded her of her maternal grandfather.

Mr. Henry taught the Sunday school class for young adults in which Ann had enrolled at the Jackson Street Church. For more than a year in Mr. Henry's class, she had wanted to privately talk to this compassionate man about some of her anxieties, but, she lacked the courage to do so. Finally, at a Sunday school social function, she found both courage and opportunity and asked if he had time to speak with her.

"Sure Ann. Time is mostly what I have. When would you like to see me?"

"Well, I work five-and-a-half days each week, and I have Jane to take care of."

Sensing her uncertainty, Wallace Henry took the lead, "How would it be if you come to my house this coming

Thursday night? Marie and I are always home on Thursdays. I may be able to get her to make us some of her fried peach pies. Would you be free to come around seven?"

"Thank you, Mr. Henry. If I have a problem getting there on time, I will be sure to call you."

Back at Aunt Bee's house, after making the appointment to visit with Mr. Henry, Ann had second thoughts about the meeting she had requested. She was troubled and in need of discussion with an older, wiser person, but she did not know how to verbalize her concerns. More and more, after returning from Ohio, she had internally wrestled with the age-old questions of "Is there life beyond this one and how does one know? If there is another life, is there some certain way to find that life? If God has all knowledge, does He not know what the future of all will be? Are all things predetermined? Does anyone in this life have the ability to influence things in the next life?"

Ann needed an older friend, but she was fearful of offending Mr. Henry. She was struggling with herself, looking for answers, and afraid of what the answers would be. Nevertheless, she decided to keep her Thursday evening appointment and arrived at the Henry home a few minutes before seven.

Wallace's wife, Marie, had baked a fresh coconut cake instead of the fried pies Mr. Henry had earlier mentioned. After some light conversation over a piece of the cake and a glass of milk, Mr. Henry led Ann into his study so they might privately talk.

In this manner, Ann came to know and greatly respect

Wallace Henry. He was the first person she had ever known who seemed to understand her, who seemed to accept her the way she was. Later events physically separated Ann from Mr. Henry, but they did not sever their emotional bond.

WALLACE HENRY: AT HOME

Three months after Ann had been arrested for killing her second husband, Job drove to Rome, Georgia, to interview Wallace Henry. Not wanting to reach the Henry residence earlier than the agreed time, he stopped in the center of the west Georgia town to again visit the statue of the wolf suckling Romulus and Remus. This statue, a replica of the original in Rome, Italy, had been a gift to the city by Italian dictator Benito Mussolini in 1929. Cooler heads of city government during World War II when the country was at war with Italy had denied the movement of some residents to destroy the statue.

Rome, Georgia, like its namesake in Italy, had been built on seven hills, divided by a river. Archeological evidence suggests both cities were first occupied by humans at least fourteen thousand years ago. As historians record events, the Rome of Georgia was founded in 1834. Gold had been discovered five years earlier in nearby Dahlonega, and the Native Americans of the area had been forced from their home by the Indian Removal Act of 1830.

The Rome of Italy was, according to historical records, founded almost 2,600 years earlier than that of Georgia. According to legend, Romulus and Remus, the twin brothers, were in dispute over which hill the Italian city should be built. This dispute led to the death of Remus, but not before the brothers had been suckled by the wolf of Palatine Hill.

Wallace Henry lived in the Blossom Hill area of Rome, Georgia. He was watering potted plants on the front porch of his small home when Job pulled into the driveway. The two men had spoken by phone twice before but had never personally met. The telephone conversations had given Job the impression that Mr. Henry was a small man as he had spoken with a soft, weak voice. The attorney was surprised to find him tall, erect, and robust, despite his age.

As the attorney came up the front steps, Mr. Henry greeted him, "Please allow me to finish watering this Cinnamon Fern before I shake your hand. It was one of my wife's favorites and, as you can see, hauling it in and out of the house, trying to keep it alive, has made an old man out of me."

The watering of the fern completed, Mr. Henry turned off the hose and wiped his hands on the legs of his khaki pants. "I'm Wallace Henry," he said, extending his hand. Welcome to my home. Let's go inside and I'll pour you a glass of iced tea, that is if you like tea."

Job Lee was fascinated with Wallace Henry and readily understood why, many years ago, his client, too, had been made captive by the man's magnetism and charm. He had driven fifty miles to interview Mr. Henry in preparation for his case.

"Mr. Henry," Job asked, "do you think Hernando de Soto came to Rome in his travels through this area?"

For the next twenty minutes, Job Lee listened as Mr. Henry shared the various theories of several historians on the route de Soto traveled in 1540. He ended with, "I'll take the risk of you not quoting me to our local Chamber of Commerce by saying I do not know. He came close to the area. How close, no one will ever know. I have lived long enough to realize that when I say what I know, I should always end the sentence with a question mark rather than a period."

For more than two hours, much longer than Lee had intended, the two men sat at the table and talked. Job found it hard to believe that anything Wallace Henry said should be ended with a question mark. With reluctance, he directed the conversation to the purpose of his visit, gathering an understanding of his client, Ann Tatum.

WALLACE HENRY INTERVIEW

LEE: Mr. Henry, how old are you?
HENRY: I am in the eighty-seventh year of life.

LEE: You appear remarkably well. How do you stay so young?
HENRY: I read and write some each day. I love writing simple poems and short stories. I try to go to my gym several days each week. I can't do too much at the gym anymore, but the young ladies at the gym like my sexy body. Trying to be a male sex symbol at age eighty-seven is not an easy assignment!

LEE: As you know, I represent Ann Albert Tatum. Ann is in serious trouble—charged with first-degree murder. I have the sworn duty to investigate her case and try to present her side of the story to the jury. I am making a recording of our conversation. Do I have your permission to continue recording the things we discuss?

HENRY: Of course. How would it be if we made our conversation a little less formal? You call me "Hank." That's what my friends call me—and I will call you "Job."

LEE: That would be fine with me. Hank, I will be very candid with you. I'm worried, very worried, not only about the outcome of this trial, but also about Ann's great depression. She has pretty much gone into a shell, and she does not want to come out. She acts as if she is willing to assist me in preparing her case, but I can't get much information from her. She tries, but seems to get lost in her effort. Sometimes, I have to ask her the same simple question several times before she attempts to answer. Sometimes the answers never come.

HENRY: Job, I will assist in any way I can. It has been many years since I last saw Ann. I never met her first husband, Lloyd Caine. I did meet Edward Tatum, her second husband, but I knew little about him. So I may not have any information that is of interest. You ask the questions, and I will answer to the best of my ability.

LEE: I would like for you to tell me what you know about Ann. I am trying to first understand my own client. If I can understand her, I may be able to get twelve people in the jury box to understand her. So, first help me understand

Ann. Tell me the things you remember about her. Tell me, as best you recall, your previous relation with her, what you saw in her and what you heard from her. Tell me the good and the bad, the ugly and the pretty that you saw in Ann.

HENRY: I first met Ann as a member of a Sunday school class that I was teaching at Jackson Street Church here in Rome. It was a young adult class. I had already retired from teaching, so the year would have been about 1948 or 49. I knew that she had previously been married, that she had a baby girl, and that she had a job at the local paper mill. She appeared painfully shy. She was always pleasant, but shy. I guess it was at least a year after I met her before she and I had a private conversation.

LEE: Tell me about that conversation. How did it come about? What was it about?

HENRY: I forget exactly how it happened. Ann overcame her shyness and made known that she would like to talk to me. Marie, my wife, was alive at the time, so I invited Ann to our home. We talked privately for an hour, or so. I tried to let Ann introduce the subject that she obviously wanted to discuss, but she seemed reluctant, even afraid, to do so. My first impression was that she was afraid of someone that she did not want to name. This was my strong first impression that evening as we talked.

LEE: Did she name someone that she was afraid of?

HENRY: No. It turned out that my impression was wrong. Ann was not afraid of any person. She was afraid of life. She was afraid of what life might do to her and her little girl. I'm sorry, but I don't recall the child's name.

LEE: Her name is Jane. What did Ann say that indicated she was afraid of life?

HENRY: She told me about her mother dying when she was a young girl. She told me of a baby sister dying a year or two after her mother died. She talked of her love for both her mother and little sister. She talked of her fear of death and her uncertainty of any life after this one. When she dwelt so much on this subject, I realized that her fear was not of someone, but of living. Life had treated her harshly and she seemed afraid of life.

LEE: Was there more discussed?

HENRY: Ann and I had several private discussions after the first one, so what we talked about on each occasion has blended together, and it is impossible to say with certainty what was said on each occasion.

LEE: That is understandable. Give me your best recollection.

HENRY: In several later discussions, Ann broadened her expressions of fear. I later realized she was not as afraid of life as she was of failure in life. In our earlier discussions, it became evident she felt she had failed in caring for her baby sister and had contributed to the baby's death. Several times, she talked of her determination not to ever fail Jane, her own baby. Slowly, I came to realize she feared failure even more than death. Possibly I split hairs in trying to distinguish being afraid of life and being afraid of failure in life. Possibly the two are inseparable.

LEE: Did she ever say what she would do should she fail in achieving some goal?

HENRY: Not that I recall. She was determined she wouldn't let failure in anything else occur in her life. She was most determined not to ever let another marriage fail. She blamed herself for the failed marriage, just as she did the death of her baby sister. Ann carried a heavy load of guilt. I didn't feel her load was justified, but it did not matter what I felt, she was the one with the burden.

LEE: Did you press her to more fully explain?
HENRY: No, I tried not to press on anything. I have found it best to just let people who need to talk, just talk. Has Ann talked to you about her fear of failure?

LEE: No, she has not. As I indicated, it's hard to get her to talk about anything.
HENRY: I see. Is Ann out of jail, awaiting trial?

LEE: Yes, she has been released on bond. She's not permitted to leave the state of Georgia.
HENRY: Job, was there any marital infidelity in Ann's marriage to Edward Tatum?

LEE: Yes. Ed had gotten involved with a woman in Memphis. Why do you ask?
HENRY: I think infidelity by her husband would have been very difficult for Ann to handle. She had already walked that bitter path in her first marriage. As my grandfather would have said, 'She had already plowed the field.' Ann was determined she would never again have a failed marriage.

LEE: I can understand, but I fear that the jurors will never understand that Ed's infidelity was a sufficient reason for Ann to kill him. Hank, there will be no dispute in the trial of this case about who did the shooting. Ann shot Ed, not once, but a total of eight times. How may that be explained?

HENRY: Job, you are the lawyer. I'm just an old man who has never been inside a courtroom. I judge you to be about thirty-five years old, fifty years younger than I. Maybe the jurors will understand Ann if you can first get them to understand themselves.

LEE: How would you accomplish that?

HENRY: I have watched just enough television trials to understand that you will have the opportunity to ask the prospective jurors some questions before the final selection of the jury is made. Is that the way it works in the Georgia courts?

LEE: Yes, we call that the *voir dire* examination. The judge will give me reasonable opportunity to ask the prospective jurors about themselves, their lives, their values, beliefs and disbeliefs. If you were Ann's attorney, what would you ask?

HENRY: Ann did what she did for a reason. If she won't talk to you, no one else will ever know her reason. I don't know how to help with that problem, but I do know that most of our acts are for a reason. It may be a good reason; it may be a bad one. My gut feeling is that Ed's unfaithfulness was a large part of Ann's reason, though I agree that shooting someone eight times for infidelity will be a difficult pill for a jury to swallow.

LEE: How would you go about getting the jurors to first understand themselves so they might understand her?

HENRY: I will answer another of your questions with a question, if you don't mind. Are you a thief?

LEE: Well, no. When I was teenager, I stole some watermelons and peaches. But that was almost twenty years ago. No, I am not a thief.

HENRY: Would you steal again?

[For several moments, the tape of the recorded conversation was silent, suggesting uncertainty on the part of the attorney. Following this pause, Job answered.]

LEE: No, I do not think I would steal again.

HENRY: I noticed you paused before answering that last question. There is a reason for that pause. None of us like to see the potential in ourselves to do the things that we condemn others for. Do you agree with that?

LEE: Yes, I agree. How does that help with the jury selection?

HENRY: Again, another question from me. You told me that you have a wife and three children. What if you could not feed them? What if you could find no honorable way to feed them and they were at the point of starvation? What if I was your next-door neighbor with a smokehouse full of meat and a pantry full of canned goods and I refused to share with my starving neighbors. If that were the situation, would you steal from me before you let your babies starve?

LEE: Yes, if those conditions existed, I would likely steal from you.

HENRY: Job, you qualify your answer. You say you would 'likely' steal from me. Is that the complete truth?

LEE: No, it is not. If those conditions existed, I would steal from you.

HENRY: Young man, I have played lawyer long enough. You have a difficult assignment and I wish both you and Ann well. All of us have the potential for good and bad. Most of us easily see our potential for good. Seeing our potential for bad is often difficult, sometimes impossible. Sometimes circumstance makes one act in a way that is completely out-of-character. The Ann I know is not a killer, yet you tell me that she killed. There must be a reason, one that the jury will hopefully understand. Let us hope her reason was a good one.

FINDING THE WATER TOO DEEP

Job Lee had gained Ann Albert Tatum as a client through his representation of Pete Atkinson, Ann's son-in-law. Pete had called Job a few hours after the Atlanta Police found Ann sitting on her kitchen floor, rocking her dead husband in her arms. After she was taken into custody for questioning, a neighbor called Jane to report the events of the afternoon. Pete, in turn, phoned the only lawyer that he had done business with.

When Job spoke with Pete, he explained that he had little criminal law experience and that a more experienced attorney should be called. At Pete's urging, Job Lee agreed to contact the police department in order to determine what had happened and to see if Ann was under arrest. This initial commitment slowly led Job more and more into Ann's legal problems and the dynamics of her life. Without realizing it, he was caught in a web, one that would pull him deeper and deeper into his client's life. This pull would increasingly take him more and more away from his own family, his other clients, and his routine of life.

Job was well entangled in this web of trying to understand and represent Ann before he recalled the admonition of his criminal law professor who told him and his classmates: "If you handle many criminal cases, sooner or later one will come along that will become your jealous mistress. There is no need for me to explain this warning, you will know when it happens, and then it will be too late. Your role as a criminal defense lawyer is not complete until you have had at least one jealous mistress."

Job was driving home after his visit with Wallace Henry when he realized he had found his jealous mistress. He recalled the warning of his law professor—that when it was realized the mistress was there, it was too late to escape her ever-tightening grip.

Through hard work and much thought, and with the cooperation of Wallace Henry and many others, Job Lee slowly came to know Ann Tatum. And, the more he knew, the more he wanted to know. His jealous mistress had become his constant companion, demanding all his time, thought, energy, and attention.

LEST WE LOSE OUR EDENS

Ann's life between the time she returned to Georgia from Ohio and the time she married Edward Tatum was largely uneventful, as society would gauge such things. She worked, helped Aunt Bee tend to household chores, took care of her child, attended her church, and found a confidant in Wallace Henry. In him, she found a degree of freedom to express her thoughts that she had never experienced before. On several occasions, she unburdened her fears and anxieties. On her fourth visit to the Henry residence, she carried a copy of the little butterfly poem that her mother had often recited to her.

"Mr. Henry, I made you a copy of the little poem my mother recited to me. I love it, and I wanted you to have a copy."

"This is a nice little poem. Who wrote it?" he asked after reading the poem.

"I don't know. My mother didn't know. She would stop her work around the house, hold me on her lap, and recite the poem to me. I loved it. I see you have several books of poems on your shelf. Do you like to read poems?"

"Yes, I do. To me, poems are about life, about our joys and sorrows. I find much peace of mind in reading poems. Do you read poetry?"

"Not really. I find most poems hard to understand. A lot of poems aren't written the way we talk, and I kind of get lost in trying to read them."

Ever the teacher, counselor, and friend, Wallace Henry reached behind his chair and pulled two books from the shelf. He handed one to Ann. "This is a selection of poems by

Elizabeth Barrett Browning," he said, "I want to give it to you, Ann. I think you will enjoy many of her poems."

"Thank you, Mr. Henry. I've never had a book of poems for my own before. The poems I've read have been at school. Do you have a favorite that you think I should start with?'

"Ann, selecting a favorite of Elizabeth Browning would be a difficult job. Her writing reflects many different moods. I suggest you start with her poem titled "Love." There is one verse in that poem worth remembering, it goes something like this:

"We live most life, whoever breathes most air."

"Why do you suggest that poem as a place for me to start?"

"I would prefer to let you read and study that poem, and you decide why I suggest it to you. It seems to fit with your life. I think you will enjoy Elizabeth Barrett's poems. The other book I have in hand contains some poems by Robert Browning. His poems have more masculine appeal, so I will keep this book for myself. However, there is one verse of his poem, "A Woman's Last Word," that I remember:

Where the apple reddens
Never pry—
Lest we lose our Edens,
*   Eve and I.*

"What did he mean by that?"

"To me, he is saying that for a full life, we must some-times take chances. Life is not without risks, but we must not let the potential for harm spoil the remainder of life."

"Mr. Henry, I know why you recited that to me."

"Why, Ann?"

"Because I got a divorce. Because I made a mistake and have been afraid to admit it. I see that now. Sometimes I think my marriage to Lloyd was a mistake, but then I look at my little girl and realize if I had not married, I would not have Jane. So, was it a mistake, after all? My thinking just takes me around in a circle."

"Ann, do you think that you will ever want to marry again?"

"I really can't answer that. I do know that if I marry again, it will be for real."

"What do you mean, 'for real'?"

"I mean it will work. It will be the real thing. I will make it forever. Mr. Henry, it is not a nice thing to say, but if I marry again, I will crawl through hell if that is what it takes to make it work."

"Ann, there are two other quotations from Robert Browning's poems that I will share with you:
Ah, but a man's reach should exceed his grasp,
 Or what's a heaven for?
The other:
Grow old with me!
The best is yet to be,
The last of life for which the first was made.

"It sounds as if Mr. Browning was willing to take chances, is that correct?"

"Yes, Ann, I think that is a fair statement about him. He knew that life had many risks, but he also knew that life could have much joy. He seems to tell us we need to run with our heads held high, and we should not be afraid to hold hands and speak of love. He seems to say that the hazardous way is sometimes best. I think Robert Browning was saying that we should do these things, and that if we fail to do them, we will likely go through life with tears of regret in our eyes. That is my interpretation."

A year after this conversation with Wallace Henry, Edward "Ed" Morris Tatum moved to Rome and took a job at the paper mill where Ann worked. Ed, four years older than Ann, was born and reared in the small town of Notasulga, Alabama. With good humor, Ed would often say, "You don't know where Notasulga is, so I'll tell you. It's exactly halfway between Liberty City and Loachapoka."

Ed was an amicable person who easily made friends. He'd joined the Marine Corp in 1942 and saw combat on three Pacific Islands, beginning with Guadalcanal. He'd served his nation both honorably and well. Following discharge from the military, he enrolled at Alabama Polytechnic Institute, now Auburn University. He was the first member of his family to attend college, and in 1949, he graduated with a degree in Mechanical Engineering. Following graduation, he got a job with a construction company in Atlanta. In 1950, he was offered a better position with the Rome Paper Mill and he took it.

Although they worked at the same place, Ann and Ed first met at the Jackson Street Baptist Church. Ed showed an immediate interest in Ann. Her interest in him developed slowly. Their first opportunity for a semi-private talk was at the church's Fourth of July picnic and softball game. Ann had five-year-old Jane with her for this outing.

Ed walked over to Ann's blanket, that was spread under a large oak tree. He brought his friendly smile with him.

"Hi, Ann. Is this your little girl?"

"Yes, this is my love. Her name is Jane. We have sandwiches and some of Aunt Bee's deviled eggs. Would you like to join us?"

"That's the best offer I've had in a long time. I'll go get us some drinks. What would you and Jane like?"

"We have some of Aunt Bee's ice tea that we'll share with you."

"Ann, I can tell you are from the South."

"How is that?"

"You say 'ice tea.' That's the South speaking. In the North, they don't know any better and they call it 'iced tea.' I would be pleased to have some of Aunt Bee's deviled eggs and ice tea."

Ann and Ed shared the food and more than two hours together. He demonstrated an easy manner and way with Jane, convincing her that he had a genuine interest in the child. During this hour, Ed shared some of his family background. This started with Ann telling Jane, "Honey, get Mr. Ed to tell you where he is from. I can't pronounce the name of the town."

Ed took the lead, saying, "Jane, I was born and grew up in a very small town in Alabama with the funny-sounding name of Notasulga. That's only one of many Indian names in Alabama. Some of the others are Coosa, Tallapoosa, Etowah, and Tuscaloosa. Now let me tell you a little story about my home town. When I was a boy about your age, my family got a dog named 'Miss Heck.' Have you ever heard of a dog named Miss Heck?"

"No sir, but I know a dog that lives across the street from Aunt Bee's house that is called 'Wags.' That's the only dog I really know."

"Well Jane, would you like to know about Miss Heck?"

"Yes, sir."

"I'll make a deal with you. If you can get your mother to pour me another glass of Aunt Bee's tea, I'll tell you about Miss Heck."

With a fresh glass of tea in hand, Ed continued, "Jane, when I was a boy, I always wanted a dog. Some of the other boys in town had dogs and I wanted one, too. It was a small town with a big, tall water tank that stood on a big vacant lot. All of us boys would play on the vacant lot and it seemed like every boy in town, except me, had a dog. I knew not only the names of all the boys, but I also knew the names of their dogs, and cats, too. I wanted a dog so bad, I could just taste it. I begged and begged my mother to let me have a dog. Do you know what she would always say?"

"No sir."

"She would look at me with a sad look in her eyes and say, 'Ed, we simply do not have the money to afford a dog. Daddy is barely making enough to feed us.' That was my mother's answer for a long, long time. Can you guess what happened?"

"No sir."

"Young lady, you are a very polite and nice girl. You always say 'Yes sir,' and 'No sir.' I'm proud of you for being so polite."

"Thank you, Mr. Ed."

"Well nice little girl, when I was six years old, a really bad storm came though Notasulga. Some people were hurt and several houses were blown away. It was scary. After the storm passed through, the sky got really dark, almost like midnight. After the darkness, the rain came. It rained and rained and rained. I was quite scared. Would you like to hear the rest of the story?"

"Oh! Yes sir. I really would!"

"Well after the storm, the darkness, and the rain left my little town, I heard a noise on our front porch. I ran and opened the door and guess what I found on our porch?"

"A dog!"

"How did you guess it? Yes, on my porch was a tiny dog, a rat terrier. Jane, I never knew where the dog came from. I knew every dog and cat that belonged in our town. This little dog, a female, was not a local dog. I have always wondered if she came to town riding on the back of the storm. There is more to the story, but I don't reckon you want to hear any more, do you?

"Oh yes! Please tell me the rest of the story!"

"Well, when I found that little dog, I set into begging, 'Oh Mama, please let me keep this dog. She has no place to go. She has no place to sleep. She has nothing to eat. Mama, please, please, please.' Jane, Mamas are special people and I knew she was going to let me keep the dog when she said, 'Oh heck, another mouth to feed.' I got to keep the dog and I named her 'Miss Heck.' This just shows us that sometimes good things can come from bad things like storms. Maybe the next time I see you, I can tell you about our milk cow, her name was 'Daisy.' Would you like to hear about her?"

"Yes sir, I sure would."

Ed Tatum shared other parts of his life with Ann and Jane that day, telling them of his grandfather moving to Notasulga after the Civil War. This grandfather had served in the Union Army and was awarded 160 acres of land in Lee County, Alabama, as compensation for his military service. He related many of his childhood experiences growing up as the only child of Walter and Peggy Tatum. He shared a humorous story of how his father had been wrongfully arrested after being mistakenly identified as a bootlegger during the Prohibition era and acquiring the name of "Wild Cat" as a consequence of the mistaken identity. He spoke of the "hard times" common to all during the years of the Great Depression. Without any sharing of details, he mentioned his years of military service, his desire to be the first of his family to attend college, and the saving grace of the GI Bill that allowed him to realize his dream. Again, without details, he briefly told of the accidental death of both his parents during his junior year at

Alabama Polytechnic Institute.

As Ed told his stories, Ann watched Jane and was somewhat saddened. The child was spellbound and, as Ann well knew, in need of a father image in her life. They parted that day with Jane looking forward to hearing the story of Daisy, the cow. Ann was afraid to open the door to her future and afraid to keep the door closed as well.

Over the first twelve months of their friendship, Ann and Ed saw each other at church functions about eight times. During this interval, Ed asked Ann for a date six times. Each time, she answered that she appreciated the invitation, but wasn't ready to date again. After the sixth rejection, Ed asked Ann, "When will you be ready to date again?"

"Ed, I don't know. I wish I did, but I simply don't know."

"Is there anything more you can tell me? You are a nice person. I really like you. Is there something wrong with me?"

"Oh no! Please don't think that. It's me. I am so unsure about myself and about my life. It is not you."

"Well, I don't see anything wrong with you. I like what I see in you. I just wish we could spend more time together."

"Ed, I guess I'm afraid to try again. My first marriage didn't work out, and I am honestly afraid to try again. It's me, not you."

Ann slowly emerged from her protective shell and started dating Ed, and much slower than he, she fell in love again. Ed had many qualities that she liked and very few she disliked. He was courteous, dependable, and honest. He was good to both Ann and her child. He lived within his budget and enjoyed a good reputation both socially and professionally. Sometimes he would consume a little more alcohol than Ann liked to see, and occasionally he would use some coarse language among selected friends, but these habits were modest and caused no problem for anyone. To her friends, she described Ed as a happy and nice man.

In late 1952, Ed was again offered a better job, this time with an Atlanta manufacturing company. The job offer included educational benefits that would enable Ed to enroll in graduate engineering studies at the Georgia Institute of Technology. He was excited about the opportunity but didn't want to move away from Ann. He went by her home the evening that he heard about the job offer. Aunt Bee served him a slice of German chocolate cake, after which he invited Ann to join him in one of Aunt Bee's front porch rocking chairs.

On the porch, they found Socks, Aunt Bee's old tomcat asleep in one of the rockers. Ed picked him up, took the chair, and re-positioned Socks in his lap. Gently stroking the cat's back and talking to Socks, "Old fellow" he said, "I hope you've had a good day and you will have a better tomorrow. I hope no dog has chased you up a tree; you are too old for that. Now continue your sleep while I talk to this pretty girl."

Socks, anticipating this command, was already asleep in Ed's lap. Instead of talking to the pretty girl, Ed fell silent as they watched the day's fading light. Ann broke the silence.

"You've got something on your mind besides petting Socks?"

"Yes. Do you remember the story I told Jane about my little dog named Miss Heck?"

"I do. That's a neat story. Thank you for sharing it with

both of us."

"Well, today I feel the same way I felt when I found Miss Heck."

"What do you mean?"

"I was so excited that I found her and was so scared that I wouldn't be able to keep her. That's the way I felt then. That's the way I feel now. I'm a little boy again, wondering if I can keep Miss Heck."

"What is it, Ed?"

"I received a wonderful job opportunity today."

"Tell me about it."

"It is with a fairly new, but growing, manufacturing company that makes heavy, dirt-moving equipment. Their new facility is in Atlanta. Taking the job gives me an opportunity to start with the company on the ground floor and work my way up. They'll pay my tuition and furnish my books if I pursue my master's degree."

"Ed, that is wonderful! I am happy for you."

"Well, there is one hitch."

"What is that?"

"I can't go unless you and Jane go with me."

For the past few months, Ann had felt that the day of reckoning was approaching. The relationship had deepened to the point that she felt a decision about remarrying was inevitable. Even so, she was not prepared.

"Ed, are you asking me to marry you?"

"Yes, that is exactly what I'm doing. I know this isn't a very romantic way to do it, but I want you as my wife. I want Jane as my child. I want all of us to move to Atlanta together and live happily ever after. Honey, I need both of you by my side. I want to keep Miss Heck, have her as my own. Will you marry me?"

"Give me a few days, Ed. Give me a few days."

Two nights later Ann visited Mr. Henry in his study. "Ann," he said, "I can tell you are worried. What is it?"

"Ed has asked me to marry him and move to Atlanta."

"I thought it might be that. Have you made a decision?"

"No. That's why I need to talk to you."

"My young friend this is a decision only you can make."

"Yes, I know. But, I always feel better after I have talked to you. I've talked to Daddy and Aunt Bee. I don't want to talk to the preacher at our church. I want to marry Ed, but I am afraid to."

"Ann, I have found it helpful in making hard choices to ask, 'What is the worst thing that can happen to me if I do this?' And then ask, 'If the worst happens, can I live with it?' So I ask you, if you marry Ed, what would be the worst possible result and could you live with that result?"

"Mr. Henry, the worst thing would be for a new marriage not to last. For it not to be forever. I don't know if I could live with that."

"You say you want to marry Ed, but you're afraid to, that you are reluctant."

"Yes."

"Robert Frost wrote a poem he called "Reluctance." In this poem, he deals with the same emotions that now pull you in different directions. Allow me to read just the last part of what he wrote:

Ah, when to the heart of man
Was it ever less than a treason
To go with the drift of things,
To yield with a grace to reason,
And bow and accept the end
 Of love or a season?

"Mr. Henry, I don't understand what he meant."

"Ann, it means whatever you want it to mean."

As Ann left Mr. Henry's home that evening, he gave her the small book of selected Frost poems.

Over the next few days, Ann was drawn to a line in Frost's poem, "The Death of the Hired Man." The line read:

Home is the place where when you have to go there, they have to take you in.

The line seemed to speak to Ann. Aunt Bee's house was warm and friendly, nice in many ways, but it was not home. Jane needed a home. Ed needed a home. Ann read the poem again and again. Each time, she was pulled to the same line and her recurring thoughts of the need of a home to call her own. Several times she recalled Ed saying he hoped to keep Miss Heck as his own.

The following weekend, Ann went back to Mr. Henry's house to talk to him about the Frost poem and her need for a home. She had decided to marry Ed. In parting that day, Wallace Henry gave her a warm hug and said,

"Ann, I always wish you well. You take life very seriously. Sometimes I think you are a little unfair to yourself. So, in addition to wishing you well, I wish you will always be good to yourself."

In late January 1953, Ed and Ann were married at the Floyd County Courthouse in Rome. Three weeks later, they moved to Atlanta. Ann married with the determination that her marriage to Ed would be, in her words, "the real thing." As she had told Wallace Henry, she would crawl through hell if that is what it took to make this marriage last.

To describe the next eighteen years of the life of Ann and her family would be like describing the lives of millions of Americans during this particular time. There were a few bumps in the marital road that they jointly shared, adjusted to, and put behind them. They first rented an apartment on Briarcliff Road in northeast Atlanta. After two years, they were able to make the down-payment on a small, but nice, home in the same area. Ed received regular promotions in his work with modest increases in pay. The couple lived a simple, but good, life together.

On occasions, at social functions, Ed would consume a little too much alcohol, but he always willingly surrendered the car keys so Ann could drive them home. His selective use of modest profanity continued, but his crude language was never directed toward any individual nor intended to offend. All who knew Ann and Ed during this time described their lives and relationship as "wholesome, respectful, loving, and caring. There was nothing they could not handle; they seemed a happy couple."

CARL SCOTT INTERVIEW

Other than family members, no one knew Ed Tatum better than Carl Scott.

LEE: Tell me about your acquaintance with Edward Tatum.
SCOTT: We were the same age, entered the first grade together. Lived just four houses apart in Notasulga until the war. Ed and I entered college together at Auburn. He came to Atlanta to work, then took the job with the Rome Paper Mill. I stayed at Auburn for my master's degree. After Auburn, I took a job in Chattanooga. In early 1952, I was hired by the new equipment company in Atlanta. Later that year, the company was looking for another mechanical engineer. I told the personnel director about Ed and they offered him the job.

LEE: So, the two of you grew up together, went to school together, and then worked together?
SCOTT: That's right. We worked together until Ed moved to Memphis in 1970.

LEE: At work, how frequently did you see him?
SCOTT: Just about every day for sixteen or seventeen years. For the first twelve years, our desks sat side by side. For the remainder of the time, our offices were just two doors apart.

LEE: During those years and apart from work, what contacts did you have with Ed?
SCOTT: Our families were close. Several times each year we

visited in each other's homes. We shared family outings with each other. Three times we went for a visit to Notasulga. Ed's parents were dead. Mine were still alive and living in Notasulga. We wanted our kids to see where we grew up. Ed and I remained close.

LEE: Was there anything about Ed's behavior that suggested marital infidelity?

SCOTT: Never. Ed was a cut-up, sometimes a clown and a joker, but he never indicated a desire to jump over the marital fence. Each August, we would attend the Southeastern Machine Manufacturers convention at Hilton Head. This was an all-male affair and the vendors who sold machine parts to the manufacturers flooded the convention with booze and women. On these occasions, sex was available for the asking. All you had to do was wink. Sometimes Ed would laugh and joke with those girls, but he never left the room with them.

LEE: How would you characterize the relationship of Ed and Ann?

SCOTT: There is only one way. It was good. They loved and respected each other. Whatever problems they had were resolved by agreement. They did not fuss or fight. They were good to each other.

LEE: Did you see either of them after Ed moved to Memphis?

SCOTT: I saw Ed only once. That was in early 1971 when he was home one weekend. I saw Ann several times when my wife and I went by for a visit.

LEE: Did you notice any changes in Ann?

SCOTT: Not until a few days before Thanksgiving, 1971. My wife had bought a turkey for Ann and her family. I was shocked to see the changes that had taken place since I had seen her about two months earlier. She had lost a lot of weight, her tremor was much worse, and she looked old and tired.

LEE: Did she say anything about her problem?
SCOTT: No, and it would not have been nice for me to ask. I knew something was wrong, but I did not know what. When I got back home, I called Ed to express my concern. Ed said that he, too, was concerned about Ann, but he did not say what the problem was. My wife went to see Ann several times after that, before Ed died, and Ann always acted as if all was normal.

LEE: Have you seen Ann since Ed died?
SCOTT: Three times Betty, that's my wife, and I have gone by to see her, but she was not herself. She seemed a different person. She seemed to be someplace else. We called Jane several times and she told us Ann was under a doctor's care. Frankly, Betty and I didn't know how to handle the situation. Both Ed and Ann were close friends and we didn't know how to act. It was and is a very awkward situation. We decided to just back away for the time being and give things time to fall in place. It seems like a play, like some kind of drama, that had been half played out and then someone rewrote the script, changing everybody's part and now no one knows their lines. Nobody knows what they are supposed to say or do next. But these changes took place after Ed took the job in Memphis. Until then, they had a healthy, happy family.

DEATH'S BROAD REACH

In 1967, Dana enrolled as a freshman at Ponce De Leon High School in Atlanta. She was a good student and looked much like her father. She had his friendly personality, and Ed was extremely proud of her. She was well-liked by her classmates and respected by her teachers.

Dana had an extremely close relationship with her father, of this no one had any doubt, but when she was in the middle of her sophomore year at Auburn, February 1972, her world fell apart. Her father, Ed Tatum was killed by her mother, Ann Albert Tatum.

In July 1972, five months after her father died, Dana was interviewed by the psychiatrist, Dr. Carl Battle. His discussion with her was particularly painful. She had made three previous trips to the doctor's office to be interviewed, only to find that she could not control her emotions to the extent that she could talk. The doctor's extensive interview notes were interlaced with parenthetical notes such as "cries profusely," "had to stop for control," "could not continue for five minutes."

BATTLE: Dana, describe your father.
D. TATUM: Which one?

BATTLE: Do you have more than one?
D. TATUM: Yes sir, it seems that way.

BATTLE: Tell me about the one you knew best.
D. TATUM: He was a great Daddy. A Great Daddy.

BATTLE: What made him great?

D. TATUM: He spoiled me. Let me get away with too much.

BATTLE: Like what?

D. TATUM: Just about everything.

BATTLE: Did this get you in trouble?

D. TATUM: Nothing serious. Sometimes it would get me in trouble with Mother. She knew that he was letting me take advantage of things. Sometimes she would talk to me, telling me that I was taking advantage of him.

BATTLE: Did this cause problems between your mother and father?

D. TATUM: Not really. Daddy knew I was getting away with too much. He agreed with Mother. When Mother would say something about it, he would just laugh and say something funny that would make all of us laugh. It was no big deal.

BATTLE: What else made him a great Daddy?

D. TATUM: He was dependable. He was always there when we needed him. I knew I could always have help from him when I needed it.

BATTLE: Did he have occasion to discipline you?

D. TATUM: He sure did. If I did something that was wrong, he would be the first to get on my case. I wouldn't like it at the time, but I knew he was right.

BATTLE: Did he ever use corporal punishment? Give you a spanking or a switching?

D. Tatum: Daddy never did anything like that. He could just give me that "Daddy look" and that was enough. I pretty much knew my limits. Sometimes I would fudge a little, but he let me know how far to go. I have no recollection of him ever even acting like he was going to give me a spanking. That wasn't his way of doing things.

Battle: What were your Daddy's good qualities and characteristics? Give me one-word descriptions.
D. Tatum: Are we still talking about the Daddy I liked best?

Battle: Yes. We will talk about the other Daddy later.
D. Tatum: His good qualities. Let me think of one-word answers.

Battle: Dana, take all the time you wish. Do you want to take a break before you answer?
D. Tatum: No. I am sorry that I get upset when I try to talk about Daddy and Mother. I am okay. His good qualities: dependable, honest, funny, happy, always there when needed, I guess that is another way of saying dependable. Friends and neighbors respected him. I'm sorry. I'm not giving you one-word answers.

Battle: Dana, you are doing just fine. Answer as you wish.
D. Tatum: I guess the best thing was that we all knew he loved us.

Battle: Who is "us?"
D. Tatum: Mother, Jane, and me. Those were the main ones. He loved other family members. I am sure he had some

friends that he also loved, but not in the same way that he loved us.

BATTLE: How did you know that your Daddy loved you, Jane, and your Mother?

D. TATUM: The same way you know when the sun is shining. You can feel it. You can see it. Sometimes you even seem to taste it. I am not giving very good answers to your question, am I?

BATTLE: Young lady, you are giving splendid answers. I know exactly what you mean. You mentioned a moment ago that your daddy was respected by his friends and neighbors. What about respect from his immediate family?

D. TATUM: Oh, Dr. Battle! I did not mean to limit that. The daddy I liked best had the respect of all of us. How could it have been otherwise? He was a good man. He was good to all of us. How can anyone not respect goodness?

BATTLE: Dana, you said that your daddy never spanked you. How did he treat others? Did he have physical confrontations with other people?

D. TATUM: Dr. Battle, he was not that kind of person. Sometimes he might strongly disagree with someone and would let them know it. But, he never threatened to get physical. He was not that sort of person.

BATTLE: What of your mother? Did your parents have serious confrontations? Any violence or threat of violence?

D. TATUM: Never, Daddy never threatened to do Mother any harm.

At this point, Dana was unable to continue. Her interview resumed two days later.

BATTLE: Dana, we were last talking about any violence between your mother and father. Do you feel like continuing that discussion?

D. TATUM: Yes, sir. I am sorry that I got upset. Mother, like Daddy, is not a violent person. She is the gentlest person I have ever known. She would do no harm to anyone, particularly Daddy. Dr. Battle, Mother loved him. She worshiped him. She thought he hung the moon. She was so proud of him, so proud of our family. She devoted her life to us. My mother is not a violent person, she…

BATTLE: Dana, let's take a short break. I am going to get a Coke, would you like one?

D. TATUM: No, thank you.

Dr. Battle left the room, leaving Dana alone. When he returned, it was obvious she had been crying.

BATTLE: Thank you for letting me get a drink Dana. Do you feel like continuing?

D. TATUM: Yes, sir.

BATTLE: You were telling me about your mother not being a violent person.

D. TATUM: Dr. Battle, I am very confused. I don't know which way to turn. I feel lost. Completely lost. I know my mother, just as I knew my father. They never fussed and fought with each other. Never. Never. Never. But Mother shot and killed my daddy. How can I say she wasn't a violent person if she did that? I love both my parents. Daddy is now dead. Mother killed him. I still love both of them. It seems as if Daddy is still alive. Mother is alive and it seems as if she is the one who is dead. I am so confused. I am just lost. A little girl is lost in the woods. I don't even know who I am. Sometimes it seems like the entire world has turned upside down and it is on top of me.

Again, the interview was halted so Dana could take a break.

BATTLE: Dana, let's continue talking a little about the Daddy that you liked. What were the bad qualities and characteristics of the Daddy you liked?

D. TATUM: Dr. Battle, back to your question about Daddy showing any violence. The only time I ever heard him really get upset with Mother was one day when he left his fishing rods laying in the driveway behind the car and Mother accidentally backed over them. Daddy got angry and said, "God damn, you backed over my fishing gear!" That is the only time in my life I heard him swear at Mother. Later, he apologized to Mother for saying that. Later, after he thought about it, he realized it was his fault. Daddy was not a violent man. He would not think of ever hitting Mother. I'm sorry, I forgot your question.

BATTLE: I was asking about any bad qualities of your father, the father that you liked.

D. TATUM: I didn't see any bad in my daddy until the last year or so of his life. But that was the different Daddy, the one I didn't like. Mother thought he sometimes used crude language, a little profanity, but she should have heard some of the boys I went to school with and she would know Daddy was just a freshman in that department. Mother thought Daddy sometimes drank a little too much. But, again, she should see what some of the school kids were doing.

BATTLE: Did you ever see your father when he was intoxicated?

D. TATUM: Never. Mother had some kind of hang-up about drinking. I think her first husband, Jane's daddy, maybe drank too much. I think that may have been a problem in her first marriage. Mother never talked very much about that time of her life. But my daddy seldom drank. Sometimes, in the summertime, when he was hot from mowing the yard, he would drink a beer or two. It's hard for me to identify bad qualities in my daddy, except for the last part of his life. During the good part, I simply didn't see any bad in him.

BATTLE: Dana, tell me about your mother. First of all, do you see her in two parts, the way you see your father? Is there a Mother that you like and one that you don't like?

D. TATUM: I don't like what she did to him. I don't like what he did to her. So, is there a Mother that I do not like? Dr. Battle, here is where I get lost. Here is where I feel alone in a dense forest.

BATTLE: Explain what you mean.

D. TATUM: The Mother who killed Daddy is not the Mother I know. The Daddy who treated Mother the way he did at the last is not the Daddy I know. They are both strangers to me, people I have never known. So, do I see a Mother I like?

Yes, I do. Do I see a Mother I do not like? I guess my answer is both yes and no.

BATTLE: What do you mean?

D. TATUM: I love the Mother I have always known. I don't love the Mother who killed my daddy.

BATTLE: Dana, are you saying that you love your mother, but you don't love what she did?

D. TATUM: Yes! That is exactly what I am saying. I had never thought of it, but that is exactly what I mean.

BATTLE: Keeping that distinction in mind, tell me about the good qualities of the mother you love.

D. TATUM: That is easy. Kind, gentle, loving, considerate, quiet, tender, compassionate, caring, devoted. Her family was her home. Daddy was her life. Jane and I were her life. Her world centered on the three of us. Mother didn't want things beyond us. She was determined that we would be a happy family.

BATTLE: What are your Mother's bad qualities?

D. TATUM: She killed Daddy.

BATTLE: Are you afraid that she might hurt you or someone else?

D. TATUM: Herself.

BATTLE: What do you mean?

D. TATUM: Every day now, I fear that she will hurt herself. She will not hurt anyone else, but I fear for her.

BATTLE: Has she talked to you about hurting herself?

D. TATUM: No. But, I can tell. I told you about how alone I feel now. Mother is more alone than I am. She is all alone in her world, and there is no one there.

BATTLE: Does she talk to you?

D. TATUM: She answers my questions, but she really doesn't talk.

BATTLE: Dana, we are almost finished now, but there is one important area we need to discuss. You told me about the Daddy that you love and you also said something to the effect that he became a different Daddy, one that you did not like. I don't recall exactly how you stated that. Do I recall correctly what you said?

D. TATUM: Yes, sir.

BATTLE: Would you like to tell me about this other Daddy now, or would you like to come back to see me on a later day and tell me?

D. TATUM: Could I use your bathroom first?

Dana excuses herself to go to the toilet but stays there an unusually long time. The nurse goes to check, finds her crying profusely, almost hysterically, and advises Dr. Battle: "Dana says she can't talk about the Daddy she does not like. It is too painful. Dr. Battle, this child has suffered so much; we need to stop for today."

The doctor agreed, and the interview was discontinued.

RELATIONSHIPS CHANGE

At age twenty-two, in 1968, Jane married and moved to the small town of Carrollton, Georgia, where her husband, Pete Atkinson, owned and operated a modest retail business. Both Ed and Ann approved of the marriage and pledged their support.

In June 1972, Job Lee interviewed Jane Caine Atkinson, Ann's first child. Lee had once represented Pete Atkinson's small retail business in Carrollton, Georgia. He and Jane had met socially several times before, and it had been at Jane's urging that her husband had called Job for assistance when she first learned the man she considered her father had been killed and her mother had been taken into custody by the Atlanta Police.

Both Jane and Job knew that today's meeting in Job's office would not be of a social nature. Both were aware, keenly so, that the death of Edward Tatum and Job's role in defending Ann had re-arranged their relationship. Both now wore different hats. Job represented "hope" in a new, frightening, desperate situation that Jane and her family had never known before. Job was no longer the friendly face that assisted Pete, Jane's husband, in routine small business matters. He could no longer laugh, joke, and wear a happy smile when they met. Jane looked at Job across his desk and realized both she and Job were changed by events beyond their control and they could never be the same.

Job was also aware of the altered relationship. He was mindful that Jane, in an unexplainable manner, was embarrassed to talk to him about her family tragedy and that she now saw him in a different light. He sensed Jane's irrational feelings of personal guilt and shame related to the death of the man she considered her father.

The relationship between the Atkinson and Lee families could no longer be casual and open. Events beyond their control had forever altered their lives and relationship. Both regretted this, but there was nothing they could do.

Job was also aware of his own limitations, his own lack of criminal law experience, and the limited ability of the client to fairly measure the competency of the attorney. Again, he remembered the words of Richard Cramer regarding the profession of law and its interplay with private life.

MENTOR REMEMBERED

When Job opened his office in Carrollton in the summer of 1962, Richard Cramer, a retired trial lawyer from Augusta, Georgia, lived on a farm a few miles southeast of Carrollton. Cramer was often considered strange, if not eccentric. He wore old, faded overalls, seldom shaved, drove an old Hudson automobile no one knew the age of, and came to Carrollton only on Tuesdays and Thursdays. Cramer often used Latin terms when speaking, but no one in town knew if he used them correctly.

Job had opened his office for the practice of law on a Monday. The following day, Richard Cramer walked into his office, right past Job's receptionist without speaking, and entered Job's private office. Job was pleased to receive his visit.

"Boy," Cramer said, "what makes you think you can be a lawyer?"

"Well, Mr. Cramer, I graduated from law school and passed the bar exam. I now have my license."

"Hell boy, I have known hundreds who have done the same thing, but that didn't make them a lawyer."

"What is your definition of a lawyer, Mr. Cramer?'

"It's a man who has sense enough to pour piss out of a boot without having to read the directions on the heel. It's a man who has grit in his craw and lead in his pencil."

"There were two girls in my graduating class. What about women lawyers?"

Cramer paused in his answer, and when the answer came, Job realized it was the serious, meditative side to this old man that most residents of the town considered strange.

"Job, the day for women in law, medicine, government, and commerce is dawning. They will bring in a new day. Most men are afraid of this; I think it will be a good thing. Men, me included, have driven the wagon for a long time. In many ways we have not done a very good job. The boys down at the barbershop and pool hall will not agree with me, but I say we need the woman's help."

"Have you ever seen a woman trial lawyer?"

"Only two. One in Augusta, twenty years ago. The other in Savannah, thirty-five years ago. Both of them beat my tail. But, the female attorney's day is coming. You've heard it said that women and blacks should be kept in their 'place.' Well, their 'place' is changing and it should." He looked intently at

Job. "Now, what kind of lawyer do you want to be? Now that you have that fancy diploma and license, what the hell are you going to do with it?"

"Mr. Cramer, I'm just getting started, so I really don't know what sort of practice I'll have. I'm not sure I have enough grit in my craw to be a trial lawyer. I understand trial work is very demanding. You were a trial lawyer, were you not?"

Again, Richard Cramer took a long time to answer. When he did, his answer seemed to come from a different time and age, and when he spoke, his words didn't come from an unshaven old man wearing ragged overalls. His words seemed to come from a place beyond the present. Maybe from yesterday. Maybe from tomorrow. But, not solely from today.

"Yes, Job. Most people considered me a trial lawyer. That's what I was, whatever I was called, and that is what I did. I didn't see myself as a trial lawyer. Do we ever see ourselves for what we are? I think not. I think we are so close that we cannot see, hear, smell, or taste what we are doing. I never saw myself as a trial lawyer. I saw myself as a poor farm boy who had come to town to work, to find a job, and to make a living, and that is what I did. You are right about trial work being hard. Son, it consumes you. It eats you up. You get lost in it; you seem to drown in it. Yes, it takes grit. It is in many ways cruel. It is cruel to the clients, cruel to the lawyer, and cruel to his family. Sometimes you get so lost in it you completely forget your family. Family members speak to you, but you are too lost in your thoughts to hear. That's wrong. But that is the way it is, or at least that is the way it was with me.

I can't really tell you how things are to others; I am limited to telling you how things were with me. Sometimes I think I know how things are with others, but I really don't. Life is a personal thing."

"Do you regret having been a trial lawyer?"

"No. How does anyone regret having seen the sunshine, having been to the mountaintop and seen the other side? How can anyone forget having weathered storms and lived to see another day? Life is a mix. Trial work is a mix. My trial practice in Augusta was a general one, mostly criminal, but also enough civil work to expose me to a cross-section of the human race and all the problems, all the unexpected, and funny things that come with the human race. Job, I have laughed with many clients. With more than a few, I have cried. My trial practice was a great teacher. To my thinking, a good trial lawyer must be aggressive. When he, or she, sees daylight, it is time to run for it. If someone is in his way, there must be a willingness to run over that person, but do it in a way that does not offend. Now that takes special talent. Being able to run over someone's ass and do it in a non-offensive way is difficult. It is hard to hit a fellow in his jaw and make him like it. But to be a good trial lawyer, you must have that ability. You do not want to appear to be a bully, but you have to have that bully instinct. I guess I am saying that you have to have a little streak of meanness in you. You don't want it to show, but it has to be a part of you."

"I would think it impossible to run over the other lawyer and make him like it."

"Son, you are right about that. I overstated my case when

101

I said that. Like everyone else, old lawyers often talk too damn much. When you kick the other fellow's ass, he'll never like it but if you do it the right way, he'll respect you. Respect is what you strive for. One way that I got respect was being well prepared for trial. I tried to know more about the case than anyone in the courtroom. I tried to outwork the other lawyer in preparation. As a group, lawyers are lazy bastards. Most of them want to sit on their ass and fail to prepare their cases the way they should. To get respect, be prepared to try your case. In every manner, let the other lawyer know that you are ready for trial, that you look forward to meeting in the courtroom, toe-to-toe and jaw-to-jaw. Don't ever go to the other lawyer wanting to settle your case. Just get ready for trial and let the other lazy lawyer come to you. This will earn respect."

"Mr. Cramer, I really appreciate the opportunity to talk to you about law. There is little trial practice here in Carroll County, or at least there doesn't seem to be much court work. I'm still learning my way around. It was just yesterday that I opened my door and hung out my shingle. What advice would you give me?"

"Son, it does not do much good to give advice. Most of the time the one giving it is wrong. The rest of the time, the one seeking it doesn't listen or follow. I've had several young lawyers ask me that same question. I always tell the asking person that my advice is not worth a bucket of cold spit. In addition to being well prepared and willing to try your case, about the only thing I would say to you is never compromise yourself and never let your client's hopes get too high."

"Sir, if you would, please explain what you mean."

"About never compromise yourself, I mean be a straight-shooter. When you tell a judge, or the other lawyer, or your client, or your neighbor something, always let them know you will do what you promised. Keep your word. Never compromise your integrity. There will be times, however, when the unexpected happens and you cannot keep your word. When that happens, seek out the person you have given your word to, look them in the eye, and explain why you can't do what you said you would do. By your words and actions, let others know they can trust Job Lee."

"What did you mean about not letting the client's hopes get too high?"

"Job, why do clients come to see the lawyer in the first place? They seek you out because they have their tail in a crack and the crack is pinching. The bigger the problem, the greater the need for help. Lawyers are a bunch of parasites; they make their living off of the troubles of the human race. You mention Carrollton being a small town and there being little court work. Son, there are people living here, and wherever there are people, there will be tails in cracks. We don't know about it yet, but as we talk, it is likely someone in Carrollton is lying, cheating, stealing, flimflamming, or trying to bed another man's wife. People find a way to get in trouble and when they do, they get their hopes up by calling on a lawyer. When one of these clients comes to your office seeking help, when they have stolen, cheated, or been caught fanning the covers with another man's wife, they will come to you with hope in their eye. Be careful not to give them too much hope. Be careful not to build them up for a fall."

"Mr. Cramer, I'm sorry, but I don't fully understand what you're telling me about a client's hope."

"I am saying that people in trouble are desperate people. The greater the trouble, like being charged with murder, the greater the desperation and the need for help. Desperate people are looking for hope, for a way out of their trap. They are prone to see the lawyer as a savior, someone who can work some miracle and make their troubles go away. They see the lawyer as a miracle-man. Those who are in this trap are very vulnerable. They are dead-in-the-water and see sharks swimming all around them. They are desperate for hope. Some unethical lawyers take advantage of this desperation by gouging the clients for money, for all they have and can borrow. Don't get me started on that subject. Job, with the desperate client, just keep in mind they are desperate and do not take advantage. Offering too much hope is as bad as taking too much money, maybe worse. Just tell your client that you will do your best, and then do it."

THE LAWYER'S ANXIETY

Several times, after committing to represent Ann Tatum, Job Lee remembered Richard Cramer telling him that people in trouble are desperate people. Now, four months after Ann Tatum had been arrested for murder, her daughter Jane Atkinson was waiting in Job Lee's office. She had been invited there to talk about her mother and the death of Edward Tatum. As she waited, the frightening impact of why she was there seemed overwhelming. She was not there to talk to Job Lee, her family friend. She was not there to talk to her husband's attorney about some minor business matter. She realized there would be little, if any, superficial talk of Job's wife and children and if such talk was had, it would not be heard or remembered. Everything had changed. Jane was there as a different person, one who waited to talk to a different lawyer.

Jane could not fix the date of the great changes in her life. Sometimes, she thought it was February 1972 when her mother shot and killed the man she knew only as "father."

In Lee's office, Jane looked at the dress and shoes she was wearing. Her clothes were clean, but nothing more. Her hair was clean, but nothing more. Uncertainty, anxiety, fear, and depression had become the reality that had wormed its way into her life. Often now, she could not sleep. Often she neglected doing the things that once seemed important and without realizing what was happening, the circle of desperation spread. It ensnared everyone around her, her family, and also her lawyer. Job feared that his commitment to represent Ann was a mistake, and he doubted his ability to effectively help her. Richard Cramer has warned him not to let the hopes of those he represented get too high, and these thoughts ran through his mind when he stepped into his reception room and invited Jane into his private office.

INTERVIEW WITH JANE ATKINSON

LEE: Jane, thank you for coming to talk to me. How is your mother doing?

ATKINSON: Job, things are not good. Mother has lost so much weight her clothes just hang on her. Her right hand shakes so much from the Parkinson's she can no longer write her name.

LEE: How much worse has the Parkinson's gotten?

ATKINSON: Stress seems her worst enemy. At times, Mother's tremor is uncontrollable. She can't even hold a cup or glass in her right hand now. She has to eat with her left hand, using a spoon.

LEE: When was she first diagnosed?

ATKINSON: It was early 1968, about the time Pete and I became engaged. Daddy was so sweet and considerate when Mother was diagnosed with Parkinson's.

LEE: What did he do?

ATKINSON: Daddy was really a funny man, and he was a very considerate person. I know you find that hard to believe after learning of the things he did to Mother and Dana the last year of his life. But Daddy had changed by then.

LEE: Have you always called him 'Daddy?'

ATKINSON: Yes, always. Job, he was my daddy. Not biologically, but that didn't matter. He was my daddy. I belonged to him and he belonged to me. In his eyes and ways, I was just like Dana.

LEE: You were telling me how he reacted when he learned your mother had Parkinson's.

ATKINSON: Daddy could make everyone laugh. When he found out about Mother's health problem, he dressed in some ragged overalls, put one of Mother's kitchen pots on his head and came into the den where Mother, Dana, and I were seated. He pretended that he was Johnny Appleseed. He said that Johnny had traveled over much of the Eastern part of America, but he had never seen the Grand Canyon. He wanted to take his three beautiful girls to the Grand Canyon. He wanted to rent a motorhome and travel for a month. Daddy got down on his knees with that pan on his head and pretended he was proposing marriage to Mother. He told her that he understood she had some health problem that made some parts of her body shake. He said he hoped going to the Grand Canyon would make Mother's butt shake, because he loved it when a pretty woman shook her butt at him. He was hilarious, making all of us laugh. There was no way he could have handled the Parkinson's news any better.

LEE: Did you make the Canyon trip?

ATKINSON: Oh, yes. We made it in a rented motorhome, just the way Johnny Appleseed had suggested. Job, my Daddy was a good and decent man. I will always love him. If I live a hundred years, I will never understand how he could have changed so much after he moved to Memphis.

LEE: It seems like you and Pete married about three or four years ago. Is that correct?

ATKINSON: Yes, in 1968.

LEE: How frequently did you see your parents after you married and moved to Carrollton?

ATKINSON: Maybe an average of once a month, plus birthdays and holidays. Daddy took the new job in Memphis in the summer of 1970. I would see him on the weekends he came back home.

LEE: Was this to be a permanent job?

ATKINSON: Yes. It was a good opportunity for him. He felt he had advanced as far as he could go with his old job, and he was excited about moving forward. So was Mother.

LEE: Why didn't she move to Memphis with him?

ATKINSON: Dana was going into her senior year at Ponce de Leon High. She wanted to graduate with the same class that she started with. Mother and Daddy talked about this. Daddy always gave in to Dana, and to me, too. He wanted Dana to graduate with her class. So, they agreed that Daddy would take a small apartment in Memphis for a year. Mother and Dana would continue to live in Atlanta until Dana graduated. There was no problem about this. Everyone was in agreement.

LEE: What were the plans after Dana graduated?
ATKINSON: She wanted to attend Auburn University. That's where Daddy went to school. Dana had her heart set on this school and both Daddy and Mother wanted it for her. After high school graduation, Mother would sell the Atlanta house and they would use the money to buy another house in Memphis.

LEE: How many times has your Mother seen Dr. Battle?
ATKINSON: I believe four. I've driven her two times, and I think Dana has taken her two times. I believe he thinks she might be suicidal. He doesn't say that, but he suggests that someone should try to stay with her at all times.

LEE: Do you think she might take her own life?
ATKINSON: Job, I don't like to think that would happen. No one wants to think like that. But, Mother keeps going downhill. Every time I see her, she has slid further into a dark pit. I keep hoping to see my real mother, but she doesn't exist. Yes, I fear for her life, though I think I understand suicide a little better now.

LEE: Jane, do you think of taking your own life after all this tragedy in your family?
ATKINSON: No, that is not what I mean when I say I think I understand suicide better. Until all this happened to us, until Daddy changed the way he did, until Mother did such a violent thing, I couldn't understand why any rational person

would take his or her own life. I think I see now why they would.

LEE: Are you talking about your mother?

ATKINSON: Yes, my dear, dear mother. Job, she is dead already. The district attorney wants to convict her of murder so she may be punished. This is almost a joke. How do you punish someone who is dead already? Mother sees no tomorrow. She sees no sunshine. She hears no birds singing. She no longer sees the roses in the front yard. To her, everything is black. She looks only inward at herself, and she no longer likes what she sees. I fear that she sees death as the way out of her trap, and it may be the more attractive path to follow. Yes, I think I understand suicide better now.

LEE: Jane, we must understand that the district attorney is just doing his job. It's not a personal thing with him.

ATKINSON: I understand. I'm just scared, frightened, and confused. I am somewhat lost myself. I'm walking a road I never thought I would travel. Not in my wildest dreams would I have ever thought Mother would kill Daddy. Mother is a tender person. She cries when a baby bird falls from its nest. She once found a baby squirrel on the ground in back of the house and tried to raise it on a bottle. When it died, Mother cried as if one of us had died.

LEE: What is your understanding of what happened to your Daddy after he moved to Memphis?

ATKINSON: I only know bits and pieces of what may have happened. Pete and I had married and I was living in Carrollton when Daddy took the new job, so I was somewhat out of the loop. Dana had completed her junior year when Daddy moved. I think that was either May or June. He said he would drive home to Atlanta on the weekends, and he did this for about six months. It was a pretty long drive, almost 400 miles, so it was understandable if he didn't get back some weekends.

LEE: Did you see him on any of these weekends?
ATKINSON: Several. I remember Daddy was back home for a long weekend on the Fourth of July. We all went on a picnic at Stone Mountain, just like old times. We even stayed for the laser show that night. My crazy Daddy had sneaked a Casper the Ghost mask into the bag of sandwiches. Mother wanted someone to ask the blessing before we ate our sandwiches. She asked Daddy and he asked me. When I finished and everyone opened their eyes, Daddy was wearing the Casper mask. Job, you never really got to know Daddy, but he was such a happy, funny man.

LEE: When did your Daddy start to change?
ATKINSON: I guess it was sometime after he came home for Independence Day. I wasn't at home so I wasn't aware of what was taking place when the troubles first began. My first awareness of the changes did not, at the time, seem important. I would know that Daddy was supposed to be back home for a weekend, and Mother would call and tell me that he was tied up at work and couldn't come. That's the way it began. Pete and I didn't think anything about it at the time. To Atlanta and back to Memphis is nearly an 800-mile trip and that's a long way to travel just to spend two nights. When Daddy came, he would not get home until almost

midnight on Friday and then had to start back to Memphis early Sunday afternoon.

LEE: When did your mother take her job with the insurance agency?

ATKINSON: She started part-time with the McCurry Agency when Dana was a freshman in high school. I was working there and learned about an available part-time clerk position. Dana was about fifteen and busy doing her own thing. I guess this would have been in 1967, not too long before Pete and I married. I told Mother about the job, talked to my boss about Mother, and she took the job.

LEE: Had she worked outside the home before?

ATKINSON: After she married Daddy and they moved to Atlanta, Mother did some part-time work. I was little and I don't remember where. When she got pregnant with Dana, she quit that job and stayed home until she took the part-time work with McCurry.

LEE: Did your father object to her working, or want her to work more? I guess I am asking if money was a problem in their marriage? With many couples it is.

ATKINSON: Job, both Mother and Daddy lived within their means. They never had much money in the bank, but they always managed their budget. Neither of them wasted money. Daddy's only splurging was for his fishing tackle and an occasional six-pack of beer. Mother's spending was for the family and her home. You can never know how much Mother loved her home.

LEE: Explain.

ATKINSON: Home was Mother's life, and she was secure there. Home was a fortress, a place of peace and security.

LEE: I have a difficult thing to say, and I do not have a good way to say it. Please do not be upset and please hear me out in what I tell you. Will you do that for me?

ATKINSON: Job, has something else happened to Mother?

LEE: No, thank God. Enough has already happened and I am trying to avoid another mishap. What I need to talk to you about is my concern that Ann is not being represented in a way that serves her best interest.

ATKINSON: You confuse me. I don't understand what you are saying.

LEE: I am talking about me. I am very troubled by the realization that your mother needs a more experienced lawyer. This really bothers me. Both ethically and morally, I am compelled to say this. Your mother needs better representation than I can give. Jane, the further I go into this case, the more I realize that I simply do not have the experience that Ann so badly needs.

ATKINSON: This is confusing! We are pleased that you are her lawyer. We are the ones who came to you. Has something happened we aren't aware of?

LEE: Jane, it means a lot to me that you and Pete asked me to represent your mother. I really mean that! But it is not a matter of my being thankful that you have confidence in me. The paramount consideration is what is best for my client.

How Ann's best interest is served. My oath of office as an attorney demands that I do my best for my client. This case is a very difficult one. This belief compels me to say I think it would be in your mother's best interest if she had some other attorney represent her in the trial. I sincerely hope you will understand that I say this out of concern for Ann. The simple truth is, she needs better than I can provide.

ATKINSON: Job, are you giving up on Mother?

LEE: No, not at all. But this needs to be discussed with you. I've tried to talk to Ann about this, but she doesn't seem to understand.

ATKINSON: I don't either.

LEE: Jane, I have very little experience in criminal trial work. I've tried a few criminal cases, but never a murder trial. As you know, I mostly represent clients like Pete in commercial, business matters. I simply don't have the experience that is needed to properly represent your mother. Her situation is a very serious one.

ATKINSON: Job, Mother would never understand if you dropped her as a client. No matter how good your reasons for doing so, she would never understand.

LEE: Yes, I know. I've tried to talk to her about my concerns, about her great need for a more experienced lawyer and she simply doesn't seem to understand. Jane, she seems in a world unto herself, a world that no one can get into. I want you and Pete to understand that it is very much in Ann's interest to have an experienced criminal attorney represent her. My duty as an attorney demands that I make this recommendation.

ATKINSON: Who would you recommend?

LEE: I don't know, yet. First, I have to get Ann's agreement that I withdraw and that someone else step in. I don't want to add to your mother's anxiety and hurt her by dwelling on this subject. But, her trial will be scheduled in a few months and a lot of preparation needs to be made. If you can, help me get Ann to understand that she needs another attorney. So far, I haven't gotten very far when I've attempted to talk to her.

ATKINSON: What about all the work that you have already done? You have already spent many hours talking to different people, investigating and arranging for Mother to see Dr. Battle.

LEE: Thus far, everyone I have talked with has consented to my making a tape of our discussions, just as I am now recording our talk. My secretary has transcribed all of these talks and I would deliver a copy of my files, including the transcripts of the interviews, to the new attorney. Of course, I would assist a new lawyer for your mother in every possible manner.

ATKINSON: Have you taped your discussions with Mother?

LEE: Yes.

ATKINSON: Job, what does she say happened the day she killed Daddy? She has never told Dana and me what really happened.

Lee: Jane, my discussions with Ann are confidential. I'm not at liberty to tell anyone what she's told me, except another attorney who agrees to represent her. It would be unethical and highly improper for me to divulge such things. I hope you, Pete, and Dana understand this.

FAITHFUL NEIGHBOR'S TOUCH

Dana made plans to return to school. Ann seemed somewhat involved in the planning and preparation and showed an occasional interest in her roses and hummingbird feeders. At other times, however, she was passive and indifferent. After Dana went back to Auburn, Ann again withdrew into her shell of darkness, that solitary place where there was no light, no home, and no tomorrow.

Ann continued living in the house where Ed had died and was seldom seen outside the dwelling. The days and weeks before her trial, time seemed suspended. She was oblivious to both clock and calendar. Almost daily, Ethel Mc-Coy, with her knitting in hand, came, made tea, and silently prayed for her friend.

In mid-August, Dr. Battle noted that Ann had related her dream of being a hummingbird that flew south over the ocean in migration. "The bird flew, and flew, and flew," she said. "It felt . . . I can't say how it felt, but the little bird just wanted to fly away."

TRIBULATION WITHOUT TREASURE

Often during the summer months of 1972, Ann struggled with many confusing forces that seemed both irrational and unreal. As her meetings with Job Lee and Dr. Battle increased, she became more and more aware that others were depending on her to remember and relate the events that led to the shooting of Ed. She knew that she had been arrested and would stand trial for his death, and she realized, too, that her attorney needed the benefit of her recollections. She had a lifelong habit of trying to please others, of being a giver, and now, with others begging her to give, she was unable to deliver. Adding to her anxiety was the slow realization that she alone had the information being sought.

Adding to Ann's dilemma was the matter of changing attorneys. She liked Job Lee. He was a considerate, even compassionate man. Many questions confounded her. Job was the only lawyer she knew. If she lost him, to whom would she turn? How could she pay another lawyer? Why change a known for an unknown? How would she go about finding another lawyer? How are things like that done? These questions flooded her mind. Job's explanation of the reasons for a change made no sense, yet she knew Job was sincere.

The question of Dana going back to college in September seemed the most troubling problem of all. Ann wrestled with this problem, not as a chronically ill person nor as a client charged with a serious crime trying to comply with the lawyer's requests for more and more information, but as a mother. All of her life she had wanted to be a mother. Not just an average, run-of-the-mill mother, but a good, caring, protective, even perfect mother. This compelling demand had started when her baby sister was born and it had never relinquished its hold. Jane was on her own, married to a good man, and living in her own home. But Dana was still under the same roof and torn by events beyond her comprehension and control. Dana was still her baby. No matter how dark the day might otherwise be, Ann's determination to be a good mother never wavered. To fully understand Ann Elizabeth Albert Tatum, it would be necessary to understand her need to be a perfect mother. She had raised the bar too high by setting an unreachable goal. Still, with Ann, that is to beg the question rather than answer. The bar was set, and she wanted to hurdle it.

Dana and her father had planned for her to attend her daddy's school, and Ann had fully supported this arrangement. The first year of college had been completed. Now, in the second year, Ann's suggestion of obtaining the loan value of her life insurance policy seemed the only way to pay expenses—yet, for reasons Ann could not fathom, Dana resisted that suggestion. Dana told her mother in early August that she would seek the advice of Dr. Battle.

Often, during the summer months, Ann would be reminded that her Parkinson's disease, already the master of her right side, was slowly making claim to her left side as well. In May, she noticed her left arm not swinging in rhythm with her right footstep as she walked. This was the way the disease had started on her right side. Then, in late June, Ann noticed the beginning of a left hand tremor. Those who have had this disease are painfully aware that stress, particularly emotional stress, is a vicious enemy, but this awareness was of little value to someone like Ann who lived in a sea of emotional stress.

During the heat of July and August, little things gave way to big things. In July, Ann started a search for the butterfly poem her mother had copied for her. It was one of only a few samples of her mother's writing. For three days she searched but did not find, the little poem, and for three days and nights, her Parkinson's tremor was violent, sometimes racking her entire body.

Ann found herself in late July frequently seated at her kitchen table, looking at the floor. She would look at the spot where Ed had fallen, the spot where she cradled his head in her arms as the police rushed into the house. She could still see the outline of Ed's blood on the floor, although it had been cleaned long ago. The summer of 1972 was a time of unrelenting darkness.

During the months that followed, Dana, Jane, the doctor, lawyers, and friends would look for signs of light, but they saw only the prevailing darkness in which Ann lived. She kept herself physically clean, but paid little attention to her home. Only twice had she walked into her yard to cut some roses.

On September 7, Dana kissed her mother goodbye, got into a friend's car, and returned to Auburn for her second year of college. As Dana rode away, she wondered if she would ever see her mother alive again. Dr. Battle had been right. Dana's going back to school proved to be good medicine for her sick mother. The plan for Dana to attend her daddy's school was back on track. Dana's return to school provided some ray of light. This was not a dramatic, noticeable change, only a slight one, but when one lives in darkness, each bit of light helps.

CAUGHT IN A WEB

In July, Job Lee again attempted to talk to Ann about withdrawing from the case and her getting a more experienced trial lawyer. He knew her case would soon be up for trial and a change of attorney, if made, needed prompt attention. After talking to Ann about making this change, Job was still uncertain as to what his client's wishes were. She seemed to agree with everything he said. If he talked about making a change, she seemed to agree. If he talked about his remaining on the case, she again seemed to agree.

Job suffered mixed emotions. Like a moth drawn to a lantern's glow, Ann's case became his constant companion. The more he learned of Ann and her life, the greater his interest became. His emotions told him to stay the course, to see the case to its conclusion. The competitive spirit of a trial lawyer had staked its claim on him. His law professors had warned him of this danger. The words of both his ethics professor and of Richard Cramer, the retired trial lawyer, kept ringing in his ears: *"You must always do what's best for the client."* His emotions begged him to *stay*. Though his logic told him that the best interest of the client deserved better than he could provide and that he should *go*. But leaving the case was not a simple matter. He would need the consent of both his client and of the trial judge before he could withdraw. Ann's consent would have to be clear and unequivocal, and she seemed unable to give that. She seemed to say both "yes" and "no" to the idea of changing attorneys.

Job sought Jane's assistance in trying to ascertain Ann's wishes, though Jane's effort was no more productive than his own. In his dilemma, he sought the opinion of the State Bar Ethics Commission, asking, in essence, "What should I do?" The Commission's answer was filled with legal double-talk and was of no real help.

In another manner, Job was trapped. He had appeared as Ann's attorney at her arraignment and entered her plea of *not guilty*. This appearance, and several subsequent appearances in court on her behalf for the hearing of various motions and preliminary matters, had "locked" him into the case. He was now the "Attorney of Record"—the one the trial judge relied on to speak for the client. Thus, he had a dual obligation—one to his client, the other to the court—ensnared by duty to both client and court.

SAMUEL GRAVES AND THE OXEN ON THE HILL

In mid-August, Job, with Ann's confused concurrence, contacted Samuel Graves, an experienced criminal defense attorney in Atlanta. Mr. Graves was the head of the city's largest criminal defense firm, and a veteran of many murder trials, both in Georgia and across the Southeast. As a general rule, though, he was also very expensive and money was something Ann did not have.

Thus far, Job had provided his services with payment of only a $500 fee; he was aware Ann didn't have the means to pay more. But to Job, the small fee was not an issue; Ann needed a more experienced attorney, one like Sam Graves. On occasion, if the case was an interesting and challenging one, Graves would undertake representation without compensation. Job hoped he would be challenged by Ann's case and eager to participate in what some saw as an impossible defense. He called to set up an appointment.

Job knew of Sam Graves but had never met him, and when he arrived at his firm, he found its lobby twice the size of his entire office. He was surprised by Graves' appearance, as well as his individual office and its furnishings.

Job had expected a giant, but Graves was a small man, approaching seventy, and almost frail. He spoke softly and was hard to hear. He wore plain tan cotton trousers with a faded white cotton shirt, open at the neck. His dress was far from the expensive attire that Job expected. Nothing about the successful trial lawyer matched Job Lee's preconceptions.

Grave's private office was very small, even smaller than Job's, and there was hardly room to accommodate more than three visitors. His office furnishings were obviously old, some appearing to be antique. Sam Graves sat in what appeared to be the world's first swivel-chair, its bottom caned with old-fashioned white oak strips like those Job had first seen at his grandfather's house when he was a boy. The desk was of the same vintage and made of plain, old, battered oak. Everything about the office, including Graves, seemed a scene from a Norman Rockwell painting.

Job's first impression was negative. He wondered why a renowned criminal defense lawyer dressed so casually and had such a diminutive office. He wondered if Sam Graves deserved the invitation to defend Ann Tatum.

Then, Graves began to talk. His voice was so soft that Job found himself edging forward in his chair to listen closely and not miss a word. Graves spoke with sincerity and a quiet conviction, and Job quickly understood why a judge and a trial jury might be persuaded by this man's argument. Graves took time to explain his office furniture. The desk, the swivel, cane-bottomed chair, several paintings on the walls, and numerous other items had belonged to Grave's great-grandfather, a lawyer who once lived and practiced in South Carolina. These items, in turn, had passed through the hands of his grandfather and father, both attorneys in South Carolina.

Job had expected a hurried visit with this interesting and busy lawyer. Instead, he found a man who acted as if he had the remainder of his life reserved to talk to him. Sam Graves inquired about Job's life, his experiences, his likes and dislikes. He wanted to know about Job's family, his wife, and his children. Here was a man who was at ease with himself, with who he was and what he was, where he was, and who he was with.

Job had visited a few other offices of lawyers with large reputations. The walls of these other famous lawyers had been covered with diplomas, citations, certificates, and photographs of the famous lawyer shaking hands with governors, senators, even presidents. None of these things were seen in Grave's office.

On the wall behind Grave's chair was a painting of a yoke of oxen pulling a two-wheel cart over the top of a hill. The frame of the painting, like the remainder of his furnishings, bore signs of great age. On the opposite wall, in front of Sam Graves, was a framed black and white photograph of a black man who appeared to be about twenty years old. This picture, framed in wood not as old as the other, was of a poor quality and obviously had been poorly preserved before it was framed.

Noticing Job looking at this painting of the ox cart and then the picture of the black man, Sam Graves spoke. "The ox cart was painted by my grandmother for my paternal grandfather. His name was Winston Graves. He practiced law in Columbia, South Carolina, for almost fifty years. He gave me this painting when I hung my shingle out. Told me 'Son, I want you to have this painting. You notice the oxen are going over a hill into either a sunrise or a sunset, you can't tell which. I want you to keep this in your office until it starts to look like a sunset and then you will know it is time to quit.' Job, several times in my practice it has almost looked like a sunset and quitting time."

"What made you feel that way?"

"A trial lawyer is, in the final analysis, a professional gambler. I've won some cases I shouldn't have won. I've lost cases I should've won. And then there have been cases that were taken away from me. The wrinkled picture of the black man on the wall behind you is one of the cases taken away from me. It was one of the cases that made the painting look like a sunset, a time for me to find something else to do."

"Would you mind telling me about that man?"

"Job, the honest answer is both yes and no. His name was Jacob Cunningham. The Cunningham name came from the Cunningham Plantation south of Jackson, Mississippi, where his ancestors were slaves. In some ways I wish I had never known the man. In other ways I never want to forget him. That's the reason I give you the yes and no answer."

"I'm sorry. I did not mean to lead you to things you would like to forget."

"No apology necessary. The case of Jacob Cunningham is one I need to remember. One I need to tell others about in hope they, too, will remember. Jacob's picture was sent to me by his mother after Jacob died. His mother enclosed the wrinkled picture in an envelope too small to contain it. That's the reason for the crease down the middle of the picture. The mother's note was simple, it said: "Thank you. Here's a picture of my boy.""

"What happened to Jacob?"

"He was from the Pinola Community, south of Jackson. The picture must have been made not too long before he volunteered for the United States Army in 1942. Jacob trained at Fort Jackson and was assigned to a transportation unit as a truck driver. He served his country by helping deliver supplies to soldiers on the front lines in Europe and was seriously injured by mortar fire in January 1945. He was sent home, spent several months in a rehabilitation hospital in

Philadelphia, and was honorably discharged from service in late August that year.

Not long after coming back home to Pinola, he was arrested, charged with raping a white girl outside a Jackson nightclub. Contacted by a Jackson attorney, I agreed to go to Jackson to assist in the defense. None of the Jackson attorneys, all white, wanted to have anything to do with the case. The memory of the Scottsboro Trials of Alabama was still in the minds of many. I went to Jackson, spent more than a month there. I developed absolute proof that Jacob could not have possibly been the one who committed the rape. There was no doubt. The girl had been raped about eight o'clock at night on September 3rd. She was drunk, out-of-her-mind drunk, when it happened. I had six reputable men, all white and residents of the county, prepared to testify that Jacob worked with them repairing a syrup mill, at Prentiss, Mississippi, from late morning until after nine that night of September 3rd. Prentiss was sixty miles south of where the rape occurred. Jacob was wrongly accused. Six years later, he was vindicated when a white man confessed to the rape.

Job, Jacob was an innocent man, and I could have proved it. But Jacob's case was taken from me when, on the Monday morning the case was supposed to begin, a note was slipped under the door of my hotel room. The note said, 'Nigger lover, you can go back to Georgia. We have done tried and convicted your nigger.' Jacob had been forcibly taken from the Rankin County jail and hanged to an oak tree about three miles north of Jackson by an angry lynch mob. I would like to think it never happened, but it did. I keep Jacob's picture on my wall as a reminder to do my best not to let it happen again. So, that's the story of my two wall decorations. I have come close, but I have never fully decided the ox should walk into a sunset."

By the time Sam Graves finished talking, Job had formed a second opinion of the man who sat before him. Graves was no longer a frail old man wearing plain cotton clothes. His office was no longer an out-of-date scene of yesterday. Job realized that Graves was a master of persuasion, the very man Ann needed by her side in the courtroom. He also knew that Graves understood the difference between the value and the price of things, a rare quality that would be evident to all who met him.

Job outlined, as best he knew it, the situation that led to Ann killing her husband. At the outset, he stated that neither Ann nor her family had any money for attorneys or investigative fees. He explained that as far as he knew, not even Dr. Battle had been paid for his services.

Sam Graves seemed unconcerned, and wanted to hear more about Ann's case.

As Job summarized it, Graves listened, eyes closed, not taking notes, but Job knew he was most attentive to what was being said.

"Mr. Graves, I appreciate the opportunity to meet you and thank you for taking the time to listen to me. I'm over my head in this case. I have no real criminal trial experience, and Ann Tatum needs far better representation than I can give. With the client's permission, I ask that you take Ann as a client and allow me to withdraw from the case."

"Before I answer, may I ask you a few questions?"

"Yes, sir."

"This shooting occurred in the family home?"

"Yes, sir."

"No one else was present?"

"That is my understanding."

"What does the client say about that?"

"She says no one else was present, but you must know that it is very difficult to get Ann to talk about what happened. She is a very gentle lady. I have every reason to believe she wants to fully cooperate with me in preparing her case, yet she doesn't seem to be able to verbalize and give me details. She seems to try, but something seems to hold her words captive."

"Job, some things in life are too painful to talk about. It took the first fifty years of my life to understand that. Did you say there was no evidence of self-defense?"

"None has been found. The autopsy shows that Ed Tatum was shot once in his chest and seven times in his back. He left a trail of blood down a hallway and part way across the kitchen floor before he fell and died. The police found a 22-caliber, semi-automatic pistol on a bed in the far corner of the house, back in the direction the trail of blood took. Eight spent 22-caliber shell casings were found, some on the bed and others next to the bed on the floor. The physical evidence indicates the shooting started in the bedroom with Ed Tatum standing near its door, and Ann standing, diagonally, in the same room some fifteen or twenty feet away. The subsequent shots had to have been fired at a greater distance. Edward

Tatum was going away from Ann Tatum. She apparently remained in the same place."

"Any signs of a struggle or a fight? Anything broken or overturned?"

"No, sir."

"What about any history of marital fights? Any calls to the police about domestic violence?

"None. I've talked to several friends and family members, and none have indicated any physical abuse or even any threat of such within this family. In truth, they all say that Ann and Ed appeared happy for most of their marriage. They were both passive in nature."

"Any history of violence by either with other people?"

"None."

"What does Ann say about the actual shooting?"

"About all she has said thus far is that she didn't expect Ed to come home that day. He was living in Memphis. She told me she remembers going to the back bedroom and getting the pistol out of the nightstand drawer, intending to kill herself. She says she has no recollection of firing the pistol. She remembers having the pistol to take her own life and the next thing she remembers is kneeling on the kitchen floor holding Ed's head in her lap and the police coming into the house."

"Your client doesn't give you much to work with, does she?"

"Not much. That's why she needs you as her lawyer, not me. Do you think it could be possible that she has no memory of firing the pistol?"

"It is not important what I think. The important thing is

129

what the jury thinks. Yes, I personally believe that memory can be a problem here. I think some things are so horrible our brain pushes them completely out of our mind. It seems some memories are unbearable. Maybe in time, she will recall. How long has she been seeing Carl Battle?

"I didn't bring that file with me, but I would say about three months. Thus far, I haven't gotten much out of Dr. Battle. Do you think she has the right doctor?

"Oh, yes. You have one of the city's best. It doesn't surprise me that you haven't heard much from him. Just give him time. You've got the right man on the job."

"Do you know him personally? Have you used him as an expert witness?"

"Yes, to both of your questions. He is most competent and highly respected. The good part, from Ann's point of view, is that he has appeared in court many times as a witness for the prosecution and only a few times as a witness for the defense. The State will never attempt to paint him as a 'hired-gun' for the defense. We don't know yet if his testimony will be of benefit, but he takes his time about forming opinions, and if he has favorable testimony to give on Ann's behalf, it will be both strong and believable."

"Mr. Graves, will you take Ann as your client?"

"Let me think about it for a few days. I won't keep you waiting long. A decision needs to be made. If I agree to the representation, will you continue as lead counsel and let me come in as your assistant?"

"Mr. Graves that would be like me trying to tell Noah about a flood! You have forgotten more about criminal trials than I'll ever know. I'm not even qualified to carry your dinner bucket."

"Job, the arrangement I suggest would likely serve the best interest of the client."

"I'm sorry, but I don't see how that could be."

"Permit me to share my thinking. Remember what I said about Carl Battle not appearing to be a hired gun. Often, old criminal trial lawyers, rightly or wrongly, are viewed by both the jury and the public as being nothing except a hired gun. Some judges allow such argument, some do not. Be that as it may, if I come on board, it would be in Ann's best interest that I bring with me the least possible impression of being a gunfighter who was hired by some rich lady. I know Ann doesn't have any money, but there is always the possibility of it being perceived so. In the trial of any case, the perception of truth is what wins or loses the contest. Sometimes the perception is very different from the real thing. For this reason, if I got in the saddle with you, I would want us to ride double, but I would want you in front."

"Mr. Graves, you flatter me by suggesting that I be lead counsel, but that would be quite awkward for me."

"Job, in the courtroom, there is no time for the attorney to be embarrassed about the pecking order. Besides, there's another reason why I suggest the possibility of coming in as your assistant. Want to hear it?"

"I want to hear anything you have to say."

"Job, so far your case has attracted little media attention. I don't follow the media accounts of many events, but I can almost tell you how this case has been treated by the news media thus far. For a day or so after the shooting, it attracted attention on the second or third page of the local papers. The local television people tried to fan the fire for a little longer, and then it disappeared and now continues to be out of sight. Am I right thus far?"

"Yes, sir."

"I predict that by the time this case begins, it will be high profile. By the time the jury is selected, the local media will treat it as if Queen Elizabeth had been shot."

"Why do you say that, Mr. Graves?"

"If you don't mind, just call me Sam. I say the case will obtain celebrity status because Aaron Bailey will anoint it. He'll put his hands on it and bless it into a big-name case."

"You mean the District Attorney Aaron Bailey?"

"That's the one."

"His assistant, Wayman Burris, is named the attorney of record. He's attended all the preliminary matters. I assumed Mr. Burris would handle the trial."

"Job, you don't understand Aaron. He's got the itch to be the governor of Georgia. I mean no disrespect. Aaron Bailey is a very good district attorney, but when a man has the itch for a higher office, he has to find some way to scratch it. Aaron picks and chooses the cases he wants to personally handle. Over the almost eight years that he's been our DA, he's established a good record of wins. He wants to have an excellent record of cases he's won, without any losses. When a trial attorney runs for higher office, talking about his wins is his way of scratching that itch. There's nothing wrong with that; it's simply how the system works."

"But how does this relate to Ann's case?"

"Mind you, I am only predicting that Aaron will be the lead prosecuting attorney when this case goes to trial. I don't mean to give you an anxiety attack in saying this, but Aaron will see this case as a sure win for the state of Georgia. In Bridge language, he'll see it as a lay-down hand. For him, Ann's case will represent another notch on the handle of his pistol. If he can make her case more high-profile, then the bigger the notch on the butt of his pistol if he wins a conviction."

"Sam, do you see this case as a lay-down hand for the State?"

"Job, I've reached the time of my life where I see no black or white. Everything now seems a shade of gray. As I said, I've lost cases that I felt should have been won. I have won cases where everything seemed to point toward the loss column. Some years ago, I quit trying to guess whether the umpire would call the pitch a ball or a strike even before the ball was thrown. This is a tough case. The lady shot her husband eight times and there is no evidence of self-defense. She first shot him when he was fifteen or twenty feet away. She shot him seven more times in the back as he tried to escape what Aaron Bailey will label, 'Her fury! Her anger! Her determination to see that he was dead! Dead! Dead!' Job, I can hear Aaron now as he pounds the podium, putting another notch in his pistol butt, all the while scratching his itch to be governor. Again, I mean no personal disrespect for Aaron. I've heard him before, and if I get in this case, I think I will hear him again. He is a very good attorney. I respect him both as a person and as a very worthy opponent. Does he have a lay-down hand? I don't know; I no longer see in terms of black and white."

"Mr. Graves, Sam, it is almost four o'clock. You said you had an appointment that must be kept across town at five. I'll take my leave and hope that you will represent Ann."

"Thank you Job. I've been keeping my eye on the clock. That appointment is a very important one. My grandson, age seven, has a T-ball game scheduled. To a man of my age, watching kids play T-ball is a lot more exciting than many of the things I recall doing as a young man. Thank you for coming by. You'll hear from me soon."

On the way out, Job paused at the door to Sam's office to take another look at the oxen pulling the cart over the hill.

RIPENED BY AFFLICTION

Although plagued by uncertainty and frightened by his lack of criminal law experience, Job realized that Ann's case was extending both his reach and grasp. He knew that carrying a heavy load could not only strengthen the back but also mature the mind. The secret of this success, however, seemed to be the manner the load was carried. If anyone knew how to carry the burdens of life, it would be Jennifer Cosby, a legal secretary who worked in Sam Graves's office. Job and virtually all lawyers in the Atlanta area had heard of her. The visit to Sam's office provided an opportunity for Job to meet her.

Ms. Cosby was ninety-six years old and had been continuously employed as a legal secretary in Atlanta for more than seventy-four years. She had never married though she was wed to the legal profession for three quarters of a century. As he was leaving Sam Graves's office, Job stopped at the receptionist's desk and inquired if Ms. Cosby was in and if she might be available for a brief meeting.

"No," the young receptionist said. "Ms. Cosby pretty much sets her own schedule. She usually comes in early and leaves early. Shall I ask her to call?"

"No. I'm Job Lee from Carrollton. Please tell her I'd love to meet her."

"I'm sure she will be around and I'll tell her you inquired."

Upon leaving Sam Grave's office, Job drove past the Georgia Tech Campus, past Grant Field. He recalled his childhood dream of playing football there for Coach Bobby Dodd. On impulse, he pulled into the stadium parking lot, parked his car, and found a quiet bench beneath an old oak. His visit with Sam Graves and his effort to meet Ms. Cosby who had seen so much of life had put him in a meditative mood.

Job considered the pressures that Ann's case had placed on him and wondered how those pressures were affecting him. John Donne had written that "affliction is a treasure, and scarce any man hath enough of it. No man hath affliction enough that is not matured and ripened by it, and made fit for God by that affliction."

Job thought of the afflictions that the death of Ed Tatum had worked on Ann, Jane, Dana, and now on him and his family. He wondered if any of the afflicted were being ripened and made more fit to meet God, and if God would approve or disapprove of this kind of thinking.

After his reverie was broken, Job walked closer to Grant Field, stopped in front of a stadium gate and thought of the kids who had hoped they would someday grow up and play football for coaches Dodd, Butts, or Bryant. When Job got back in his car, he made a mental note to ask Ms. Cosby if she thought affliction could be a treasure, and, if so, did it occur by one's will, or by chance?

Memory took Job back to New Orleans, back to law school and his courtship of Sally, his Georgia Cajun Woman. He was sorry he had not taken the time to do more with Sally for the tenth anniversary of their marriage. He had let Ann's case command too much of his time. The personal note and flowers given her for the occasion seemed too little for so much received. Sally, in the past ten years had presented him with three splendid children, Henry in January 1964, Elizabeth in February 1966, and, Robert in January 1967. Now, the demands of law were separating him not only from Sally, but also from his children. Job resolved to spend more time with his family, but his resolution did not answer the question of how he would find the time.

EMERGENT MEDIATIONS AND AN OPINION

Between the Chattahoochee River and Vila Rica, Job's thoughts returned to Ann and his visit to Atlanta. His discussion with Sam Graves had taken some unusual turns. Graves had kept the door open to the possibility that he would come into the case on Ann's behalf, but his suggestion that Job also remain as lead attorney was puzzling.

Stopping at Bob's Convenience Store on the east side of Carrollton en route home he was greeted by Bob LeCroy, the storeowner, a high school classmate and a client of Job's.

"What you doing on my side of town, Job?"

"Two things. First, I've been to Atlanta to see a big-town lawyer. Second, I owe you a phone call."

"What happened buddy that sent you looking for a lawyer? Did Sally catch you with your britches unzipped?"

"No, it's not that simple. I was looking for a lawyer to represent a client. Mind if I use you as sort of a sounding board on a case that has me bothered?"

"Hell, I've been used for everything else, might as well try that, too. Shoot."

"Ed, do you remember the news reports back in February about the lady in Atlanta shooting her husband several times and killing him?"

"Hell Job, them folks in Atlanta always shoot several times. They got plenty of money for bullets. Us country boys are more conservative. We don't waste ammo. We make every shot count. But to answer your question, I don't recall any specific shooting in Atlanta, unless I was the one being shot at."

"You may remember that TV-33 got their story about this case all wrong. They reported the man who was killed had been shot eighteen times and they had to correct the story the next day by reporting he had been shot only eight times."

"Only eight times, my ass. When you get shot more than

twice, you stop counting. Yeah, I remember something about it now. I heard it was Pete Atkinson's relative, mother, mother-in-law, something like that. Is that the case you're talking about?"

"That's the one. What do you think a jury will do to that lady?"

"Why do you ask? You involved in it?"

"Yes, I am. I don't know if I'll stay in it, though. It looks like I will. I'm just using you as a sounding board, trying to get a feel for public opinion."

"Job, if I was on that jury, I would vote to fine her $500 for wasting ammo and not being able to do it in one shot. Then I would vote to fry her ass for killing her husband. We don't want Georgia women to get the impression they can get away with killing their man. Are you representing that woman?"

"At this time, I am. I thought I might be getting out, but it looks like I'm staying in."

"Ole buddy, if you can get out, get out. The jury's gonna tear up that woman's ass worse than Sherman tore up Georgia."

"Thanks for your opinion and advice. Now my second reason for stopping. You called me several days ago and I have been too busy to call you back. What did you need?"

"Ole buddy, just forget that call. I was hot-under-the-collar about a guy givin' me a bad check for some beer. I was thinkin' about whupping his ass and wanted to know how much the judge would fine me if I did it. The fellow made his check good and I've cooled off. It wasn't a good idea to begin with."

"Let me have a six-pack of beer, I don't care what brand."

When Job arrived home, Sally and the three kids, now eight, six, and five, were playing kickball in the yard. Mindful of his recent resolution while stuck in traffic on the way home, Job handed Sally the six-pack.

"Here babe, take this in for me so I can play with the kids. Come out and join us."

The beer put away, Sally rejoined the game. She was pleased to see Job play with the children and to hear their excited voices and laughter. More and more now, she was increasingly concerned about Job. He seemed preoccupied, at times almost distant. She gladly took part in the game, exercising her long legs and joining in the family laughter. It was after nine before the long, summer day lost its light and ushered them inside.

Sally and the kids had already eaten, saving Job a plate. While Job ate, she got the kids bathed and in bed. It was past ten when she joined Job in the family room.

"Would you like one of those beers? You look tired. It's been a long day for you."

"No, thanks. I had one with my supper, that's enough for tonight. Honey, I had a most interesting and unexpected development in Ann's case today."

"Tell me about it."

"I met and talked with Sam Graves for a long time. He is one of the most interesting people I have ever met. You would love meeting him, I hope that can happen."

"Tell me more about Mr. Graves."

"His reputation is as big as Stone Mountain. This led me

to believe I would find a big man in a big office. There are more than seventy lawyers in his firm so in that sense he has a big office. But, his private office is small, even smaller than mine. Rather than being physically big, he is no taller than I am and on the slim side. Even his office furniture did not match his reputation. It was old and handed down from his father and grandfathers. They were all lawyers. You should see the old swivel chair he sits in. It must have been on Noah's Ark. And, the way he was dressed did not match what I expected either. The few hot-shot lawyers I know are fancy dressers; they try to dazzle you with their dress and cars. Sam Graves is not that way. He had on khaki pants, an old white shirt, and no tie. Had he not told me who he was, I would have thought he was the janitor. On the wall behind his chair, he had a painting of oxen pulling a two-wheel cart over a hill into what could either be a sunrise or a sunset. The painting had been made by his grandmother for his grandfather. His grandfather had given it to him, telling him that when it started to look like a sunset it would be time to quit law. That was a really neat thing for a grandfather to say. When I first went into Graves' private office and met him, I formed a very negative opinion. I thought, 'What is a man like this doing practicing law in a situation like this?' But the more he talked, the more he told me about his family, himself, and his furniture, the more impressed I became. Honey, I've never met a lawyer like Sam Graves."

"Job, it's been a long time since I saw you so enthusiastic over anything. I'm glad to see that."

"But that's not all of it. You've got to hear his voice. It's impossible to describe the way he talks. You have to hear it to understand. It seems as if he whispers, but he is not really whispering. His voice carries well, but it seems like a whisper. The way he talks makes you want to lean forward in your chair so you can get closer to what he says. You could sit normally and hear, but something makes you want to get closer. It's hard to explain. And his eyes, they talk, too. At first you do not notice his eyes and then it dawns on you that his eyes are saying the same thing as his mouth. Sally, Sam Graves is one of the most powerful speakers I've ever heard."

"You said he spoke softly."

"I do not mean powerful in volume. I mean powerful in content. His soft spoken words have power, the power to lift you out of your chair so you can get closer, so you can hear more. His words make you want more and his eyes do the same thing."

"You obviously like Mr. Graves."

"Yes. Yes, I do. But it is more than liking him. There is something intangible about what I felt when he talked to me. I guess 'awe' is the word I'm looking for. Not awe of fear, but awe of wonder. He has a magic about him. A magic of truth. Everything seems to tell you what he says is true. He does not use fancy words, just plain, simple, everyday words. You've got to see and hear."

"I'm glad you met Mr. Graves. What did he say about taking Ann's case?"

"You won't believe this part."

"Try me."

"He didn't say yes. He didn't say no."

"That's not hard to believe."

"He said he would think about it, but if he came in, he wanted to be my associate. He wanted me to remain lead attorney. Can you imagine that? Me, the leader, Sam Graves assisting! Honey, that would be like me pitching baseball and Mickey Mantle being the hitter. I was amazed that he suggested, even insisted, on that arrangement if he came on board as part of the defense. I could hardly believe what he suggested in spite of his way of making you believe every word that comes from his mouth. He said it would be best if we did it that way so the jury would be less inclined to see him as a hired gun for the defense."

"So, Mr. Graves may come into the case. I hope that works out. It would be a great opportunity for you to work with him. Oh, I almost forgot to tell you, Dr. Battle called today. He said he was putting his report in the morning mail and you should have it tomorrow. May I tell you something else?"

"Sure."

"Honey, I'm not complaining, so don't take it that way. I just want you to know of late I've been missing you in my life and how glad I am tonight to feel you back in. Thank you for sharing your day with me. It made me feel good."

"I know Sally. On the way home I was thinking the same thing. I sometimes get lost in Ann's case and seem to forget everything else. I'm going to try to do better."

"Job, you're doing just fine. Did you get to meet the long-time secretary in Mr. Graves's office, the one you told me about?"

"No, she had gone for the day. I understand she pretty much goes and comes as she wishes. It is hard to believe she has been a legal secretary as long as she has. I bet when she says 'jump,' every damn lawyer in that office asks 'how high?' I'm sorry I did not meet her. Maybe the next time. She would be a great teacher. Sally, come over here and sit on my lap for a few minutes."

"Baby, Sam Graves was leaving his office for his grandson's T-ball game. He said at his age T-ball was more exciting than some of the things he once did as a young man."

When Job reached beneath Sally's blouse and skillfully unsnapped her bra, Sally reached over, turned off the reading light, and said "Welcome home Job, I'm glad you're not T-ball age."

As Job got ready to leave his house the next morning, Sally pinched him and asked, "Ready for more T-ball?"

"Not this morning, babe. I've got to run." He walked outside to get in his car and Sally called out to him.

"Don't forget Dr. Battle's report is coming today. And even though you don't like T-ball, you sure hit a homerun last night."

Job smiled all the way to his office. Once there, he wondered if Ann and Ed had enjoyed such silly times as he and Sally shared.

Job sent his secretary to the local post office at 10:30 to pick up the morning mail, but there was no report from Dr. Battle.

Job had lunch with two business clients and the local city court judge. Each ordered the Thursday Special: chicken pot pie and three vegetables. The city judge, watching his waist-line, read the morning Atlanta paper, sharing what he read while his colleagues ate their banana pudding.

"Listen to this. Abe Kronenberg, in his *Political Talk* column, writes, 'District Attorney Aaron Bailey discounts rumor that he wants the governor's chair. Says he has commitment to complete the term of office to which he was elected.' Fellows, when they talk like that, they are already running for something bigger. Have you ever heard of anyone seeking a lesser office?"

Job smiled and remembered yesterday's talk with Sam Graves. To create a diversion, Job steered the conversation to college football and the upcoming season.

The afternoon mail brought Dr. Battle's expected letter. Job took particular note of a very important statement in the doctor's report:

Job, Mrs. Tatum seems pleased that daughter plans to go back to college next month. This, one of few positive developments. Patient suppresses emotions to extreme degree. Little progress in opening doors that need to be opened. (We have discussed this before.) To your question: "Is client mentally able to reasonably assist her attorney in preparation for and trial of case?" Answer is: "At present, no." More later.

THESE THINGS I WILL DO

On August 21, 1972, Job Lee received the following letter from Sam Graves:

Job,

> *Thank you for talking to me about the Tatum case. First, you sell yourself short. You can handle this case without an old man tugging at your elbow during the trial. But, if you want me there, I am willing to get in the saddle with you on these terms:*
>
> *(1) You will be lead attorney and handle all pretrial discovery and preparation, including all preliminary court appearances.*
> *(2) I will be available to you for discussions and planning as you need.*
> *(3) I will appear with you for trial, making my formal appearance on the day the trial begins.*
> *(4) I will make the opening statement to the jury for the defense and you will handle final summation.*
> *(5) I will undertake this representation without expectation of compensation.*

Job, you may have seen the article in the paper a few days ago about Aaron Bailey and the governor's chair. He has that itch and will likely, at the last moment, take charge of the prosecution, and bring one or two assistants to the trial with him. The assistants will do the work where there are no cameras present. Aaron will be there to take the bows for the cameras before, during, and after (if he wins) the trial.

If my prediction comes true, this is another reason that you do not need me in the case. It may well be to Mrs. Tatum's advantage with the jury if it appears that Goliath (Aaron Bailey and assistants) do battle with David (you, without me at your side). Sometimes appearing the weaker has strong jury appeal, making the weaker the stronger. Just a thought. Let me hear from you.

Regards,
Sam Graves
P.S.

Wish you could have seen my grandson play T-ball. On his first time at bat, he hit the ball and then ran to third base rather than first. I laughed so much I almost pissed in my pants.

COMMITMENTS OLD AND NEW

Job discussed Grave's proposal with both Ann and Jane and they agreed to the terms of engagement. It wasn't what Job had expected to accomplish, but he was still relieved. Being on the same side of a case with Sam Graves would be a tremendous help, no matter what the pecking order.

During the next three months, Job worked as he had never worked before. In many ways, he was walking on unfamiliar ground. Criminal law and procedure was not his field. Slowly, he worked his way past the "trapped" feeling he'd had. He vacillated in his resolve to devote more time and attention to his wife and family. For a few days, he disciplined himself by leaving his office no later than six each evening. Then, without realizing what was happening, the cycle would renew. Ann's case would reassert its claim and it would be eight, nine, or even ten o'clock before he even noticed the clock. The long days left him very tired. Sally was concerned but made no complaint.

Not only did this case rob Job of energy, it also became increasingly expensive. Opportunities to serve new clients were, of necessity, declined. Some obligations to serve existing clients could be deferred but some could not.

BOB LECROY

Bob LeCroy, Job's high school classmate, owner of the convenience store on the east side of town, had become one of Job's first clients and had remained a client over Job's ten years of practice. He was often a rough and tumble fellow with a quick temper, and often crude in his language. In early October, when Job had more than he could do, Bob called at the early morning hour of 1:30. He was in the Carrollton jail and charged with assault and battery on Phil Price, another resident of Carrollton who had been a classmate of both Bob and Job. Bob and Phil had gotten into a dispute in a poker game that evolved into a fight and serious injury to Phil. Job could not decline Bob's call for help. Several days were consumed in getting this dispute between friends resolved and the criminal charges in city court dismissed.

MARY HORN

Ten days after getting Bob LeCroy's problem resolved, Roger Horn, a retired lawyer called Job.

"Job, my wife has her drawers in a wad over a traffic ticket. Can you see her and take care of her problem. She's driving me nuts."

Job couldn't say "no" to this request. Roger Horn was an old family friend and had referred several clients.

The next day, Mary Horn was in Job's office. She was ninety-one and always wore hat and gloves when outside her home. The cause for her visit and for her "drawers being in a wad" as her husband put it was a traffic ticket issued by a young Carrollton policeman. The story Mary privately told Job and the story that was told when she and her attorney went to the city court four days later was the same.

From the witness chair in the city court, again wearing her hat and gloves, Mary told the judge what had happened. On the Saturday morning she was ticketed for speeding and for failure to obey an officer, along with reckless driving, and resisting arrest, Mary was on her way to the grocery store. She explained to the city judge that she went to the grocery store every Saturday morning. On this particular morning, a young policeman had signaled her to "stop" at an intersection to allow the participants of a 10K road-run to pass. When the first group of runners was safely past, the policeman waved his hand, signaling Mary to proceed through the intersection. A second group of runners was approaching and Mary failed to accelerate fast enough to please the officer. Thus it was that Mary was greatly humiliated by the policeman blowing his whistle at her and urging her to drive just a little faster.

As Mary said several times from the witness chair: "Men do not blow their whistles at ladies. I will not stand for it. I will not have it. I was not reared that way. Yes, I said those exact words to that officer standing there blowing his whistle and waving at me. Yes, just as he said, when I got to the middle of the intersection, I stopped beside the officer and I shook my finger at him. I said, 'Young man, that is rude. You shut up.' It was rude. I shall not tolerate such conduct. I will do the same any time a man whistles at me."

After properly chastising the young policeman, Mary had put her old, long, black Buick back in gear, and proceeded, at twenty miles per hour toward the grocery store. The intersection policeman forgot his duty to the road runners, climbed on his motorcycle, turned on its "whistle" and gave chase to Mary. Two patrol cars turned on their "whistles" and joined in the twenty mile per hour chase. Being a lady who would never dignify a whistle, Mary proceeded on her way to the grocery store. She never made it. Two other police cars, their "whistles" screaming offensively, approached Mary from the opposite direction and blocked her path, whereupon, with all whistles stopped, the officers gave Mary the citations.

Asked on the witness stand why she did not stop for the police cars, Mary truthfully said, "I had become frightened. The officer in the intersection seemed angry. I decided not to stop until I could do so in a place where others were present. I was greatly humiliated by all those whistles and I was frightened."

Virtually everyone in Carrollton knew Mary. The judge had known her for years. By this time, in the simple, rather informal trial, the judge was convinced that Mary had, in fact, been offended by being whistled at. He realized she had become frightened and was looking for a "safe" place to stop.

The story was told and everyone in the courtroom, except Mary, saw humor in the entire episode. Even the young policeman who had blown the first "whistle" now saw Mary as a figurative great-grandmother and was no longer upset by her actions.

After Mary finished testifying, the kind judge gave the prosecuting attorney a "knowing look" and asked, "Would you like a few minutes to privately speak to the officers?" A private conference between the city attorney and the police officers was held, after which the city attorney moved to dismiss the charges against Mary.

VENTURE OF YOUTH

Shortly after Mary Horn's case was dismissed, another distracting event took Job away from Ann's case. This time the added pressure was forced on him by the very person who was most concerned Job was working too hard, his wife, Sally.

It had been another long, hard day and before Job could even start eating the late dinner that was saved for him, Sally said, "Honey, I know you already have more than you can do, but you have to help Sammy Whitmore. Leona came to see me today and she is embarrassed to tears and beside herself with fear of Sammy being kicked out of school."

Job and Sally had no closer friends than Robert and Leona Whitmore. Robert, some twenty years older than Job, had been Job's Boy Scout leader, Sunday school teacher, and high school science teacher. Leona Whitmore was Sally's confidant and friend, almost a surrogate mother. Job and Sally were well acquainted with the three Whitmore children, Sammy, now age twenty-three, was the oldest of the three. He was in his last year of pre-med studies at Emory University, an honor student, and had been accepted for admission to the School of Medicine, University of Virginia, in 1973.

Having missed lunch and hungry, Job shoveled in two quick bites of the food Sally had set before him, quickly swallowed and asked "What has happened to Sammy?"

"Job, Leona is so upset, she can hardly talk about it."

"Honey, you can talk about it. What has happened?""

I'm so upset, I can't talk about it, either."

"Well, I guess that lets me off the hook. I don't know anything about it, so I can't help."

Job scooped in a load of mashed-potato and gravy before Sally gained enough composure to say, "Sammy has been arrested!"

About half the potato-gravy mix came out of Job's mouth with his surprised response of, "What for?"

Sally's answer of "Public Drunkenness," almost got the remainder of his potatoes and gravy.

Job quickly finished his late evening meal and within an hour was back in his office talking to Sammy Whitmore. In hand, Sammy had a citation charging him with the offense of "Public Drunkenness on Carroll County Road #10." He was directed to appear in the Carroll County District Court at 10 a.m. the following Thursday to answer the charge.

Although greatly embarrassed, Sammy told Job what had happened. Long before Sammy finished his narrative, Job had decided to take Sammy's case. A conviction would represent a grave injustice and possibly do irreparable harm to a fine young man.

The following Thursday, Job and his client appeared in the District Court, entered a plea of "Not guilty," and the simple, but humorous, trial began. State Troopers Baker and Elmore, the arresting officers, appeared as prosecution witnesses for the State. Both troopers were young and inexperienced.

Trooper Baker, the older of the two, was called as the first witness. Baker was not far into telling the Judge what happened before Judge McDonald realized, as Job had realized when Sammy privately told him the story, the primary purpose of the state troopers on the evening of Sammy's arrest was not to enforce the laws of Georgia, but to try to catch young lovers in an embarrassing circumstance.

Josh Gillespie, who served as County Prosecuting Attorney called Trooper Baker to the witness chair and said, "Trooper Baker, in your own words tell Judge McDonald what happened that caused you and Trooper Elmore to make this arrest.

"Well Mr. Gillespie," Baker said, "it was like this. On the evening of this arrest, Trooper Elmore and I were on patrol in the west part of the County. As we were going east on that part of County Road 10 that is frequently called Beer Can Alley Road, we spotted a light blue '67 Chevrolet parked in a cotton field off to our right. It matched the description of a stolen car that we had a report on, so we took our flashlights and went into the cotton field to investigate. When we got to the car, we noticed the back door was standing open and the back seat of the car was missing. We heard some noise further down in the cotton patch and went to investigate. About twenty-five or thirty yards further, we found the back seat of the car with a nude female and male more or less stacked-up on top of it. The nude male on top was mooning the moon above while attending to more pressing business below. When the beam of my light fully illuminated his fanny, he grabbed up his pants, took one jump that covered about three cotton rows, got his left leg in the left leg of his pants and took another three row jump, got his right leg in the right side of his pants and from then on he was jumping about six cotton rows at the time. We gave chase. He ran onto Beer Can Alley Road, where we caught him. His face was flushed and he looked like he might have been drinking. So we gave him the citation to appear for drunkenness.

By this time, everyone in the courtroom, except Sammy Whitmore, was enjoying the show. When Josh Gillespie rested his case, Job addressed the Judge: "Judge McDonald, I move for a judgment of acquittal on the grounds there is a fatal variance between what has been charged and what has been proven. My client stands charged with being drunk on County Road #10. The proof that has been offered shows that he was arrested not on road #10, but on a piece of ground that was once a part of #10. In fact, that portion of the road was abandoned and officially vacated as part of the county road system in 1963 when the new County Road #10 was constructed. I have a certified copy of the official resolution of vacation in hand to provide to the court, and I have the County Engineer on standby to be called as a witness. If called, he will testify that the place where this young man was arrested was not on a public road but in a privately owned cotton field. In the interest of time, I ask the judge to take judicial notice that the arrest was made on privately owned property and grant my motion for acquittal.

Judge McDonald looked to Josh Gillespie. "Josh," he said, "I am inclined to grant the motion for acquittal. I am aware that a portion of County Road 10 was officially vacated in 1963 when the new road 10 was constructed. I can't tell you that I am certain that this portion was abandoned as Mr. Lee says. But I can tell you that I have personal awareness this part of the old road has not been used as a county road since the new Road 10 was opened. It is common knowledge the area known as Beer Can Alley Road is frequently used for young people, and a few old ones, too, to meet and do the things that people frequently like to do under the cover of darkness. You would not be aware that parts of the old County Road 10 had been vacated. That happened before you became an attorney. Whether or not you are aware that Beer Can Alley Road is now used for the doing of the things most people like to do in the dark is none of my business, and I do not want to know. I might add that what people do in a cotton field, out of public view, is rarely the business of the State Troopers, and as a general proposition, they should not try to make it their business. If you seriously object to my taking judicial notice of this portion of the road having been abandoned, I'll allow Mr. Lee to call the County Engineer to offer formal proof. What do you say to the motion?"

Josh Gillespie looked at the Judge and said, "Mr. Lee is

an honorable man. I'm sure he would not misrepresent this matter to the court. I do not object to you taking judicial notice of the things requested."

Judge McDonald granted Job's motion. The case was over. Sammy was "not guilty" and free to go back to school, and later on to medical school where he became an orthopedic surgeon. The case was also rewarding to Job, both in the present and in the future. Not only had he obtained a good result for his young client, he had found humor and a needed escape from Ann's problems in doing so. Most of the humor and the thing that he frequently recalled with a smile, was an epilogue to the case.

As soon as Judge McDonald granted his motion for acquittal, and before anyone could get to their feet to leave the courtroom, Job put on his most serious face, and in his most indignant voice again addressed Judge McDonald: "Judge, I move the court to issue a bench warrant for the arrest of Troopers Baker and Elmore."

Everyone in the courtroom was surprised. The troopers were both surprised and shocked. With a puzzled look, Judge McDonald tucked his chin to his chest and over the top of his half-lenses glasses said, "Mr. Lee, this is highly unusual. What would you have me charge them with?"

"Disturbing the peace your honor, disturbing the peace," Job replied.

Immediately catching the pun, the Judge said "I think they might be guilty, but I don't think I'll charge them."

Job went home and told Sally that Sammy had been acquitted. Thirty minutes later he was back in his office working on Ann's case.

UNABLE TO REMOVE HIS EYE FROM THE COMET

Ann's case was of a new and different variety. It was time consuming. Problems of old clients and friends continued at their normal pace. Old allegiances could not be ignored. Simple cases, like those of Mary and Sammy, were humorous, but Job needed both time and income, not laughter. He held a wolf by its ears and he could not afford to turn loose. His income was greatly reduced and very quickly he accumulated a backlog of recorded interviews that needed to be transcribed into printed form. Marie Watson, his only employee, served as both receptionist and secretary.

The state was required to furnish Job with witness statements and investigative materials of an exculpatory nature. Feeling very confident of obtaining a conviction, the district attorney's office essentially furnished Job with copies of all materials the office had collected, and this left him swamped with paperwork to examine.

With Ann's consent, her medical files were copied by her doctors and shared with Job. These had to be reviewed and relevant information summarized and transcribed.

Job had the advantage of having personal involvement in many important interviews. This gave him firsthand knowledge of what had been said. Sam Graves did not have this advantage and with his commitment to participate in the case, the need to transcribe all recordings became critical. Very quickly, Ms. Watson was overwhelmed in her efforts to help Job keep his new jealous mistress happy while still trying to fulfill his responsibilities to old clients. In order to clear the backlog of transcriptions and to try to keep abreast in transcribing new recordings, Job was forced to use the part-time services of four different secretaries.

Three weeks after Sam Graves agreed to assist Job in Ann's defense, he received his first collection of transcripts and summaries, together with this letter from Job:

Dear Sam,

I enclose the first installment of promised transcripts and summaries. Aaron Bailey's office is trying to cover me up with paper.

Different part-time secretaries have made these transcriptions. I regret that this has resulted in a variety of formats. But the content is accurate, so I guess the form is not so important.

I will forward additional transcripts and summaries as they are generated.

Best,
Job Lee

Four days later, this same note came back to Job. At the foot, Sam Graves had added:

Job, received and thanks. Don't worry about the format. My grandfather (an old South Carolina attorney) told me that some people say 'possum,' others say 'opossum,' but they are all talking about the same ugly critter. ~ Sam

Later in life, Job would remember the three months before Ann's trial as being the most hectic of his entire legal career. During that time, he interviewed, among others: Dot Carey,

Ann's co-worker at the McCurry Agency; Ethel McCoy, Ann's long-time next-door neighbor; and Mary Mills, the lady who had recently moved into the house across the street from the Tatum home. Transcripts of these three interviews were collectively filed as "Potential Trial Witnesses."

DOT CAREY: CO-WORKER, SEPTEMBER 26, 1972

The first file document was the interview with Dot Carey:

LEE: Please tell me about your relationship with Ann Tatum—how you knew her and for how long.
CAREY: I met her when she first started as a part-time worker at the McCurry Agency. I guess that was three or four years ago. She became full-time later. Maybe that was two years ago. I am not too good at dates, so don't hold me to that.

LEE: No problem. Just give me your best recollection.
CAREY: Except for holidays and vacations, I saw Ann pretty much five days a week during this entire time. A few times we had some catching-up to do and we would work a half-day some Saturdays.
LEE: What were her job duties and how did she perform?
CAREY: She started out mostly as a file clerk and then she moved to bookkeeping, doing most receivables and payables. From time to time, when someone was out, she handled the phone and reception desk. What was the rest of your question?

LEE: I was inquiring about her performance.

CAREY: Until about the middle of last year, she did her work very well. There was never any problem with her performance. Our office is loosely organized. We don't have an organizational chart. More or less, I was Ann's supervisor. I didn't have that title, but that is what I did. Understand?

LEE: Yes. What happened at the middle of last year and how did her work performance change?

CAREY: I don't know what happened, but something obviously did.

LEE: Explain.

CAREY: The first thing that I noticed was that Anne's Parkinson's, would sometimes be much worse than at other times. Her right hand would shake more. Next, I noticed she started losing weight. These were gradual things. After several weeks, maybe two months, I knew that something was going on with her, I didn't know what and I still don't know. But I could tell Ann got to where she wouldn't eat her sandwich at lunch. She always brought her own lunch, and some days she wouldn't eat any of it. She seemed to start downhill and never stopped.

LEE: Did she ever talk about her family?

CAREY: Her family is about the only thing that she talked about. That's why it's so hard for us to understand why she killed Ed. I never personally knew him, but through Ann, I felt as if I did. She was devoted to Ed and her girls. She really had no other interests. All she ever wanted was her family. You men don't understand us women. We can tell about another woman, what she wants, and whom she wants. I will believe to my dying day that all Ann wanted was her family.

LEE: Were you aware of her plan to move to Memphis?
CAREY: Oh, yes. Ann told all of us about Ed's new job, her plans to stay in Atlanta until Dana graduated, and then she would move with him. She was a little sad about pulling up her roots, but wherever Ed went, that's where she wanted to go.

LEE: Did she ever say anything that suggested her husband ever abused her, or threatened abuse?
CAREY: Never.

LEE: Back to what you were saying about how things started to change with Ann. I believe you said you first noticed this about the middle of last year. Dana graduated in May.
CAREY: It was around that time. There was no dramatic event or fixed time. Around that time, Ann started losing weight, losing energy, and seemed to be tired a lot of the time. As the year went on, she got worse and worse. She didn't complain. Ann is a very private person; she doesn't reveal her emotions. But, even with that, there were times she seemed on top of the world, times she seemed like her old self.
LEE: Can you associate these times when she seemed like her old self with any other events in her life?
CAREY: Yes. Sometimes she would say that Ed might lose his job in Memphis and she might not move. There were several times she so indicated. At times when she talked about Ed coming back to Atlanta to live, she would be happy. Then,

there would be times when she would indicate she'd soon put their house on the market for sale and she would be moving to Memphis after all. She would be very happy when she talked about moving to Memphis. Her mood changes were very strange. They all centered on her plans to be with Ed. I couldn't follow what her thinking was. At times, she was high, at other times low, very low.

LEE: How many times did you see these mood changes?
CAREY: I didn't keep count. I guess during the last six months of last year and the first six weeks of this year, Ann was on the peaks and then in the valleys six or eight times. Mr. Lee, during the last part of last year and this year, Ann has been in a pitiful condition. Really, really bad shape. She lost so much weight that the rest of us at the office thought she might have some form of cancer. Yet, she came to work each day and didn't take any sick days, even though she looked like a walking skeleton. By this time, her right hand shook so badly that she couldn't even write her name. If she wanted to give someone a written note, she had to type it. We knew something was bad wrong, but we didn't know what.

LEE: Did anyone in the office talk to her about her condition?
CAREY: Several of us who were close to her tried, but she would always pat you on your hand, sometimes on your cheek, and say, "Honey, I'm just fine. Just fine." Ann is a very affectionate person. She seems to love everyone.

LEE: I understand that you drove Ann back to her house the day Ed was killed. Tell me about that day.
CAREY: It was February 18, 1972. I'll never forget that day

as long as I live. I live about a mile from Ann's house. Most of the time, I would pick her up and we would ride to the office together. She would help me with gas costs, sort of a car-pool arrangement. When she had some running around to do after work, she would drive her own car. That was another thing; we all got worried about her even trying to drive. I'm sorry, I lost my train of thought. Ann drove her own car on the 18th, the day Ed died. She was having a really bad day. At lunchtime, even though she brought her usual sandwich, I offered to drop her off at her house on my way home, so she might rest, and I'd stop by to pick her up on my way back to the office. She agreed to do that, and she took her sandwich back home with her. I dropped her off at her house about 12:15 and drove on to my home. When I returned to pick her up, her yard was filled with police cars and all traffic was turned away. I had no idea what had happened, and I went back to the office since I couldn't get to her house. It wasn't until the six o'clock news before any of us knew someone had died. I was afraid it was Ann. The news people didn't know who it was either, until later that night. They said it was a man that had died. I still didn't know who.

LEE: Why did you think it might have been Ann?

CAREY: If you had seen Ann the few months and weeks leading up to that day, you would understand. She had become a zombie. Most of her life had left her. She was pitiful.

ETHEL McCOY: FAITHFUL FRIEND,
SEPTEMBER 3, 1972

LEE: Thank you, Mrs. McCoy, for talking to me. You are aware I will record our conversation and my secretary will prepare a transcript for my use.

McCOY: Yes, that was explained to me.

LEE: If at any time you want a copy of either the tape or the transcript, let me know and it will be provided. Our discussion will be very informal. Let's start with you giving me a history of your relation with Ann and her family.

McCOY: They moved in next door to Walter and me about 1954. I'm not sure about the exact date. We've lived next door to them since that date, and they have always been good neighbors. There's never been any friction between our families all this time. They were just a young couple, and only had one child then, Jane. She was maybe eight or nine. I later learned that Jane was Ann's child by a previous marriage. I think Dana was born maybe nine or ten months after they came to the neighborhood.

LEE: Please allow me to interrupt. You mentioned Jane. Tell me about Ed's relationship with her.

McCOY: He treated her exactly the way he treated Dana after she came along; he treated her like a daughter. He was always, up until about the last year, a truly loving, caring, devoted father to both girls. I am sure they'll tell you the same thing. Ann and Ed were about twenty-five years younger than Walter and me. Our three children were grown and out on their own. It was a time of my life when I was lonesome for a child to have around. That happens when your children marry and move away. I missed our three. I sort of adopted Ann. We bonded together and have stayed bonded all these years.

LEE: What was your relation with Ed?
McCOY: It was a good one. He was always considerate and respectful. He bonded more to Walter. They fished together every chance they got. They'd come home from a fishing trip and see which one could tell the biggest yarn about catching the biggest fish. We were good to Ed and he was good to us. I'll never understand what happened to Ed. Life has many mysteries.

LEE: Did Ann ever talk to you about her past, her life before she moved to Atlanta?
McCOY: Not for a long time. Ann is a quiet person, somewhat shy. For the first few years, she had a new baby to care for and was busy establishing her home. It was after Dana started school that we became really close. Mr. Lee, may I ask you a question?

LEE: Of course.
McCOY: I don't feel comfortable talking to you about the personal things Ann told me. She spoke to me in confidence and I don't want to betray her.
LEE: I both understand and respect that. Now may I share something with you?
McCOY: Of course you may.

LEE: I also have a confidential relation with Ann, an attorney-client relation, so I must be careful how I say this to you. I must not betray the confidence of my client. I'll put it this way. As her attorney, I have a serious problem. Several serious problems. First, I have a client who is charged with murder. Second, I need to know all that I can about her background and what happened to cause her to kill her husband. Thus far, my client has been unable to communicate with me in a meaningful way. Out of respect for Dana's feelings, I have not pushed her to share whatever she may know. Dana, like Ann and Jane, has been devastated by what happened. This case will likely be set for trial before the end of the year, and time for preparation is getting short. Before trial, I'll attempt an in-depth discussion with Dana about what she knows that may be of benefit. When and if Ann will be able to reasonably assist me in preparing her defense, I don't know. Thus, through you, and others, I attempt to gather facts that may help my client. Yes, I have several serious problems.

McCoy: Mr. Lee, has Ann not told you of the things that Ed was doing, the way he treated her the several months before he was killed?

LEE: Mrs. McCoy, I must not share with you anything that Ann has told me in confidence. I can say that I need all the information I can gather about Ann, her life, any problems she may have had with Ed, anything that may help twelve people in a jury box understand what happened and why Ann shot her husband. I can say that I'm desperate for information of this nature. While I'm not at liberty to tell you the things Ann has told me in confidence, I can say she has not been able to tell me very much. She seems to try, but doesn't seem to be able to do so.

McCoy: Do you mind if I privately talk to Ann, telling her that you asked me to share our previous private talks with you? Do you mind if I seek her permission to do this?

Lee: Has Ann told you she is seeing a doctor?
McCoy: Yes. I now visit her most every day. I go to her house. She no longer comes next door to mine. She has told me about Dr. Battle, if that is who you mean.

Lee: Yes, I made reference to him. Before encouraging you to speak to Ann about sharing the things she's told you, I think it best that we get Dr. Battle's agreement that this would be a good approach. We don't want to harm any treatment plan that he has underway. Would you be willing to talk to Dr. Battle about this approach?
McCoy: Of course. Will you arrange an appointment?

Lee: I will arrange that and let you know.

Job came away from this interview with Ethel McCoy greatly impressed with the intellect, poise, and dignity of this lady. He sensed that she might have desperately sought information about Ann, her life, and family. He had tried enough cases to know that how a witness says something was often more important than what the witness said. Mrs. McCoy, like Sam Graves, had a way of speaking that made one want to listen. Job immediately called Dr. Battle's office and requested an appointment for Mrs. McCoy.

MARY MILLS, OCTOBER 6, 1972

LEE: Mrs. Mills, I represent Ann Tatum. I am sure you're aware that she is charged with a serious criminal offense. Do I have your permission to record our conversation?
MILLS: Yes, you do.

LEE: I understand that you live directly across the street from Ann's house. Please tell me how long you have lived there and describe your relation with the Tatum family.
MILLS: My husband, Anthony, and I moved there in late April, last year. He is disabled and seldom gets out of the house. I don't think he ever met either Ann or Dana. I just barely know them. I've never been in their house nor have they been in mine. I stay inside most of the time with Anthony. Once or twice, last fall, I stepped across the street to introduce myself to Ann as she left or returned from work. Ethel McCoy told me that Ann worked with an insurance agency. I never met Edward Tatum, but I believe Ethel told me that he worked in Memphis. So, my acquaintance with Ann and Dana is pretty much limited to our waving to each other across the street. I'm afraid that I can't be of any help to you.

LEE: Let me ask you about the events of February 18 this year. Did you see or hear anything out of the ordinary that day?
MILLS: Yes. The police, a Detective Parker, questioned me and I gave him a statement.

LEE: Tell me, as best you recall, what you told the detective.
MILLS: It was during the lunch hour, maybe about 12:30. I

had fed Anthony his lunch and gotten him down for his afternoon nap. It was a warm day and I had some tulip bulbs I wanted to get in the flowerbed beside our driveway. When I went outside to plant the bulbs, I noticed a strange car in Ann's driveway. Ann's car was usually in her drive if she was at home. She seldom put her car in her garage. This strange car was dark blue or black in color and had a Tennessee license plate. Someone was seated in the passenger seat, but the back of the car was to me and I couldn't tell whether it was a man or woman. But someone was in the car. I thought it might be burglars, so I went into the house for a pencil and pad, came back out and noted the tag number.

LEE: Do you still have the tag number?
MILLS: Yes, I gave the number to Detective Parker. He wrote it down and suggested that I keep my original note. It's at home.

LEE: When you return home, will you call me back with that number? Did you see or hear anything else that day?
MILLS: Another thing that attracted my attention was that Ann's garage door was open. She has a garage door that slides up and down, and it was open. She seldom parks her car in the garage, but when she leaves home, it's her custom to leave the door closed. That was one of the reasons I thought it might be a burglar.

LEE: Anything else?
MILLS: About the time I finished recording the tag number, I heard what sounded like firecrackers exploding. It was difficult to tell the direction of the noise. I wasn't sure what was

going on and I went inside to call the police. I reported what I had seen and heard and went back to my front door. I didn't go back outside, but when I got back to the door, the dark car was gone from the driveway. In a few minutes, the first police car arrived and the officer went into the garage and, I guess, into the house. From my door, I couldn't see the door of Ann's house that opens into the garage. Shortly thereafter, other police cars arrived. By this time, Anthony was awake and calling me. That's all I know, Mr. Lee.

LEE: Thank you Mrs. Mills, You have been very helpful. Please remember to share that tag number with me.

At the end of this transcript, Job added: Note to file: Follow up on automobile in driveway. What make and model car did Ed Tatum drive? Someone had to drive this car away! Why? Who?

WHO BENDS NOT AN EAR TO ANY BELL?

Keeping the appointment that Job Lee made for her, Ethel McCoy met with Dr. Battle on October 13. The doctor added this brief note to his file on Ann Tatum:

Ethel Sammons McCoy, neighbor of Ann Tatum for 18 years, deliberate, organized, "almost like her mother." Confirms some patient statements. Wants to talk to patient, seeking her permission to share previous, private discussions with attorney. I advised I had no objection to proposal.

On October 14, Dr. Battle posted a letter to Job Lee.

Job,

To reply to your recent inquiries:

Patient continues to suppress traumatic event and things leading thereto. Although not a strong believer in hypnoses, some colleagues report favorable results. I may consider this, but prefer more conventional approach. I understand your need for details of events. Please give me early notice of any trial date. On the positive side, patient shows slight signs of addressing and confronting painful memories. Only time will tell.
You asked about patient cooperation. I have no reason to believe she intentionally conceals or desires to mislead. To the contrary, she gives every indication of desiring to cooperate. Job, some things the human mind must address slowly, otherwise it would be too painful to cope with. I don't yet know the extent of this lady's wounds, but I do know they are very deep and real.

About your desire to have a detailed discussion with Dana. First, she is not my patient. I have met her briefly two times and had a more extensive conversation a third time. My observations, as opposed to a professional opinion: Dana, too, is deeply wounded. She was very close to the father whom her mother killed. She is equally close to her mother. She has not withdrawn into a protective shell as her mother has. Thus, she is more vulnerable and doesn't enjoy the protection that suppression often affords. Strongly suggest that you defer as long as possible before pressing Dana for information.

I met with Ethel McCoy a few days past, an impressive lady. She posed the question of her asking patient's permission to divulge content of private discussions the two of them have shared. I see no potential for harm to patient if this is done, and I told Mrs. McCoy so. I did not tell Mrs. McCoy, but such a talk may have the positive benefit of helping Mrs. Tatum escape from her present protective cocoon.

ETHEL McCOY'S SECOND INTERVIEW: OCTOBER 25, 1972

Eleven days after Dr. Battle's letter to Job, Ethel McCoy, wearing her low-heel walking shoes, drove her 1961 Chevrolet to Job's office and went in to talk with him. It was not a pleasant mission, but an important one. The restraint of her breaching the confidence of a friend had been removed and she had information that Ann's lawyer needed. She came resolved to truthfully tell what she knew.

Once in his office, she said, "Job, this remark is not directed toward you, but this is not a pleasant trip for me. Tragedy holds no pleasure. My friends have suffered, so if you please, let's get right to work on the things I'm here for. I hope I do not sound rude. That is not my intent. I guess I rush because of the pain I suffer, pain that Ann's family, Ed's family, all of us suffer, so please ask your questions, and I will answer. Then I'll go back home and cry."

"I understand," Job said as he turned on the recording machine.

LEE: Let me thank you for the times you've driven Ann to my office since Dana has gone back to school.
McCOY: Job, I am glad to be of help. Ann, Jane, and Dana are just like family to me. Did Dr. Battle tell you that I had talked to him?

LEE: Yes, he said that your talking to Ann about sharing previous talks between the two of you would do no harm and might be of benefit. Two days ago, when you last brought Ann to see me, I again tried with little success to get her to share the things that were taking place in her marriage. Mrs. McCoy, I need your help. May I explain why?
McCOY: I wish you would.

LEE: For Ann's trial, we'll start out with twelve strangers in the jury box. None of them will know her or anything about her. These strangers will hold Ann's fate in their hands. At the end of the trial, they will have to vote as to what her fate will be. The facts against Ann seem overwhelming. After the State finishes presenting its testimony and evidence, what will the jurors know about the case? One, they will know that apparently Ann and Ed were alone in the house. Two, they will know that Ed was shot eight times, once in his chest and seven times as he attempted to run away. Three, they will know that Ann's fingerprints and part of her palm print are on the pistol. Four, they will know that three of the eight bullets taken from Ed's body were so distorted that no reliable ballistics test could be made on them; however, the ballistics on the other five bullets show they were fired from the pistol bearing Ann's prints. Do you see the difficult position Ann is in?

McCoy: Yes, I do. What are you going to say on her behalf? Ann told me that another attorney, a Mr. Graves, would also represent her. What is Mr. Graves going to say?

Lee: Mrs. McCoy, you ask the very question that we attorneys ask. What can we say? Allow me to add another part of the trial picture about what the attorneys say before, during the trial, and after. First, we'll speak directly to the jury before the testimony begins. In this opening statement, we'll be permitted to tell the jury what we expect the evidence and testimony will show. We are allowed to paint a word picture of what we think the facts of the case are. This opening statement is very important for the simple reason that first impressions are always important. We want to make, if possible, a positive first impression on Ann's behalf. Second, during the trial, Mr. Graves and I will be limited to simply asking questions. During this part of the proceedings, we may speak to the judge, but not to the jury. During this part of the trial, the facts presented by the State will be speaking very strongly against Ann. What favorable facts do we have to present on Ann's behalf? We can show that for all her life, she had been a peaceable, non-aggressive person. But showing this does not overcome the shock of what she did. Sam Graves and I are searching for facts that will speak favorably for Ann. Facts that will help the jury see Ann's actions in an understandable light. Gaining the favor and consideration of the jury is what it's all about. The jurors have the vote—the only vote that really counts. We look to Ann and Dana, and to people like you, to reveal favorable facts on behalf of our client. Jane had married and moved away, so she has little information that will be of material benefit to Ann. But first, we attorneys must know what the facts are and then we prepare a way to present those facts to the jury.

McCoy: You mentioned that you and Mr. Graves will get to talk to the jury a second time.

Lee: Yes, this is after all the witnesses have testified, after all the documents and exhibits have been admitted into evidence, and after all the facts for and against Ann have been presented to the jury. Before the jury goes to the jury room to vote, we attorneys, both for the State and the defense, have the opportunity to make a final statement to the jury. Often this is called the "final argument." This, too, is an important part of the trial. It gives us an opportunity to make a "final impression" on the jury. I strongly believe that people are often powerfully influenced with first and last impressions.

McCoy: Do you and Mr. Graves know what you will say in your final argument?

Lee: Mrs. McCoy, to be very truthful, thus far we don't know what we can say to the jury at any time that is likely to make a difference. On the surface, it appears Ann was the aggressor and acted without any threat to her person. There was no evidence of any fight. I can get little information from Ann, but she does indicate that Ed did not threaten her. She indicates that he never threatened to do her any physical harm.

McCoy: Job, is physical life more important than the will to live?
Lee: I'm sorry, but I don't understand your question.

McCoy: I was really just talking to myself. I was just pondering the question of which is the greater wrong?
Lee: I'm still not able to understand what you're saying.

McCoy: Until Ann killed Ed, I had never thought of it before. Since then, I've often wondered if it's worse to kill someone's will to live than it is to take someone's physical life?
Lee: How does this question relate to Ann and Ed?

McCoy: It relates directly to them. The things Ed was doing to Ann is what brought the question to my mind. Until then, until I saw what was happening, I had never thought of it before.

THE KISS OF ANGELS

Through Ethel McCoy, the neighbor who was like a mother to Ann, Job started to develop an understanding of Ann's reason for doing what she did. Job remembered talking to Wallace Henry, Ann's old Sunday school teacher and friend, and his statement that Ann must have had some reason for doing what she'd done. Job also remembered that Mr. Henry said he hoped she had acted for a good reason as opposed to a bad one. The things Mrs. McCoy told him might make Ann's actions at least partly understandable, but not forgivable. Mrs. McCoy's knowledge of critical events did not include the day Ed Tatum died in the house next door; but the things she did know were like the dawning of morning, some of the darkness that surrounded Ann's reason for shooting her husband began to fade. Only Ann had knowledge of the events that led her to such a violent act, and, thus far, she had not been able to tell.

Job's productive talk with Mrs. McCoy was on Wednesday. His children, Henry, Elizabeth, and Robert were excused from school the following Thursday and Friday for fall break. After his lengthy discussion with Mrs. McCoy, Job drove home where Sally and the kids waited for their planned drive to Columbus, Georgia. They were to take the children to Sally's parents for a long weekend visit in Valdosta. Job had surprised Sally a week before with his suggestion to spend three nights at Calloway Gardens.

"We have not been there in several years," he said. "We need some time to ourselves."

"I'm one hundred percent in favor of that," Sally said. "What do you think about leaving Robert? Two nights away from us has pretty much been his limit."

"He's in kindergarten now and will take it like a soldier. Mark my words."

"He's just a baby, Job."

"Let's play it cool, act like there is nothing to it. I speak from experience."

"What do you mean?"

"When I was about five, maybe four, my aunt and uncle came from Spartanburg for a visit and asked me to go back home with them for a visit at their place. I was all for it. Mother packed my bag and got me ready. I was in the back seat of their car, all set and ready to go until Mother came to the open car window where I sat, stuck her head through the window, and said, 'Kiss me bye, Job.' That ended my trip away from home. My trip did not reach the end of the driveway. Out of that car window I came, straight into my Mother's arms. So let's just be cool. When we get Robert in your parent's car at Columbus, don't lean in the window and invite a kiss. I've been there, and trying it that way won't work."

"Sounds like a good plan. I'll try to be cool."

After the children were in their grandparents' car at Columbus and ready to leave, Job laughed and spoke to Sally.

"Honey, don't fool around with the window."

Henry, now eight and inquisitive like his father, asked.

"Daddy, what do you mean about not fooling around with the window?"

"Son, it's a private joke between your mother and me. I'll tell you about it when you're old and gray."

"By that time, you'll be dead."

"I know. That's when I'll tell you."

Just as Job had predicted, Robert, his brother and sister, drove away.

Sally took the wheel of their car. "Job, I'll drive. You've had a long day. How long will it take us to get to Calloway Gardens?"

"It's not too far. We should be there in forty-five minutes, maybe a little more."

"Did you talk to Mrs. McCoy again today? I didn't want to ask when the kids were around."

"Yes. I had a very good talk with her. I didn't know it before, but she is a retired college professor. She shared some things that give me a better understanding of Ann."

"Do you feel like talking about what she said?"

"It's a long story, too long to tell before we get to Calloway. Let me save it for tomorrow."

"No problem."

"There's one thing I want you to be thinking about before I tell you about my talk with Mrs. McCoy."

"What's that?"

"Which is worst: The taking of one's physical life or the taking of one's will to live?"

"Job, that's a dark subject. Very depressing just to think about it."

"Yes, I'm beginning to know."

Sally and Job rode silently on to Calloway Gardens.

The next morning, over breakfast, Job asked, "You said you would try to find out who wrote the little butterfly poem that Ann was enchanted by. Did you find anything?"

"I turned the search over to Margaret Chapman at the library. She says it was written by Christina Rossetti, an English poet. Margaret sent me a copy; it's at the house. The poem is short, but a little longer than the version Ann had."

"Thanks. When we get home, give me the copy. I don't know how I can do it, but maybe there's some way I can use the poem in Ann's trial. But, let's not talk about a trial. After we finish eating, let's go see the Calloway butterflies. Their butterfly house is huge and filled with butterflies."

Sally agreed to the proposal and smiled to herself with the realization that, try as he may, Job could not get away from Ann's trial. He was a man possessed and would be until the trial was over. Sometimes, she had nagging doubts that it would be over even when it was over.

The visit with the butterflies was followed by a walk through the large rose garden of Calloway. The roses, in their last splendor of the season, were almost breath-taking. The Ruby-Throated Hummingbirds, fattening their bodies on nectar, preparing for their long flight south, darted and danced their way from bush to bush. Job paused.

"What are you waiting for, Job?"

"Just a minute, babe. I'm composing something for you. Walk on ahead, I'll catch you in a minute."

Sally walked to a large water oak tree at the end of the garden and took a seat on a bench to wait. In a few minutes, Job joined her.

"I love you Sally. Ann has her butterfly poem. I've composed a poem for you. Want to hear it?"

"You bet, I do."

"It's in my head, I'll make it better when I can write it down, but it will go something like this:

> *Blue skies,*
> *Little girls and doll carriages,*
> *Boys skipping rocks across a pond.*
> *Sunshine, roses, and hummingbirds.*

The warmth of your smile and love,
A day God has kissed,
I was with you.

"You like it?"

"I love it and I love you," Sally said.

At mid-morning and back in their room, Sally said, "Job, you were talking in your sleep again last night. Several times it sounded as if you said, 'Help me if you can.' I think you're working too hard on this case. It worries me to see you so preoccupied. Honey, I'm not complaining. I'm just worried about you."

"I know Sally. I know you're right, but I can't help doing what I am doing. Do you remember my telling you about my talk with Mr. Henry, the old man who lives in Rome?"

"Yes, you said he was a very nice person."

"He told me Ann acted for a reason and I needed to find out what the reason was."

"Sounds like a good suggestion to me."

"Yes, it was. But, at the time Mr. Henry said that, I found it a little strange the way he said it. He said it in a way that seemed as if he knew the reason but couldn't tell me. His saying it the way he did gave me an eerie feeling."

"I thought you were impressed with his openness, his sincerity."

"I was, very much so. He is a very mature, wise person. It was just a feeling on my part that gave me the strange, spooky impression he knew some things about Ann and her life that he couldn't tell me, like he had a sort of extra-sensory perception and saw some things that others couldn't."

"Job, what brought all this to mind? When you were talking in your sleep last night, asking someone to help you, were you thinking about Mr. Henry?"

"Babe, I don't know who I was thinking about, nor do I remember what I was dreaming about. My talk with Mrs. McCoy yesterday brought Mr. Henry to mind."

"How so?"

"It was strange. Mrs. McCoy gave me some good insight into Ann's life and what had been going on in her marriage. She opened some doors and gave me a better understanding of Ann and Ed, and of life."

"How does Mr. Henry fit into this?"

"That's the strange part. It's eerie. As Mrs. McCoy spoke to me, it seemed as if Mr. Henry was speaking to me at the same time. He seemed to say, 'Job, this is the reason. This is the reason. Look further Job, look further.' Honey, I got the same eerie feeling that I had when I first spoke directly to Mr. Henry."

"Baby, do you recall telling me about the old lady who knew Ann as a little girl, the lady who came to help with the washing and ironing when Ann was young?"

"Yes, I remember. I've talked to so many people, I can't place her name right now, but I remember her. She didn't know her exact age, but she gave great details of her life as a sharecropper's wife. She's the one who used the expression about having the 'misery,' or 'misery of the spirit.' Oh, now I remember her name. It's Mrs. Glover. Mrs. Hattie Glover. Is that the lady you mean?"

"Yes, that's the one. Do you remember the other thing she

told you that you sort of laughed about?"

"No, I don't remember laughing about anything she said to me."

"Job, you don't remember because you don't believe."

"What in the world are you talking about?"

"You don't believe in angels, that's what! You said that lady talked to you about Ann not crying when her baby sister died. She said the death angels weren't able to comfort Ann because she wouldn't let them see the tears on her cheek. You remember that?"

"Yes, I remember."

"You remember laughing about that?"

"Sally, I wasn't laughing at the lady. I just found what she said amusing, both tender and amusing. But, I wasn't laughing at her. I was just amused by her unusual expression. I found it interesting."

"Job, it's something to believe in, not to be amused by."

"What are you talking about and how does this relate to Mr. Henry?"

"Remember last Sunday when our preacher talked about David lifting up his eyes and seeing the angel of the Lord standing between Heaven and Earth?"

"Yes, I remember that. But, you know I have a hard time believing all that I read in the Old Testament. I have some problems with the New Testament, too. What has all this got to do with the little lady who talked about the angels not seeing tears on Ann's face when her sister died? What does this have to do with Mr. Henry?"

"You were telling me about the strange feeling you had

when you talked to Mrs. McCoy. That reminded me of the preacher's talk about the angel and David. I have an easier time than you in believing things like that. I'm glad you talked to Mrs. McCoy and she was able to help you better understand Ann and her life, and I'm glad you talked to Mr. Henry, too. Sometimes it's good to talk to people who give you a strange, even spooky, feeling. Maybe you'll talk to an angel in your sleep."

"If an angel talks to me in my sleep, I hope that he, she, it . . . Honey, what gender is an angel?"

"There you go again, talking like a lawyer. Each time I think I have moved you one foot forward in your belief, you take two steps backward. Just treat angels in the masculine. That will make you feel better and the angels will understand."

"Girl, you have some excellent suggestions, so, if an angel talks to me, I hope he will tell me what happened in Ann's house that day. That was the one very important thing Mrs. McCoy did not know."

In bed Saturday night, Sally approached the question Job had asked on their arrival at Callaway.

"Job, I have thought about the question you asked, if it were worse to take one's physical life than to take one's spirit of life. I think you expressed it a little differently, but it was something like that."

"That's what I meant."

"You are obviously talking about Ann."

"Yes."

"That's a serious question."

"I know. I had never thought about it until Mrs. McCoy

mentioned it. I forget just how she expressed it, but she suggested Ann's spirit, her will to live, her love of life was taken from her. Mrs. McCoy did not say which was worse. She raised the subject as a question, not an answer. What is your answer?"

"I'm like Mrs. McCoy. I see the question, but I do not see any good answer. If you don't have physical life, what is left? If you have physical life, but no spirit for life, you have only misery and what kind of life is that? What do you think?"

"I am struggling to find the answer."

Sally's parents brought the children to Callaway Gardens on Sunday, in time for all the family to have lunch together before going back to their homes. Job, Sally, and the kids were hardly on the road going north before Henry asked.

"Daddy what was that private joke about Mama watching out for the window, you promised to tell me."

"Son, I promised to tell you when you are old and gray. Don't rush life. You will be there before you know it."

COMING OF THE HARVEST

On Monday following his return from Callaway Gardens, Job received notice that Ann's trial was scheduled to begin on December 18. After talking to Mrs. McCoy, he was armed with specific information of prior events and occurrences between Ann and her husband, things that Ann had shared with Mrs. McCoy as events had occurred, before she killed Ed and before she shut down emotionally. The fact Job finally knew about Ann's previous problems opened the door for Ann to talk about the last eighteen months of her marriage to Ed. Slowly, he began to realize what Mrs. McCoy was talking about when she raised the question of which is the greater wrong, the taking of one's will to live or the taking of one's physical life?

In spite of the progress in getting her to discuss her life with Ed and the things that went wrong during 1971 and early 1972, Job knew that Ann was still suppressing some things that were likely valuable to her defense.

On the same day Job received the notice that Ann's case was scheduled for trial, he called Sam Graves. "Sam, I received notice that Ann's case will be set for December 18. We've drawn Judge Ernest Johnson. What do you know about him?"

"We could have done better and we could have done worse. He's been on the bench about fifteen or so years. His father was a fundamentalist preacher, and sometimes that fundamentalist background comes through in Judge Johnson's rulings and the sentences he imposes. He's pretty much a law-and-order man. On the positive side, he tries to be fair with both camps. To my thinking, the most important quality a judge can have is a keen sense of fairness, and Judge Johnson has that. I've always enjoyed a decent relation with him."

"I've tried to keep you abreast with the trial preparation, sending you synopses of statements and objectives. I am mindful that I committed to handle the preparation for trial. Even so, Sam, I need your help with something, if you can find the time to spare."

"Job, we'll make the time. What may I help with?"

"You said that you wanted to meet with Ann and Dana a week before the trial. Did you get a chance to read my interview notes of October 18 with Mrs. McCoy?"

"Not yet. I've had a lot on my plate. Is there something urgent?"

"Sam, you've been handling criminal trials for so long you've forgotten how urgent everything seems to an inexperienced lawyer like me. I would like to bring Ann and Dana to your office during the Thanksgiving holiday, while Dana is home from school. Do you have any available time?"

"Job, how does ten o'clock the Friday after Thanksgiving sound to you?"

"Great! I had another conference with Mrs. McCoy just last week. That interview tape is being transcribed and a copy will be in your hands in a couple of days. To save you time, the transcript of October 18 does not give us anything to work with. This later transcript, the one we are presently preparing, gives us considerable insight into some things. If you have time, I think it would be helpful if you read Ethel McCoy's second interview transcript before you meet with Ann and Dana."

"You bet I will. I will see you the day after Thanksgiving. Job. One other thing I'm compelled to mention."

"Have I messed something up?"

"To the contrary. I just wanted to tell you that you are doing a good job with a difficult assignment."

"Thank you, Sam. Coming from you, that means a lot."

OUT OF DARKNESS, A GLIMMER OF LIGHT

Job agreed to drive Ann and Dana for a scheduled meeting at Sam Graves' downtown Atlanta office though they had some trouble getting there. When passing through the Sand Hill community, Job had to pull to the side of the highway to replace a flat tire with his spare. Then, just as they got into Douglasville, west of Atlanta, the spare tire went flat and he was stranded.

Job found a telephone booth to call Sam's office, but the switchboard was closed for the holiday and he never made it through to Sam's personal telephone line. He next called his home number three times, hoping Sally could come to his rescue. After the third try, he remembered Sally and the children had planned to visit Grant Park Zoo, and they obviously were executing that plan. Walking a half-mile, he found a small automotive body shop that seemed open for business. It was open, but for automotive body repairs, not fixing flats. Job paid the repairman fifty dollars to get his car mobile again. In spite of the gentle nature of Sam Graves, Job could not but wonder, "What will the most famous criminal defense lawyer in the South think of being delayed so long by a country lawyer who was stranded on the road trying to fix a flat tire?"

After what seemed an eternity, Job's tire was repaired and, more than two hours late, with Ann and Dana, he arrived at Sam's office. When they finally arrived, Sam Graves waved off all apologies. Laughing, he said, "Job, I wish my maternal grandfather who, as a doctor, traveled by horse and buggy could have been here to witness your frustration over a flat tire. He sometimes used unneeded profanity when talking about motor vehicles, describing them as 'Tomfool contraptions that won't survive.' He called me Samuel, would spit his tobacco, hitch-up his pants, and say, 'Mark my words Samuel. Those contraptions ain't natural and they won't last. There will be mules and wagons parked around every courthouse when you die, with nary a horseless carriage in sight.' He used some other language about motor vehicles that I best not repeat. Had Grandpa been here when you came in with an embarrassed look on your face, he would have nudged me in the ribs with his elbow and whispered, 'I told you so.'"

Sam Graves could not have been more gracious. At the outset, Dana was somewhat intimidated, not by Sam Graves, but by the occasion for the meeting. Ann was subdued. Her right hand shook violently, and she walked with uncertainty. Dana was wearing a light wool skirt, a neat blue blouse, and a darker blue jacket. Ann's dress was clean, but somewhat wrinkled. She wore a heavier, long coat.

Noticing Dana looking at the picture of the black man on the wall, Sam addressed her: "That is a picture of a young man I once represented. It's a long story and I will not burden you with it at this time. Someday, when we have more time, I hope you will come back to see me, I would like to tell you about the man. His name was Jacob Cunningham. For now, I would like to pick your mind on football. Your Auburn Tigers just beat the Georgia Bulldogs. They've won all their games this year, except LSU, and are scheduled to play the Crimson Tide next week. Who's going to win?"

"Auburn, I hope. Who are you pulling for?"

"Dana, I don't have a dog in that fight, so I'm not picking a winner."

"I've not had time to get too involved in football, but I hope Auburn will win. Mr. Graves, I really like your office."

"Let me tell you about a few of the things in my office. My old desk and chair belonged to my grandfather, a lawyer who practiced in South Carolina. He never went to law school; rather he 'read law' as an apprentice in his father's law office. It is my understanding this desk was hand-made about 1844 from the log of a big water oak that that grew near Charleston. I've been told hundreds of gallons of whiskey have passed over this desk, not as bootleg whiskey, but as payment for legal services rendered. The whiskey received would, in turn, be traded for needed goods and services. The drawers of this old desk are an aggravation. They get stuck, and sometimes won't open and close. My swivel chair, hand-made from red oak, is about twenty years younger. The caning in the chair has been replaced several times. The last time, about twenty years ago, I had to ship the chair to a man in Waynesboro to get it re-caned. Couldn't find anyone in Atlanta who knew how to do it."

Other than shaking Sam's hand and saying hello when she came into the office, Ann had remained passive, seeming to listen at times, and at other times looking at the ox team painting behind Sam. The subject of chair caning aroused her attention.

"Mr. Graves," Ann said, "my grandpa Albert knew how to cane. He used both white oak strips and hickory bark strips. I loved to watch him work. He liked to use the hickory bark for chairs and the white oak for cotton baskets. I remember one time he had sixteen rocking chairs to cane at the same time. They belonged to a hotel at Menlo. He had so many rocking chairs in his shop, on the porch, and in the house that my grandmother said there was not enough room for the cat to chase a mouse."

"Ann, I'm not acquainted with hickory bark caning. The Campbell Folk School in North Carolina has caning classes. I have taken their blacksmithing class and been tempted to try their caning class so I can cane my own chair. I noticed you looking at the yoke of oxen pulling the cart over the hill into the sunrise. That painting was done by my grandmother and given to me by my grandfather."

Job noticed that Sam, in the description of the painting, had styled it a more optimistic "sunrise," rather than a possibly darker "sunset."

From the caning and painting, Sam guided Ann into a discussion of handmade quilts and the different kinds of quilting frames. He then engaged her in a discussion of apple trees. This evolved into the varied uses of the apple. They covered applesauce, apple pie, apple strudel, apple dumplings, apple cider and ended with the making of apple vinegar and its many uses. Job was awed by both his knowledge and his skill in getting a lady who lived in a shell to talk.

Learning that Dana was taking algebra, Sam tested his own memory on the subject.

"Are algebra teachers still teaching Horner's Method to determine the square root of a number?"

"Yes, sir. We covered that. I'm not sure I understand how to do it, though."

"Dana, I'm not sure I remember how to do it, either. Let's see if we can work it together."

Together they solved a problem, and Sam Graves continued his control of the conversation with Dana.

"Have you read about Socrates and his life?"

"No, sir."

"Read about him sometime. He's fascinating. None of his writings have been found, so all we know of him is what others wrote about him. While waiting for your arrival, I had the pleasure of rereading some of Plato's writings about the trial of Socrates. Dana, he was accused of impiety and of corrupting the youth of Greece. In answering the accusations that were made, he personally spoke to the Senate, which was a political body that acted as a court hearing the charges against him." Sensing Dana had a question, Sam Graves paused.

"Mr. Graves, if the senate acted as a court, that would not be a separation of powers, would it?"

"That's a very good observation. Even in our present government, our U. S. Senate may be converted into a judicial body, a court, to try the case of a president who has been impeached. Sometimes the separation of powers is not a complete separation and your question was a good one. In his trial, Socrates acted as his own attorney, too. That was different from the way we usually do things. Pleading his own case, Socrates made a powerful appeal on his own behalf. He said something like this:

My accusers have spoken so skillfully against me that I am almost persuaded that I am guilty. They have warned you to beware of my eloquence, to be careful of my ability to persuade you of my innocence. 'Eloquence' is the word they used. Yet, I have but to speak a few words to you for you to realize that I am anything but eloquent—unless you equate truth with eloquence and if that be the equation, then I am truly eloquent."

Dana was immediately captured by Sam's charm and magic. "Mr. Graves." she said, "I do not believe Socrates had your eloquence."

"Dana," he answered, "you are a young lady after an old man's heart. What a wonderful compliment. I read a lot, and in my work it is necessary to remember and verbalize things. It comes with practice and experience."

Wanting to keep Ann in the conversation, Sam Graves got her to relate childhood memories of gathering eggs at the hen house and feeding the pigs with leftover table scraps. Between the eggs and pigs, he discussed his mother's method of pickling peaches and how to make her prized coconut pound cake.

Job watched and listened in amazement as this seasoned veteran of criminal trials put everyone at ease. He gently introduced the subject of death by relating how, forty-six years earlier, his small son, Jacob, had died an accidental death in a motor vehicle accident. Everyone present knew he spoke truthfully when he said, "The death of my son, even though many years ago, has left a tear in my eye and a tear in my heart."

Using the information that Ethel McCoy had provided, Sam Graves, sometimes speaking so quietly it was hard to hear, walked Ann and Dana though the events of 1971 and through February 18, 1972. In this painful and often emotional experience, Sam didn't lead the discussion, but instead seemed to follow. He opened doors to memories that Job had found tightly closed.

The heart and soul of a family tragedy was revealed. As Ann related events of which Dana had no prior knowledge, Dana, now a sophomore in college sometimes seemed a little girl again. Sometimes she would buckle in disbelief. At other times she seemed to look for a hiding place, a sound-proof room where no more could be heard. Often, she attempted to bury her face in her hands. Dana loved her daddy, just as she loved her mother and wanted good things for both of them. At other times, when Ann, in what seemed a distant voice talked, Dana felt as if her daddy were present, and she listened for him to say, "No. It was not that way. It did not happen like that."

Dana seemed to hold on to some hope that her daddy was there, that he would speak, and everyone would be happy again. She listened, but her daddy didn't speak, only her mother.

As Ann slowly and painfully related bits and pieces of what happened the day she killed Ed, Dana began to see her mother in a new light, a light that comes only from understanding.

Ann's first description of an event was often confusing, disjointed, often incoherent, and always discomforting. Under the compassionate, skillful questioning of Sam Graves, Dana's mother was transfigured. She was no longer the mother she did not like. Ann was the mother she loved, the mother who loved her daddy, even as he died, and even after his death.

The talk in Graves' office that afternoon followed no plan and established no recognizable pattern. Often statements by Ann had no connection to what had been said before. Sam never interrupted what she was saying. He took no notes, just listened and remembered. Often his follow-up question came much later. When he returned to a subject, it was with apology for his own lack of understanding. No mention was made of the up-coming trial. No mention was made of how best to be a good witness. In every manner, Sam conveyed the genuine impression that he was not shocked or offended by anything Ann had done. He tried to gain understanding by showing understanding.

To say the afternoon, after the small talk of introduction,

was difficult for both Ann and Dana is a gross understatement. Truth suffers no harm to say it was difficult for both in different ways. Ann remembered the events her child described and related. Even so, as Dana brought to Ann's memory events of the months before Ed died, old wounds were re-opened and laid raw again. When Dana spoke, Ann often tried not to let her tears show. Repeatedly, she silently wiped the tears from her cheeks with the back of her hand, ignoring the nearby box of tissue. Ann understood her daughter's love for the father who was no longer there. Dana had not heard her mother describe the events of the day her daddy died. She had never wanted to know any details.

The realization that Dana did not know the circumstances made the telling even more difficult for Ann. Driven by a mother's instinct to protect her child, she attempted to soften the blows by adopting a strange voice. She described events as if talking about the lives of strangers, as if she were telling a make-believe story. Even when she wept, Ann spoke without emotion. In spite of her efforts to protect Dana by subterfuge of voice and expression, all present knew she was not talking about others. She was talking about her own family, the husband she had dearly loved, the daughter who now sat beside her, hiding her face in her hands and wanting to close her ears so she could not hear. She was talking about a new part of herself, a part she did not know existed, and as she talked, she saw again a circle of blood on her kitchen floor. It was Ed's blood, and she was sitting in the middle of it.

In spite of the raw emotions turned loose and the accompanying pain, the afternoon had therapeutic value. Some, but not all, of the dark and ugly truths were turned loose. Tears were shed and grieving, much needed by Ann, began.

Ann had not given a complete picture. More questions were raised than answered, but she was far removed from being prepared or capable of being an effective witness in a court of law with all its ritual, pomp, and ceremony. The lawyers knew Dana would likely be able to tell her part of the story to twelve strangers with a stern judge looking over her shoulder. Sam knew the flood gate had been partly opened and with good fortune and much hard work by Job, she might be able to speak on her own behalf at her trial.

Ann, of course, was a different matter. Although she had spoken in a surreal manner, at least she had spoken, but this was only a first step. Sam knew the floodgate had only been cracked, not opened. In trying to protect Dana, Ann spoke as someone unknown before. The jury needed to hear the old Ann, the one who had resolved that if she ever married again, she would walk through hell to make her marriage work. The jury needed to understand that Ann's home was a sacred place, not a pool of blood. Sam knew it would require hard work on Job's part to peel away the veneer of guilt and shame that held Ann captive in a new-found hell. Older and wiser and more experienced than Job, Sam understood that the jury might take ten minutes of Ann's life as representative of the whole. The trial was only a month away. Much work had to be done before Ann could be a viable witness. Sam silently wished both Job and Ann good luck.

Job had been a third row spectator in the afternoon drama of Ann and Dana. As Sam patiently and skillfully led Ann in opening doors that concealed dark truths, he was again reminded of a conversation with Richard Cramer who had spoken about reticent, shy, and hesitant clients or witnesses. "Job," he'd said, "some folks have what I call the lockjaw. You can't get'm to talk. When you get into that situation, you've got to find a way to break the inertia that binds them. Once you've got them talking, some of them never want to stop."

Job had intended to make notes of what was said in the afternoon's conference, but he'd become so engrossed with what was being said and the way Sam managed the conversation's flow, he forgot his plan. He was relieved that Sam would be by his side in the courtroom to question Ann. With Sam there and the inertia of silence broken, he knew Ann would be in good hands. He wanted to call Sally to let her know that, at last, Ann was beginning to shed some light on the dark question of "why." He knew only a part of the confusing story had been told.

Job had three weeks remaining to work with Ann as he tried to prepare her to meet Cramer's definition of a good witness. Before anyone was aware, it was past seven o'clock in the evening. Sam insisted that his three visitors allow him to treat them to dinner at a nearby restaurant. But first, he pulled Job to the side for a private conversation.

"Job, what are your thoughts about what we know thus far?"

"Sam, I know for certain that we've made a mistake in agreeing that I be lead counsel. You amaze me. You got more out of Ann and Dana in a few hours than I've been able to get from them in ten months. Ann does not need me. She needs

197

you. Only you."

"Job, we made a deal, and we're sticking with it. You've done a great job in finding the key to opening some doors of understanding. You found Ethel McCoy. This is your case; I'm just the water-boy. I have a few things that I want to suggest to you, but we've had a long day. I'll call you and we can have a long talk. Let's take Ann and Dana for a nice dinner at this restaurant down the street. First, let me call my wife. That T-ball grandson I told you about is now a basketball star. I want to find out how his team did this afternoon."

"I need to call Sally. She took the kids to the park today and I need to see if they're home."

"Use the phone in the conference room, down the hall, second door on the right. You'll have privacy there. Ann and Dana have gone to the lady's room. I'll meet all of you in the reception room. Job, we've made some progress today. Ann has opened up a little. There is more to be told, and time will tell if it's good or bad. Go call your wife and remember that sometimes a good day starts with a flat tire."

Sally answered the phone after its first ring.

"Hi, babe. I wanted to be sure you and the kids were home."

"I'm glad you called, I was beginning to get worried."

"I was late getting Ann and Dana to Sam's office. I will tell you about that. We've had a good day with Ann and Dana. Sam did all the work. I'll tell you about that, too. He wants us to have dinner with him, so I'll be late getting home. I love you, Cajun Woman."

"I love you, hard-working barrister."

Over dinner, Sam related some of the cases he had tried and, without divulging names, told of some of the interesting people he had represented. He carefully avoided lawyer stories about cases involving violence.

During the dinner hour, Ann again withdrew into her protective shell. Dana, and to some extent, Job, had grown accustomed to this noticeable habit. At Graves' office, just two hours before dinner, she had, in some ways, reasonably communicated with Sam Graves. Now, she was quiet. Again Job wondered if she would be able to cope with the pressure of a trial in open court.

After dinner and back at the parking garage where Job had left his car, Sam maneuvered Dana aside a few minutes and out of Ann's hearing.

"Are you back in class on Monday?"

"Classes begin then, but my first one is not until Tuesday."

"When will you be released for the Christmas holidays?"

"On December twelfth. I think that's on a Tuesday."

"Dana, your father's death has placed a great burden on your shoulders. I want to privately tell you that you are doing a great job in handling the weight you now carry. You and I hardly know each other, but I'm very proud of you."

"Thank you Mr. Graves. That means a lot to me. Daddy used to say things like that to me."

"Today's been very difficult for both you and your mother. I was pleased that both of you talked to us about painful things. We all needed that. Your mother will likely go in and out of the shell she has lived in for the past months. I think it would be wise if everyone let her choose the time when she wants to talk about the things that happened in her life. I suspect the next few days will be difficult for your mother."

"Why do you say that?"

"I may be wrong, I often am. But your mother is now beginning to face some facts that will cause her to suffer even more than she has suffered. I think she will have a difficult time, but I also think she will handle her difficulty well. I've detained you long enough. Let's get back to Job and Ann. It's time for all of us to go home."

Ann remained quiet as Job drove them home. He and Dana talked some, but the long day seemed to have worn on both of them. It was around midnight when he stopped at Ann's house. He still had another forty-five minutes to arrive at his own carport, where Sally greeted him at the door. Almost immediately she recognized Job's mood change.

"Honey, when you called, you seemed upbeat and excited. Now you seem dejected. Has something happened?"

"I'm not sure. During the afternoon, Ann was opening up, telling us things we needed to know. Over dinner, she became quiet again, saying little. It's hard to understand."

"You need to study the Bible more."

"Why?"

"You need to refresh your memory of your namesake. Job was known for his patience. Remember?"

"Babe, you're right. You're always right. It's been a long day. In many ways, a good day. Now let's get in bed and snuggle close to each other. I need that and more patience."

Job was surprised when Sam Graves called early Sunday evening on November 26, two days after the long conference in his office.

"I apologize for calling on Sunday. I hope I'm not catching you at a bad time."

"Not at all. It's a little surprising that a lawyer whose name appears at the head of a long list of lawyers is working on a Sunday night. I thought only us country lawyers had to work like that."

"Job, don't ever make the mistake of being the senior member of a firm. All it means is that you have to work harder. I like to come to the office when no one else is here. I can get more done when it's quiet. I came in to dictate my notes on the talk we had with Ann and Dana two days ago. We made some progress, but we still have a long way to go before Ann can be an effective witness on her own behalf."

"How should I handle her?"

"That's a tough question. If pushed too hard, she may regress. If not pushed at all, she may not improve. That's a lawyer's way of saying, 'I don't know.' Job, old lawyers are great ones for telling the young lawyer, 'If it were me, I would do so and so.' That said, I think Ann will best respond to patience on your part and repetitions on her part. She clearly has a story to tell and she needs to tell it well. Good storytellers become good by practice, by telling their story again and again. Ann's story is a painful one. As painful as I have ever heard. Her pain is so great and so obvious it overpowers the listener to the point that her story may not be heard. Get her to tell you that story again and again. See if you can get her to tell it until she no longer feels the pain of telling. You've got a difficult assignment. Now, let me get to the purpose of my

Sunday night call. In your closing arguments, do you use a transcript of the testimony?"

"Sam, I have had a few cases where I wished I had a transcript, but I've never had a client who could afford the cost."

"I like to use an official transcript of testimony when I argue a case. I like to be able to tell the jury that I have requested the official court reporter to transcribe all the testimony and that what I argue is taken from the official court record. Being able to do this has a strong appeal to the jury. That way, they know I'm not relying on a memory that may be faulty. I suggest we make arrangement with the reporter to prepare a transcript for us."

"Sam, Ann doesn't have the money to pay the reporter for that service and, frankly, I don't either. You are representing Ann without compensation. The five hundred dollars that I was initially paid has long since been used. Ann doesn't have any money to pay either of us. I would love to have the transcript, but financially it is simply out of reach."

"Job, my maternal grandfather was a sharecrop farmer, and one of the finest men I have ever known. Many times during his life, he would tell me about oxen, how strong and durable they were. To make his points, he would use many expressions about the ox. In times of high excitement or protest, he'd say, 'It all depends on whose ox is getting gored.' In times of a friend being in need, he would say, 'It makes you feel good when you can help a neighbor get his ox out of the ditch.' I think it will make me feel good to help get this ox out of the ditch. Before trial begins, I want you to contact Judge Johnson's court reporter; her name is Marie Moore. Tell her I want my usual transcript prepared. She'll know what I want; she's done it before. Tell her to send me the bill."

"Sam, that is very generous."

"Job, when you can, in your practice of law and life, help others get their ox out of the ditch. Grandpa was right, it makes you feel good."

Three weeks before the meeting at Sam Graves' office, Job and Sam had talked by phone about an investigative problem Job had concerning the Tennessee tag number of the automobile Mrs. Mills saw parked in Ann's driveway the day Ed Tatum was killed. Job was unable to get any cooperation from the Tennessee Department of Motor Vehicles to determine the owner of the car.

Sam suggested Job contact Robert Parker, the detective Mrs. Mills had given the tag number to. "I have worked with Detective Parker many times before and found him to be honest and forthright when asked for information. In the statement she gave, Mrs. Mills said she'd given the tag number to Detective Parker. He is a good officer so you can bet he followed that lead. He will share what he can that doesn't jeopardize the State's case. He may not tell you all that he knows, but what he does tell you, you can depend on it."

Job followed the suggestion and visited Detective Parker on November 18, at the North Side Station of the Atlanta Police Department. He found Parker reading the third volume of Gibbon's *The Decline and Fall of the Roman Empire*.

"Hi Mr. Lee. I'm Robert Parker. My friends call me 'Bud.' Some call me a lot worse. You're representing Ann Tatum?"

"Yes, and I wanted to ask you about something."

"I'll help you any way I ethically can. You've got a tough assignment in handling that defense, but that's not my call. I just try to do my job and let others do theirs. How may I help you?"

"Before I get to what I want to ask you, may I ask about this picture on your desk? Is that a picture of you?"

"Yes. I keep it there as a reminder not to be foolish. That picture was made after I graduated from high school and thought I would be a rodeo star. The bull I was riding was named 'Greasy Spot.' The photographer who made that picture had to be quick, because in less than three seconds Greasy Spot had thrown my tail into the second row of grandstand seats. That ended my desire to be a rodeo man. Have you ever tried riding a crossbred bucking bull?"

"No, I've never been that daring."

"I have. I was that foolish, but never again. How can I help you?"

Following the contact with John Parker, Job had noted: *11-18-72—Talked to Robert Parker about tag #AEC 964. Car, 1970 Dk. Blue Buick, was titled to M. C. Walker, Ellendale community NE of Memphis. Car sold to used-car dealer in Memphis 10-22-72. Walker and wife, Sara, had marital problems, maybe separated. Both left Ellendale and whereabouts unknown. Parker says he was unable to directly connect the other occupant (apparently Sara Walker) of the car with event of death. Circumstances suggest possible relation between Ed Tatum and Sara Walker, who was probably in the car. Nothing suggests that she ever entered the Tatum residence.*

On Saturday, the day after the meeting in Sam's office, Job

added this to the foregoing note:

Thanks to the expert and gentle hand of Sam Graves yesterday, Ann gave us the car connection that Parker was unable to establish.

LAWYER TEAM LOST

The four weeks before Ann's trial date rushed by. In large measure, Job Lee neglected his other clients and their problems as he was held captive by Ann's case. Sally had never seen him so engrossed in his work, and even her playful suggestions of a T-ball game went unnoticed.

During the weeks preceding the trial, Job read and re-read all interview notes, every report from Dr. Battle, and his outline of the order in which his witnesses would be called. It pleased Job that Sam Graves was committed to making the opening statement. Several times he considered asking Graves to handle the final argument, but he knew Sam wanted him to deliver Ann's final plea to the jury. Maybe Sam had a reason for wanting it that way.

Job was discouraged with the results of his conferences with Ann after their meeting in Sam's office on November 24. He had left that evening with considerable hope Ann could escape the darkness that held her and, in her trial, be an effective witness on her own behalf. Since that meeting, however, her ability to relate events in a meaningful, coherent manner had not improved. She still seemed to speak of the tragic events of February 18 in an adopted voice, as if rehearsed. At other times, her pain of telling overwhelmed the listener, and her story was not heard. Job knew it was necessary that she suppress her emotions to be able to describe what had happened, but he also knew that to be effective with the jury a show of some honest emotion was necessary. He wanted his client to be prepared, but he did not want her to be programmed for trial.

During the week of December 11, Job and Sam Graves exchanged daily phone calls, reviewed the evidence they planned to present to the jury, discussed the order in which their case would be presented, and the role that each attorney would play in the drama. In addition to being an outstanding trial lawyer, Sam was also a teacher.

"Job," Sam said, "we have discussed our closing argument. You will recall, from the very beginning, I've insisted that you handle the closing argument. I had a reason for taking that position. Where there are two or more lawyers on the same side, invariably the case 'belongs' to just one of the lawyers. Without exception, one, and one only, of the lawyers has put his heart and soul into the case, while the others have played a secondary role. It's a lot like a parent/child relation, the one lawyer being the parent and the client who is confronted with possible loss of liberty or life being the child. No one can match the plea of a good parent trying to save the life of a child in danger. Job, you are the parent, Ann has become your child. It was that way when I first met you and it remains that way. That's my reason for insisting you handle the closing argument."

"Will Judge Johnson limit our time of argument?"

"No, he may suggest a time limit, but he will let each side

make the final decision on how long closing should be."

"Sam, you have a way with words that I can't match. Ann needs your help with the closing argument. Could we agree on sharing the argument, with you taking the first part and me following you?"

"I'll make a partial concession. Let's agree that I'll evaluate the situation at the close of the case and if I think I can make a positive contribution in sharing the argument, I'll take not more than twenty minutes to open the closing statement and surrender the remainder of argument time to you. Is that a fair arrangement?"

"Thank you, Sam. That makes me feel better."

"One other thing about the closing argument. I've told you that I often make extensive use of the court reporter's transcript of the testimony in my closing arguments. Keep in mind, doing it this way is my style, my way of doing things. Just because it is my way does not mean it is the right way for anyone else. In fact, for the other person, it may be the wrong way. Job, be yourself. Don't try to adopt another's style. Remember you are the parent and don't be afraid to plead for your child."

On Saturday, December 16, Job forced himself away from Ann's case long enough to take Sally to a mall on the west side of Atlanta for some last minute Christmas shopping. En route back home, Sally listened to a radio newscast about the astronauts of Apollo 17 who had completed their three-day visit to the moon's surface and were on their way home with a collection of rocks and soil. Sally thought of the astronauts, their families, and the fear and anxiety they must have suffered over the past few days. She thought of the joy and excitement that had to be theirs in knowing the dangerous moon-mission was almost over. "Honey," she said to Job, "it seems as if the astronauts will be safely home for Christmas. I'll be happy to have you safely back home, too. It seems you've been gone for a long time. The kids and I will be so happy when you really get back with us again. So often now, even when your body is with us, your spirit is not there. I don't say that to complain, only to explain that we really miss you."

Sally watched Job's face and waited for his reply. For a few moments she watched the far-away look in his eyes and realized he had not heard what she had said. Job had never been so "far-away" before. Ann's trial was to begin on Monday. Maybe it would last only a few days and Job would be released from this strange power that now held him captive. She reached over and patted her husband's knee. In silence, Job drove the remaining twenty miles home.

Back home Sally prepared dinner as Job reviewed some of his trial notes. Sally understood the man she knew as her husband was absent. His body was present, but Job, like the returning astronauts had been, was away in space. She sat down beside him.

"Honey, it was sweet of you to say you wanted to go to church with us, tomorrow—I appreciate you saying that. But, you do not need to be in church. You need to be at your office, doing your final review. Let's plan on you doing that. I will take the kids to both Sunday school and the morning worship. Starting next year, we can all resolve to go to church together each Sunday. Will you, for me, agree to my suggestion about tomorrow?"

"Sally, you talk like an angel."

"I may be one."

Sunday night, Job's trial plan started to fall apart. He had spent the greater part of the day in his office and was still there when Sam Graves called around 10 o'clock that night.

"Job, I have bad news. I have involuntarily been taken off of Ann's case. I'm calling from Peachtree Hospital, scheduled for rectal surgery at seven tomorrow morning. The doctors say I have no choice if I want to live more than another two or three months. I am sorry to let you and Ann down in this manner."

"Oh no, Sam, that's terrible. Surgery? Really? I'll ask Judge Johnson for a continuance of the case. This is the first time we've been set for trial. Surely the judge will grant my motion."

"Job, don't do that. A continuance is not in the client's best interest. I advise against any delay."

"Would you mind telling me why?"

"My reasons are simple and threefold. First, you have prepared this case for trial. You know it backward and forward. You will be better prepared than the District Attorney's office. Aaron Bailey may still come in. As far as I know he still has the governor's itch. If I didn't think Ann would be well represented by you, I would tell you so. You are well prepared, and I'm certain you will do an excellent job."

"What is your second reason for my not requesting a continuance?"

"My second is more important than the first. Much more important. I speak of client interest. We must ever be mindful of what is best for the people we represent. You've told me that Ann has not made much progress with her ability to relate the events of the day Ed Tatum died. I wish she could do a better job in telling her side of the story, but we can't expect her to do the impossible and it is likely that she will do the best she can. Keep in mind that we lawyers do not create our clients and witnesses. We take them as we find them. Both Ann and Dana are now as ready to face the uncertainty that goes with any trial as they will ever be. They have conditioned themselves for a trial beginning tomorrow. Job, as you know, better than I, Ann is a delicate person. I am not at all sure she can weather the storm that would go with a delay, another long wait, and again prepare herself emotionally for a later time. It is my strong belief that she will make her best appearance in court next week."

"And your last reason?"

"Most attorneys would laugh at my last reason. This case is set for trial beginning just seven days before Christmas. It's my belief that most people in our country become a little more charitable and compassionate during the Christmas holiday. A later jury might not have that trace of Christmas spirit that this one may have. Ann needs all the Christmas spirit she can get."

"Sam, I don't know what to say."

"Good. Say nothing. Go to court tomorrow and do your best. Job, I've got to get off this phone, another nurse is here for some more blood. If these good people do not bleed me

210

to death, tomorrow I start a battle against rectal cancer. Tomorrow, you do battle for Ann Tatum. I expect both of us to win. May I make one suggestion about your opening statement to the jury?"

"Yes sir, I need all the help I can get."

"I suggest that you keep it as brief as possible. Be careful not to make any false promise to the jury. I know you wouldn't do this intentionally, but be careful not to do so inadvertently. Limit what you say to things you will prove. Promise only those things you are very certain you can demonstrate. If you can't prove all that you say you will, it'll come back to haunt you when the District Attorney makes his final argument—and that office always has the right of speaking the last words."

"Thank you, Sam. I needed that. I couldn't have gotten this far without you."

"My pleasure, Job. Now, one other thing. Listen carefully to the things the District Attorney says in his opening statement. He may overreach and make some promises he can't keep. Equally important, in his opening statement, listen for some word or phrase that he uses that you may seize on and use to your advantage during the trial. Sometimes a single word becomes the central focus of a trial. Look for that word or phrase. If the District Attorney presents it, grab hold, cultivate, and nourish it. Make it into a theme song, but do it in a subtle manner. It's really rather simple. Now good night, Job, and good luck tomorrow."

Job Lee set the phone back in its cradle and stared down at his notes. He didn't know how or when this unexpected development should be shared with Ann or what her reaction might be. It wasn't news that he wanted to share by phone and it was too late to drive to her home for a personal visit. It would have to be shared with the client at the courthouse the next day, just before the proceedings were set to begin.

It was late Sunday night and as Job drove the short distance from his office to his home, he felt alone in the world. He needed Sam Graves by his side. He needed his guidance, maturity, and experience. Most of all, he needed Sam's wonderful voice asking Ann the questions. Sam had talents that he didn't have and would never have. He had grown dependent on Sam. Now the security of this experienced trial lawyer had suddenly been snatched away. Sally was waiting for him at the door and saw the distress on his face.

"Has something happened to Ann?"

"Indirectly, yes. Sam Graves is in the hospital, facing surgery in the morning."

"How terrible! What is his condition?"

Sally sat beside Job as he told her what had happened, patting his knee as he talked. She and Job had grown together, gaining a little more understanding each year. Their growth in understanding, each of the other, was largely due to Sally's dedicated effort to that purpose. She had insights that Job didn't have. In many ways, she understood him better than he understood himself.

Several times before, Sally had heard Job tell the story of his "getting lost" at a large church in Atlanta when he was five years old. In his story, Job's mother was only a few feet away and he was not lost at all, except in his mind. It was a story of the human feelings of desperation being the same whether based on fact or fantasy.

"Do you remember when you got lost at Trinity Church when you were a little boy?"

"Yes,"

"Just remember that experience. Remember you were lost only in your mind. It's time to get in bed. You've got a big week in front of you. You can handle it. You can do it. You're not lost."

THE TRIAL

Monday, December 18, 1972, broke with a cloudy sky and a strong touch of winter weather in the air. Job met Ann, Dana, Jane, and the witnesses subpoenaed in the courtroom at 9:30. The judge would call his docket at 10 o'clock, and Judge Johnson's office had already advised Job that his case would be the first one for trial. It was the only murder case on the judge's calendar for that week, and Job knew that it would take more than an hour for the judge to call out the remainder of the cases that followed his. He decided to use that time to tell Ann that Sam Graves was in the hospital, likely in surgery even as they spoke. He was fearful of what Ann's reaction might be. Would she accept this setback or would she fall apart? Job held his breath.

District Attorney Aaron Bailey wasn't seen in the courtroom when Judge Johnson called Ann's case. Job and the Assistant District Attorney both approached the bench and announced they were "Ready for trial." The judge handed both attorneys a list of fifty names from which twelve would be selected as jurors and then instructed both attorneys to stand by while he moved onto other matters with other attorneys.

The time of jury selection was largely a matter of discretion with the trial judge. Depending on the nature and complexity of the case, some judges arranged for jury selection in advance of the trial date. Sam Graves, with his good understanding of judicial habits, had informed Job that Judge Johnson would attend the jury selection on the trial date. In large measure Job had counted on Sam Graves handling the jury selection. Now Job was standing alone. He was pleasantly surprised when Sam's paralegal arrived, bringing background information on more than half the jury panel from which fourteen men and women would be selected to sit in the jury box and hear the evidence in the case. Before jury deliberations began, two of the original fourteen would be excused from further service and the remaining twelve jurors would hold Ann's fate in their hands. The background information on the prospective jurors was of great benefit to Job. Even from the hospital, Sam Graves was doing all that he could for Ann. The rest was up to Job.

Job escorted Ann, Dana, Jane, Ethel McCoy, and the paralegal into an empty room reserved for the trial attorney and broke the news about Sam Graves.

Ann's reaction was surprisingly calm. She told the paralegal to give Mr. Graves her best wishes, and added that she would pray for his recovery. She then reached over, patted Job on his arm, and said, "You will do just fine." Job found no comfort in the realization that Sally and Sam Graves had told him the same thing.

Ann, though neatly dressed, made a pitiful appearance. Two years earlier, she had carried a well-portioned 130 pounds on her five feet five inch body. Now, she sometimes weighed ninety pounds and on occasion even less. She was forty-three years old, though most people would have taken her to be more than sixty.

Ann's Parkinson's disease had steadily progressed in taking control of the right side of her body. As she walked, her right arm hung loosely and lifeless by her side. Her right and dominant hand was sometimes relaxed and still and other times shook violently. It had been more than a year since she was able to sign her name. Now, she wasn't able to print it. Yet, despite her appearance during the week of her trial, she exhibited a quiet dignity and appeared to be the caretaker of those around her. The reporter for a local television station, reporting the progress of the trial, described Ann best by saying, "Ann Tatum, accused of viciously murdering her husband, gives every outward appearance of being a lady, someone one would expect to see in church rather than the courtroom."

At 11:15, the court bailiff came to the room and announced that Judge Johnson was ready for attorneys and parties to return to the courtroom. Job guided Ann to the counsel table closest to the witness box. The jury box, facing toward the judge's bench, was to their right. The District Attorney's table was across an open area and directly in front of them. They were in place when Aaron Bailey, followed by the assistant that had handled all preliminary matters, strode into the courtroom and took the opposing counsel table.

Judge Johnson looked up from reading the most recent edition of *The Emery Law Review* to see Bailey. Being a member of the opposing political party and wanting to make a little political dig, the judge smiled at the district attorney and quipped, "Mr. Bailey, does some higher calling bring you to my courtroom today?"

All the attorneys knew what the judge was doing, and everyone, except Bailey and his assistant, laughed. The laughter quickly died and a somber atmosphere of murder and death set in. There would be no more smiles during this trial, only tears.

Ann sat quietly by the side of her attorney. When her right hand developed a violent shaking, she would remove it from the sight of others by placing that hand on her knee, under the table.

The judge marked his place in the law review article, put it aside and directed the bailiff. "Bring in the jury panel."

In less than two minutes, fifty adult residents of Fulton County, Georgia, were seated in the two front rows, immediately behind the jury box. From this panel, a trial jury would be selected by a process of elimination. Both sets of attorneys were handed a list of the names, addresses, and types of employment, if any, of the fifty panel members. On the list, a number preceded each name and none of the fifty knew "their number." Alternating, the attorneys would call out the number of the prospective juror he wanted to eliminate from Ann's case.

In preliminary questions by the judge, it was determined that one prospective juror had a serious hearing disability and another wasn't a permanent resident of Fulton County. The judge excused these two from further consideration, reducing the panel to forty-eight. He turned to Aaron Bailey.

"The State may *voir dire*."

Although Job had never tried a murder case before, he knew the importance of the *voir dire* examination. It was the opportunity of the lawyer to learn more about the prospective jurors who would decide his client's fate by asking questions to the panel. The panel members were under oath to truthfully answer all questions relating to their fitness and qualifications to serve as a juror. Job also knew the experienced trial lawyer often used *voir dire* examination to pre-condition the juror's mindset in a way that might make it receptive to the lawyer's trial theory. Otherwise stated, the trial lawyer is a salesman, trying to get the jury to "buy" what he attempts to sell. The skillful lawyer's questions can sometimes get the prospective juror to look with favor on both the product and the salesman even before the juror is chosen for the trial. It's a form of attempted brainwashing, and it quickly became evident that Aaron Bailey was a super-salesman.

Bailey, following the judge's lead, got to his feet, and walked to the short rail that divided the room—judge, court reporter, bailiff, lawyers and clients on one side, the spectators on the other. For the moment, the jury panel sat on the spectator side. Soon fourteen of their number would be chosen to cross over the bar, the dividing rail, and join the other participants in this drama.

Bailey was tall, almost six-four, slender, and handsome in his dark gray suit. His *voir dire* questions had two purposes: One was to find qualified jurors who would hear the evidence with an open mind and render a verdict based solely on the evidence presented. The second, concealed, purpose of the same question was subliminal in nature. It was to start the jurors thinking about the horrors of unlawful conduct, the compelling interest of society to prevent one person killing another, and the ever-present need for a law-abiding society. Bailey would like to have very conservative jurors decide Ann's fate. He did not say so, but fourteen old bankers who had been victims of crime would have pleased him. Bailey wanted jurors who saw all things in either black or white, with no shades of gray. He wanted jurors who believed that all questions had a ready, simple answer.

When Bailey completed his *voir dire* exam, Judge Johnson turned in Job's direction with a knowing look.

"Mr. Lee, you may ask."

Job was ill-at-ease and not prepared. Sam Graves was supposed to handle the *voir dire* examination, but Sam was no longer a part of the plan. It was only between the early morning hours of one and three that Job had formulated his plan for *voir dire*. During these hours, he remembered Richard Cramer talking to him about the force of inertia sometimes holding a human tongue silent, not allowing it to speak of painful things. Cramer had also told Job about the power of inertia to keep a moving body in motion, not allowing it to come to rest. It was this latter inertial power he feared in Ann's case. He was fearful that, from the start, her jury would develop a mindset that could never be overcome. He knew the fact that Ann had fired eight bullets into the body of Ed Tatum might close the jury's minds to all else that followed, and he knew the sound of eight bullets being fired was one of the first things Bailey would let the jury hear.

In the early morning hours Job decided that unless Bailey mentioned the subject in *voir dire* examination, he would be the one who broke the ice of the eight bullets fired. He decided it best to get the bad news in the open as soon as possible in the hope that time would permit a breaking of inertial motion. He decided it best that the bad news come from him, rather than Bailey. He, too, would play the attorney's game of asking *voir dire* questions with a dual purpose. He would ask questions that, on the one hand, inquired if the juror would enter the trial with an open mind, and a willingness to keep it open until all the evidence had been presented. On the other hand, he wanted his questions to make the jurors wonder if there were such a thing as an open mind? Wasn't the concept merely a fiction? Isn't the mind, the brain, filled with preconceptions, beliefs, notions, and convictions, some accurate, some erroneous, every day? Is it humanly possible to comply with the judge's instruction that a juror must reserve judgment until all evidence has been presented? Job wanted the jurors to think about these things.

Where Bailey wanted conservative jurors who saw only black and white, Job wanted jurors who saw mostly gray, jurors who saw danger in fixed opinions rather than comfort. He wanted jurors who would try to understand why the eight bullets were fired rather than being carried away with the sound of the pistol being fired.

As Aaron Bailey finished his questions to the jury panel, Job once more remembered the counsel of Richard Cramer who had told him: "Job, trial lawyers often get too damn fancy in their talks to the jury. Most of the time, they use a hundred words where ten, or less, would do a better job. Keep it simple. Don't try to dazzle them with a lot of fancy mouth work. Talk to the jury in the same way you've been talking to other people all of your life." Job tried to follow his old friend's advice.

Job's *voir dire* examination was a clever one. Even Aaron Bailey, veteran of many trials, admired Job's approach.

"Ladies and gentlemen," Job said, "Judge Johnson will tell you that our law requires all jurors to enter a trial with an open mind and to keep an open mind, reserving all judgment until all evidence has been presented. In other words, you are expected to keep your mind open to all evidence, but closed to all judgment until the judge tells you it is time for you to form a judgment. How many of you think you can follow that requirement?"

The collective hands of all forty-eight jurors were raised in a show of consent.

"How many of you," Job asked, "have practiced that manner of judgment-making thus far in your life, seeing and hearing things happen but not forming any opinion about what you have seen and heard until all parts of the event have played out? For example: When you have seen another car driver speeding and driving in a reckless manner, have any of you thought, 'He's going to have a wreck.' Or have you thought, 'I'll not form an opinion on that. I'll wait until everything happens and then I'll decide if he is going to have a wreck.' Another example. When you have seen a small child suddenly dash into the street in front of a rapidly on-coming car, have you not immediately formed a judgment of 'Oh, my God! That child is going to be hit by that car? Under this last example, how many of you would have failed to immediately form a judgment that the child was in grave danger even before the car hits the child? If you had not immediately formed the judgment under that circumstance, let me see your hand."

Not a single hand was raised.

"Is it not a life-long habit for each of us to frequently form judgments and opinions in a progressive manner? As things happen, as events of life are unfolding, we form opinions. Sometimes these early judgments are right, sometimes wrong. Often, later events prove our first opinion wrong and we change our thinking. Is it not true that for most of our lives, we have formed judgments more-or-less on an installment plan, often finding our final opinion to be completely at odds with our first judgment?"

This question prompted an exchange between Job and some of the panel members. After considerable discussion, most panel members acknowledged that they usually formed judgments contemporaneous with the event and modified their judgment as later events required. In the final analysis, most agreed the concept of keeping an open mind was a legal fiction, not a reality.

Job then fired the telling shot across the courtroom.

'I want to ask each of you a very important question about your ability to reserve judgment. The judge will tell you that you must reserve judgment until the end of this trial. I am sure each of you will do your best to give Ann Tatum, this lady who sits before you, a fair and impartial trial. In asking my next question, I do not imply that you will not try to be fair, so don't think that. I'm not asking about what you want to do. I'm asking about your ability to do. For example, suppose I want to be able to sing and play the piano, but I don't have the ability to do either. Please carefully think about the distinction that I make. My question is a difficult one. Plainly put, I ask each of you to assume that your son, your brother, your husband, or your father has been shot and killed, not by just one bullet, but by eight. If that happened to you, would you have the ability to wait until all the truth was known about the circumstance of death before you formed an opinion about the death? Would you be able to keep a completely open mind until all the facts were known? Until all the story was told?"

Even before Job finished his question, Aaron Bailey was on his feet seeking the judge's attention. This led to a sidebar conference between the judge and the lawyers. Bailey objected.

'Judge, the question assumes facts that will not be part of the evidence. The question assumes a relative of a juror has been killed. That is not the case before the court."

"Mr. Bailey, the question is designed to test the ability of the jurors to reserve judgment. They will be instructed that they must do that very thing. I will allow the question. Mr.

Lee, your question is both proper and clever, but do not push your luck too far with this line of questioning."

Job's question led to a lively exchange with some of the jurors. The bottom line of the discussion suggested the jurors would find it difficult to reserve all judgment under the assumed facts, but they would try.

In conclusion, Job said, "Yes, I understand it would be difficult, but all of you have indicated you would do your best to reserve judgment. My final statement is that Ann Tatum will depend on each juror to try and reserve judgment. Will you keep your word to do that very thing? Do you have the ability to do that? We all have different talents and abilities. If you were to ask me to play and sing for you, I would have to tell you I do not have that ability. Not having a particular ability is not something to be ashamed of. We are all different people. If you do not have the ability to break a life-long habit of making judgments as-you-go, tell me now. Your silence will be treated as your promise to reserve judgment to the best of your ability. Your silence will be your promise to Ann Tatum."

Job stood silently before the jury panel for several long moments.

"Thank you for your promise."

Back at his table and seated by Ann, Job glanced across the room toward Aaron Bailey. Bailey looked Job's way and mouthed something. Job was not sure what Bailey said. It seemed to be "Good job."

By 1:30 that afternoon, fourteen people, twelve jurors and two alternates, had been selected and placed in the jury box. At this point, Sam's paralegal left the courtroom, leaving Job Lee and his client on their own.

Suddenly Job felt all alone. To his left sat a man wearing a black robe and a stern disinterested expression on his face. This man was not there to help Job or anyone else. He was the umpire, the referee. His job was to determine whether the pitch was a 'strike or a ball' or whether the 'toe stepped on the line.'

Across the room, facing in Job's direction, sat two men. Both were older and more experienced than Job and they were not his allies. They had guns that pointed in his direction. In addition to the guns of age and experience, they were armed with the financial strength of the state of Georgia. On a moment's notice, investigators across Georgia and adjoining states could look for new witnesses and for evidence that would disprove or cast in doubt anything Job presented to the jury. These men across the room could afford to buy legal and scientific research. Job had no investigator, no partner. He owed three ladies who had helped transcribe recorded statements into manuscripts $425.00. His office utility bill was past-due, and he had $216.39 in his office bank account.

To Job's far right, packed tightly together, side-by-side like sardines in a can, sat two rows of strangers. In theory, they were to be impartial. They were not supposed to have a 'dog in the fight.' They were supposed to be the super-humans who came into the arena with open minds, free of all biases and prejudices. But Job knew this was more fiction than fact. Honesty, truthfulness, bias and prejudice were relative things. Some of these fourteen persons had already begun to form opinions, for they were, of course, human, and Job knew that to have any chance of success, most of the close calls on the balls and strikes had to go his way, and the pitcher had to make some bad throws. He had to go twelve for twelve at the plate.

AARON BAILEY'S OPENING STATEMENT

Job's *voir dire* talk of eight bullets pumped into a hypothetical body did not muffle the cannon of Aaron Bailey's opening statement to the selected jury.

Ladies and gentlemen, through its witnesses and evidence, the State of Georgia will prove to you beyond all reasonable doubt that Ann Albert Tatum shot and killed her husband, Edward Wesley Tatum, on February 18, 1972. The evidence will clearly show that Ed Tatum was in his own home, standing some fifteen or twenty feet away, when the defendant raised her pistol, took deliberate aim, and shot her husband in the chest. The evidence we present for the State will show that the defendant was not satisfied with shooting him once, after which he turned his back and tried to flee. We will prove that the defendant shot him seven more times in the back as he made a valiant effort to save his life by running away. We don't know what evidence, if any, will be offered by the defense. Should the defense contend that the defendant acted in self-defense, the State will prove that no other deadly weapons were found in the house, except two butcher knives that were neatly stored away among other kitchen utensils. No weapon, other than the one that carried the fingerprints of the defendant, was found in the house. The evidence will show no sign of a fight or scuffle. There will be nothing presented to suggest any struggle taking place in that home on February 18, 1972. No furniture was overturned, no chairs knocked over, no books pulled from the shelf. We will present numerous pictures of all rooms of the house. All photographs will show a home that was neatly arranged and nothing that would suggest a fight of self-defense. We will show you that Ann Albert Tatum committed an act of cold-blooded murder against her husband. At the conclusion of this case, the State will ask you to return a verdict of first-degree murder.

DEATH EMPLOYS SEVERAL TRANSLATORS

Job Lee listened with considerable admiration of Bailey's style and manner. He had never met him before, but he immediately knew that he was confronted with a most worthy opponent. Following Sam's suggestion, Job listened for some word or phrase that Bailey may use that he might turn to his client's advantage. He thought he had found what he sought. After jotting a few more notes on the outline in front of him, he rose from his chair to make his opening statement.

Drawing on things Richard Cramer had told him years earlier and following Sam's more recent suggestion, Job decided to make his opening statement brief. Walking to the front of the jury box, he paused and turned toward Ann who was seated on the right end of the table. He stood there, looking at his client for a long time, not saying a word, just looking at the once-dignified lady, who now seemed more skeleton than human. His eyes pulled all other eyes in the room toward her.

Ever so slowly, he addressed the jury.

DEATH DIMINISHES ALL

Ladies and gentlemen of the jury, I am Job Lee of Carrollton, Georgia. I represent Ann Tatum.

First, let me tell you that Ann will take the stand and testify in this case. The law does not require her to do this, but of her own free will, she has chosen do so.

Next, Ann will not deny shooting Edward Tatum, nor will she tell you that she did shoot him. All that she will be able to honestly tell you is that she does not remember shooting the man she truly loved. If pressed on this issue, Ann will agree that all the evidence suggests that she fired the pistol.

So, as Ann's attorney, I tell you at the beginning of this trial that all evidence clearly leads any rational person to the conclusion that Ann Tatum shot Ed Tatum once in the chest and seven times in the back. I tell you that now and I will tell you that when the trial concludes.

This case will boil down to the question of why? Why did Ann kill the one person she loved above all others? What made her do it, and should she be found guilty of murder for doing so? Your questions will be just that simple. Your questions will be just that serious and complex.

I must commend Mr. Bailey on his opening statement to you. He is a splendid trial attorney and a most worthy opponent. However, I take serious issue with what he said in his opening remarks in one particular. To be sure not to misquote him, I wrote his words down. Mr. Bailey told you, "There will be nothing presented to suggest any struggle taking place in that home of February 18, 1972."

During this trial, I ask that you remember those words, that no struggle took place. I want you to contrast those words with the evidence that will be presented to you.

Ladies and gentlemen, it is my belief that the evidence and testimony that you receive will in fact show a struggle taking place in that home, not only on February 18, but also for months before that date. The evidence will show a struggle the likes of which the human mind can hardly conceive. The evidence will show you a struggle for life, for dignity, for respect, for compassion, and a struggle for love. The evidence will show you a never-ending struggle for the preservation of the most precious of things, the will to live and the spirit of life.

After you hear the evidence, it will be your solemn duty to decide if you want to label the product and result of this struggle murder, or if you will want to say, "We understand."

With the opening statements concluded, Judge Johnson instructed the District Attorney to call his first witness. It was 2:30 in the afternoon, seven days before Christmas.

THOMAS McGEE

Uniformed police officer Thomas McGee was sworn in as the first witness. Bailey asked if he had occasion to go to the Tatum house on February 18, 1972.

"Yes," he replied. "I received a call from the dispatcher at 12:42 p.m., concerning possible gun shots at that address. I arrived at 12:46. There were no vehicles present and the garage door was standing open. I went into the garage and found an open door that led into what proved to be a kitchen. Going into the kitchen I found a white male lying on the kitchen floor in a pool of blood. A white female was sitting on the floor with him, attempting to hold his head in her lap."

Bailey interrupted. "Is the white female that you saw that day present here in the courtroom? If so, point her out."

"I now know the lady to be Ann Albert Tatum. She is here, seated beside her attorney, Mr. Job Lee."

"Thank you, Officer McGee. Please proceed with what you saw and did that day."

"I didn't see any weapons in the kitchen area. The dispatch suggested gunshots, and the man on the floor in a pool of blood suggested possible gunshots. I had no way of knowing if there were others in the house. Several times, I asked Mrs. Tatum if there was anyone else in the house."

"What was her answer?"

"She acted as if she didn't hear me. She acted as if I wasn't there. She was crying softly, and she kept saying quietly to the man in her arms, Edward Tatum, 'I love you.' Not getting any response from Mrs. Tatum and thinking it possible that another person might be in the home, I backed away. I went back into the garage and called dispatch for back-up and an ambulance."

The testimony of two other uniformed officers followed next, and they, too, described the activities at Ann's home. They had searched the house for other individuals and found no one besides Ann and her dead husband. While these officers were present, the ambulance arrived and the emergency medical personnel determined that the man on the floor, Ed Tatum, was dead.

SERGEANT HENRY MALONE

When Sergeant Henry Malone took the stand, he stated that "Mrs. Tatum was seated on the floor, holding her husband's head when I arrived. She stayed there as we searched the house. When the emergency medical people arrived, we had to physically lift Mrs. Tatum off the floor and away so the ambulance attendant could make an examination of the man on the floor. At the time, we didn't know who he was. After they determined him to be dead, I tried to get Mrs. Tatum to identify the man. She seemed not to understand me. She just kept crying quietly and saying, 'I love you. You have come home.'"

"Sgt. Malone, what did you do next?"

"After securing the house and determining there had been a homicide, I directed that Mrs. Tatum be taken into protective custody. Another unit, another officer, transported her to the Northeast Station. I notified Homicide Division, and directed that all uniformed officers vacate the crime scene. I waited outside the home until Detective Robert Parker and the crime scene unit arrived. At that point, my work was finished and I had no further contact with the case."

Job, in cross-examining Sgt. Malone, asked him to describe Ann's appearance that day, along with anything she said and any specific actions.

"Mr. Lee, she was obviously very upset and confused. She was seated in a pool of blood, holding the head of a dead man in her arms. She just sat there, patting the man's cheek, telling him that she loved him, and telling him how glad she was that he had come back home. Several times, she told him how happy she was that he was back home. She acted as if there was no one else in the house, except the two of them."

Bailey called the crime scene investigators as his next two witnesses, and they provided insight into the physical evidence found at the crime scene. They identified numerous photographs of the home's interior. Pictures of all the rooms in the house were taken from various angles, identified and introduced.

The officers described how they took measurements of all the rooms and the hallway of the house and also prepared a scale drawing of the floor plan that was admitted into evidence.

Through these witnesses, five photographs of Ed Tatum's body were introduced into evidence. The pictures depicted Ed lying face down, slightly on his left side, with his head turned to the right. His upper body lay in a large circle of blood that, around the front of his face, had a "smeared" appearance on the floor. This smear was identified as the place where Ann sat as she cradled Ed's head in her arms. The State made an attempt to submit Ann's bloodstained dress as evidence, but Judge Johnson ruled the dress to be inadmissible as evidence for murder.

Another photograph showed the kitchen table, located about three feet from Ed's head. On the table were a partially eaten sandwich, a partially filled glass of milk, and the little butterfly poem that Ann's mother had written down for her a few months before her death in 1941.

It was past five o'clock when the photographs were introduced into evidence and Judge Johnson announced, "Ladies and gentlemen of the jury, this seems a good place to stop for the day. I'm going to release you to go to your separate homes for the evening. I've already explained to you the importance of not allowing any person to talk to you, or to talk in your presence, about this case. Do not read anything about it and do not listen to any radio or television broadcast about the case. Should anything occur in your presence that is contrary to this instruction, you are to immediately bring such occurrence to my attention. Please report back to the jury room by 8:45 tomorrow morning. Trial will resume at 9:00. The court stands in recess until that time."

As the jurors left for the jury room to gather their hats, purses, and coats, Job gathered his notes and files and placed them in an old, battered briefcase that Richard Cramer had given him. The briefcase, wide at the bottom and narrow at the top, must have been fifty years old when Cramer gave it to him. "Boy," he'd said, "I brought you my old grip. She's of the topside load variety, not one of these flat lay down on her belly kind like you see around today's courtrooms. A lawyer's briefcase, like the lawyer, ought to stand up and be proud of what they're doing. I want you to have this one. I have no further need of her. She's served me well. Maybe she'll do the same for you."

Job released the lock of Cramer's "grip," pulled the two handles in opposing directions, and placed Ann's files inside. He thought of how, during the testimony, she sat quietly at the table, her trembling right hand in her lap under the table. He had not had time to observe her closely. Listening to the testimony and making notes had demanded his undivided attention. On the few occasions he did look her way, she seemed removed from the present, almost as if she were an observer of the trial rather than its centerpiece. Her appearance was cause for concern. He was fearful the jurors might get the impression that she didn't give a damn, but trial activity didn't allow time to dwell on such thoughts.

Now, the first day of trial was over. Job remembered Cramer had told him there would be times when he would be scared as hell. There would be times when he felt the urge to soil his pants, or to run and hide.

"The courtroom doesn't allow the luxury of doing either." Cramer had said. "You have to learn to take the licks without flinching. You can't duck or dodge. You have to stand up and be proud of what you're doing. The jury will be watching both you and your client. They will be looking for signs of fear and if they see it, they'll wonder what you're afraid of. They'll wonder if you have something to hide, something you don't want them to see. Every case is a representation of life. Every life is a combination of good and bad, pretty and ugly, sweet and bitter. Every judge you meet and every juror you stand before will have been a human being long before they became judge or juror. So, in the trial, be prepared to face the ugly that will be presented against your client. We're all ugly in some way or another. All judges and jurors are ugly in some manner. Stand up and be proud of what you are doing."

Cramer had also warned Job that "the darkest day of your life will be the end of the first day of trial when you are repre-

senting someone who is charged with a serious criminal offense. In a case where the stakes are high, where all the chips
are on the table and life is gambled, the first day will end in
darkness. You will have to sit there that first day and take all
the shots. The district attorney will be doing all the shooting. You won't be able to shoot back. You can't even draw
your weapon. You'll just have to sit there and take it. You
can't hide. You can't cow. You can't hunker down. You just
take it. You'll suffer what the old folks call a serious sinking
feeling, but you can't tuck your tail between your legs and
run. You'll leave the courthouse at the end of that first day
in total darkness, even if the sun has not set. You don't know
what darkness is until you see the end of the first day of trial
when you are defending someone in a serious criminal case."

Job placed his hand on Ann's shoulder. "Come my
friend," he said, "it's time for a rest."

Ann rose from her chair and gave a gentle smile, but she
acted confused. She acted as if she didn't realize the trial was
over for the day. Job was concerned. He had never seen Ann
act this way. He took her arm. "The judge has released us for
the day," he said. "It's time to go home."

By the time Job and Ann walked to the back of the courtroom to meet Jane, Dana, and Mrs. McCoy, Ann seemed to
have returned to the present time and place. Job wondered
where she had been. He wondered if she would be able to
maintain her composure, to return to the courtroom and
withstand the avalanche of ugly facts that would swirl around
her head.

At the back of the courtroom, the lights were on, but the

room seemed dark. It seemed as if the darkness would prevail for a long time, and he would never again see the light of day. This was the total darkness of which Cramer spoke.

Job, Ann, Dana, Mrs. McCoy and Jane walked together to the parking garage. The four ladies got in Jane's car, and they all parted company for the day. Job drove to his home, the opening statement of the district attorney and the testimony of the police officers running through his mind.

Sally was in the kitchen the next morning when Job came in for his first cup of coffee. "Are you ready for your second day of trial?" she asked.

"I'm ready. I slept better than I thought I would."

"You talked in your sleep."

"I hope I didn't tell any secrets and get myself in trouble. What did I say?"

"Nothing that made any sense. Just a lot of mumbo jumbo. I called Sam Grave's office mid-afternoon yesterday. They had not heard anything about his surgery. I'll try again this afternoon. Honey, you better eat your breakfast. You said you needed to be at the courthouse by 8:30. It's almost 6:45 and traffic will be heavy this morning."

SECOND DAY OF TRIAL

On Tuesday, December 19, Job and Ann took their seats in the courtroom a few minutes before 9:00. Job opened his old briefcase and placed his files on the table. He felt as if he held Ann's life in his hands. He knew more shots would be fired his way. Heavy artillery. Large shells that could do real damage.

Job knew that Detective Parker would be called to the witness stand. He knew that Detective Parker was capable, experienced, honest, and believable, but he resolved not to dodge or duck, not to run or hide, not to show fear, but to do his best.

At 9:05, Judge Johnson took his seat, looked toward the district attorney and said, "The State may proceed."

Detective Parker was called to the stand and placed under oath to tell the truth.

DETECTIVE ROBERT PARKER

"I am Robert Parker, Senior Homicide Detective with the Atlanta Police Department. I have worked homicide for almost twenty years. Prior to that, I worked Uniform Division for eighteen years. I hold a Bachelor of Science degree from Georgia State University, and I am a graduate of the F.B.I. Academy. I have also regularly attended investigative seminars and special studies courses. I have investigated more than 200 homicides. I don't recall the exact number."

"Thank you, Detective Parker," Bailey said. "What can you tell the court about February 18 of this year?"

"Responding to a call from Uniform Division, I went to the home of Ann Albert Tatum on February 18, 1972, arriving there at approximately 1320 hours. That would be 1:20 p.m."

"Please tell us what you found and what you did."

"On arrival, I found Sgt. Malone, Uniform Division, in the front yard. He briefed me, advising there was a dead man in the house and that a white female, whose name was not then known, but believed to be Ann Tatum, had been removed to protective custody. I later determined that this lady was, in fact, Ann Albert Tatum.

"Sgt. Malone turned the case over to me, and crime scene investigators arrived about the same time as I did. I directed them to conduct their usual investigation and to report anything that appeared to be of special interest. May I use the photographs and the floor plan to aid and give better understanding of my testimony?"

Judge Johnson turned to Job Lee and asked, "Do you have any objections to their use in this manner?"

Lee answered no, and Detective Parker continued.

"I entered the house from the garage, going into a kitchen area. This photograph shows the kitchen table, a partly eaten sandwich, a glass of what appeared to be milk, and a page from a note pad with some writing on it. The writing, in pencil, was some little poem.

"Just beyond the kitchen table, as I traveled north to south through the house, on the floor was the body of a white male. These pictures show him as I first saw him that day. I later learned this was the body of Edward Tatum, the husband of Ann Albert Tatum.

"A trail of what appeared to be blood on the floor led from the body, down a hallway to the south, to the door of the second bedroom on the right as one traveled that hall, north to south. These two photographs show the hallway and the blood on the floor. Later lab reports show the blood on the hallway floor to be that of Edward Tatum.

"Following the blood trail, I entered through the door of the second bedroom on the right. These photographs show the bed, with its head against the south wall. A 22-semi-automatic revolver was found lying near the pillow on the southwest portion of the bed, its carriage bolt locked in the "open" position. Eight spent shell casings, 22-caliber, were found, some on the bed and others on the floor in the southwest part of the bedroom. These photographs show the pistol and shell casings as I found them."

"Mr. Parker, based on your experience and your investigation, do you have a judgment as to where Edward Tatum was when he was first shot?"

"The pathology report suggests he was shot while standing. The report also shows that he was shot once in the chest and seven times in the back, but it does not indicate which shots came first. The physical evidence suggests that Mr. Tatum was standing close to the door of the second bedroom when first shot in his chest, and that the other shots were fired after he had turned and started going north down the hallway. It is my opinion that this is the way it happened."

"Do you have an opinion as to the location and position of the person who fired the shots?"

"The pathology report suggests that the person firing the pistol was standing. The location of the spent shell casings suggests that person was standing on the west side of the bed, near the southwest corner of the room."

"Do you have a judgment as to the distance that separated Ed Tatum and the person pulling the trigger?"

"It was a large bedroom, the largest in the house. The diagonal measurement of the room, for the northeast corner, next to the door, to the southwest corner, where some of the spent casings were found, measured twenty feet, three inches. It is my judgment that the distance that separated the two when the shooting began was not less than fifteen feet and not more than twenty feet. This was at the time of the first shot. Mr. Tatum obviously tried to run away, and the subsequent shots would have been at a greater distance. Everything suggests that the person firing the shots remained relatively stationary, not moving to any great extent."

"Detective Parker, you said something to the effect that when you saw the pistol on the bed, its carriage bolt was locked open. Explain what you mean and explain how the bolt could be locked in an open position."

"This was a clip-fed, semi-automatic pistol. Newton's Law of Physics states that for every action, there is an equal and opposite reaction, and that law is definitely at work in this type weapon. When the bullet is discharged from the firing chamber, the projectile is forced down the barrel of the pistol. The powder discharge propels the carriage bolt backwards, in the opposite direction of the projectile. The carriage bolt is spring loaded, which means that when it goes backward as far as the pistol frame allows, the spring then forces the bolt back in the direction from which it came. As the bolt goes forward, it forces the next round of ammunition from the clip and moves it forward into the firing chamber. If the trigger is pulled again, this new round in the chamber is fired and the process of action and reaction, so long as the trigger keeps being pulled, is repeated. When the clip is emptied and the last round in the firing chamber is discharged, the pistol is designed so the carriage bolt becomes locked in the open position. This tells the person firing the weapon that there are no more rounds in the weapon. As the photographs show, the bolt on this weapon was in its locked, open position when I first saw it."

"Were fingerprints found on the pistol that you found on the bed?"

"Yes. The lab reports indicate that the prints found on the pistol match part of the palm and three of the fingers of the right hand of Ann Albert Tatum."

"Did your investigation show anything in the house to be out of place or disturbed?"

"Mr. Bailey, I am sorry but I cannot answer that question, not knowing where things in that house were usually kept."

"I agree, it was a poor question. I'll rephrase. Did you find anything that suggested a fight, a physical disturbance, anything that indicated the person firing the weapon acted in self-defense?"

"Of course, there was a dead man on the floor. That strongly suggested violent behavior. Other than the dead man, the blood, and the pistol and spent casings, I found nothing else that suggested a physical confrontation. There was nothing overturned or broken. Usually a physical contest leaves some signs. Other than what I have described, I found nothing else."

"Did your investigation indicate the presence of any other person being in the Tatum residence at or about the time that Ed Tatum was killed, other than the victim and his wife?"

"No. May I refer to my investigative notes?"

Judge Johnson answered, "Detective Parker, if you need your notes to refresh your recollection, you may use them."

Robert Parker reviewed his notes, then continued his testimony.

"On February 19, the day after Mr. Tatum died, I was told by Mary Mills, a lady who lived across the street from the Tatum residence, that she had seen a dark late model vehicle parked in the driveway of the Tatum residence. She saw someone seated in the car, but could not make an identification of the person. She indicated the vehicle left shortly after she heard what seemed like firecrackers exploding. Mrs. Mills gave me the tag number of this vehicle, and I traced the Tennessee tag number that she gave me. The tag had been issued to M. C. Walker, whose general delivery address was Ellendale, Tennessee. Mr. Walker had sold the vehicle to a used car dealer in that area in late March of 1972. He and his wife, Sara Walker, had moved from the area sometime after this vehicle had been seen at the Tatum residence, though I wasn't able to establish where Mr. and Mrs. Walker had moved. It was rumored that they had possibly separated from each other, but this rumor has not been confirmed.

"Mr. Tatum owned a 1969 Ford that was found parked at his Memphis apartment, so it appears that he probably arrived at his home that day in the Buick that was seen in the driveway. I wasn't able to establish anything further on the Walker family and other than the presence of the vehicle, nothing suggested that anyone in the vehicle was involved in the events inside the house. It's obvious that someone drove the Buick away from the Tatum home that day, but I found nothing inside the home that suggested any third party was involved in the immediate events that led to Mr. Tatum's death. Collectively, my investigation did not suggest the presence of any other person inside the Tatum home at the time of the occurrence."

UNDERSTANDING THE BELL'S TOLL

It was late in the second day of trial before Job Lee had the opportunity to cross-examine Detective Parker. He kept the cross-examination brief.

"Mr. Parker, thank you for the professional service that you render, year after year, for all of us."

Parker, a veteran of many criminal trials, looked a little surprised by Job's gentle approach. He smiled and said, "Mr. Lee, I just try to do my job in an honest way."

"Mr. Parker, that's obvious to all of us. You have our gratitude."

Job took a small slip of paper from his case notes and walked toward the witness stand. "Let me hand you this old and worn piece of paper," he said. "Do you recognize this as being the paper that you found on the kitchen table, along with the sandwich and glass of milk, the day you went into the Tatum residence?"

"I can't be sure. At the time, the paper on the table did not seem important, and, frankly, I paid little attention to it. I left it where I found it. It appears to be the same paper that's shown in one of the photographs. If you say that it is the same, I will take your word for it."

"I cannot personally tell you that it's the same. I've been told it is the same, and I will connect this with a later witness."

Job handed Mr. Parker three of the photographs and continued. "Please look at these three photographs and tell the jury what they show."

"This first one was taken from the hallway that I described, looking into the first bedroom on the right, as one walks north-to-south in the Tatum home. This second one shows the bed and nightstand in that first bedroom. So, the first picture shows the doorway and the second picture shows the interior of that room."

"Mr. Parker, tell the jury what the third picture shows."

"It's a picture made in the same bedroom, the first one on the right as one goes down the hall. The picture shows a stuffed chair that sat beside the door of the bedroom. The stuffed chair was inside the room and to the immediate left of anyone going into the room. The pictures show a wad of crumpled-up money lying on the cushion of the chair."

"Why was the picture taken?"

"It was standard procedure for any crime scene. After the picture was taken, I called Detective Adams into the room with me, so the money might be counted and sealed as possible evidence and for safekeeping. This, too, was standard procedure. We counted the money, sealed it in an envelope, and both of us initialed where it was sealed. The envelope was turned into the evidence room at the station."

"How much money did you find in the chair?"

Parker looked again at his investigative notes. "A total of $192. Eight twenties, three tens, and two one-dollar bills."

"And you say that the money, when first seen, was on the cushion of the chair? I believe you described it as being in wadded, crumpled-up form, as the third picture shows it to be?'

"Yes, that is correct. As the picture shows, it was not neatly placed there. It was wrinkled, as it would have been if I had found it in the bottom of my wife's purse." Detective Parker smiled and said, "If you're a married man, you'll know what I'm talking about."

"Yes, I know what you mean," Job said, smiling back. "In your judgment, Mr. Parker, would a man carrying the same money in his pants pocket, rather than in his wallet, would it give the same wadded, crumpled appearance?"

"I would think so."

"Did you later release the $192 and, if so, to whom and why?"

"Yes, I released it. About three months ago, in reviewing the evidence and preparing for a possible trial, I discovered the money was still in the evidence locker. I had not connected the money in any way to the homicide, and frankly, I thought Mrs. Tatum might have use for what appeared to be her money. Sometimes things get stored away in an evidence room and forgotten. I talked to my captain, and with his consent, I contacted you, as Mrs. Tatum's attorney, and asked if you could receive it on her behalf."

"That you did, Mr. Parker, that you did. It is one of my

reasons for thanking you for your service and your honesty." Job handed Detective Parker a white, sealed envelope. "Do you recognize this envelope as being the one containing the $192 that you delivered about three months ago? Is it in the same sealed condition as it was when you gave it to me?

Examining the envelope, Parker answered, "Yes, it is the same, and has not been opened."

"Mr. Parker, please open the envelope and tell the jury what you find inside."

Opening the envelope, Parker removed the money and counted it out loud. "There are eight twenties, three tens, and two one-dollar bills."

"Thank you, Mr. Parker. Now I want to further question you about the appearance of this $192 when you first saw it on the seat of the stuffed chair. Please look at this photograph of the money, as you first saw it in the chair. You've already indicated that the money was wadded up, as the photograph shows. Do I understand that the wadded, crumpled money that you found that day had an appearance that was consistent with it having possibly been carried in the bottom of a woman's purse?"

"Yes, it had that appearance. That was my first impression."

"And, you have already admitted, the appearance of the wadded money was also consistent with the possibility that it had been removed from the pocket of a man's pants."

"Yes sir, the appearance of the money was equally consistent with both possibilities."

"Of course, Mr. Parker, you were not there when the

money was put, or placed, or thrown onto the chair, were you?"

"No sir, Mr. Lee."

"Mr. Parker, I will ask you a hypothetical question. Was the appearance of the crumpled-up money also consistent with the possibility of it having been thrown onto the chair by Edward Tatum?"

The District Attorney objected. "The hypothetical question assumes facts that are not in evidence."

Job assured the judge that the missing facts would be provided by subsequent witnesses, and with that assurance, the judge allowed the witness to answer the questions.

"Mr. Parker, to be sure you understand what was asked, I will repeat the question about the money. Was the appearance of the wadded or crumpled money consistent with the possibility that it had been thrown onto the chair by Edward Tatum?"

"Of course, I was not there when it happened, but the wadded money in the chair was consistent with the possibility that it had been thrown there by Mr. Tatum before he died."

"Mr. Parker, one more hypothetical question. Was the appearance of the money in the chair consistent with the possibility that Edward Tatum had told his wife, 'If you're going to kill yourself, here's some money for your God damned funeral,' as he threw the money onto the chair?"

"Yes sir, the appearance of the money would be consistent with it having been placed in the chair in that manner."

"Thank you, Detective Parker." Job turned his attention to

the judge. "Your Honor, I offer this envelope and its contents as Defendant's Exhibit No. 1. I have no further questions."

A SHARING HEART

It was 5:20 p.m., the end of the second day of trial, and the judge adjourned the court until 9:30 the next morning.

Sometime that afternoon, an older gentleman had quietly entered the courtroom and taken a seat on the back row. As Ann and Job Lee walked toward the exit door at the end of the day, the gentleman stepped forward in front of Ann.

"My dear, it's been a long time since I've seen you, and I decided I had to correct that situation. Have you been reading the Browning poems I gave you?"

"Mr. Henry! Mr. Wallace Henry! It is so good to see you." Ann fell into his arms and he held her while she cried.

After both Ann and Mr. Henry regained their composure, he extended his hand to Job.

"Job, it's good to see you again. I drove down from Rome this morning. As Lincoln would say, I had 'a-purpose' to be here with Ann and her girls. I'd like to take them to supper and catch up, if that doesn't interfere with your plans. Could you join us?"

"Thank you Mr. Henry. I think it would be wonderful for you to take these ladies out to eat. I've got several notes that I need to review tonight, and for that reason I decline your kind offer, but thank you. And thank you so much for coming to support Ann." Turning to Ann and her girls, Job added, "We start at 9:30 tomorrow morning. Try to get a good night's rest and meet me in the attorney's room at 9 o'clock."

ALL MANKIND IS OF ONE AUTHOR

Job never knew what Mr. Henry and Ann discussed that night, or if they discussed anything. He thought it inappropriate to ask. But overnight, something happened to Ann. During the last six weeks before the trial began, she, with the support of Dr. Battle and Ethel McCoy, had slowly gained partial control of her emotions. The meeting in Sam Graves's office, three weeks earlier, had provided much needed information, but was only the starting place. It often seemed as if it were a two-step forward, one-step backward progression. This frustration notwithstanding, during those six weeks, in discussions with Ann, Dana, Jane, and Ethel, Job had been able to put many parts of the puzzle together, and slowly gained an understanding of his client and the circumstances under which her husband had died.

In spite of this, Ann had retained a reserve, a stiffness, a wall of separation between herself and the persons she spoke with. In a mechanical manner, she had been able to relate the things that had happened between her and Ed, but, even at best, it was not meaningful communication. It never quite put the listener at ease. Something intangible was always held back as if Ann's method of describing events seemed to come from a spectator rather than from a participant. Job could not define the communication problem, but he was keenly aware that the real Ann Tatum was not speaking. The real person seemed more shadow than substance.

After dinner with Mr. Henry, Job immediately noticed a change in Ann. She looked the same. She was the same walking skeleton, and she still tended to drag her right foot when she walked. Her right hand still shook at intervals, but she was a different person. Overnight, she had become someone the listener wanted to hear. She still spoke with her same soft voice, but there was an unexplainable difference.

After they talked for a few minutes and before leaving the attorney's room for the courtroom, Ann stopped Job and gave him a tight hug.

"Job, you don't need to worry about me. I've made my peace with all who matter."

THE THIRD DAY OF TRIAL

It was the third day of Ann's trial, and Job Lee was largely passive. He listened along with the jury as Aaron Bailey applied all the finishing touches to what appeared to be an open-and-shut case of cold-blooded murder. A pathologist testified as to the cause of death, and Bailey placed emphasis on the gory details of the eight gunshot wounds.

Other witnesses completed painting the picture of Ed Tatum's death with their testimony, and by the end of the day, Bailey had dotted all the i's and crossed all the t's of the State's case against Ann Tatum. Shortly after 4 o'clock, the State announced that it had rested its case.

Wallace Henry was again seated on the back row, and once more, he treated Ann and her daughters to dinner after court recessed. Job Lee and Aaron Bailey stayed behind for a conference with the judge.

BAILEY'S MOTION DENIED

After the courtroom had cleared of everyone except the court reporter and the attorneys, Judge Johnson spoke.

"Mr. Bailey, I understand you have a motion that you want considered outside the hearing of the jury. State your motion."

"Your honor, I just came into this case on Monday. In reviewing the file, I see that the defense has entered a special plea of not guilty by reason of insanity."

"Yes, that plea was entered some weeks ago."

"Your Honor, the State moves to strike that plea."

"What are your grounds that support a motion to strike?"

"It was not timely filed. The late filing denied the State the opportunity to have the defendant examined by an expert of the State's choosing."

"Mr. Bailey, this plea was made and entered on October 13, 1972. This trial began on December 18, 1972. I count that to be more than six weeks. Does not Local Court Rule No. 9 require the filing of special pleas not less than forty-two days before the trial commences?"

"Yes, sir, that is what the rule provides."

"Mr. Bailey, I count from October 13 to December 18

as being more than forty-two days. Do you get a different count?"

"No sir, your Honor. In the alternative to my motion to strike, I move the court to delay this trial until next Monday and order the defendant to make herself available for mental evaluation by a doctor of the State's choosing during the interim."

"Aaron, let me get this straight. You're asking me to stop a trial, after you have rested your case, so the State can do something it should have done weeks ago? Do my ears deceive me ? Is that what you are asking?"

Job Lee stood silent during this exchange. He might have been a young and somewhat inexperienced lawyer, but he knew that when the judge was making an argument against the other side, it was best to stand mute.

"Yes, Judge, that's what I am asking. I just got into this case, and I've only just learned of the insanity defense."

"You just got in?"

"Yes sir, on Monday."

"Did the District Attorney's office not present this case to the Grand Jury for indictment?"

"Yes, sir."

"Has not your office had exclusive control of this case from its beginning?"

"Yes, sir."

"Have you not been the head of that office for several years?"

"Yes, sir."

Aaron Bailey was a veteran of many criminal trials and

fully understood the roles of all the participants in a trial. He knew successful trial lawyers had to be assertive, sometimes asking for rulings from the judge that had little chance of being granted. He also knew that a trial lawyer had to respectfully accept the judge's denial of the request. He knew that each judge had a different way of denying a request. Sometimes it was simply a statement of "Motion denied." Sometimes it was with a taunting cat and mouse game. By this time, in the dialogue between Judge Johnson and Aaron Bailey, it was evident to all that Bailey's motions would be denied. It was equally evident the Judge had chosen to inflict a little pain on Bailey for having made a ridiculous request. Trial judges develop ways to apply a whip that leaves no scars, and Bailey was beginning to feel the whip.

Veteran trial lawyers like Aaron Bailey develop a thick skin that does not flinch or quiver when a whip of ridicule or sarcasm is applied. Having started the charade, Bailey had no choice but to take the medicine as Judge Johnson continued.

"Before Monday, when you first appeared as trial counsel, could you not have read the court file at any time you wanted to?"

"Yes, sir."

"Do I recall correctly that this past August and part of September you took an extended vacation of some six or seven weeks? Does my memory fail me?"

"No, sir."

"Mr. Bailey, before I rule on your motions, do you mind if I offer you a suggestion?"

"Judge, I am always pleased to receive your suggestions."

"Good. I strongly suggest that the next time you come to my court, you best read your file and prepare your case before you reach the midway point of the trial. Your motions are denied. Trial will resume at 9:30 tomorrow morning."

TO LISTEN: TO UNDERSTAND

For the first time since he met Ann Tatum, Job felt good about the case as he drove home to Sally that evening. Ann was much improved in her manner of speaking, and now her voice carried the conviction of speaking the simple truth. She had told Job that he need not worry about her. She said she had found peace with those who mattered. Moreover, the young lawyer had witnessed his adversary, Aaron Bailey, bear the brunt of the judge's attack. It always made a young lawyer feel good to see an older lawyer get his ass chewed.

Back home, Sally was pleased to see the smile that lingered on Job's face. "Good to see you smiling. Did you have a good day?"

"Not with the testimony. Bailey fired the rest of his ammunition my way and rested the State's case."

"And that made you smile?"

"Babe, you've heard the expression that misery loves company. Bailey gave me misery all day. Then he made a ridiculous motion and the judge chewed his fanny out. I guess it is juvenile on my part, but seeing Bailey catch some of the misery seemed to relieve some of mine."

"Job, I know our budget is stretched, but if Margaret

Landman gets back home from school in time, could I get her to keep the kids so I can watch some of your trial?"

"My good wife, we are stretched, but not broken. If you can arrange it, do it."

That night after dinner, after he and Sally had gone to bed, Job described the marked change he'd seen in Ann.

"I have talked to you before about Ann not being able to tell me the things I needed to know about her relationship with her husband."

"Yes, but you told me she had overcome her shame, guilt, or whatever it was."

"That is correct, she has, but something else has changed with her, something that I can't accurately describe. She was different today."

"Was she on the witness stand today? I'm sure that would be a most difficult time for her. That experience would change me, too."

"No. I haven't called any of my witnesses to the stand. I'll have Jane, Dana, and Dot Carey testify tomorrow. Maybe Mrs. McCoy, too. It will be at least Friday before Ann testifies. Her change has been for the better, not the worse. Sometime yesterday afternoon, Mr. Henry, Ann's old Sunday school teacher, came down for part of the trial. He was there in the courtroom at the end of the day."

"Is that the man you said she was so fond of?"

"Yes, he lives in Rome. He came down for the trial. He was back again today. Yesterday evening, he took Ann, Jane, and Dana out to dinner. Then this morning, when I first saw Ann, I saw a change in her."

"What kind of change? You're not making sense."

"You're right, it makes no sense. I can't even describe the change that I see or whatever it is. Ann is just different, but in a very positive way. Today, for the first time since I've known her, she seems at peace with herself. She said so. She told me not to worry about her. She said she was at peace with all those who matter, or something like that."

"What brought this on?"

"I don't know. I suspect Mr. Henry said or did something, but it would be improper for me to ask. I just like what I see. She speaks differently now. Her words are the same, but they don't sound the same."

"The lady has been through so much. Do you think the change will last when she goes on the witness stand?"

"I sure hope so. The way someone says something often makes a stronger impression than what they say. Today, for the first time, I feel that Ann can tell her side of the story in a way that will make the jury listen. I hope this change is not only good for the rest of the trial, but also good for the rest of her life. Sally, Ann Tatum is one of the most gentle and kind people I have ever known. And now something has come over her that I think will allow others to see that side of her, too."

"How old is Mr. Henry?"

"I believe he told me that he was eighty-plus. I don't exactly recall. Why do you ask?"

"You remember laughing about the lady who said Ann would not let the death angel see her tears when her little sister died?"

'I told you I wasn't laughing at the lady. I just found what she said unusual. But what's this got to do with Mr. Henry?"

"Do you agree some things happen in life that are beyond human understanding?"

"Now, you're the one who's not making any sense. We were talking about Mr. Henry."

"Did you not say that Mr. Henry was her Sunday school teacher years ago?"

"Yes, that's correct."

"Well, my dear husband, I believe in angels. It may be of help if you did, too. I'll be glad when this trial is over and you have enough energy for another game of T-ball. Now let's turn out the light and get some sleep. You have a busy day tomorrow."

Thursday, the fourth day of trial, began earlier than expected. Robert, Job's youngest son, developed an upset stomach during the night. Sally took charge of the problem. Even so, Job's rest was disturbed and, after helping Sally change the sheets on Robert's bed, he could not get back to sleep. The State had fired its guns at Ann, loudly so, and rested its case. Today would mark the beginning of Ann's defense. Would the jury listen? Would they understand? Had the noise of the State's cannons deafened their ears? These thoughts flooded Job's mind as he lay in bed, trying to go back to sleep after Robert's bed was cleaned. Job thought of one of Winston Churchill's war speeches when it appeared England would fall to the enemy. He recalled Churchill asking: "Is this the end of the beginning or is it the beginning of the end?" Job carried these questions with him as he drove to Atlanta.

Job had asked Ann, Dana, Jane, and Ethel McCoy to meet him in the attorney's room at 8:30 a.m., an hour before court began. They were held up in a traffic jam, though, and it was 8:45 before they arrived. This reduced the time for the last-minute review with any of the witnesses Job expected to call that day.

THE DEMONSTRABLE HEART OF SADNESS

Ethel McCoy was seated at the head of the small conference table in the attorney's room when Job walked in. Jane and Dana were seated beside the table, facing the door. Ann sat opposite her girls with her back to Job as he entered the room.

Richard Cramer had told Job, "Boy, in a murder trial, by the time the District Attorney finishes presenting his case, he'll have the accused wearing horns. He'll have the defendant looking like a devil, maybe looking like Lucifer himself. The first thing the defense lawyer needs to do is to dehorn his client. You've got to get those horns off so the jury can see the defendant as a human being." In a more refined and dignified manner, Sam Graves had given Job the same advice.

Job saw no horns on the back of Ann's head as he stepped into the attorney's room, but Job had come to know his client. Over the past few months, he had seen Ann change from being a defendant to a person. Now, he understood what Richard Cramer was talking about. The evidence presented against her had been brutal, shocking by all standards of decency. At the beginning of this fourth day of trial, some, or all, or the jurors more than likely saw Ann with horns.

Job stepped to the back of Ann's chair, rested a hand on each of her shoulders and spoke to Mrs. McCoy, Dana, and Jane: "This lady who sits in front of me is a human being. Jane, you and Dana see her as your mother. Mrs. McCoy, you see her as your neighbor and friend. One cannot be a mother, a neighbor, a friend without being human. I rest my hands on her shoulders, her very human shoulders."

Job continued. "Mr. John Compton, a retired plumber is one of the jurors. You will soon face him from the witness stand. He sits in the front row, third seat from the right. Mr. Compton wears a stern face. He seldom smiles. Most of the time, he appears almost angry. Mr. Compton suffered a stroke that permanently damaged some of the muscles in his face. He no longer has the ability to wear a happy face. He is a human being. How does he see this lady that sits before me? He does not view this lady as mother, neighbor, or friend. Does he see Ann Tatum as a human being, or does he see her as something less than human?

"When you are in the witness box, you will face Mrs. Alice Thompson, a widow, a grandmother and retired nurse. Mrs. Thompson sits in the second row, fourth seat from the left. She is very active in her church. She strongly believes in the commandment not to kill. How does Mrs. Thompson see Ann Tatum? Does she view Ann as a human being?

"Seated in the witness box, you will likely feel as if you are in a strange and different world. You will be in a formal, regulated place and, if not careful, you may be intimidated by the formality of the trial. The judge is formal in his manners and speech. You cannot communicate with the jury in the same way that you have talked to others all your life. You are allowed to only answer the questions that are put to you.

"In spite of this, I want you to keep in mind that the trial is a human process. Mr. Compton, Mrs. Thompson, Judge Johnson, and you and I are humans. Each of you know Ann Tatum is a human being. I want the jurors to come to know her as a human. Thus far, they have heard terrible things about her. Now it is our turn to present evidence to the jury. Now it is our time to get the jury to see this lady as a mother, neighbor, friend, and, yes, even as a loving, faithful, and devoted wife."

Job paused in his talk, took his hands from Ann's shoulders, and walked to the opposite side of the table. Facing his client across the table, he again spoke to Jane, Dana, and Mrs. McCoy:

"Forgive me. I realize I was talking to myself more than to you. I sincerely want the jury to see my client the way I see her. I got carried away in my thoughts.

"When you are on the witness stand, I want you to listen carefully to all of the questions. Take your time and answer truthfully. If you don't know the answer to a question, just remember that the truthful answer is, 'I do not know.' Don't feel obligated to supply an answer simply because a question is asked. There are many questions in life that seem to have no answer. Just be yourself and tell the truth."

Ann rose from her chair, came around the table to where

Job stood and gently patted his arm, saying, "Job, you are not to worry about me. I'm at peace with myself and with the people who have a vote about my future. I'll be just fine, and I want you to be fine, too."

Job was relieved to see that Ann still retained her recently-found inner peace. The District Attorney had fired his big guns. Now it was Job's turn to return fire. The preparation time had ended, now the presentation. It was time to go into the courtroom, time to see if the jury could be persuaded to see Ann without horns. "It's almost time to begin," Job said, and led the way out of the attorney's room toward the courtroom door.

"Mr. Henry called just as I was leaving my house," Ann whispered as they passed through the courtroom door. "He said to tell you that he might be a little late getting to the courtroom, but he wanted you to know that he would be there."

Job was surprised when he walked into the courtroom to see Mr. Henry already seated in the back row seat he had claimed since the start of the trial. He carried a small book in his hand, titled "Selected Works of Robert Browning."

To Job's further surprise, Sally was seated beside Mr. Henry.

Sally gave Job a quick hug and said, "At the last minute I got a sitter for the kids and decided to come and meet Mr. Henry and help with moral support today. I guess you'll take all the help you can get? I wanted to see you present your side of the case."

Job hugged her back.

"Pretty girl, I'll take all the help I can get from this world or from angels." He glanced at Mr. Henry, then winked at Sally and made his way to the counsel table.

When Job paused in the back of the courtroom to greet Mr. Henry and Sally, Ethel McCoy took Ann aside, reached into a small bag, and removed an inexpensive silver chain and small, ceramic butterfly.

"Wallace Henry brought this for you last night," she said as she placed it around Ann's neck. "He wanted you to wear it today."

Before the judge took the bench, the court reporter handed Job a large envelope. "This is the transcript of all testimony of yesterday," she said. "The envelope I handed you yesterday had all the testimony of Monday and Tuesday. I will transcribe it and get the remainder typed as quickly as I can."

As Marie Moore, the court reporter, started to leave, Job said, "I know you will be pleased to know Sam Graves is doing nicely after his surgery. I understand you are long-time friends."

"Yes, friends of many years. I'm sorry he couldn't join you for this trial."

"I'll have three or four witnesses today and about the same tomorrow. I suspect Judge Johnson will bring us back to finish on Saturday. Will you be able to transcribe and type all this testimony overnight?"

The court reporter smiled and said, "For Sam Graves, I have done it before."

LISTENING TO THE BELL

All parties and attorneys were at their respective tables when Judge Johnson, dressed in his somber black robe, took the bench and addressed the courtroom.

"Ladies and gentlemen of the jury, I commend you on the close attention you have given the State as it presented its case. The State has now rested and the defendant, Ann Tatum, has the opportunity to present her case. The defendant has no obligation to present any evidence or testimony. It is the burden of the State of Georgia to prove, beyond a reasonable doubt, that the defendant is guilty of the crime with which she is charged. The defendant has no duty to prove her innocence. Should the defendant elect to present evidence and testimony, it is the duty of you, the jury, to give her evidence and testimony the same careful attention that you have given to the State's case."

Turning to Job Lee, the judge said, "Mr. Lee, what is your pleasure?"

"The defense calls Jane Atkinson."

The special defense of not guilty by reason of insanity opened the door to Ann's life history, particularly any history that might leave emotional scars. Job wanted to use Jane's voice to introduce to the jury parts of Ann's earlier life.

"Would you please state your name and address."

"Jane Tatum Atkinson. I live at 118 Scott Street, Carrollton, Georgia."

"Are you related to this lady who sits beside me?"

"She is my mother."

"Were you related to Edward Tatum?"

"He was my daddy."

"So the jury will understand, wasn't your maiden name "Caine?""

"Yes."

"Were you adopted by Edward Tatum?"

"Mr. Lee, that depends on what you mean by 'adopted.'"

"Explain what you mean."

"There is no piece of paper in any courthouse or public office that says I was legally adopted. But there are many memories. He was my daddy in every way possible. When Mother and Daddy married, I became his child. I remained his child. I am still his child and will be forever. The papers in the public offices identify me as 'Caine.' But those papers do not know me. The people who prepared the official records have never seen me, and they have never talked to me. Until I married, I always used the name 'Tatum.' I did that because in all ways that really matter, I was Jane Tatum. In all ways that count, I was adopted by my daddy."

"What is your age?'

"Twenty-six."

"How long have you lived in Carrollton and what caused you to move there?"

"I married Pete Atkinson about four years ago. He had a business in Carrollton and I have lived there with Pete since we married."

"Where did you live before moving to Carrollton and with whom?"

"When I was a baby, Mother took me to live with her daddy and her aunt who lived in Rome, Georgia. That is my first memory of a home. Next, we moved to an apartment here in Atlanta. Then Mama and Daddy bought the house that Mama lives in now."

"When you say 'Daddy,' who is the person you refer to?"

"The only Daddy I ever had."

"Would that be Edward Tatum?"

"Yes."

"Tell the jury what your formal education and work experience has been."

"Eight years ago, I graduated from Ponce De Leon High School. Mama and Daddy wanted me to go to college, but I didn't want to. We compromised by my going to a secretarial business school not too far from where we lived. Following business school, I worked for the McCurry Insurance Agency until three months before Pete and I married. I have worked in Pete's retail business since we married."

"Jane, what is your first memory of your mother?"

"I was about four years old. We were living with my Aunt Bee in Rome. Mama and Aunt Bee were sitting at the kitchen table, talking. I was playing with some jar rings and lids in the pantry. Aunt Bee was talking to Mama about the cost of food and clothes for me. She was encouraging Mama to try to get my biological father who lived in Ohio to assist in the cost of my clothes and food. Mama kept saying, "Let him keep his money. All I want is my little girl."

Jane paused to look at her Mother who was softly crying.

"Mama, I have never told you I remember that. I'm sorry to make you cry. Mr. Lee, that is my earliest memory of Mama. What Mama said at the kitchen table that day pretty well describes her. It tells you the kind of person she was, the kind of person she is, and will always be."

"Explain your answer."

"Mama's wishes have always been simple. Her wishes in life have always centered on her family. Family was her life that day I played in Aunt Bee's pantry and family has remained her life ever since."

"What is your first memory of the man you always call Daddy, Edward Tatum."

"That memory, too, comes from Rome. Mama and Daddy were not married then. Mama and I were at a picnic, sitting on one of Aunt Bee's blankets. A happy, smiling man came to where we sat. He drank some of Aunt Bee's ice-tea. He sat with us a long time and told me a story about a little dog that came to his house when he was a little boy. His story was so interesting, I wanted to hear another story. Job, the man was Ed Tatum. He became my daddy not too long after that. That first memory of Daddy, like my first memory of Mama, pretty well describes him for the remainder of his life. Up until about a year and a half before Daddy died, he remained a happy, smiling man. Up until he changed, he was always my happy, loving, smiling daddy."

"Describe the relationship of your Mother and Daddy until both of them changed."

"It was very good. Mama had her family. Daddy had his work and a few fishing ventures with Mr. McCoy, a neighbor. Mama enjoyed her home and family. Daddy would laugh at most everything and sometimes cut the fool. They did not hit any big bumps in the road. Their relationship was good."

"Before they changed, did either ever physically abuse the other."

"Never."

"Did either ever threaten abuse?"

"Never."

"Did either ever verbally abuse the other."

"Never."

"Did either parent ever have confrontations with non-family members?"

"The only thing I remember was when I was about eleven, Daddy saw a drunk man beating a child with a stick. Daddy got between the man and the child and told the man that he would have to whip him before he could whip the child any more. That's the only time I saw Daddy come close to getting in a fight."

"When did you first notice the changes that you say took place with both your parents?"

"This was after I married and moved to Carrollton, so I picked up on things gradually. Daddy had moved to

Memphis. Mama and Dana stayed in Atlanta. This was all planned. I was living in Carrollton and not seeing them too much. I noticed that Mama's Parkinson's was getting worse. Daddy started to miss coming back home for the weekends. He missed Dana's graduation that he had promised to attend. Job, I was out of the loop. When I visited Mama, I could see the change in her, but she denied having a problem. Mama is like that. She doesn't complain. Even at Christmas, 1971, I remember her patting my face and telling me that everything was all right. Mama kept things bottled up."

"Had any particular problem between your parents come to your attention before Christmas, 1971?"

"In early August, Dana called me and told me about a phone call Mama had received from a Mr. Walker about a month before. Mama had asked Dana not to tell me, but she did anyway. It was at that time everything seemed to go up and down, around and around. Once started, it never quit. I was not there, so I got just bits and pieces of what was going on."

"Explain."

"Daddy started playing a very mean game with Mama. Mr. Walker, the man who called, had told Mama that his wife and Daddy were having an affair. Daddy, at first denied any affair. Then he said it was over. Then he would say he was moving back to Atlanta. Then he would say he wanted Mama to come to Memphis to live with him. He would build Mama's hopes up and then let them fall. I tried to call Mama often. She continued to work all this time. But she was up and down like an elevator. Daddy would give her hope and then snatch the hope away. My poor Mama became a nervous wreck. I'm sorry. I'm upset. Could I be excused for a few minutes?"

LOVE OF MAMA AND DADDY

After a ten minute break, Judge Johnson called the court to order.

"Mrs. Atkinson, we will proceed. If you need another break, just look my way. Do you feel like going further at this time?"

"Yes. Thank you Judge Johnson."

"As I was saying, during the last few months before Daddy died, Mama's moods were up and down. Sometimes as high as the sky when she thought her marriage could be saved and her family held together. Sometimes when Daddy pulled the rug from beneath her feet and she thought her family was lost, she would be deeper than the ocean. My daddy had changed and Mama changed too."

"Jane, what are your present feelings toward both your daddy and your mother."

"I feel the same toward both of them. Even though Daddy is dead, I do not see him dead. I see him as alive as when he held my hand when I was a little girl, back when he told me stories. I see him as the loving father he always was.

I love both Mama and Daddy. I grieve over the changes in both. I'm hurt by the things Daddy did to Mama. I hurt over what Mama did to Daddy. There is much that I do not understand, but they are my parents and I love them. All Mama ever wanted was her family, and it's now broken into shards."

A QUESTION NOT ASKED

After Job finished questioning Jane, Aaron Bailey walked toward Jane and the witness chair where she was seated. Without the benefit of notes, he accurately reconstructed the substance of what Jane had said with his rhetorical questions.

"Mrs. Atkinson, I'm Aaron Bailey. I represent the people of Georgia in this case. I have listened carefully to your testimony, taking note of the substance of what you have said. To be sure the people of Georgia have heard correctly, I will try to restate the substance of your testimony, asking if you agree with what I say. Will you work with me in doing this?"

"Yes."

"You have stated that you always considered Edward Tatum to be your father. You have treated him that way. You have always loved him, you still love him, and you always will love him. Do I recall your testimony correctly?"

"Yes."

"You have told the jury that changes took place in the lives of both your daddy and mother and these changes started to appear after Edward Tatum took the job in Memphis. Am I correct?"

"Yes, Mr. Bailey."

"And, you have said during the time of these changes in the lives of your parents, you were living in Carrollton. Is my memory of what you said still accurate?"

"Yes."

"What is the driving distance between your house in Carrollton and the house where Edward Tatum died in Atlanta?"

"I really don't know. I'm not very good in estimating distance."

"If I told you the distance is slightly more than fifty-eight miles, would you agree with that?"

"Yes, sir. That sounds about right."

"And, you have told the jury that when these changes were taking place, Edward Tatum was living and working in Memphis, more than 350 miles away from where you lived."

"Yes."

"You have said you did not personally see your father more than a dozen times after he moved to Memphis and that you saw your mother an average of once each month during all this time. Am I still correct?"

"Yes, sir."

"With these things agreed to, don't you further agree that your opportunity to see changes in both your father and your mother was very limited?"

"That is true."

Bailey next moved to a subject that caused Job concern, the special defense of "Not Guilty by Reason of Insanity." Before asserting this defense, Job had discussed it with Ann, Jane, and Dana. The custom and practice of society in general was to be ashamed of, to hide and conceal anything that suggested mental defect or disease. To proclaim and to seek advantage of mental illness was, to most at the time, foreign and repulsive, Jane, in particular, had resisted the concept of asserting an insanity defense. For this reason, in his direct examination of Jane, Job had stayed away from the subject. Now, Bailey was moving to that subject and Job feared what Jane might say.

"Mrs. Atkinson, I must confess the District Attorney's Office has made an extensive search of your mother's family and of her ancestors. My office has established a family tree on your mother's side, going back three prior generations. The interest of the people of Georgia demanded a search of this nature. Do you know what we were looking for?"

"No."

"We were trying to see if there was any history of mental illness on your mother's side of the family and we found none. In fairness to the question and to be sure our search reached the right answer, do you know of any of your mother's ancestors ever having suffered a mental disease or defect."

"No, I've never heard of any."

Job breathed a sigh of relief when Bailey announced that he had no more questions. On direct examination, Job had intentionally omitted asking Jane's opinion on the insanity issue. He knew Jane found the subject repulsive and her answer to a question on the subject would be weak, if not harmful to the defense. Bailey, not knowing what Jane's answer would be, took what he could by establishing a lack of mental illness within the family and avoided Jane's opinion about Ann's sanity. Job called for his next witness.

DANA TATUM

"Your honor, the defense calls Dana Tatum."

After identifying herself as the daughter of Ed and Ann Tatum, Dana told the jury of the family plan that her father would take the job in Memphis while she and her mother would remain in Atlanta for Dana's senior year of high school, after which she and her mother would move to Memphis to join her father. She told of the family plan that she would enroll in college at Auburn after her high school graduation.

After these preliminary matters, Job Lee asked Dana to describe what she liked best about her father.

"Mr. Lee, there were many, many things that I loved about Daddy. I guess the best thing was his laugh. His ability to make me laugh, to make Mama laugh. Up until near the end, Daddy was such a happy man. Next best, I loved the things he and I did together, just the two of us. I loved it when he took me places, when we went to playgrounds and parks together. I loved when we went fishing together. I was very close to my daddy."

"You said he was a happy person up until near the end. What did you mean by that?"

"Daddy started to change after he moved to Memphis. He went there just after I finished my junior year of high school. After moving there . . . . " Dana's words vanished beneath sobs.

Judge Johnson gave her a moment, then said, "Young lady, do we need to stop for a rest? Anytime you need to rest, just look my way and we'll stop and take a rest."

Dana regaining her composure and continued, "Thank you, Judge. I'm okay now. I was trying to tell about my daddy changing. For the first few months that he was living in Memphis, he'd come home on some weekends. At first I didn't notice any changes in him. The big change took place after I graduated from high school in May of 1970."

"Did your daddy come home for your graduation?"

"No. Daddy had promised to come, but he called the day before and talked to me. He said he was sorry that he had to work and assured me we'd still make the trip to Auburn that we'd planned."

"Was there discussion that evening about your moving to Memphis?"

"Yes, it was still the plan that we would sell the house and move and I would go to Auburn in September. Daddy told Mama to list the house with a real estate agent. He said he was ready to get his family back together again."

"Dana, when did you become aware that major changes were taking place?"

"The first big thing that really upset me was when Mama and I found out that Daddy had taken the money from the education account." Dana's voice quivered. "Mr. Lee, I can't talk about that without crying. I'm sorry."

"That's fine, Dana. So the jurors will understand the order in which things developed, is it fair to say that the plan to sell the Atlanta house when you graduated did not materialize as planned?"

"That is correct."

"Is it also true that even though it was determined that the money had been removed from the education account, you were still able to enroll at Auburn in the fall of 1970?"

"Yes."

"Dana, I am aware that the money missing from the account was a painful experience. So, we'll move on to other things and maybe come back to this money issue later. Did you learn that your father was involved with another woman?"

"Yes sir. That was last July. I mean July of 1971, not this year."

"What happened at that time?"

"Mr. Lee, July 23, 1971, is when Mama's world started falling apart."

"How do you fix the date?"

"July 23rd is the birthdate of my friend, Julie Adams. We have shared birthdays for as long as I can remember. I went to Julie's house that night. It was almost midnight when I got home and I went to Mama's bed to tell her that I was back, but she wasn't in her bed. I found her sitting in the living room, in the dark, seated on the sofa next to the telephone table. When I turned on the light, I could tell she'd been crying, but she wouldn't tell me what she was crying about. She just insisted that I go to bed. That's when Mama's world started to cave in. I didn't know it at the time, but that weekend was the big beginning."

"Did your mother tell you what the problem was?"

"Not until Sunday night. When I got up Saturday morning, Mama was still sitting next to the phone. Except for going to the bathroom, she sat by the phone all day Saturday,

all that night, and all Sunday. She said that Daddy was supposed to call her and she didn't want to miss his call. I knew something was bad wrong, but Mama wouldn't tell me what it was."

"Did she finally tell you?"

"Yes. Late Sunday afternoon, she was still seated by the phone. I told her I was going to call Jane and let her know something was wrong. When I reached for the phone, I saw Mama's little poem about the butterfly on the table and I saw another piece of paper beside it. The other paper had the name of M. C. Walker written on it, together with a telephone number. When I asked Mama about that name and number, she cried and cried and cried. I thought she'd never stop crying. She kept saying that Daddy was going to call her. Over and over, she told me not to use the phone, that Daddy was going to call."

At this point, Judge Johnson, sensing Dana's emotions and tension, declared a late-morning recess of court. Ten minutes later the trial resumed.

"You were telling the jury about your conversation with your mother in the late afternoon of Sunday, July 25th. Dana, please continue with your statement."

"I couldn't get Mama under control. Finally, I told her

I was going next door and use Mrs. McCoy's phone to call Jane. I also said I was going to get Mrs. McCoy to come to our house and talk to Mama. When I said this, Mama picked up the paper with Mr. Walker's name and number and told me what had happened."

"What did she tell you?"

"She said that Mr. Walker had called her on Friday night when I was at Julie's party and told her his wife, Sara Walker, was having an affair with Daddy. Mama said she had called Daddy as soon as she talked to Mr. Walker. She said Daddy told her that he'd call her right back, but he never did. She said she was waiting by the phone for when he called back."

"Your mother had waited by the phone almost forty-eight hours for him to call. Is that right?"

"Yes, Mr. Lee. Mama's waiting for Daddy to call had just begun. From that weekend until now, she has waited for Daddy to call. In the following months, there were many times that Daddy said he was coming home and never showed up. Mama would be so excited when he'd promise we were going to be a family again. She would get the house ready. She'd get herself ready, prepare his favorite foods, and then he wouldn't come as he promised. Mama's life just went up and down, up and down."

"Dana, did you ever talk to your father about his involvement with Mrs. Walker?"

"I tried to, but he wouldn't talk to me about it. All he ever said was that adults make mistakes."

Realizing Dana had gained composure by talking about one painful memory, Job returned to the issue of the missing college money.

"If you can talk about it now, Dana, please tell the jury about your college money and how that affected your mother."

"For almost as long as I can remember, Daddy and I talked about me going to school at Auburn. That's where he went to school. When I was little, he and Mama started a savings account for my college education, and Mama worked part-time so she could contribute to my college fund. In August 1970, when my tuition for the first quarter at Auburn was due, Mama discovered that Daddy had withdrawn the money and closed the account. Mr. Lee, this hurt me very much. It hurt Mama. I would never have thought Daddy would do something like that."

"Were you able to enroll at Auburn as you had planned?"

"Yes. Mrs. McCoy, our next door neighbor, paid for my books and tuition for my first year and each month she sent me a check for $100."

"You have enrolled at Auburn for your second year. How has that been managed?"

"Before Mama and Daddy married, my grandfather, her father, purchased a paid-up two-thousand-dollar life insurance policy for Mama. Mama took the cash value of that policy and is using it to pay this year's tuition and books. I work part-time in the laboratory on Ag Hill at Auburn to help with my room and food."

"Dana, did you notice any changes in your mother's emotional or mental condition over the last seven or eight months before your father died?"

"Yes, many."

"In your own words, tell the jury what you observed."

"Mr. Lee, after Mama found out about Daddy and Mrs. Walker, she started to change. Both Mama and Daddy changed so much in such a short time, it now seems as if both Daddy and Mama are gone. It seems. . . . " Again, Dana's words were replaced by tears.

THE WORDS OF A GENTLE TOUCH

Judge Johnson interrupted and called for another recess, giving Job and Dana a break from the emotional testimony. As Job led Ann and Dana out of the courtroom, they passed Wallace Henry. He occupied the back-row seat he had claimed for the duration of the trial. As Dana walked by, Mr. Henry reached for and touched Dana's left hand. Nothing was said by either, except the words of a gentle touch.

Outside the courtroom and at the door of the attorney's room, speaking to Job and Jane, Ann requested the opportunity to speak to Dana alone. Once inside the attorney's room with Dana, Ann held her close and said nothing. Like Mr. Henry, she used the words of gentle touch as Dana wept.

MAMA: ONCE MORE THE BUTTERFLY

Following the recess with Dana back in the witness chair, Job Lee brought her back to the point where she left off.

"Dana, you were telling us that now it seems as if both your parents are gone. Please tell the jury what you mean."

"My daddy is dead. My mother is more dead than alive. My world has changed so much in such a short time. After Mama found out about Mrs. Walker, her life just seemed to leave her. She would spontaneously burst out crying and cry for long periods at a time. She became withdrawn. Many times she acted as if she didn't know what she was doing. She became forgetful, which was not at all like her. Her Parkinson's became much worse. Sometimes she was so depressed that I feared for her life."

"Dana, did your mother ever threaten suicide?"

"Not in so many words. But, yes, I could sense some of the things she was thinking."

"Give us an example of what you mean."

"Thanksgiving of 1971 is an example. Daddy had promised to come home for the holiday dinner. I came home from Auburn to see him and be with Mama, but Daddy didn't come. He didn't call. Mama tried to call him, but his number didn't answer. Mama and I ate our Thanksgiving Dinner alone. It was so sad. Mr. Lee, I love my daddy. I love my mama. . . . "

"Dana, do you need to take a break?"

"No, let me finish what I was trying to say. Some things are hard to put into words. After eating Thanksgiving dinner, Mama and I sat on the sofa and she recited the little butterfly poem to me. This is a poem her mother had taught her. Mother must have recited that poem to me a thousand times. Well, not that many, but at least a hundred times in my life.

After we had dinner, she again recited the poem:

Brown and furry
Little caterpillar in a hurry
Take your walk
To shady leaf or stalk
Spin and die
And live again, a butterfly.

"After reciting the poem, Mama reached over and patted me on my knee and said, 'Is it not a beautiful thought that a lowly worm can someday become a butterfly?' Mr. Lee, Mama was that lowly worm she was talking about. She didn't say that, but it's what she meant. I know she had hope of someday becoming a butterfly."

"Thank you, Dana." Then turning his attention to the judge and Aaron Bailey, Job announced, "I have no further questions."

TREADS LIGHTLY

Aaron Bailey, sensing that the jury would be offended by any vigorous cross-examination of the daughter of the deceased, asked Dana very few questions, though there was one telling exchange when Bailey asked Dana about Ann's waiting for the telephone call from Ed.

"Miss Tatum, you told Mr. Lee that since July 23, 1971, when Mr. M. C. Walker called your mother about the affair, that your mother called your father and he was supposed to call her back. Do you remember saying that?"

"Yes sir, Mr. Bailey. Mama said that Daddy promised to call her back, and she'd been waiting by the phone for his call.

281

Is that what you are asking about?"

"Yes, young lady. Please understand that all of us in the courtroom know this is a very difficult situation for you, and none of us want to add to your pain. But I wanted to ask you what you meant by that statement."

"I am sorry, Mr. Bailey, but I'm confused about what you're asking."

"Dana, it was a poor question on my part. Let me try again: You were talking about the weekend of July 23, 1971, and you said something to the effect that 'since that weekend until now, your mother has been waiting for your daddy to call.' Do you suggest that even now, when your father is dead, that your mother expects him to call?"

"Mr. Bailey, if you understood Mama, you would understand. Daddy was her life, and for the rest of her life, she will always be waiting for Daddy to call."

Following the noon recess, Mr. Henry returned to the courthouse with a single yellow rose for Dana. He also gave her the book of Browning's poems that he had been reading for the last couple of days.

DOT CAREY

Job's next witness was Dot Carey, who worked with Ann at the McCurry Agency. She testified as to Ann's marked deterioration in health over the last months of Ed's life and of taking Ann back to her house at noon the day Ed was killed.

"Mrs. Carey, explain the changes you observed in Ann

during the last part of 1971 and the first part of 1972, and explain how it came about that you drove Ann to her house the day Ed Tatum died."

"Starting in the fall months, Ann began to lose weight and the tremor in her hand became much worse. She started kind of shuffling her right foot when she walked, and she became more and more withdrawn. Ann is a very private person. She didn't talk about her problems. At first, the rest of us at the office thought her Parkinson's was just getting worse, but as time went by, we knew that something else was going on in her life, but we didn't know exactly what it was."

"Mrs. Carey, when you say 'we,' who are you talking about?"

"The ladies at the office. You men will never understand us ladies. Most of us talk about our families, our lives, and our world. The other ladies and I knew that something was wrong with Ann. We could just tell. We figured it had something to do with Ed, but Ann never said that was it."

"How did the deterioration of her health affect her job performance?"

"Ann never knew it, but she almost lost her job. Mr. McCurry, the owner of the agency, talked to me about letting Ann go and getting someone else to do her work. I knew Dana was in school and that Ann needed the income, so I assured Mr. McCurry that all of Ann's work would be done, even if some of us had to stay over, without pay, to finish her assignments. Yes, her work suffered, but the rest of us pitched in. Ann is the kind of person who would help, and we wanted to help her."

"Describe her emotional state during this time."

"Ann tried not to show her emotions, but she became more and more withdrawn. She never let herself cry at her desk, but sometimes she would go into the ladies room and cry. I found her crying there eight, ten or more times. Others in the office did the same thing. Mr. Lee, Ann Tatum became more of a shadow than a person. Like a shadow, we knew she was there, but like a shadow we couldn't touch her. We knew Ann was living in hell, but we didn't know the extent of her hell."

"How long have you worked in the same office with Ann?"

"Gosh, I really don't recall. She started part-time and then became full-time. I guess she first started about the time Dana entered high school. That's the way most of us women fix dates. We relate dates to our kids. Dana has been out of high school a year and a half now, so I guess Ann worked with me about four or five years before Ed died."

"And what about her emotions, did you notice changes?"

"She didn't show emotions. She showed a lack of emotions. More and more, she withdrew into herself. The biggest change was about her family."

"What do you mean, about her family?"

"Mr. Lee, Ann's family was her life. She didn't care about having a big house, or fancy furniture, or expensive clothes. She didn't give a rip about things like that. She just wanted a happy, healthy family. That is what she had always talked about, yet during the last few months before Ed died, she stopped talking about her family. She stopped talking about selling her house and moving to Memphis. That's the way her emotions changed. She simply stopped talking about the things she so dearly loved."

"Was it your opinion she suffered some mental illness?"

"I can't speak to that. What is a mental illness? Do not all of us, at times, suffer a mental illness? Did she act like what some of us call 'crazy?' No, she didn't. She always seemed to know who she was and what she was supposed to be doing. Sometimes she didn't seem to be able to do the things she was supposed to do, but I always felt she knew what she was supposed to do. The best that I can do in describing her emotional state is to say that she simply withdrew into a shell. I guess her shell was her sanctuary, her place of safety, and she didn't want to come out."

"Tell the jury about the day you drove her home, the day Ed Tatum died."

"Ann had brought her sandwich with her that day. She usually brought something for lunch that she could eat at the office. She was having a really bad, bad day. I had some errands to run after work, so Ann had driven her own car. Most of the time, she and I carpooled since we live near each other. But that day, she drove herself. Like I said, she was having a very difficult day. I asked Mr. McCurry if Ann and I could take an extra thirty minutes for lunch. He agreed. I fibbed to Ann by telling her I had to go back home for something and suggested she ride back to her house with me, eat her sandwich there, and rest. After a while I would come back and pick her up for our return to the office. She agreed and I dropped her off at her house and drove on to my house."

"When you dropped her off, did you see any motor vehicles at her house?"

"No. Her overhead garage door was closed. She seldom parked in the garage anyway. There were no vehicles in the drive or at the curb in front. I think I told you Ann had driven her car to the office, so her car was not there."

"How long was it before you came back to pick her up?"

"I would guess about forty-five minutes. It could have been more or less. When I returned, the front of the house was covered with police and emergency vehicles and I was turned away."

Dot Carey's testimony gave the District Attorney an opening that he wanted to emphasize.

DAMAGING TESTIMONY

After Job finished questioning Dot Carey, Aaron Bailey started his cross-examination.

"Mrs. Carey, you have stated that it was your opinion that Ann Tatum always knew what she was supposed to do?"

"Yes, to me it appeared that way."

"Well if she appeared to always know what she was supposed to do, would it be your opinion that she always knew what she was supposed not to do?"

"Yes, that would be my opinion."

"Would it be your opinion that on February 18, 1972, that she knew she was not supposed to shoot her husband in his chest?"

"Yes, I think Ann knew she was not supposed to do that."

"Is it your opinion that Ann Albert Tatum knew that she was not supposed to shoot her husband seven more times in his back as he tried to run away?"

"Yes, I think Ann knew she was not supposed to do that."

"At that date and time, is it your opinion that Ann Albert Tatum knew right from wrong?"

"Yes, I think Ann knew what was right and what was wrong. Mr. Bailey, Ann has always been a person of high morals. I have never had occasion to question her morals or her values. Ann is a good person."

"Yet, she shot her husband eight times?"

"Yes sir, it appears that way. This, I'll never comprehend."

NOT THE TIME TO PANIC

Job Lee fully understood the practical effect of Dot Carey's statement about Ann being able to distinguish right from wrong.

This distinction went to the very heart of the defense strategy of *not guilty by reason of insanity*. For more than 150 years, the legal and medical professions had wrestled with the concept that one should not be held legally responsible for one's action if such actions were the product of a diseased mind. One of the major problems between the medical and legal professions on this subject concerned language—the legal profession used legal terms to define the subject.

In most cases where insanity was asserted as a defense,

the lawyers, not understanding the language of the medical profession, adopted and argued the issue of insanity in moral terms of "knowing right from wrong." To the doctors, one's moral standards had no bearing on one's state of mental health.

On the difficult issues of degrees of mental impairment and the beginning and end points of such impairment, the standards adopted by most of the courts had evaded rather than answered these questions by adopting a simplistic standard of "what was the mental condition at the time of the occurrence in question?" It was Job Lee's belief, and hope, that Judge Johnson would instruct the jury about this matter.

Job also knew that the judge would instruct the jury that they might consider the opinions of lay people, such as Dot Carey, on the complicated issue of mental capacity. Mrs. Carey's testimony about Ann's knowing the difference between right and wrong when she shot Ed eight times was a great body-blow to the defense. But, Job realized that the middle of the trial was not the time to stop and lick one's wounds. The judge and jury waited for him to call his next witness. Lee intended to call three more witnesses for the defense.

"Your honor, the defense calls Ethel McCoy."

ETHEL McCOY AT EIGHTY-NINE

"Please state you name, address, and tell us what acquaintance you have with Ann Tatum and her family."

Mrs. McCoy was a small woman, barely five feet tall.

She wore an old business-style lady's suit and a faded blue button-down sweater underneath her jacket. Instead of answering Lee's question, she gained favor with everyone in the courtroom by turning toward Judge Johnson and saying, "Young man, you keep this courtroom colder than a meat locker."

"Thank you for calling me a young man," answered the judge. "You're not the first to rightfully complain about the temperature. It seems we can send people to the moon, but can't regulate courtroom temperatures. I'll ask the bailiff to check with the maintenance people to see if anything can be done."

"Thank you, your Honor. My circulation isn't as good as it used to be and I tend to get cold. In fact, it seems that very little about me is as good as it once was."

The judge continued the dialogue. "The lawyers will ask you this anyway, so I may as well save us all some time. How old are you, and can you tell us a little about your life?"

Smiling nicely, Mrs. McCoy replied, "I was born at my grandfather's house in rural west Alabama 89 years ago. My father inherited the farm when my grandfather died, and what proved to be a small oil deposit was found on the farm when I was young. The oil income lasted long enough for me to earn degrees at the University of Mississippi, Tulane University, and the University of Texas. I have served as Professor of Latin and Greek at several universities, and I retired from teaching in 1950. My husband and I had five children, two of whom have predeceased us. We have lived quietly and simply, avoiding cocktail parties as if they carried the plague.

There, young man, you have my life story."

Job Lee sensed that the jury liked Ethel McCoy and her "take-charge" style, even taking charge of the judge, and it appeared obvious that Judge Johnson liked her, too. She seemed to be everyone's great-grandmother.

With a smile, the judge said, "Thank you, Professor. I'll see if I can get the heat turned up in this room before we all freeze. Now Mr. Lee will have some questions for you."

From the outset, Aaron Bailey sensed that Mrs. McCoy represented a danger to the State's campaign for a guilty verdict. There was an appearance, a bearing about her that both commanded respect and dominated the moment. Mr. Bailey, as do all trial attorneys, wanted to be the dominant one. Dominance was an essential part of the trial process, and Aaron Bailey, with his eye on the Governor's chair, did not want to play second fiddle. Yet, with Mrs. McCoy, he seemed to sense that anyone who matched wits with her was likely to occupy the second chair. That's why, early in her testimony with Job Lee, Bailey whispered to his Assistant District Attorney, Wayman Burris, "I want you to handle this lady's cross-examination, but be careful."

Mrs. McCoy, in plain and simple language, told the jury of the Tatum family moving next door and of the warm relationship she had with Ann, Ed, and their girls. She described the passing years of interrelationships of the two families as "very good years."

"Mrs. McCoy, over these years," Job asked, "did you notice, other than normal aging, any changes in either Ann or Ed Tatum?"

"In Ed, no. He moved to Memphis around the middle of 1970, and I only saw him a few times after that."

"What were your personal feelings toward Ed?"

"I always enjoyed a good relationship with him. He was a very friendly, happy person, and very easy to like. He was closer to my husband than to me. They were fishing buddies. I personally never had a moment of difference with Ed. We respected each other and acted accordingly."

"Tell us about your personal relation with Ann."

"Very, very close. In some ways, Ann has been closer to me than my own two daughters. Mr. Lee, you are a young man, but time will teach you that sometimes one may be closer to other young people than they are to their own brood of chicks. Sometimes the parent/child relation precludes too much closeness."

"Other than aging, have you noticed changes in Ann?"

Before answering, Mrs. McCoy turned in the witness chair and looked silently at Ann. The silence became deafening before she looked back to Job.

"Yes, there have been changes. Changes that tear at both her heart and mine."

"Fix the dates as best you can, and tell us about these changes."

"I was aware of Ed taking the job and moving to Memphis and of Ann's plan to join him there after Dana finished high school. I hated to see them go, but life has taught me that chicks leave the nest. Ann was happy with the plan. To understand Ann, one must understand her values."

"What were her values?"

291

"I can spell her main value in one word, 'Family.'"

"What do you mean by that?"

"All that Ann ever wanted was a healthy, happy family. She had no desire for the frills, bells, and whistles of life. She merely wanted the wonderful peace-of-mind of having her family near. It was when she started losing her family that her life started a nose-dive that seems without end."

"When did you first notice this nose-dive?"

"It's impossible to fix an exact date. By the time Dana graduated from high school, I noticed Ann was more and more withdrawn. She started losing weight and her hand-tremor, at times, became much worse. I knew something had gone wrong."

"Did she talk to you about any trouble?"

"Not at first. Ann always liked to wear a happy face when it came to her family. It is about the time that Dana graduated from high school that Ann started sharing some of her personal problems with me."

"Would you mind sharing with the jury some of the things Ann told you?"

"To give you an honest answer, yes, I would mind. Ann talked to me in confidence. For me to tell such things would make me feel I was breaching Ann's trust in me. If I must tell these things, I must ask Ann's forgiveness in my doing so."

"Mrs. McCoy, I think everyone in the room both understands and appreciates your sense of trust. Let's wait and see if Ann can relate such things on her own behalf. If, for any reason, Ann isn't able to provide these answers, I may need to recall you as a witness at a later time."

"Thank you, Mr. Lee."

"Now, I want to ask you questions about Ann's apparent mental stability in February 1972. You have already told the jury that Ann became more and more depressed and often very forgetful, sometimes not appearing to fully understand what was going on around her. In February, what was your opinion about her mental capacity?"

"Mr. Lee, let's use plain language. Are you asking me if I thought Ann was crazy?"

"If you prefer to use that term, yes."

"No, that is a term I do not like, but it is often used. In my life, I've done many crazy things. I'll bet you and Mr. Bailey have too. I'll even be so bold as to suggest that Judge Johnson has done some crazy things. Does that make any of us crazy? I think not. Mr. Lee, are you asking me if I think Ann shot Ed of her own free will and accord?"

"Yes, that is what I ask."

"Mr. Lee, Ann shooting Ed was very wrong. Let me be understood about that. Ed was a human being. For anyone to intentionally take his life was wrong. Did the loving, tender, caring Ann that I've always known intentionally kill him? Should I live a million years, I'll never believe that. Call it what you may. Call it crazy if you wish. Call it mental derangement or impairment. Use whatever silly words the human tongue can speak, but when Ann killed the man she dearly loved, forces beyond her control were in command."

"Thank you, Mrs. McCoy. No further questions."

Assistant District Attorney Wayman Burris carefully undertook the cross-examination, but Ethel McCoy maintained her control of the courtroom throughout her time on the stand.

"Dr. McCoy, Dana Tatum told this jury that her mother had been waiting and expecting Ed Tatum to call her since the weekend of July 23, 1971. Dana told the jury that even though her father is dead, her mother still expects her father to call. Is it your opinion that Ann Tatum still expects her dead husband to call her?"

"Mr. Burris, are you now asking if I think Ann is crazy? We have already, as my daddy would say, hoed that row of beans."

"No, I merely ask if it is your opinion that Ann expects a dead man to speak to her?"

"In Greek Literature, I have read of such things."

"That is very interesting. Tell us what you've read."

"It will be a rather long answer."

"Mrs. McCoy, if you can tell us how a dead man might talk, we'll take all the time you wish."

Aaron Bailey tugged Burris' elbow, trying to urge him to withdraw the question, but Ethel McCoy had already started her answer.

"Many years ago, more than 200 years before Christ, Callimachus, a famous Greek poet, lived at Alexandria, Egypt. Across the Mediterranean Sea, in ancient Caria, lived his friend, Heraclitus. As time and circumstance permitted, the two would visit each other and enjoy long talks into the night. The mode of travel was slow and the distance that separated them was great.

"One sad day, Callimachus received word that his old

friend had died. For weeks after hearing this, Callimachus was disturbed. Often in the middle of the night he would hear his friend's voice in the song of the night birds.

"Callimachus took his quill and paper and wrote a beautiful poem about the voice of the dead man who still spoke to him. The translation from Greek goes something like this:

They told me, Heraclitus, they told me you were dead,
They brought me bitter news to hear and bitter tears to shed.
I wept, as I remembered, how often you and I
Had tired the sun with talking and sent him down the sky.

And now that thou art lying, my dear old Carian guest,
A handful of grey ashes, long long ago at rest.
Still are thy pleasant voices, the nightingales awake,
For death, he taketh all away, but them he cannot take.

"Yes, Mr. Burris, I think Callimachus heard the voice of his dead friend. And yes, Mr. Burris, I think Ann yet listens for Ed's voice, and I think she always will. One always wants to hear the voice of a loved one."

OLD FRIEND'S STEADY HAND

Once again, Wallace Henry was seated in his back row seat as Ann, her girls, Ethel McCoy, and Job left the courtroom at the end of the day's trial. He asked Mrs. McCoy where he could find a copy of the poem she had recited to Mr. Burris.

"Do you believe the dead can speak, Mr. Henry?"

"After hearing you, I think they can."

"Good," she replied. "I'll get a copy for you. Now, let's get out of here. This room is still cold enough to hang a fresh-killed hog."

JOB'S THOUGHTS ALLOW NO REST

Job Lee hadn't slept well since the beginning of the trial. During his hours in court, the adrenalin rush kept him alert to everything that was taking place in the courtroom. As Ann's attorney, he gave her the very best that he had to give. He didn't realize how tired he was this day until the judge rapped his gavel to signal the end of the day's testimony.

The jurors had given Ethel McCoy their undivided attention during her testimony. Job was preoccupied with speculations of how they perceived her. *How did the jurors view what she had said? Were they favorably impressed? Did they find her believable?* These were the questions that kept him from hearing his wife as she spoke to him over dinner.

"Job, you're not listening to me. Remember what you once told me about the warning of your law professor?"

"Babe, I'm sorry. I know. What did you say?"

"You told me one of your professors had warned that someday a case would become your jealous mistress. Remember?"

"Yes, it was Professor McGee. He was a former federal prosecutor who participated in German war crime cases. In that caustic manner of his, he warned that it would happen to all of us, and that when we realized we had the mistress it would be too late to do anything about it."

"Do you realize it now?"

"Do you mean Ann's case?"

"My love, do you have any other?"

"You're right, Sally. My other few trial cases are on the backburner until this is over. Ann's case has seduced me. It's even taken me away from you. I'm sorry to be so preoccupied."

"I understand, Job. I'm actually pleased that Ann has you. Just remember, no matter how far your work takes you away, I'm here waiting your return."

"Sally, this lifetime will never allow me to forget you. I hope you have Margaret lined up to keep the kids so I can have you with me for the rest of the trial," Job said as he reached for Sally's hand.

She let him squeeze her hand tight and said, "Come on, honey, it's almost midnight. Let's go to bed and let me hold you close."

THE COMET RETURNS TO EARTH

Job had called all but two witnesses: Dr. Battle and Ann. He knew Dr. Battle would make a good impression on the jury and he wanted the last impression of his case to be a strong one. Initially, he'd planned on using the doctor as his last witness and Ann next-to-last, but after Ann had devel-

297

oped this inward calmness that he hadn't seen before, he reconsidered. Physically and outwardly, Ann Tatum was a pitiful wreck. Now, with this mysterious change, which Sally suggested was the work of an angel, Job toyed with the notion of making Ann his last witness, rather than next-to-last.

Job was on his third cup of coffee the Friday morning when Sally came into his study.

"I see you're up early again. Will the trial finish today?"

"I don't think so. I still have Dr. Battle and Ann to present. Their testimony will likely take more than a full day, and the District Attorney may call some rebuttal witnesses. The judge is holding our feet to the fire by telling the lawyers that we are going to continue the trial until it is finished, even if we have to work on Sunday and Christmas day. He may be bluffing. Judges try to move things along. We might finish the testimony sometime tomorrow."

"How do you feel?"

"Scared to death. I'm in over my head. I wish Sam Graves were sitting at the table with me. Did you reach his wife yesterday?"

"No, she is still at the hospital with Sam. His secretary says he continues to improve, and there is talk in the office of sending Jennifer Cosby to the hospital to get him out of bed."

"Jennifer Cosby?"

"Yes, the little lady who has been a legal secretary for seventy-five years. Sam's secretary says her bark can move Stone Mountain. I'll try to reach Sam's wife again today. The court reporter told me that her office door is never locked and I can use the phone whenever I wish."

"If Jennifer Cosby told me to get out of bed, I'd quickly do it. Babe, I'm glad you're getting to see part of the trial."

"Job, you said you were scared to death about Ann's case. I've heard you say it's not the lawyer's job to make the difficult decision of whether the defendant is guilty or not. More than once, you've told me that it's the responsibility of the jury. Is it the question of guilt that scares you?"

"Yes, it is. It's easy to be philosophical until push comes to shove, and then things become difficult. Sally, I've allowed myself to identify too closely with Ann Tatum, and I've gotten too close for my own good."

"That may be good for her, though."

"How so?"

"It means you have your heart in it, and the jury will know that. Is Ann going to testify today?"

"That was my plan, but I'm having second thoughts. She's changed, I don't understand why, but there's something different about her. I told you about it."

"Will Mr. Henry be back today?"

"I think so. Ethel McCoy promised to bring a poem for him. Why do you ask?"

"I just do. If Mr. Henry is back, it doesn't matter when she testifies. If he is there, she'll do just fine."

"I guess this is more of your angel stuff."

"That's right. This is some more of my angel stuff. Now we had better get going or we're going to be late."

Before leaving home, Job made a phone call to Ann's doctor.

"Dr. Battle, this is Job Lee. We're in the final stages of

Ann's trial, and if you can come to the courthouse first thing this morning, I can put you on as the first witness of the day."

"Sure, Job. What time do you need me?"

"Can you be there by 9:00? That will give us some time before the judge comes in at 9:30. I have one or two things I want to ask you before you take the stand."

"I'll be there. This is in Judge Johnson's courtroom?"

"Yes. I know you're busy, Dr. Battle, so I'll get you on and off the stand as quickly as I can. Even so, your testimony may take the better part of the day."

"Job, take all the time you need."

FIFTH DAY OF TRIAL

The change in the jury was noticeable. The newness of the courtroom was gone. The formality of court procedure had become the expected. The once amusing sound of the bailiff rattling the keys in his pocket as he walked had become somewhat irritating. Judge Johnson's stiffness as he sat behind the bench had disappeared. The jurors called each other by first name and knew something of each other's private lives. Notwithstanding the judge's contrary instruction, the jurors' private comments were occasionally exchanged about what a witness had said and if the testimony was believable. Christmas was just three days away. Would they finish soon? Some had more shopping that still needed to be done. Some wondered if Ann Tatum would testify. Her attorney, in his opening statement had said she would. What would she say?

What could she say that would make a difference? All wanted to hear Ann's side of the story. Some of the jurors were tired and just wanted to go home, but none had lost their interest in knowing why Ed had been killed.

Dr. Battle took the witness stand on Friday morning and told the jury of his medical training and experience.

"I was born in Williston, North Dakota. I graduated from the University of North Dakota, in 1937. I graduated from The Minnesota School of Medicine in 1940 and did an internship and residency at Simmons Clinic for Mental Illness in Seattle, Washington. I went into the Army in 1943, specializing in the study and treatment of soldiers suffering from what was commonly called 'shell shock.' In late 1944, I was seriously wounded and honorably discharged from service. After service, I completed another residency at Menninger Clinic in Topeka, Kansas. At Menninger, I met and married a pretty girl from Atlanta. I opened my practice in Atlanta in 1947. Atlanta has been my home ever since."

Dr. Battle looked the part of being a doctor. He was distinguished in appearance with a head full of gray hair that was almost white. For reading, he slipped on his half-circle glasses that rested on the tip of his nose. He had an easy, quick smile that put his audience at ease.

Wanting to avoid the appearance of the doctor being a "hired gun" for the defense, Job was careful to first question Battle about the number of times he had offered expert testimony in a courtroom.

"Dr. Battle, have you testified as an expert in criminal trials before?"

"Yes, on quite a few occasions."

"Do you remember how many times?"

"Not really. I pay no attention to such matters. Possibly twenty or more."

"Have you been called as a witness by both the defense and the State of Georgia?"

"Yes. Over the past twenty-five years, both the prosecution and the defense have called me. I would guess that I have been called by the State about seventy-five percent of the time. Mr. Bailey has called me in on several of the cases he's handled. Others in his office have called on me. Don't ask me the numbers. I don't keep a record."

"Are you being paid by anyone to appear as a witness in this case?"

"No."

"Do you expect to be paid by anyone in the future for being a witness in this case?"

"No."

"Thank you, Doctor. Now, can you tell me if Ann Albert Tatum, the lady seated beside me, is your patient?"

"Yes. She was referred to me by her family physician, Dr. Shelby Lamar. He called on April 21, 1972, and I first met with her on April 24, 1972. Since that date, I have seen Mrs. Tatum a total of fourteen times. Her last visit to my office was on December 6, 1972."

"Did Dr. Lamar provide you with a medical history of Ann Tatum?"

"Yes, he reported that Mrs. Tatum had enjoyed reasonably good physical health until the middle of 1971. She had contracted Category One Parkinson's disease some five years ago. This problem was not life-threatening and Mrs. Tatum did not see Dr. Lamar between the dates of August 1970 and October 1971. During this interim, her only contact with Dr. Lamar's office was for renewals of a prescription of Carbidopa-Levodopa 25-100 four times a day that he ordered for her Parkinson's disease in 1966."

"Dr. Battle, does this medicine impair one's mental capacity?"

"No, it helps to control the tremors of Parkinson's. Parkinson's is a chronic, progressive disease. It is not curable. This medicine treats the symptoms. It tends to lower one's blood pressure and may cause dizziness, but it does not impair one's mental capacity."

"Thank you. Please continue with the medical history Dr. Lamar provided."

"Dr. Lamar saw her on October 7, 1971, and noted in the patient's chart: 'fourteen pounds weight loss, marked tremor increase, withdrawn, no objective finding. Suggested sleep medication; patient declined.' Dr. Lamar saw her again on November 3, December 17, 1971, and January 17, 1972. He noted a continued loss of weight, symptoms of severe depression, and on her visits in December and January, suggested that she see a mental health specialist. She declined. His notes of December read: 'Possibly suicidal.' His notes on January 17, 1972, read: 'patient likely suicidal, declines referral to mental health specialist.'"

"Dr. Battle, did Dr. Lamar's record contain other notes of interest to you?"

"Yes. On February 29, 1972 Dr. Lamar's nurse noted on the chart that on the 22nd, Jane, the patient's daughter called to say it was urgent that her mother see Dr. Lamar. An appointment was made for that day. As before, Jane called shortly before the appointment time and said her mother refused to come.

The last entry in Dr. Lamar's record was given to me is dated April 21, 1972, and it reads: 'Without appointment, patient brought to office by neighbor identified as Ethel McCoy. Mrs. McCoy's insistence that I see Mrs. Tatum—'even if it takes all night'—was well taken. Examination revealed patient in complete withdrawal, complete introspection. Called Carl Battle. He will see her Monday.'

"When Dr. Lamar called, did he say anything about Ann being charged with a crime?"

"Yes. When asking if I could see Mrs. Tatum, he explained that she had been charged with the murder of her husband. He said he felt that she might take her own life even before her husband died, and with the recent events, his concerns were greatly increased. I agreed to see her three days later, April 24."

"What were your initial observations of Ann Tatum?"

"Her physical condition was much the same as she appears at this time. Noticeably thin, marked hand tremor, irregular walking motion on her right side. Very reticent."

"Explain her reticence."

"Ann Tatum is highly resistant to a discussion of any personal problem."

"What about any family problem?'

"Mr. Lee, her family is her person. She does not separate

her persona from that of her family. To her, they are one and the same."

"Do you have a judgment as to why that is so?"

"Yes. Mrs. Tatum was twelve years old when her mother died. Her death cast the young Ann into the role of mother to a two-year-old baby sister. The baby sister died within a year or two of their mother's death, and Ann unfairly blamed herself for the death of her younger sister. She went on to marry young, during which time she had a baby and a husband who drank and cheated. She walked away from that marriage, taking only her baby girl and not asking for child support. It is my opinion that these three events—the deaths of her mother and her baby sister and then her failed early marriage, set her on a most difficult path for life."

"What do you mean in saying these events put her on a difficult path?"

"Mr. Lee, I don't mean to belittle the teachings of the Bible, when it says something to the effect that 'Blessed are the peacemakers for they shall see the kingdom of God.' That statement, as far as it goes, may well be the truth. I personally hope so. But the statement omits another truth. It is my judgment that the life of the peacemaker is often hell on this earth."

"Please explain."

"At some point in her life Ann Tatum took a vow to be a peacemaker. It was not an open vow. She didn't make a verbal declaration, but she took a secret, personal vow that if she ever married again, come hell or high water, she would make it last. She vowed to do whatever it took to make another marriage a permanent one. She assumed one of life's most difficult roles, that of being a peacemaker."

"In your judgment, does she see herself as a peacemaker?"

"Not at all. That is part of a peacemaker's problem. They don't see themselves. They see others. It's the others they want to please, not themselves."

"I see, Doctor. Did you obtain a personal history from Ann Tatum?"

"With some difficulty, yes."

"What was the difficulty? Did she fail to cooperate with you?"

"Oh, no. She wanted to fully assist me. She wanted in all things to please me, which, again, is the nature of a peacemaker."

"What was the difficulty?"

"May I start at the beginning and give a narrative answer?"

"Please do."

"In the care of my patients, I try to let them come to me. I try not to press for details or answers. So it was with Mrs. Tatum. When I first met with her, I concurred with Dr. Lamar's opinion that she was likely suicidal. I didn't tell her that, but I felt she was a strong candidate for self-destruction. She didn't want to tell me things and I did not press for information. It was evident from the start that she was in great emotional pain. Ann Tatum sets high standards for herself, high values. To understand Mrs. Tatum, one must understand how she viewed her home."

"Explain what you mean."

"Early in life, probably about the time her first marriage ended, she became determined that her home would, at all costs, be protected. Early in life she determined to do whatever it took to have and protect the place of security that she called 'home.' The better I came to know and understand Mrs. Tatum, the more evident it became that she was and is a peacemaker whose mission in life is to have a safe, secure home and family. She wanted this, not for herself, but for those she sought to protect, her daughters and husband."

"Back, for a moment, to the extent of her cooperation with you. Did there come a time in your treatment when it was your opinion that she became fully cooperative?"

"Fully, no. To the extent of which she is able, yes."

"Explain what you mean."

"Mr. Lee, there are some things in life that are simply too painful to talk about. Some things hurt too much to relate to others. I dare say that virtually everyone in this courtroom has, at some time during life, said or done something they found too painful to talk about, something they never shared with others. Ann Tatum carries with her some memories she cannot handle. Those memories are a real and present threat to her. Those hidden memories are threats of death, and to preserve her own life, she conceals them, even from herself. Slowly, over the months that I've treated Mrs. Tatum, she has overcome parts of her reluctance to relive some of the things she has experienced. For that reason, I say to the extent that she is able, she has cooperated with me. This is not to question her honesty with me. It is simply to question her ability to recall and to relate. It's a question of her capacity. She's done her best, and I cannot ask more than that."

"What history of marital discord did you obtain from her?"

"In our last two visits, she was able to relate most of this experience. She related the family plan of moving to Memphis after their daughter graduated from high school, the disruption of those plans and the changes in her husband, beginning in late 1970 and greatly increasing in July 1971. She told me of her husband's promises to return to the family and the number of times he broke those promises. It's my judgment that she was subjected to mental abuse by her husband beyond her ability to handle."

"Explain."

"My patient related a series of broken promises by Mr. Tatum. She told me of his becoming involved with another woman and his boasting to her of the youth and charm of the younger woman he was involved with. She told me of his firm promise, on several occasions, to end his affair and return to his family, only to betray those promises. She told me of hope restored, then of hope destroyed again. It is my judgment that she was subjected to mental abuse beyond her capacity to handle."

"What, in your medical judgment, was the result of this repeated mental abuse?"

"Ann Tatum related the events of February 18, 1972, to me. She told me of her husband bringing his girlfriend to their home, and that she has no memory of anything that happened afterward, including killing her husband. In her subconscious mind, I think she recalls that tragic moment, but I think the horror of what she did will not permit her conscious mind to bring that memory to the surface."

"What else did she relate to you about the events of February 18?"

"She told me that she took the pistol from a nightstand drawer, intending to kill herself, and that her next recollection was of sitting on the floor beside her husband. Mr. Lee, it is my judgment that Ann Tatum was emotionally and mentally pushed beyond her ability to handle the stress of her family breaking apart, and that her mental dam broke. Each of us has a breaking point. If we are pushed beyond that point, we react in a manner that is both out of character and beyond our control."

"Dr. Battle, assume for the sake of the question that Ann Tatum shot her husband once in the chest and seven more times in his back. Assuming that, and based on your experience and the history of your patient, in your judgment, did Ann Tatum know right from wrong when she was shooting her husband?"

"Mr. Lee, here is where the legal profession and the medical profession find their differences on this subject. Concepts of 'right and wrong' are moral ones and very inexact concepts at that. They are concepts with many meanings. At the time in question, Ann Tatum was not thinking in terms of right or wrong. At the time, she was not in control of her thinking. Other forces had taken charge. Did she know right from wrong? No. At the time, she knew neither right nor wrong. Her mental dam had broken, and she was part of a flood."

LAWYERS PLAY THEIR ROLE

Before finishing with Dr. Battle, Job traced the entirety of Ann's life. The defense of *not guilty by reason of insanity* had opened a legal door that permitted the jury to consider all aspects of Ann's life that might have a bearing on the question of sanity.

Aaron Bailey did his best with objections to limit the scope of this testimony, while Job Lee did his best to keep the door open. In the legal tug-of-war on this subject, Bailey was at a marked disadvantage. He had to be careful not to appear to the jury as an obstructionist, a man who objected to anything and everything. This concern demanded a measured use of "objections" by the seasoned District Attorney.

After Job finished questioning Dr. Battle, he turned his witness over to Aaron Bailey, but before Bailey could ask his first cross-examination question, Judge Johnson called the two lawyers to his bench for a side-bar discussion.

Leaning across his bench and carefully whispering so the jurors could not hear, the Judge, talking to Aaron Bailey said, "I am satisfied that the defense has presented sufficient evidence to entitle the jury to consider the question of insanity. I am not at all sure the jury will find the evidence sufficient, but they are entitled to consider the question in their deliberations. Mr. Bailey, how long do you think your cross-examination of Dr. Battle will last? I will not hold you to your answer, but I would appreciate your best estimate."

"Not more than two hours, your Honor."

"Do you expect to call a rebuttal expert?"

"No sir, at present I have no such intent. However, I would like to reserve that right, should I change my mind."

"Your right is reserved."

Addressing both attorneys, Judge Johnson advised, "It's almost 2:00 p.m.. If the State can keep it down to two hours on cross with Dr. Battle, I'll adjourn court early so I can review with you what I expect to tell the jury about the insanity defense. Before you argue your case, you are entitled to know what my instruction to the jury will be on that subject."

Job Lee was grateful to know that the Judge would hold such a pre-charge conference. He didn't want to tell the jury what he expected the Judge to tell them about the insanity defense and then have the Judge instruct them differently.

The Judge released them from the sidebar, and Job returned to his seat next to Ann. Aaron Bailey returned to his position in front of the witness stand.

"Good afternoon, Dr. Battle. We've known each other several years now."

"Good afternoon to you, too, Aaron. It's nice to see you again."

"Dr. Battle, you told the jury that when it comes to the question of insanity, the legal and medical professions speak two different languages. Did I understand you correctly?"

"I was speaking figuratively. To borrow from Winston Churchill when he spoke of Great Britain and the United States being two nations separated by a common language, that is what I meant about our two professions. We both speak in the same tongue. We just attach different meanings to the same words."

"Does the medical profession attach better definitions?"

"My friend, your use of the word 'better' illustrates my point. Our legal system is largely founded on moral convictions, particularly when it comes to what the legal system calls 'insanity.' My profession tries—it doesn't always have success, but it tries—to deal in scientific terms, terms with a reasonably fixed meaning."

"Dr. Battle, you have also said that Ann Albert Tatum was a very controlled person, that she kept her emotions under wraps, completely bottled-up."

"Yes, that is my opinion."

"If that were the case, how does one explain that she obviously shot her husband once in his chest and seven more times in his back as he tried to flee? The evidence shows nothing to suggest she acted in self-defense. There is no evidence that Edward Tatum ever, during the entire marriage, physically abused his wife. There is no evidence that he ever threatened to do so. How do you reconcile your statement that the defendant was a very controlled person with her killing her husband in such a violent manner?"

"All of us need to understand that we have a breaking point. Even a twenty-four-inch I-beam made of the hardest steel known to man has a breaking point. If enough stress is applied, both man and steel break. I agree with you. There is nothing to suggest that Mr. Tatum ever physically abused his wife, or even threatened physical abuse."

"Is that what the defendant told you? Did she say there had never been any physical abuse?"

"Yes, those are her words."

"In her talks with you, did she ever use the word 'abuse' in describing Edward Tatum?"

"No."

"So, Ann Tatum made no complaint of abuse."

"She made no complaint. She's not the complaining kind. Had she been a complainer, a fighter, her husband would likely be alive today."

"Surely, Dr. Battle, you do not suggest that her non-aggressive nature—her kindness, if you would—killed her husband."

"Aaron, you have said it better than I could."

"So, Doctor, you would have this jury believe that Mrs. Tatum killed her husband out of kindness?"

"No, that's not what I'm saying. What I'm saying is that had Mrs. Tatum been a more assertive person, she would have released her emotions along the way. She would have complained, fussed, even fought with her husband and vented some of her hurt and sorrow. Had she released some of her pain, she likely would not have finally exploded in such an out-of-character manner."

"Dr. Battle, you seem to take us back to square one. You seem to say she killed her husband because she was such a kind and gentle person. You seem to say she shot him eight times out of kindness."

"Mr. Bailey, you are a clever man with words, and in that department I am not your match. Mrs. Tatum suffered no physical abuse. She suffered much worse, great mental abuse. The bruise left by physical abuse fades and is gone within a few days. The unseen bruises of mental abuse sometimes last forever. When any human being is subjected to enough mental abuse, they break. No matter how loving, gentle, or kind they may be, they break. Sometimes they take their own life. Sometimes they take the life of another. It is my opinion that on February 18, 1972, Ann Tatum intended to take her own life and that her emotional explosion caused her to take the life of her husband instead."

"Ahh, my good doctor, now you seem to say that Edward Tatum interfered with her aim of the pistol, that instead of shooting herself, her husband caused her to change the direction of the pistol barrel, one-hundred and eighty degrees, and shoot him instead of herself."

"Mr. Bailey, as I said, you are a clever man with words. You, again, have said it better than I."

INSANITY MAY BE CONSIDERED

At 4:15 that afternoon, Dr. Battle was released from the witness stand. Before taking a matter up with the lawyers, the judge spoke to the jury.

"Ladies and Gentlemen, it is late in the week and approaching a major holiday for most, if not all, of you. I am informed there will be at least one more witness whose testimony will be lengthy. I am inclined to continue with this trial tomorrow, and even Sunday if necessary. But I must be considerate of your wishes as well as my inclination. It is very important to both the State of Georgia and to the defendant that your verdict be based on the evidence. This requires good memory on the part of each of you of what has been said and done. Should we recess now, it will be Tuesday before we could resume. I would like to avoid such a long break in the trial by coming back tomorrow and Sunday, if necessary. Would doing this work an undue hardship on any of you? If so, step to the bench so we can discuss your situation privately."

As the judge waited, some of the jurors put their heads together for a hushed, private discussion. After a few moments, the juror seated near the middle of the back row took control.

"Judge Johnson, we would like to come back tomorrow and see if we can finish."

Job was mildly disturbed with the way the juror made the statement. He thought he had seen the man look in Aaron Bailey's direction and smile as he made the announcement. The judge warmly thanked the jury for their favorable consideration and dismissed them for the day.

"Thank you ladies and gentlemen. We will try to get started by 9 o'clock, so try to be in the jurors' room a little before that time. The bailiff will come for you when we are ready to resume. Mr. Bailey and Mr. Lee, I have a matter to discuss with you. Please meet me in chambers in fifteen minutes."

As he'd promised, Judge Johnson invited the lawyers into his chambers for a discussion of what the jury would be told regarding the defense of *not guilty by reason of insanity*.

Two times before, Judge Johnson, in private discussions with the attorneys, had inquired if there had been any discussion of Ann agreeing to a plea bargain. Thus far, neither the State nor the Defense had shown an interest in this possibility. Aaron Bailey did not want to plea bargain this case because he wanted another notch in his gun-butt and a shot at the governor's chair. Job Lee didn't want to make any sort of deal because, at first, he couldn't even get a good understanding of the facts from his own client. Now with better understanding, Job had developed slight hope for an acquittal if his client could just hold up on the witness stand. He knew this was a big "if," but with it, he finally felt there was a remote chance that Ann would be vindicated.

Judge Johnson, before getting to the discussion of insanity, again introduced the subject of a possible plea bargain. He encouraged Job and Bailey to enter into a private discussion in which each would consider the possibility of a settlement.

Bailey was quick to reply. "Judge, this lady shot her husband eight..."

The judge smiled and interrupted; "Aaron, you're talking to me now, not the jury."

"I'm sorry, you're right. I was beginning my closing argument. The State must proceed to the jury with this case. There is no way I could justify a plea bargain."

"I understand," said the judge. "Now, let's talk about the insanity defense and what my charge to the jury will be. Mr. Lee, we have heard your expert on the subject. It is my opinion that his testimony is very weak, but I am inclined to let the insanity defense go to the jury based on what Dr. Battle has said, whether I find it a strong defense or not. Mr. Bailey, what do you say on the subject?"

"Judge, I don't feel the Defense has met its burden of

proof. At its very best, Dr. Battle's testimony makes out a case for temporary insanity, and Georgia does not recognize temporary insanity as a defense. Insanity is a special defense and the defendant has the burden of proving what she asserts."

Job, realizing the judge was already committed to letting the jury consider the insanity defense based on Dr. Battle's testimony, thought it best to leave that issue alone. Once again, he felt the Judge was making his argument for him. He remembered what Sam Graves had said: "If Judge Johnson commits to a favorable position, leave him alone. Don't give him the opportunity to change his mind." Job chose his words carefully,

"Your Honor, I agree that Georgia does not recognize temporary insanity as a defense, but our appellate courts split hairs in taking this position. I have carefully researched this issue, and the case law is often confusing on the subject. I think the case of *Simmons vs. Georgia*, written in 1939, most clearly states Georgia's stance on the issue. That case holds that the key thing for the jury to do is to look to the moment of the occurrence in making the decision about insanity. In the *Simmons* case, a murder trial, the trial judge instructed the jury:

> *Gentlemen of the jury, the defendant has entered a special plea of not guilty by reason of insanity. Insanity may be shown in many ways. In your deliberations, you are not limited to the opinions of expert witnesses. You should consider all the evidence and testimony that tends to prove or disprove insanity. Our law does not require a fixed time or duration of insanity to be proven. If you are reasonably sat-*

isfied that at the time of the occurrence the defendant was not of sound mind, that is legally sufficient and if you are so satisfied, then your verdict should be for the defendant, even though you might think the defendant is presently sane or even though you might think the defendant was sane immediately before or immediately after the occurrence.

"Mr. Bailey," said Judge Johnson, "our courts do split hairs on the subject of temporary insanity. Our reported decisions say such is not a defense, yet as in *Simmons*, they narrow the gap by saying the jury should look to the moment of the occurrence. As far as I know, *Simmons* is still the law of our state. Do you agree or disagree?"

"Judge, our appellate courts, time and again, have held that temporary..."

"Mr. Bailey, you are preaching to the choir. Do you agree or disagree that *Simmons* is still the law of our state?"

Job Lee tried not to show his pleasure when Bailey answered, "Judge, that is still the law of Georgia."

"Gentlemen, I will so instruct the jury and you may, if you wish, so argue your case. Mr. Lee, how many more witnesses will you present and how long do you think it will take?"

"Judge, I have one final witness I'd like to call. The defendant will take the stand tomorrow, and I believe her direct testimony may take the better part of the day. At present, I do not anticipate any other witnesses."

"Gentlemen, if this case is not finished by five tomorrow afternoon, we will come back to finish on Sunday."

Job Lee smiled to himself when the Judge made this announcement. He had read that Bailey's political party had scheduled a Christmas party on St. Simons Island that weekend. He wondered if the Judge had read the same news article.

THIS LAST LAMENTING KISS

Saturday morning, the sixth day of trial, broke with an overcast sky and threat of rain. The impending downpour notwithstanding, two neighborhood boys, members of the high school track team, were running in the park as Job and Sally drove by on their way to Atlanta. The two boys seemed happy as they ran and laughed in freedom. Job understood that the cards were stacked against Ann. He wondered how she would perform on the witness stand. Could this be the beginning of her last days of freedom? As they passed the jogging boys, Sally broke the silence.

"Wasn't that the Peterson boy running in the park?"

"Yes, he's a senior this year."

"Honey, you did a good job when you represented him. That was three years ago and he has not been in any trouble since he was placed on probation. It must be rewarding to know that you help people who have made mistakes that got them in trouble."

Job made no reply to Sally's comment. He knew she was trying to boost his morale and he appreciated her effort. He also knew that when the Peterson boy got in trouble, he was only fifteen years old and his trouble came from shoplifting a ten cent package of chewing gum.

The Saturday morning traffic was light, enabling Job and Sally to arrive at the courthouse a little after 8:00 a.m. Ann, her girls, Mr. Henry, and Mrs. McCoy had not arrived. Job took Sally to the second floor of the building where the photographs of Georgia servicemen who had been awarded the Congressional Medal of Honor were on display.

"Babe, when I come to this courthouse, I always like to visit this floor as a reminder that freedom is not cheap. These people you see paid a heavy price so you and I might come here in freedom today."

Knowing that Job had Ann on his mind, Sally made no reply as they walked hand-in-hand past the photographs to the elevator and onto the sixth floor where Ann and the others now waited.

Since the meeting in Sam Graves' office three weeks earlier, Ann had visited Job's office seven times. Following Sam's suggestion, he tried to get Ann to the point that she could truthfully tell her side of the story without the distracting influence of pain. In these meetings, he always emphasized the importance of telling only the truth. Time and again, he told his emaciated client, "Just tell the truth. Don't guess. Don't speculate. Don't let the other attorney put words in your mouth. Your voice is weak, so speak loud enough that everyone can hear you. Listen carefully to each question. Be just as cooperative with the other attorney as you are with me. Treat both of us exactly the same."

In these office meetings, Ann had improved in her ability to tell her story, but she had never mastered her pain. In Job's office, her words never seemed to be her own. During the week of the trial, Ann had changed in an intangible and mysterious way. Job had seen this change, but the demands of the trial denied him opportunity to hear Ann's story in the voice of one who now said, "Don't worry about me. I've made my peace with all who matter."

Before going into the courtroom, Job and Ann left the others and went into the attorney's room. Once inside, and before Job could speak, Ann gathered Job into her arms, gave him a long, tight hug, and said, "Job, I am at peace. Try not to worry about me."

Job said not a word and led Ann and the others into the courtroom. Marie Moore handed him an envelope containing the transcript of Dr. Battle's testimony. In spite of Ann's words, Job was worried.

At 9:05, the court bailiff announced, "All rise and come to order. Court is in session. Judge Johnson presiding."

SHADY LEAF AND STALK

Job Lee called Ann Albert Tatum to the witness stand. She was forty-three years old, but most would have thought she was much older. Her walk from the counsel table to the witness box was somewhat uncertain. At times, the right side of her body, both hand and leg, refused to cooperate with the remainder of her body. She was dressed warmly, wearing one of Ethel McCoy's heavy sweaters that buttoned down the front. Mr. Henry's thoughtful butterfly necklace was all but concealed by her clothing.

Dr. Shelby Lamar had seen Ann ten days before the trial began. His records of that date show her weight to be ninety-two pounds, and her blood pressure as "105/63." The doctor's note in the patient chart read: "Pt advised to reduce beta-blocker 4 x 24."

In spite of her shuffling walk and her trembling hand, Ann impressed everyone with her quiet dignity. In all that she said and did, she gave the impression that she was a lady. Many with the same poor health and physical weakness would have made others ill at ease, but with Ann, these factors didn't distract. Physically, Ann had once been considered a most attractive person. Most of that physical beauty was now a thing of the past, and her future was in the hands of the jurors who sat quietly in the jury box watching and listening.

Job questioned Ann for a total of five hours and twenty minutes. In a soft voice that was sometimes hard to hear, Ann outlined for the jury the story of her life. Several times, a juror on the back row of the jury box had to signal that he couldn't hear what she was saying. With obvious sincerity, Ann would apologize and try to speak a little louder. It was obvious to everyone in the courtroom that loudness, like a foreign language she couldn't speak, was not her style. Some of the jurors knew that loss of speaking volume was also a symptom of Parkinson's disease and beyond Ann's ability to control.

Ann told the jury of her dream that her marriage to Edward Tatum would be for a lifetime. She didn't use those words, but one could tell that she saw the death of her baby sister, Betsy, and her failed first marriage to a cheating husband as her walk to the shady leaf or stalk, there to spin and die. One could tell that she viewed her marriage to Ed as the time of life when she would live again, a butterfly.

At 4:05 that afternoon, Job Lee turned to Aaron Bailey and said, "Your witness, counsel."

Bailey asked permission from the judge to approach the bench, and Judge Johnson signaled both attorneys forward. At sidebar, Bailey spoke, "Judge, it is after 4:00 p.m. It's Saturday, and my cross-examination will take several hours. The jurors are tired. We are all tired. I move the court to recess until 9:30 a.m. Tuesday. That will allow all the jurors to have some time for Christmas with their families and all of us to get some rest. I know you have already discussed this matter with the jury, but I respectfully request you to reconsider your decision to come back tomorrow."

The judge looked to Job Lee for a reply.

Job, too, was tired. A break in the trial had much appeal, but he was concerned about Ann. Thus far, she had held up remarkably well. What would be her condition in two days? His better judgment told him it was best to let the case go forward and come back on Sunday to finish.

Job reminded the Judge of his previous statement, replying, "Your Honor, you had told us to be prepared to try this case over the weekend if that were necessary. I have prepared for that and would prefer that we proceed."

"Those were my words, and that is what we will do. Mr. Bailey, proceed with your examination."

Job took his seat at the counsel table, and he was worried. Ann had been on the witness stand for a long time. She had to be very tired. How long would the Judge allow Bailey's cross-examination to continue before court was recessed for the day? How much longer could Ann retain her poise? Would she become too fatigued? Confused? Irritated by an aggressive cross-examination?

With only a ten-minute break, Aaron Bailey cross-examined Ann for four hours and twenty-five minutes, ending at 8:50 p.m. His cross-examination ended with this series of questions and answers:

"Mrs. Tatum, you say that you intended to take your own life, is that correct?"

"Yes, sir."

"You say that you thought that your husband had brought his girlfriend into your home?"

"Yes, sir. I thought that he had."

"Do you have any proof that had happened?"

"No, only what Ed said he was going to do."

"Did you see his lady friend in your home?"

"No."

"Did you hear her steps as she walked in your home?"

"No. I heard footsteps, but I cannot say whose they were. I saw Ed when he came to the bedroom door."

"Do you even know of anyone else who says they saw Mrs. Walker in your home that day, or any other day?"

"No."

"And you say that you intended to kill yourself because you thought Mrs. Walker had come into your home?"

"Mr. Bailey, I thought she had."

"Did you even see Mrs. Walker outside your home that day? Did you see her in the yard, in the driveway, or even out in the street in front of your house?"

"No, sir."

"So, what your testimony boils down to is that you would have the jury believe that you intended to kill yourself because a lady you never saw was in your house, but instead of killing yourself, you killed your husband. Is that not what you are saying?"

"Mr. Bailey, I have no recollection of killing Ed."

"Do you deny killing him?"

"I wish I could. I wish with all my heart that I could deny that. But everything shows that I did. I simply cannot remember doing so. Mr. Bailey, I am not trying to evade your question. I know that I have sworn to tell the truth. The horrible truth is that everything shows I killed Ed. I just can't remember doing so."

"Do you remember taking the pistol from the nightstand drawer?"

"Yes, sir."

"Do you remember firing the pistol, not just once, but eight times?"

"No, sir. That part I do not remember."

"Do you remember when the policeman came into your house and what you were doing at that time?"

"Yes, sir. I was sitting on the floor with Ed."

It was a few minutes before nine that night when Judge Johnson addressed the jury. "Ladies and Gentlemen, it has been a long day. The defense has rested its case. I thank you for giving the defense the same careful attention that you gave to the State's case. I previously told both you and the attorneys that we would come back tomorrow to finish this case. Before making that decision final, again I ask each of you, would coming back tomorrow work a hardship? If so, please step to my bench so we may privately discuss your situation."

The jurors looked at each other for a few moments and exchanged muffled comments among themselves. Job Lee, during the trial, had been watching the juror who occupied the second seat on the back row of the jury box. In the jury selection process, this lady had identified herself as "Alice Bentley," a retired elementary school teacher. Job had a hunch that the jurors might select Mrs. Bentley as the foreperson of the jury, as she had kept copious notes as evidence and witness testimony were presented. Job was glad that the court reporter was preparing a transcript of testimony, but he was concerned that possibly some of Mrs. Bentley's notes might conflict with those of the reporter.

After the judge's question and a few private exchanges between the jurors, Mrs. Bentley took the lead, "Judge Johnson, we would like to come back tomorrow and try to finish the case."

"Very well," answered the Judge, "we are adjourned until 9:30 a.m. tomorrow morning. As I have instructed you all week, I again instruct you not to read nor listen to any news accounts about this case. Do not discuss the case with anyone nor permit anyone to discuss the case in your presence. Drive carefully on your way home and I will see you tomorrow morning."

As he was leaving the courtroom, Marie Moore, the court reporter told Job, "I'll have the complete transcript ready by 8:00 a.m. tomorrow if you would like to come in early." Job quickly agreed to the arrangement.

Ann, Jane, Mrs. McCoy, and Dana had left the lobby area when Job emerged from the courtroom. Sally and Wallace Henry were waiting for him outside the door.

Job was hungry for second and third opinions. First, he turned to Mr. Henry. "How did Ann do today?"

"She was a little hard to hear at times, but my old ears don't work as well as they used to. It was a long day for her, and for you. I suspect both of you are very tired."

This was not the information that Job sought. He tried again, "Mr. Henry, what was your impression of both what she said and how she said it?"

"Job, I think she gave us understanding. I think everyone who listened now knows much more about life and themselves. You may recall our first meeting in which I said Ann acted for a reason, and I had hoped it was a good reason. Today, I think she gave her reason very well. The more difficult part of the question is, was it a good reason? It is very difficult to find many good reasons for taking a human life, and I think Ann made it understandable. Did she make it forgivable? I hope she did."

Sally intervened. "Mr. Henry, as Ann was leaving, she showed me the little butterfly and chain that you brought her. That was very thoughtful."

"Ann is a very nice person, Sally. The simple gift was my

way of letting her know that I care and that I understand."

Wallace Henry walked with Job and Sally to the nearby parking garage. Job's car was obtained and Sally offered to drive Mr. Henry to his hotel. Each of the three was silent during the ten minute drive, each was lost in thought. As Mr. Henry got out of Job's car, he paused at Job's window for a moment, as if to gather his thoughts. He reached through the window, gently gripped Job's shoulder.

"Job, it is well to remember that few things are ever as good or as bad as they seem at the moment. Drive carefully going home and I'll see you in the morning."

They rode silently until Sally passed the small town of Douglasville, west of Atlanta. It was Job who broke the silence. "Honey, thank you for driving. I am grateful for your support. What did you think of Ann's testimony?"

"To answer bluntly and in a way my mother would not approve, I think the son-of-a-bitch needed killing."

"What's makes you say that?"

"I just say it. Mr. Henry thought the same thing."

"That's not what he said to me. You heard what he said."

"He didn't say that to me either, but that's what he thought."

Job, puzzled by Sally's strong expression, fell silent. Sally must have sensed that he needed to think on some subject other than the one he had wrestled with all week.

As they approached the Sand Hill community, some eight miles from Carrollton, Sally asked: "Remember that old church on St. Charles Avenue in New Orleans where we used to park and cuddle when we were in school?"

"How could I ever forget? What brings that to mind?"

"This old church at Sand Hill always reminds me of the New Orleans church and our heavy petting."

"If I had had my way, it would have been more than heavy petting."

"Would you like to park behind this Sand Hill Church tonight and smooch a little, like old times?"

"You were mighty good on that smooching, but not willing on anything else."

"Maybe you didn't try hard enough. Want to stop tonight and I'll give you a second chance?"

"Sally, you are too good for me. Thank you. But I don't think I have the energy tonight."

"What about the second chance? I don't give many men that opportunity."

"You had better not give any other men that offer."

Sally reached over and patted Job on his knee as they drove past the old Methodist Church at Sand Hill. She honked the horn as she passed.

"Why did you blow the horn?"

Sally again patted his knee. "I was just letting the girl behind that church know that she should keep holding out and that boy will marry her."

By the time they pulled into their driveway, Job's mind was again on Ann's case and mentally he was replaying the argument he would make to the jury.

UNDERSTANDING OFTEN SOFTENS JUDGMENT

Shortly before 6:00 a.m. the next morning, Job's home telephone rang. It was Sam Graves.

"Job, I just wanted to wish you and Ann well today. My office told me that Judge Johnson was bringing everyone back for a weekend session."

"Sam, how are you doing? I've wanted to personally check on you all week and I failed to do so."

"I'm doing fine, short about eight inches of colon, but I still have enough guts left to handle most lawyers. How is it going? Did you finish with Ann's testimony?"

"Yes, Ann was on the stand all of yesterday. The judge kept us rather late, but I think she held up very well. In fact, much better than I ever believed she would. It seemed that all of the jurors gave her their undivided attention."

"Will Bailey have any rebuttal witnesses?"

"I'm not sure. The judge inquired about that yesterday, but he didn't get a firm answer."

"You seem to indicate that Ann made a positive impression. Is that your belief?"

"Yes. The jurors listened carefully. Her testimony carried a strong emotional appeal. I think she made at least some of the jurors understand why she killed her husband."

"Good. Understanding often softens judgment."

"Sam, how should I argue this case? The facts of how Ed Tatum was shot are brutal. One shot might be understood by the jury, but seven more after the first with the man trying to run away is a large pill for the jurors to swallow."

"Job, you know best. If you feel Ann's testimony was persuasive, you may consider letting the jury hear, for the second time in your argument, parts of what she told from the witness stand. Marie Moore will have the transcript ready for you. You have put your heart and soul in this case. Don't be afraid to share your emotions with the jury. They represent many combined years of human experience and reflect your heart-felt emotion. I've taken too much of your time. After you finish this case, come by to see me."

Sally drove back to Atlanta Sunday morning while Job prepared his final argument. Passing the old Methodist Church at the Sand Hill community, she again honked the car's horn, saying to the make-believe-girl behind the old church, "Keep your knees together girl. Keep them together until that boy marries you."

Job looked up and smiled.

As promised, the court reporter met Job at eight o'clock with Ann's transcribed testimony in hand. He spent the next hour and a half marking the parts that he wanted to quote to the jury. At 9:15 a.m. the bailiff advised Job that court would convene at 9:45, fifteen minutes later than scheduled. Job correctly assumed that Aaron Bailey had requested the additional time, trying to prepare a rebuttal witness.

Ann waited just inside the courtroom as Job reviewed the transcript. Dana, Jane, Ethel McCoy, Dot Carey, Sally, and Wallace Henry waited with her. For the first time, Job noted the little chain and butterfly around Ann's neck. He started to make mention of this, then had second thoughts. Later, he told Sally that when he first noticed this simple, inexpensive gift, he realized it was a gift from Mr. Henry.

It was almost ten o'clock before the bailiff called the court to order and Judge Johnson took the bench and announced, "Ladies and gentlemen, I apologize for the delay this morning. It appeared there might be an additional witness called to testify. The State has decided not to do this and has informed the court that its case is rested.

"Both sides have rested. It is time for what is commonly called the final argument. Before the attorneys make their closing statements to you, I will give you a few simple instructions as to how you should consider and treat what the attorneys say to you.

"You, and you alone, are responsible for determining what the facts are. I am the judge of the law; you are the collective judges of the facts. In determining what the facts are, you should consider only the evidence that has been presented from the witness stand. You should not use conjecture, speculation, or surmise in your search for truth.

"What the attorneys say to you is not evidence. Their statements to you about what the evidence has shown are not to be taken as correct or incorrect. It is for you, and you alone, to determine what the evidence has shown.

"I have noticed that some of you have been making notes during the trial. That is your right. But your notes are not to be taken by other jurors as being correct. Each juror is to search his or her own recollection as to what a witness said and not sacrifice your independent recollection in favor of the notes kept by another juror.

"It is the right and duty of each attorney to fairly state

their respective positions. You are to carefully consider their arguments, but always remember that the determination of what the facts are is your responsibility. After the attorneys have made their final arguments, I will then instruct you about the law of the State of Georgia and how you are to apply that law when you make your determination of the facts. Listen carefully to the attorneys. Mr. Bailey, you may proceed.

Assistant District Attorney Wayman Burris, beginning at 10:25, a.m. made the initial closing statement. He methodically traced the testimony of each of the State's witnesses and the picture he painted was not pretty. In brief, he emphasized the lack of self-defense and of Edward Tatum being shot once in his chest and seven more times in his back as he attempted to flee down the hallway and toward the kitchen door that opened into the garage.

During this argument, Ann sat beside Job and showed little emotion. She made eye contact with no one in the courtroom. At times, her right hand shook violently, as it had during the trial. When this occurred, she removed her shaking hand from the table and placed it in her lap.

Wayman Burris finished his argument at 11:50, at which time the judge recessed court for lunch, instructing the jurors to return at one o'clock.

Job, too preoccupied with his thoughts on his closing argument, stayed in the attorney's room while Ann and others went across the street to a small diner for lunch. Several of the jurors did the same, keeping their distance from Ann, Sally, and the others. Sally ordered a sandwich for Job and took it to him as the others finished lunch.

Job mumbled his thanks but was too busy to eat. He knew what he wanted to tell the jury, but he didn't know how to begin his statement.

As Sally left him to his thoughts, she said, "Mr. Henry made an interesting comment just as I was leaving to bring your sandwich to you. He asked about your study of the Book of Ruth that is found in the Bible."

"How did he know about that?"

"I don't know, but the way he asked his question, he apparently knew. He said if I had the chance, I should remind you that the Biblical Ruth lost her first husband and then found a new life for herself, pledging to follow her new people wherever they went, that their people would now be Ruth's people. I told him our Sunday school class had been studying that book for the past several months and that you and I had discussed the similarities in the lives of the Biblical Ruth and Ann. Do you not find it interesting that he made mention of this?"

As Job started to rise from his chair, Ann spontaneously reached over and gently patted the back of his hand, much as a mother would give a pat of encouragement to a nervous son.

Alice Bentley, juror and retired elementary school teacher, noticed the gesture, recalling the many times she had given a similar pat to the numerous third-grade boys she had taught.

Job Lee addressed the jury:

Ladies and Gentlemen, I am scared to death. Scared that

my best might not be good enough. Scared that I may have failed to do something that I should have done for Ann Albert Tatum. I am scared that I have done something the wrong way, in a manner that may be misunderstood. I cannot match Mr. Bailey and Mr. Burris in their experience of criminal trials, and I fear that my lack of experience may work to the detriment of my client.

I'm scared that I may cry as I talk to you today. I'll do my best not to do that. Should I lose my composure, which I hope I don't, please understand that my tears are not part of any cheap dramatics. Should I cry, please understand that the tears originate from my deep regard for my client, Ann Albert Tatum. Please, understand that.

In his opening statement, at the beginning of this trial, Mr. Bailey told you that the evidence would not show any sign of a struggle that suggested self-defense. Mr. Burris, in his closing statement, again emphasized that there was no sign of a struggle in Ann's home. I respectfully disagree with such statements. I submit that the evidence in this case shows a struggle the likes of which were beyond human endurance.

Ann's life is much like that of the Biblical Ruth. Ann lost her mother while she was just a child, and then she lost her baby sister, Betsy. She then had the misfortune of marrying a cheating and abusive husband. What then did she do? She did not seek alimony. She did not seek child support. She took her baby girl and came back home to Georgia. All that she sought was her child. Does this not speak volumes regarding the nature and character of Ann?

After these disappointments and failures in life, Ann made herself a promise. She resolved that if she ever married again, it would be forever. Like Ruth of the Bible, she determined that should she ever marry again, she would go wherever her husband wanted to go. His people would be her people. She resolved to do whatever was required of her to make the next marriage last forever. She resolved to pay the price, whatever the price may be.

Ladies and gentlemen, there is a valuable lesson for all of us in this tragedy. There are, in fact, many lessons, the first being that some people change. Edward Tatum changed. For years he was a good, faithful, loyal husband and father. And then, for reasons beyond our ability to understand, he changed. Can there be any doubt of that? It is not for us to determine why he changed, but the undisputed facts show that change. In a brief period of time, Edward Tatum became a different man. Why? No one knows. Someone, something changed him from a caring, compassionate, thoughtful person into an uncaring, thoughtless, cold, even vicious person. Not vicious in a physical manner, but vicious and uncaring in a way far more damaging. In his words and actions, Ed Tatum attacked one of Ann's most precious possessions, her will to live. I urge you to ask yourself this question: Is not the will to live more valuable than physical life itself? Is not an attack on one's desire for life a struggle of monumental proportion?

Yes, Ed Tatum changed. Of this, there can be no doubt. The second great lesson of this tragedy is that all of us have a breaking point. A point at which, if pushed beyond it, we will break and react in a manner that is completely out of character. Whatever your verdict may be in this case let us go from this courthouse with the understanding that we all have a breaking point. This lady seated here in front of you, Ann Tatum, is living proof that we have a breaking point. She is living proof that even the most gentle and kind person is capable of breaking and reacting in a violent manner. Can anyone doubt this?

It may be fairly said that Ed and Ann had a good marriage. They both respected and loved each other. They worked and planned for the future. Until July 1971, Ann's world was safe and secure. Like the Ruth of old, wherever Ed wanted to go, she wanted to go with him. His people had become her people. Her family was her life. Her home was her sanctuary and refuge. Her marriage was one that was to endure. Whatever it took, Ann was prepared to pay the price.

We will likely never know when Ed Tatum started to change, though clearly it was sometime after he moved to Memphis. We do know when Ann's world started to crumble beneath her feet. It was on a Friday night in July, 1971. Dana was away from home that evening, attending a friend's birthday party. When Dana returned home that night, she found her mother seated on the sofa, next to the telephone. Her mother sat beside that telephone all night, all the next day, all the next night, and all day Sunday. What prompted this futile wait by the telephone? What did Ann Tatum say to you from the witness chair about that? What did Ann say about the events that tore her world apart? What did she tell you about the time that forever changed her life and cast her into a pit of darkness that will last forever? You have seen this court reporter taking shorthand notes of everything that has been said in this courtroom. To be absolutely sure that I exactly quote what Ann said from the witness stand, I requested the court reporter to make a certified transcript of her testimony. I have this transcript in my hand. Here are the questions asked and the answers that were given:

Ann, tell the jury about the phone call you received in July 1971.

It was a Friday night and Dana was at Julie's birthday party when a Mr. Walker called from Memphis, telling me that Ed and his wife were having an affair. I immediately called Ed and he denied it. He said there was a mistake, that he would call Mr. Walker and then call me right back. I waited by the phone for Ed to call back. I waited for a long, long time; I don't remember how long. I kept hoping it was all a mistake. Ed did not call until Monday saying he would come home in a few days and explain how it was all a mistake.

When did you next talk to Ed?

He came home the next Friday and explained how Mr. Walker had been mistaken. Ed told me to list the house for sale and to get ready to move to Memphis. He said he was tired of living alone—that he wanted his family together again. We talked about Dana enrolling at Auburn as we had planned. Everything seemed normal again. I believed Ed. I guess I believed him because I wanted so badly to believe him. It was a lot like a parent always wanting to believe the best about their child.

Tell the jury about the college fund.

Years ago, we started a savings account that we called the "College Fund." When Dana received the registration package from Auburn, we discovered Ed had closed the savings account almost two months earlier, and there was no college fund. Ethel

338

McCoy paid for Dana's tuition and books last year. Job, there is no way for anyone to know how hurt Dana was to learn her daddy had closed that account.

Ann, you mentioned earlier that you started thinking of ways to escape. Were you thinking of taking your own *life?*

Yes, my life seemed a complete failure. I know it wasn't, but it seemed that way. Ed played games with me, saying there was no affair with Mrs. Walker. Then saying the affair was over. Then saying I was crazy to believe there had ever been an affair. Then saying he was coming back home. Then telling me to sell the house and then saying not to sell it. The thing that hurt the most was his telling me about the intimate relation he had with Mrs. Walker—the comparisons he made with what our relation had been. He said things I cannot repeat. Yes, starting in August of last year, I started thinking of a way to escape. I started to feel like a school teacher had given me a test on my life to see how I had done and I had scored a zero. That was it. I was a zero.

FINDING A WAY TO SAY

At this point, Judge Johnson interrupted Job's reading from the transcript of Ann's previous testimony and said, "Mr. Lee, I think this would be a good time for our afternoon break. We stand in recess for fifteen minutes."

During the recess, Job visited the men's room, finding Wallace Henry already there. As the two were leaving, Mr. Henry stopped Job.

"Are you talking to the jury the way you would really like to?"

"What do you mean?"

"Job, I don't know why I even asked that question. I apologize for distracting you. It just seems as if you would like to talk to them, not read to them. Talk to them from your heart. They, too, have hearts."

Job realized there was truth in what Mr. Henry said. He hadn't been talking to the jury with warmth and compassion. Many times before, in his mind, he had argued this case to the jury, but in a different way. Now, at the critical moment, he was on a different track, a track that wasn't right for this jury. Again, it seemed as if Mr. Henry had a special message that he needed to share with Job.

Job resolved to go back to the argument style that had denied him sleep for so many hours of so many nights. He resolved to no longer be afraid of losing his emotional control and shedding tears. He didn't want to cry in front of the court, but if tears came he now felt the jury would understand.

LET THE HEART SPEAK

Job went back into the courtroom and took his seat next to Ann. In a few moments, the jury was back in their box and seated.

Judge Johnson returned to the bench, looked to Aaron Bailey and asked, "Is the State ready?"

"Yes, your honor," Bailey replied.

The judge turned toward Ann and her attorney and said, "Mr. Lee, you may continue."

Several times during the trial, Ann had gently patted Job's hand. It was not a "staged" arrangement. Her pats on the hand were from her heart and everyone who had seen these gestures understood her intent. Now, when the judge told Job to continue his argument, there was a role reversal. This time, Job gently patted the back of Ann's left hand that rested on top of the table. Her trembling right hand was in her lap. Job then walked to the front of the jury box without his notes and without the transcript of testimony.

LEST IT BE TOO LATE

Ladies and gentlemen. I've told you my fears—that my effort on behalf of my client may not be sufficient, and I'll say nothing further about me. Instead, I will talk to you simply and directly about Ann Albert Tatum.

In July of 1971, when she received the call from Mr. Walker, her world started to fall apart. Long before that time, she had made herself a solemn promise that if there were a next marriage, it would last for a lifetime. For most of that second marriage, her dream seemed to have come true. She felt that she had found the real thing and then her world started crumbling beneath her feet.

For the next several months, Ann's very being cried for understanding, for explanation, for something to hold onto.

For whatever his reasons may have been, Ed Tatum changed. In changing, he also changed Ann, Jane, and Dana. You have heard the testimony of how he would promise to put his relationship with Sara Walker aside, how he would promise to come for weekend visits, how he would promise to return to his family, only to again fall under the evil spell of the illicit relationship with another woman.

You have heard Dana, Ed's daughter, tell of her love for her father and his promises to her that he would return home to stay. Dana and Ethel McCoy have told you of how happy and excited Ann would become when Ed extended one of his many false promises and how dejected she would become when he failed to keep his promise.

Throughout those months, Ann's life was not taken. Something far more valuable was taken from her. This was her spirit. Her will to live was taken. Her joy of life was taken. What is a physical life that has no joy? What is a physical life that has no sunshine, no blue skies, no flowers, no children who romp and play, no tomorrow? I beg you to ask that question of yourself.

Yes, Edward Tatum is now dead. No, Ann does not recall shooting him, but we all know that she did. In this trial, we have not played any silly game of pretending that Ann didn't kill her husband. Edward Tatum is dead. Let us join Ann, and Dana, and Jane, and Edith McCoy in wishing and hoping that Edward Tatum now rests in peace. For most of his life, he was a peaceable, caring, loving man, father, and husband. Let us all hope, and even pray, that he now has regained all those wonderful characteristics that he once had.

Accepting that Ed Tatum is dead and extending every wish

for his present peace, let us look at Ann Albert Tatum. Here she sits before you with her frail body, her trembling hand, and leg that will not work as well as they once did. But, where is she? Where is Ann Tatum? Is she here? Or, is she someplace else?

I will tell you where she is. Ann Tatum now lives in a place that I call the City of the Living Dead. The Ann Tatum who dearly loved her husband and her two daughters, that Ann Tatum is no more. Forever and ever, as long as this life lasts, she will reside in the City of the Living Dead. The Ann Tatum who loved her family, who found complete joy in being only a wife and mother, has left us.

The District Attorney has told you there was no sign of struggle in that home. May a merciful God spare all of us the struggle of Ann Tatum. For months, she begged and pleaded with Ed to leave his lover and return to her bosom. What was his answer? It was cruel in the extreme. Instead of coming back home as he so frequently promised, he taunted his wife with intimate descriptions of his love life with Sara Walker. Dare anyone say there was no struggle? He boasted of the fine and youthful body of his lover, comparing that younger body with Ann's shaking hand and breaking heart. Dare anyone say there was no struggle?

I submit that the struggle to maintain dignity, pride, and the will to live is a struggle of epic proportion. What is life without the will to live? What is life when one hides the pistol from oneself?

The District Attorney would have you believe that Ann is a violent person. You have heard both Dana and Ann tell of the two occasions that Ed came back home during the fall months, these visits filled with the promise that he had ended his affair with Sara Walker. You have heard how Sara Walker called their home four times when Ed was there, asking to speak to him. You have heard how both Ann and Dana would leave the room where the telephone was located so Ed might privately talk to his lover. You have heard Dr. Battle, Edith McCoy, and Dot Carey describe Ann as being the most gentle of people. Yet, the State of Georgia would have you believe that Ann is a violent person.

How does one reconcile a gentle, non-violent person exploding and becoming, for a few seconds of her life, a person who would shoot her husband eight times? Dr. Battle, an experienced psychiatrist who has treated many people, gave us the answer. He said that we all have a breaking point. We all have a point that when pushed beyond, we react in a manner that is completely out of character.

You've heard of Ann's pleas with her husband to return to his family. Like the Ruth of old, Ed's people were her people. Dana, Jane, Mrs. McCoy, and Dot Carey have all told you of Ann crying until there were no tears left in her body. They have told you of Ann's pleas.

Ann's pleas for Ed to stop were unanswered. Her need for understanding unabated. She couldn't eat or sleep, and she cried until every tear was wrenched from her body. Why, why, why? She found no answer; she found no peace. Often she thought of how sweet the release from misery would be if she were not alive. I have heard older people speak of "having the misery in the soul." I find it a very descriptive and meaningful expression. Ann truly had misery in her soul. Often she *thought of the escape that would come with her death. Dare anyone say there was no struggle?*

Ann's friends at work assisted her when her hands shook so badly she could not hold a pen to do her work. Her friends tried to entice her with rich foods in an effort to compensate for her loss of weight. Her kind boss looked the other way when her work was unfinished. Only a few close friends knew of her troubles, and they were concerned that Ann was at the point of taking her own life. Ann's life was in transition. I guess all of life is in transition, but not the way Ann's was. Thank God for that.

There were a series of unplanned, unexpected events that day in February. Ann drove herself to work, carrying a sandwich for her lunch. Dot, her friend who lived in the same neighborhood, decided that she wanted to go to her house during the noon break. Dot, sharing everyone's concern for Ann's health, told Ann that she was going home for lunch and invited Ann to ride with her, back to Ann's house. Dot explained that Ann could take her sandwich back home, eat it at her own home, and rest during the noon hour.

Ann agreed, and Dot dropped her at her home. This placed Ann back at home, with her car at the office. Ann, seated at the kitchen table, had eaten a few bites of her sandwich when she heard the garage door open. This was frightening, because no one was expected. In another moment, Ed opened kitchen door. Neither expected the other to be there. How quickly the unexpected may change the path of one's life.

With no word spoken, Ed walked down the hallway to the back, unused bedroom on the left. Ann heard drawers being opened, and she went to the bedroom and asked Ed what he was looking for. When informed that he was looking for in-come tax records, she inquired if they were not going to file a joint return. "I am not doing a damn thing with you" was his reply. Ann detected that Ed was mildly intoxicated, and she returned to the kitchen table and her unfinished sandwich.

In a few minutes Ed reappeared from the back bedroom, with some papers in hand. He stopped to talk, when both pru-dence and decency demanded that he leave.

"I have Sara in the car with me," he taunted. "I'm going to invite her in so you can see what a good-looking woman she is."

The shame, the humiliation, the disgrace was unthink-able. Never in her wildest moments did she think her husband would bring that woman to their home. Never would she have believed that he had such little respect for her. Ann's life, her universe, broke apart and tumbled down. Down! Down!

Her cries, tears, and pleas were met with more taunts, more insistence that she "meet Sara," "get to know her," and "see what a fine woman she is."

At this time, Ann speaks to Ed for the last time in this life. "Ed," she says, "please don't bring that woman into our home. Please don't do this. As many times as I have begged you to come home, now I am begging you to leave. I am begging you to take that woman away from our home. I don't want to see her. I don't want to see her in our home. I can't take it. I can't take any more of it. Please, Ed."

Driven beyond desperation, she told Ed she couldn't live with this and that. If Sara was brought into their home, she would kill herself. Leaving her unfinished sandwich, glass of milk, and the little handwritten poem about the butterfly on the kitchen table, she walked down the hall, stopping at the first bedroom on the right. This was Dana's room. She walked to the far side of Dana's bed and silently stood there. Why did she do this? Ann has told you that she stood there in Dana's room wondering what would happen to Dana. Would she be able to continue her education? Would she have a good life? Would Dana ever be able to recapture the loving relationship she'd always had with her father?

The pistol wasn't in Dana's room. It was in the master bedroom, the last room on the right at the end of the hall. It seems that Ann stopped in Dana's room for a last visit with her daughter. Perhaps she stopped there to say goodbye. Possibly she relived some old scenes of life with Dana. Possibly she held Dana, a baby, in her arms again. Possibly she told her little girl a story of Jack and the Beanstalk. Possibly she again recited the little poem about the butterfly. Possibly she held the child again in her arms and quieted her crying after a bad dream. Before taking her own life, she must be the Mother for a few moments. Once again, just a moment more, she must be Mother.

How many things can flood your mind as you face death? How many memories can you live? How many little girl birthdays can you recall, how many little girl dresses can you wash and iron? How many skinned knees can you still see, how many bad dreams can you quiet by holding the little girl close? These things we will never know.

There is one thing we do know. We know that Ed came to Dana's bedroom where Ann stood. We know that he stepped inside that room and added great insult and injury to a faithful wife who was already gravely injured. As Ann was saying goodbye to Dana. As Ann spent a last few moments with her child, Ed reached into his pocket and pulled out $192. Detective Parker told you about this money being found in the stuffed chair inside that room, next to the door. We do know that Ed looked his faithful wife in the eye, tossed the money in the chair and said, "If you're going to kill yourself, here is some money for your goddamned funeral."

Leaving Ann with her memories of better days and money to be buried with, Ed turned and left Dana's room. Ann remained. She heard Ed walk to the kitchen, to the garage door. She heard the door open and close and then all was silent in her home.

In her mind, Ed had gone outside to invite Sara in. He wanted Ann to see what a "fine" woman she was. He wanted Ann to see that she was younger and prettier.

We'll never know whether Sara Walker actually came inside the home that day. She was outside in her car. Ed told Ann that he was inviting her in, and he went outside after making his cruel and vicious boast. While Ed was outside, Ann went to the master bedroom where the pistol was kept in the nightstand drawer.

In the master bedroom, Ann was mindful of this being the bed she had shared with Ed. This was the bed where they had loved. This was her home, her place of safety. Now, Ed was going to violate their home by bringing another woman inside.

Ann removed the pistol from the drawer. She did so with every intention of placing the end of the barrel to her forehead and ending the living hell that now possessed her. Dare anyone say there was no struggle taking place in that home? Dare any-

one say such a thing?

Standing beside the bed, the victim of the worst struggle that the human mind can conceive, standing there with every intent of escaping from a world of torment and anguish and fleeing to a world of peace and love, Ann heard the kitchen door again open and close. She heard footsteps in the kitchen. She heard footsteps coming down the hallway.

Was Sara Walker in the house? We don't know. Ed had said he was going to invite her in. The testimony of Mary Mills, a neighbor that lived across the street, suggests that Sara Walker never entered the house. But, in Ann's mind, she was there. Sara was in her home.

Ed, back in the house, walks to the master bedroom. He gets to the door and possibly steps inside the room. Ann, with pistol in hand, stands on the far side of the bed, diagonally across the room from Ed. Is Ed there on a mission of compassion? Does he come to apologize and try to persuade his faithful wife not to take her own life? Is he there to try to protect Dana's mother? Hardly so. Sadly, tragically, cruelly, his mission is adding additional insult and humiliation. Looking across the room, he says, "Go ahead and get it over with. Me and Sara want to have a party!"

The next thing Ann remembers is sitting on the kitchen floor, cradling her dying husband's head in her lap and telling him that she loves him.

May a merciful God spare all of us in this courtroom such a struggle!

Ladies and gentlemen, I have spoken to you with emotion, sincere emotion. In the trial of this case, we all have witnessed death. The death of Edward Tatum, and I sincerely hope that he is at peace. Something happened to this man. Something changed him. For all but the last year and a half he was a very decent, caring, loving father and husband. For all those years he was a good neighbor and friend of many. I suspect that Ed Tatum was very unhappy with the person that he came to be. May he rest in peace.

But your mission as the jury in this case is not to decide the fate of Ed Tatum. Your solemn responsibility rests with deciding the fate of Ann Albert Tatum. What will you do with her?

I hope it is not your decision to punish Ann for what she's done. I do hope that will not be your decision. But, if it is so decided, how will you add to her punishment? Her life is over. She now resides in the City of the Living Dead. She is permanently consigned to that place. She cannot be recalled. She cannot be redeemed. She now and forever lives with the awareness that she killed the man she loved. She doesn't remember firing the shots, but she will forever remember it was she who took a life that was more precious to her than her own.

It's not pretty, this place of the living dead. We live in a country where the greatest possible emphasis is placed on liberty and freedom and dignity for each of us. These are great values that we hold: liberty and freedom and dignity and self-respect. The right of everyone to walk and carry themselves with their heads held high. This is the cornerstone of our system. We often fail to realize what happens when any of us lose that freedom, and that dignity, and that self-respect.

This is what happens: we move into the City of the Living Dead! Lest any of us leave this courtroom today without realizing that dignity, self-respect, pride, appreciation for life, anticipation of life, the will to live—the will to live—unless we realize those things are more important to us than physical life itself, we are making a tragic mistake. The spirit to live, the will to live is of far greater importance than a physical life. What is a physical life without those things? It is a place of the living dead. I hope we will all understand that if we do not gain anything else from this tragedy, I hope each one of us will realize that.

Possibly during the course of this trial, we have all changed. Certainly Ann has changed, changed from the whole to the fraction, changed from the light of day to the gloom of eternal night. She has been changed beyond description, beyond comprehension, beyond measure. What is a physical existence without hope, without joy, without expectation, without the light of day, without the smell of flowers, without the touch of a child, without any joy of the day, and, maybe most importantly, without the spirit to continue?

Why didn't Ed take the pistol and shoot Ann? Why didn't he take her physical life? Almost all else was dead. It would have been much easier for her had he put an end to her misery, her suffering, her shame, her humiliation, her degradation, her hurting, her crying, her pleading, and praying. Death can be sweet, even welcomed. There are many things in life worse than death. Let us all realize that.

Ed was cruel beyond measure that fateful day. He was threatening something in Ann that was much more valuable than physical life itself. He was taking away the last shred of respect she had. He was taking away the rest of her humanity, the *rest of her dignity, the rest of her pride, and he was completely killing her will to live. Does society place its stamp of approval on what Ed did and condemn Ann for her actions? I pray not.*

Today, Ann Tatum resides in a place none of us have ever known. In the truest sense, it is beyond the ability of the living to add to her punishment. On Ann's behalf, I earnestly, sincerely ask for your understanding.

I hope that by your verdict you will see fit to help rehabilitate Ann. I hope your verdict will tell her you understand. I hope your decision will tell Ann you find her to be a person of worth, of value, of dignity, of honor.

I have given Ann Tatum my best effort. She is worthy of this, and I am proud to do so. I am sure that each of you will give her your best effort as you deliberate her fate. I hope your verdict will tell Ann that unfortunate circumstances of life have caused her to spin and die, and that by your verdict you will do your best to help her live again, a butterfly.

THE .22 CALIBER RUGER SEMI-AUTOMATIC PISTOL

Bailey, in a measured, calm voice, addressed the jury:

Ladies and gentlemen, this is your home. This is where you, your family, your spouses, your children, and your friends live. By your verdict, you play a major role in deciding what your home will be. Will it be a place of safety? Will it be a place of comfort and security? Or will it be a place of the survival of the fittest? The very heart and soul of our system of government de-

pends on obedience to law by all people. If we obey our laws, we survive. If we disregard our laws, we die. It is just that simple.

Possibly this is a good time for you to recall the special oath that each of you swore when you were selected to serve on this jury. I will paraphrase what you swore to: Each of you raised your right hand to God in heaven and said that you would carefully hear and weigh the evidence; that you would follow the instructions of law that the judge gives to you; that you would uphold and defend our laws and our constitution; and that you would render a fair and just verdict in this case. In taking this oath, and in occupying the very chair that you now sit in, you are an important and essential part of our system of government. To put things bluntly, if you properly do your job, our system works and survives. If you fail to do your job as our law expects and requires, our system breaks down and, in time, fails. Soon, Judge Johnson will instruct you on the law that applies to the facts of this case. Soon, you will go into the jury room to make a decision of paramount importance. Your decision will be of supreme importance to Ann Tatum, to our community, city, and state. Your decision will be of greatest importance to our way of life. In making your decision, I am sure you will remember raising your right hand to God and the promise you made to God, to society, and to yourselves. Obedience to our laws is the heart and soul of our system. Will our laws be obeyed? Your answer to that question will be an important part of the larger answer that other jurors, like yourselves, give to like questions when one citizen takes the life of another.

Will this community be a place of safety? Will it honor law and order? Will it be a place where we feel safe when we walk the streets? Will your home be a place of safety? You, the jury, stand between law and order on the one hand, violence and death on the other. Which will you choose for your home? Your community? Your county? Your state? What is your choice? The decision is yours.

This case is not about the life of Edward Tatum. It is about his death. This case is not about whether Edward Tatum cheated on his wife. It is about his wife killing him. It is about Ann Tatum taking this pistol that I now hold in my hand and shooting her husband in the chest. He stood fifteen or twenty feet away when she deliberately raised this gun. There is no evidence that even suggests that her husband posed any physical threat to her. This case is about the defendant taking careful and deliberate aim at the chest of her husband and pulling the trigger. It is about her carefully squeezing the trigger with the full intent to take the life of another person.

But wait! There is more, much more, to her careful, calculated action. You've heard Detective Parker testify as to how this pistol works. He told you that it is a "semi-automatic" weapon. He has told you that each time this pistol is fired it requires a squeezing of the trigger by the person who holds the gun. Detective Parker is a fine police officer. He is also an expert with firearms. It is undisputed that each time a pistol of this type is fired, someone pulls the trigger.

I urge you not to forget Detective Parker's testimony about the "trigger-pressure" that was required to cause this very weapon to fire. I urge you to carefully consider the time this experienced pistol expert said would be required for Ann Tatum to fire eight times, hitting the target with each shot. I will read the court reporter's transcript of that very testimony to you. I invite your close attention to his words.

EIGHT SHOTS AND TRIGGER-PRESSURE

Detective Parker, are you familiar with the term "trigger-pressure?"

Yes.

Explain what trigger-pressure is to the jury.

All pistols have a trigger. All triggers require a certain amount of applied pressure before the weapon will fire. This is commonly called "squeezing the trigger." It takes a given amount of pressure to squeeze the trigger. This pressure is called trigger-pressure and is commonly expressed in "pounds." For example, a pistol with a four pound trigger-pressure rating means that four pounds of pressure must be applied to the trigger to make it fire.

Is there a scientific way to accurately measure the trigger-pressure that is required to fire a particular pistol?

Yes sir. That procedure was established many years ago, long before I became a policeman.

Does the trigger-pressure that is required to fire a pistol vary, or is it the same in all pistols?

Mr. Bailey, it varies not only with different brands or makes of pistols, it varies within the same make of pistols. For example, the trigger-pressure required to fire a Beretta .320 semi-automatic varies when comparing one Beretta to another Beretta.

Do pistol manufacturers establish and publish standards of trigger-pressure for particular models?

Yes, the manufacturer of a pistol gives qualified information about trigger-pressure.

How is that information qualified?

All pistol makers tell you that trigger-pressure varies with the individual weapon. The printed material will tell you the range of trigger-pressure varies with different makes of semi-automatic weapons. For example, the pressure range for one brand or make may range from 4.8 pounds to 6.9 pounds. The pressure range for a semi-automatic made by another company may have an indicated range of 6.0 pounds to 9.5 pounds.

Mr. Parker, you have testified that a Ruger .22 caliber semi-automatic pistol was used in the killing of Edward Tatum?

Yes.

Has the manufacturer of this Ruger published material about the range of trigger-pressure for this particular weapon?

Yes sir. As I recall, the manufacturer's publication gives a trigger-pressure range of about 5 pounds to 6.5 pounds. This Ruger is mostly used as a target-shooting weapon and has a relatively light trigger-pressure.

Tell the jury what this means.

It means that if you want to fire that pistol, you will need to apply not less than 5 pounds of pressure on the trigger and not more than 6.5 pounds of pressure. But, keep in mind, this information is qualified. This information gives a fair estimate, a fair guideline. With some pistols, the required pressure will be more or less than what the manufacturer specifies. Many things can influence the pressure that is required to fire a pistol.

What are some of those things?

Mr. Bailey, each gun has its own personality. One pistol of the same make will vary from other pistols of the same make. Required trigger-pressure for the same weapon is subject to change. Such things as how well a pistol is maintained, cleaned, and oiled can influence the trigger-pressure. How many times a pistol has been fired can influence the required pressure. As a general rule, the more a pistol is fired, the less trigger-pressure is required. But with some weapons, the more it is fired, the greater the pressure must be. Understanding trigger-pressure can be a tricky thing. The owner of each pistol should practice with his weapon so as to understand his pistol. If the weapon's required trigger-pressure is too light, it is considered to have a "hair-trigger" and is more dangerous to handle and fire.

Is there a scientific way to determine how many times a weapon has been fired?

Not specifically. Reasonable estimates can be established. The barrel of each pistol has what we call lands and grooves. These are the little ridges and valleys that one sees when look-ing down the barrel of a gun. I always caution people to be very careful about handling a gun, much less looking down the barrel. These lands and grooves are worn down by friction the more a weapon is fired. By measuring the lands and grooves reasonable estimates can be established as to how many times a gun has been discharged.

Did you examine the lands and grooves of the Ruger that was used to kill Edward Tatum?

I made a visual inspection. Our lab made scientific measure.

Based on this, do you have a judgment as to how many times this weapon had been fired?

Of course, I cannot give an exact number. It is completely fair to say this pistol had been fired very few times. The weapon had been well maintained. It was clean, well oiled, no sign of rust or corrosion, and the lands and grooves showed no signs of wear. That is the best I can say.

Was a trigger-pressure test performed on this particular weapon?

Yes sir.

Was this test conclusive? Did the test result in a scientific certainty?

Yes sir.

What did this test prove?

This weapon was tested eight times, the same number of shots that resulted in Mr. Tatum's death. In all eight tests, the required trigger-pressure was 6.65 pounds each time the pistol was fired.

How do these test results compare with the range of pressure indicated in the manufacturer's manual?

The test results show that the actual pressure required to fire this pistol slightly exceeded the manufacturer's specifications. *This is not surprising, as I said trigger-pressure is a tricky thing.*

Did the higher trigger-pressure affect the accuracy of the pistol?

Not the accuracy of the weapon, per se, but the higher pres-

sure could affect the accuracy of the person firing the weapon. Generally speaking, the higher the trigger-pressure, the more difficult it is for the person to hold a steady and true aim.

Mr. Parker, in your judgment, was there any change in the required trigger-pressure of this Ruger pistol between the time it was used to kill Edward Tatum and the time it was scientifically tested?

No. The trigger-pressure would have been the same both times.

Detective Parker, what is your personal experience in the use of handguns, such as the one that was used to kill Edward Tatum?

I have had extensive training in the use of handguns. Many years ago I was trained in both our police academy and the FBI school. I am required to retrain each six months. I regularly practice at our pistol range. I am a qualified handgun user and safety teacher. I don't mean to boast, but I am very good in the use of a pistol.

What is your experience in the use and firing of a semi-automatic pistol, such as the Ruger .22 caliber?

I personally carry a Browning semi-automatic. I have frequently fired the Ruger .22 caliber on the target range, but have never carried it as a sidearm. This pistol is seldom used by law enforcement officers, except for practice.

Mr. Parker, I have asked you many questions about the pistol and trigger-pressure. I have done this to ask you the most important question of all—the question of how does trigger-pressure influence marksmanship? Does trigger-pressure affect one's ability to hit an intended target?

Mr. Bailey, trigger-pressure is very, very important in the effective use of any weapon. It is even more important in the use of a pistol. This is because of the short barrel length of a handgun.

Please explain what you mean.

The objective in the use of any weapon is to hit the desired target. It is much easier to accurately aim a long-barrel weapon, such as a rifle, at the target than it is to accurately aim a short-barrel weapon, such as a pistol. The basics of the use of a handgun are, take a steady position and stance. If possible use both hands to steady the gun, take deliberate aim, control your breathing, and apply trigger-pressure in a steady, increasing manner. Apply the trigger-pressure in a way that you, the person doing the shooting, do not know exactly when the weapon will fire. You want the weapon to fire, but you want to be a little surprised when it actually does. You want to steadily increase the trigger-pressure, not in a jerky, erratic manner, but in a smooth, steady, increasing manner. Keep in mind that the pistol must be aimed at the target when it fires. The application of smooth, increasing pressure is necessary to avoid pulling the pistol off the target.

Mr. Parker, what role does trigger-pressure have in accurate shooting?

It is a critical factor. The greater the required pressure, the more difficult accurate shooting becomes. Trigger-pressure must be applied in a direction that is contrary to the direction of the target. The pressure applied in an opposition direction has a tendency to pull the pistol off target. When one fires a pistol from a right-handed position, this contrary pressure has a tendency to cause the pistol to shoot lower and to the right of the intended target. The contrary pressure must be compensated for by the person doing the firing. The greater the required trigger-pressure, the more difficult the shot becomes. Many hours of practice are required to overcome the many things that stand in the way of good marksmanship.

Detective, I have a final subject that I want you to carefully consider. Let's discuss the time that is required to accurately shoot a semi-automatic pistol eight times. Do you follow me?

Yes sir.

Assume that a Ruger .22 caliber semi-automatic pistol is being used, assume that it is fired once, hitting a man in his chest, and then, after the man turns his back and moves in the opposite direction, the same pistol is fired seven more times with each bullet hitting the man in his back. Based on your experience and qualifications, do you have a judgment as to how much time would have elapsed between the first and last of those eight shots?

Mr. Bailey, at least eight seconds would have been required, probably more, but at least eight.

Explain the reasons why that much time would be required.

There are several things. Each squeeze of the trigger is a separate and distinct action. With an automatic weapon, one pull and hold of the trigger causes the automatic to continue firing until the trigger is released or all the ammunition is fired, whichever first occurs. This was not true with a semi-automatic like the one used to kill Ed Tatum. Each time a semi-automatic pistol is fired, the trigger must be pulled. Each pull of the trigger is preceded by a command from the brain to the finger to squeeze. The muscle controlling the finger squeeze takes time to respond to the brain's command. This is called "response time." The finger must not only squeeze, it must squeeze in a deliberate, steady manner so the pistol is not pulled off the target. After the first shot, adding to the problem, in this case things become more complicated, both physical and mentally. Mentally the thought rushes in that you are shooting another human being. Very few, if any, ever develop a complete disregard for human life and this mental concept disrupts and often slows other mental operations. The first and all subsequent shots cause physical movements of both gun and hand. When the weapon is fired, it moves to some extent backward and usually slightly upward. The strongest hands and arms in the world cannot completely deny this movement and adjustment for this movement must be made. If the target is a moving one, as it was in this case after the first shot, mental and physical adjustments are demanded if the later shots are to strike the intended target. We're talking about a wife who apparently loved her husband while shooting at him. This adds to the emotional stress and tends to impair the mental process. Mr. Bailey, it is remarkable that all eight bullets hit Mr. Tatum, and it is my opinion that not less than eight seconds were required. It is my judgment that at least eight seconds elapsed, more likely closer to minimum of ten seconds.

Why do you find it remarkable that all eight bullets found the target?

I have been around many people who were experts in handgun use. I consider myself an expert. In my investigation,

I inquired of others about Mrs. Tatum, her background, and specifically about any experience that she may have had in the use of guns. My investigation led me to the conclusion—and this is the remarkable part—it led me to conclude that she had essentially no experience or training in firearms. Given all these factors, it was remarkable that all eight bullets were accurately fired. Under the same circumstance, I doubt that I could fire that well.

Mr. Parker, as a firearms expert, you have said that you find it remarkable that all eight bullets hit Mr. Tatum. Do you have other reasons for saying that?

Yes sir.

What are those reasons?

Mr. Bailey, the prints found of the pistol matched the right hand of Mrs. Tatum. I know it cannot be helped, but the Parkinson's disease that Mrs. Tatum has causes her right hand to tremor, sometimes violently. This tremor would greatly affect the ability of that hand to hold a pistol on target. Yet, eight bullets hit the target. Most anyone who is experienced in the use of handguns would say that was remarkable.

EIGHT SECONDS, MAYBE MORE

Ladies and gentlemen, I have just read to you the exact words of Detective Parker. You have heard him testify. You've seen him on the witness stand, and I'm sure you were impressed with his open and honest manner. He is truly an asset to our city. I call your particular attention to his testimony because it is of great importance. After hearing what this good officer told you, how can there be any doubt about the calculated, measured, deliberate actions of the defendant in taking the life of her husband? Think of the eight seconds—at least eight, maybe more.

In the jury room, take your watches with second hands and quietly time eight seconds. You will be surprised how long eight seconds can be. As you measure this time, think of the deliberate, calculated, intended actions that had to take place to fire each shot. Think of our need for law and order. Think of your oath as a juror to judge things fairly for both the defendant and the public. Think of your community.

As you consider what type of community you want to live in, as you consider what your verdict will mean to others, ask yourself how many times Ann Tatum took deliberate aim? How many times did she deliberately pull the trigger? How many times did she show the presence of mind, the calmness of thought to steady a shaking hand and hit a moving target as it tried to flee from her wrath?

As you decide the fate of the defendant, and the type of society that you want to live in, ask yourself how many times this lady pulled that trigger?

What does the evidence clearly show about the deliberate acts of Ann Tatum in wrongfully taking the life of her husband? The evidence is clear and certain. The facts speak for themselves. Not only did she carefully, with deadly aim, shoot her husband in his chest—she was not satisfied with that. As Edward Tatum tried to run away, as he tried to escape the rage of his wife, with his back turned, and more than twenty feet away, Ann Tatum again took deadly aim. Again, she deliberately pulled the trigger.

As Edward Tatum ran away, he increased the distance that separated him from the deadly weapon. As he increased the distance, he increased the difficulty of the person with the gun hitting the target. With each step of flight, Ann Tatum had to more carefully take her aim and pull the trigger. The greater the separation, the greater the calm, deliberate action of the person holding the gun had to be.

Ladies and gentlemen, this was no accidental killing. This was a cold and deliberate act of lifting the pistol, taking aim, and pulling the trigger. Not just once, but again, again, again, again, again, again, and again. Once in the chest, seven times in the back, the bullets found their intended target. This was not a matter of chance. This death is the product of deliberate and intended acts. This occurred in your hometown. Are you going to condone and approve such conduct?

No matter what you or I may think about the morals of Edward Tatum, no matter whether we consider him a good or a bad husband, a good or bad father, a good or bad citizen or person, these are not the issues before you. Ed Tatum is not on trial for bad morals. Of course, it is shameful that he would effectively abandon his family in favor of another man's wife. Of course it is shameful that he did and said some of the things that are attributed to him. But, we must keep in mind that Edward Tatum is not on trial. Whatever his sins, misdeeds, or mistakes may have been, he will now be tried by the court of last resort, not by a court of this world. The only issue before you is whether or not the defendant intentionally killed her husband.

Both God and our State have taken the position that we are not to kill. Now it becomes your solemn responsibility to decide a simple question: Did the defendant intentionally kill her husband? Look to the undisputed evidence to answer that question. Look to what Ann Tatum said and then look to what she did.

The defendant told you that she intended to take her own life. Let's examine that statement. The hard evidence shows that she shot her husband eight times. Now you must admit, this is a strange way of taking one's own life. Her lips tell us that she intended to kill herself and her actions tell us that she chose to accomplish this by shooting her husband eight times. One must admit that this is a strange way to commit suicide.

If the defendant had shot her husband only once, it might be logically argued that she did not intend to shoot at all. It might be, with reason, argued that the gun fired accidentally and no harm was intended. But the evidence clearly shows that the pistol was pointed, leveled, and with a steady hand, fired again, again, and again. What stronger evidence of a criminal intent can be shown? What stronger evidence of intent to do serious bodily harm, even death, can be imagined? No one would have you believe that she shot her husband for his health. Other than to cause death, what possible reason could there be for shooting eight times? To argue to the contrary defies all logic, all common sense, and all moral standards. Are you going to put your stamp of approval on these actions by voting not guilty? Is that the standard you seek for your community?

What evidence do we have that Ann Tatum shot in self-de-

fense? Absolutely none! All the evidence is to the contrary. The undisputed evidence clearly shows that never during the entire marriage did Ed Tatum physically abuse his wife. The evidence is undisputed that he never even threatened physical abuse. Whatever the faults and shortcomings of Ed Tatum, physical abuse, or even the threat of physical abuse, was not one of them.

Mr. Lee argues, and would have you believe, that Ann Tatum was insane at the time she shot and killed her husband. He would have you believe that she didn't know right from wrong at that time, that she didn't understand the nature and consequence of her acts. This contention is refuted by all logic, by all acts, and by all reason.

By her own admission, the defendant knew that the pistol that she held in her hand was a deadly weapon. By her own admission, she knew it could be used to take a life. By her own admission, she said she intended to use that pistol to take her own life. Is that not the strongest possible evidence she knew the nature and capacity of the pistol and what it could do with the assistance of a willing hand? Is that not very strong evidence that she fully understood that the pistol was an instrument of death and destruction? All logic, all reason, all human understanding shows the defendant fully understood that the pistol in her hand was an instrument of death, and she intended to use it for that purpose.

Ladies and gentlemen, I thank you for the undivided attention you have given to all the witnesses and evidence in this case. The judge will instruct you on the law that governs our lives and the law you are to apply to the facts of this case. I am confident you will listen carefully to the judge's instructions and do your very best to apply that law to the facts of this case. Among other things, the judge will tell you that you are not to allow sympathy, prejudice, or bias to influence your decision. I want you to listen carefully to the judge's instructions of law. I want you to listen carefully when he tells you that your verdict must be based on the true facts as you determine those facts to be and that sympathy, prejudice, and bias have no standing in the courtroom nor in your decision making.

Please be mindful of the deliberate steps that the defendant took as she raised this pistol and pulled the trigger eight separate times. Please be mindful that we are a nation of law, and the only way we can maintain our cherished way of life is to remain obedient to our laws. I respectfully submit that it is your sworn duty to find Ann Tatum guilty of the murder of her husband. Anything short of that will make a mockery of our system of law and justice.

IN THE PALM OF HIS HAND

Concluding his argument, Aaron Bailey placed the pistol on the evidence table that sat in front of the jury box. Eight empty shell casings had been gathered from Ann's bedroom, from where she stood the afternoon that she shot Ed. These shell casings had been introduced as evidence and were proper for the jury to see. As Bailey placed the pistol on the table, he picked up the bag containing the eight shell casings. He emptied the eight shell casings into the palm of his hand. He then, in a slow and deliberate manner, as if counting seconds of time, one by one, dropped the casings to the top of the table beside the pistol.

Aloud, he counted: "One—two—three—four—five—six—seven—eight."

In this dramatic, highly emotional, and most impressive manner, the argument for the conviction of Ann Albert Tatum was brought to a conclusion. The collective eyes of all jurors focused on the instruments of death. The slow count of one through eight echoed in their ears.

BEYOND THE CLOSE OF DAY

It was almost ten o'clock Saturday night before Judge Johnson concluded his instructions of law to the jury. He gave special attention to the instruction on how Georgia law defined insanity, how it applied to Ann's case, and then added a final word on what they would do the next day.

"Ladies and gentlemen, I have kept you a long time today. Too long, and I apologize for that. I will recess court for today, or for tonight, I should say. I want all of you to go to your homes and try to get a good night's rest. In view of the long day, we will not resume until eleven o'clock tomorrow morning. You are to report directly to the jury room at that time. The bailiff will be present to attend to your needs. There are fourteen of you now. Before you begin your deliberations tomorrow, I will excuse two of your number. These two were chosen as alternate jurors to be used in the event of some disabling event among your number. Fortunately, no one has been disabled and your number will be reduced to twelve before your deliberations begin. When the final twelve are selected, but not before, you may begin your deliberations. Thank you for your service. You are dismissed for the day."

WHAT IS REASON? WHAT IS LOVE? WHAT IS LIFE?

The jurors silently walked to the private room that had been their home-away-from-home for six days to gather their personal belongings and go their separate ways for a few hours. Each juror was sobered with the realization that tomorrow they had to make a choice. Over the past few days, they had grown increasingly accustomed to each other to the point of exchanging greetings when meeting and goodbyes when parting. Tonight, as they parted, they seemed strangers to each other, again. Their thoughts were of tomorrow.

Pete Atkinson, Jane's husband, had not been a trial witness and the keeping of his small retail business in Carrollton had precluded him the opportunity to attend the trial until late Saturday afternoon. Pete, Jane, Dana, Mrs. McCoy, and Ann drove Mr. Henry to his hotel. Except for Ann, this group was, in parting from Job and Sally, cheerless and somber. This is not to imply that Ann seemed happy and gay. Such was not the case. "Composed, collected, and serene" appeared to be better adjectives to describe her condition after a long, long day on the witness stand. She was the master of an emotional moment as she gave both Sally and Job a goodnight hug. Mr. Henry's ceramic butterfly dangled from her neck. All Ann said was, "Thank you, Job."

Job and Sally rode back to Carrolton in silence. It wasn't the time for levity or a remembrance of the times they had parked behind the old church in New Orleans. They were both exhausted, not just from the long and final day of Ann's trial, but from the strain of the last ten months. The clicking of the car's tires as they passed over the expansion joints of the concrete highway reminded Job of Bailey's slow count to eight as he dropped, one by one, the shell casings on the table in front of the jury.

Job had been reasonably satisfied with what he had argued to the jury until Aaron Bailey made his summation. The contrast of styles was dramatic. Job had not realized how much of what he had said was based on emotion, until he heard Bailey's argument that was based almost completely on logic. In retrospect, the contrast came into clear focus. All the emotion in the world could not speed the clock and the deliberate acts required for Ann to hit her target eight times with eight shots. In his mind, he knew that logic would likely trump emotion, and each time the tires hit the expansion joint, he heard the shell casings hit the table. He dared not share his thoughts, even with his wife.

Once home, Job's adrenaline was still pumping just enough to keep him from sleeping. By 2 a.m., he found himself searching out his journal.

SOUNDING THE SULLEN BELL

Dec 24, 1972: Sunday, 2 a.m.—long, long day. Argued Ann's case. Fear my best not good enough. Several times, Ann patted my hand as if to say something; what was that something that she wanted to tell me? We go back tomorrow—today—1st Sunday trial—Ann's case probably my last. Ann retains, so it seems, her newfound inner peace. A. Bailey made powerful and moving summation. He's a good trial lawyer. I feel like an old man, tired, worn-out, uncertain and afraid. Will know soon. I yet hear the sound of each empty shell as Bailey dropped them one by one on the table. Will I always hear that sound? Will Ann?

THE UNKNOWN STILL AHEAD

"Job, honey, wake up. It's almost eight o'clock."

Sally sat on the side of their bed, shaking her husband awake. She had let him sleep later than he had requested, but she knew that traffic into Atlanta would be light on Sunday morning, and there was nothing else Job could do for Ann, except wait.

"Is the coffee ready?" Job asked.

"By the time you get your shower it will be. I let you sleep a little later. You were talking in your sleep this morning, too. Get your bath. I'll be in the kitchen."

Sally had the coffee ready when Job joined her. Together, through the kitchen window, they watched their neighbors leave home, all dressed in their Sunday best.

"The McGees are off to early church," Job said. "They never miss."

"Job, I'm worried about you. You've been working so hard. Maybe next Sunday we can go to church with the Mc-Gees. I would like that." Sally seemed ready to have her husband back.

"What were you dreaming about this morning? You were mumbling something I couldn't understand."

"I had a weird dream. I was in some foreign country, Romania or Turkey or someplace like that. The people were dressed in bright colors, dressed like gypsies. They traveled in wagons and carts, pulled by horses, mules, and oxen, all except one old man who seemed to be the leader of the group. He traveled in an old, long, black Packard automobile. These people were just traveling about. They seemed to have no home, no place to stay. They were just wanderers. They had no roots. At times, I was part of the group. At other times, I was just a bystander, watching them. At times I fit in, and at other times I didn't fit. I wanted to be a part of the wanderers, yet I seemed to be afraid to join. It was a strange dream." Job sipped his coffee. "Now you tell me what it meant."

"Honey, it meant that you're tired and you need a rest. Better yet, it meant that you and I are past due for a T-ball game. Now, finish your coffee and I'll have your breakfast ready in a few minutes."

THE LAST BELL BEGINS TO TOLL

Ann, with her small group of supporters, was already in the courtroom when Job and Sally walked in. In her mind, Sally noted that Ann and Mr. Henry appeared the most relaxed of the group. She said a silent prayer for Ann, and for Job. She had never seen him so remote before. He was paying a high price for his client.

Shortly after 11:00 a.m., Judge Johnson came into the courtroom, but didn't take the bench.

Standing close to the door of his chambers, he announced, "All of the jurors have reported in, and I have excused the two alternates. The remaining twelve have started their deliberation. I will be in my chambers. You attorneys should not hesitate to call for me if the need arises."

The courtroom became a tomb. Finally, everyone was at liberty to speak, but no one did. Each person became victim to his or her own thoughts, wishes, anxieties, hopes, and fears. Time was suspended. No clocks were ticking. Minutes became hours. The jury room in which the jurors deliberated could only be entered through a door that opened into the main courtroom. The bailiff sat in a chair outside the jury room door, sometimes napping as he waited for the jury to knock on the door, signaling a need to speak to the judge, a break, or a verdict. At 2:30 that afternoon, the jury broke long enough for them to grab lunch at the diner across the street from the courthouse.

As the jurors went out of and back into the courtroom, Job carefully watched for eye contact with the jurors. He was anxious for a friendly sign, any sign of hope. He had hope that one or more of the jurors would look his way and give a silent signal of encouragement. No one looked his way.

With the jurors back in the jury room, the silence of the courtroom again became deafening. So it remained until 6:15 p.m. when Judge Johnson took the bench and announced that the jury had a question. The bailiff then led the jury into the courtroom.

Once they were in the box, the judge read the note that held the jurors' question.

"The jury asks, 'Can intent to commit murder be proven by circumstantial evidence only?'"

"Ladies and gentlemen of the jury, your question is an important one, and I will try to give you a meaningful answer. The answer to your question has some important qualifications, so please give me your undivided attention. Our law says that *intent to commit murder* may be proven by circumstantial evidence only when the circumstance is consistent with the hypothesis that the defendant intended the result that was obtained and is inconsistent with every other reasonable hypothesis.

"As with so many rules of law, this definition may leave you more confused than informed. I am somewhat reluctant to try to paraphrase this definition, fearful that I may add even more confusion. But, I will try. What does the word 'hypothesis' mean? A hypothesis is an assumption that is made to test its consequences.

"For example, when we look out our window and see the wet pavement, we assume it is raining and then we step outside to see if it is raining. In this example, if we walk outside and see the cloudy sky overhead, see the lawn is wet, see the sidewalk is wet, and see water dripping from the roof, and see no other reason for the wet pavement, we can reasonably assume that the street is wet because it has been rained on. Under this example, there is no other reasonable hypothesis. All circumstances suggest that the street is wet because it's been rained on.

"But let's enlarge my example by adding other reasonable causes for the wet street. Let's assume that in seeing the wet street from our window and wondering if it is raining, we step outside our door and see the heavy clouds overhead, see lightening in the sky, and hear the thunder roll. It sure looks and sounds like rain. These are reasonable signs of rain, but no rain is falling. We look down the street and see a street-washing machine going away from where we stand. The street washer is spraying its water onto the street. Is it reasonable to assume that the same street washer just went past the place where you now see the wet street? Is that a reasonable hypothesis that is inconsistent with rain?

"Or, to modify the example, assume that when you step outside to investigate the wet street, you see all the same signs except the street-washing machine. The street is wet.

You see and hear the lightning and thunder, but see no rain coming down. You look further and see your neighbor's lawn sprinkler is turned on. The sprinkler is not only wetting the lawn, it is also spraying out into the street. Again, this example tells us that it would be equally reasonable to believe that the street is wet because it has been raining or that it is wet because of the yard sprinkler.

"When you resume your deliberations, on the question of proving intent by circumstantial evidence, ask yourselves, is the circumstance consistent only with intent to kill? Or is there some other reasonable explanation? If there is another reasonable explanation, then the circumstance is not legally sufficient to prove intent to murder. I hope I have been helpful. You may return to your deliberations."

During these instructions to the jury, Aaron Bailey sat with his arms crossed over his chest and a look of confidence on his face. Directly across the room from Bailey, Job sat with his client. His face reflected concern, as opposed to Bailey's confidence. Ann appeared passive, even remote, as if she would not be affected by the special instruction the judge had just given.

After the jury again retired to the jury room, Sally caught Job's eye and signaled that she would like to speak to him outside the courtroom. Sally had seen the troubled expression on Job's face as the instructions were given. She knew Job too well.

Job left Ann at the table and followed Sally into the attorney's room for a private talk:

"Job, I can tell the jurors' question and the judge's answer bother you. Would you like to talk about it?"

"Not really."

"Honey, I understand. I just wanted you to know that I love you and I hate to see you in pain. If you don't want to talk now, I understand."

"Sally, I'm worried."

"I know you are. I know that look on your face. Do you want to go back into the courtroom to be with Ann?"

"Not really. I don't know what I want to do. I do know that the question that the jury asked is cause for real concern."

"Job, I heard the question and heard what the judge said, but I am afraid I don't understand what all of it means. Is that what is bothering you?"

"Yes. Very much."

"If you feel like it, tell me what you mean."

"What it means is not good. That's what it means."

"Job, you've lost me."

"Honey, it means the jury is talking about a murder conviction. It means they're trying to have the right understanding of the elements of the crime of murder. They aren't talking about an acquittal. They aren't talking about a verdict of *not guilty*. They are discussing murder and they want to be sure they get it right. Honey, it doesn't look good. For a long time, I've been afraid that my best wouldn't be good enough for Ann. Did you notice the expression on Aaron Bailey's face while the judge was answering the question about using circumstantial evidence to prove intent?"

"No, I wasn't watching him, I was looking at you. What

was he doing?"

"Sally, Aaron Bailey is a very good attorney with far more experience. He's an old pro and I could tell by the look on his face that he was pleased with the question they asked. He knew what it meant." Job looked down at his watch. "Honey, I'd better get back in the courtroom. I don't want Ann to ever think I've left her."

"Just remember, Job, I believe in angels."

THE SEVENTH DAY

Sunday proved to be another long day and all the participants, the main players, the support group, the stagehands, and the spectators, were very weary when, near midnight on Sunday night, the jury returned its verdict. The waiting was over.

The demands of the judicial system had been met. Edward Tatum was dead, and Ann Tatum was more dead than alive. Job Lee was exhausted, too tired to even talk. Sally held his hand as they walked from the courthouse to their parked car.

Job sat silently in the passenger seat as his wife drove them back to their small hometown after the verdict had been received, and Job Lee was more convinced than ever that he was a small-town lawyer and that the big city arena was not for him.

Before retiring to bed that night, Job made his final diary entry that related to Ann Tatum.

Dec-1972—Ann's case over. Bone tired. Learned a lot. Did my best. Never again. Time to put on a happy face for Christmas.

THE END OF THIS EVENTFUL HISTORY

Dana Tatum graduated from Auburn two years after the trial. She became a registered nurse and practiced pediatric nursing in New Orleans after graduation. She never married.

Jane and her husband continued to live in Carrollton until 2001 when they sold their business and moved to the mountains of North Carolina.

Job and Sally Lee live outside Augusta, Georgia, and Job continued a general practice of law in Georgia until his retirement in 2004. He and Sally adopted two children to go with the three they already had, and one of the adopted children became an attorney. After Ann's case, Job limited his trial work to civil cases, never again representing anyone charged with a criminal offense.

Ann's case had attracted at least modest attention in the Atlanta area, including Job's then-hometown of Carrollton. After the trial was over, Job refrained from discussing the facts of the case. The limited number of times he talked to anyone about what had happened to Ed and Ann centered solely on the lessons he'd learned from the tragic experience of Ann and her husband. When asked, he usually just said, "The case changed my life. It made me less certain about myself, and it taught me to never say 'never.'"

When others asked Sally about the case, she always remembered Job's troubled look when Judge Johnson gave the jury the special instructions about the proper use of circumstantial evidence to prove intent to commit murder. She retained a vivid recollection of the private talk that she and Job had in the attorney's room following this instruction. In her mind, she could see Job's reluctance to go back into the courtroom. At the time, Job had appeared torn between his fear of what the jury would do and his continuing duty to his client. At the time, Job seemed lost, not knowing which way to turn. Sally never forgot that his sense of duty prevailed in his saying: "Honey, I had better get back in the courtroom. I don't want Ann to ever think that I've left her." She also came to know that Job would never fully leave Ann.

Ann Albert Tatum survived until 2006. She never regained a zest for life. When she died, Dana and Jane buried her in the small country cemetery at Bethel Baptist Church where her mother, father, and little Betsy lay.

Job Lee had been right. Ed's death had consigned Ann to the City of The Living Dead. The jury saw it too, and they held back from punishing her further.

They did all they could to set her free by declaring her *not guilty*.

CHARACTERS

Albert, Betsy—Ann's baby sister.

Albert, Ellis "Ell"—Ann's father.

Albert, Martha—Ann's mother.

Appleby, Thrath Curry—Ann's high school teacher.

Atkinson, Jane Caine—daughter of Ann and Lloyd Caine.

Atkinson, Pete—Jane's husband.

Bailey, Aaron—District Attorney and chief prosecutor.

Battle, Dr. Carl—Ann's psychiatrist.

"Bee," Aunt—Ann's paternal aunt of Rome, Georgia .

Burris, Wayman—Assistant District Attorney.

Caine, Lloyd—Ann's first husband, father of Jane.

Carey, Dot—Ann's co-worker.

Cramer, Richard—retired trial lawyer, Job's mentor.

Gibson, Ralph—Ann's high school teacher.

Glover, Hattie—elderly friend and neighbor of Ann's family.

Graves, Sam—experienced criminal defense attorney.

Henry, Wallace—Ann's faithful friend and "Guardian Angel."

Johnson, Earnest—trial judge.

Lamar, Dr. Shelby—Ann's family physician.

Lones, William—family pastor (Bethel Baptist Church).

Lee, Job—Ann's trial lawyer.

Lee, Sally—Job's wife

McCoy, Ethel—Ann's faithful friend and neighbor, Atlanta.

Mills, Mary—Ann's new neighbor, Atlanta.

Parker, Robert—Atlanta detective, key witness in trial.

Scott, Carl—lifelong friend of Ed Tatum.

Tatum, Ann—mother of Jane and Dana, wife of Ed.

Tatum, Edward "Ed" Morris—Ann's second husband.

Tatum, Dana—daughter of Ann and Ed.

Wimberley, Dr. Charles—doctor who delivered Ann and Betsy.

20324999R10216

Made in the USA
San Bernardino, CA
07 April 2015